DRIVEN BY DESTINY

TRACKING TROUBLE
BOOK 3

LINDSAY BUROKER

1

WITH THE SUMMER SUN WARMING HER BACK, ARWEN FORESTER knelt on the earthen roof of her father's house, distractedly picking lingonberries. She was watching the half-dragon, Azerdash Starblade, construct a magical regeneration pool on the back half of the farm.

He stood shirtless in the cavity he'd hollowed out beside the pumpkin patch, his eyes closed, his arms spread as he gripped a small spherical artifact. Tendrils of power emanated from it, twining with his own significant power and working together to infuse the earth with magic. Though Starblade barely moved, the sweat dampening his skin attested to the effort it took to create the pool.

"Maybe I should bring him some lemonade," Arwen mused.

It was a three-day process, and he'd been at it all morning. Maybe he would enjoy a break and a refreshment. And while he drank, he would gaze at her with his violet eyes, perhaps showing his appreciation while stepping close and touching her cheek. He might like the feel of her skin and forget that he found her mongrel dark-elven blood distasteful. He might also forget that he'd said numerous times that he had no romantic interest in her.

A black Jeep rolled up the long gravel driveway, and Arwen pushed away her silly thoughts. She was supposed to be picking berries for the sauce for tonight's big dinner, not fantasizing about something that wouldn't come to pass.

Sensing Val Thorvald and Matti Puletasi in the Jeep, Arwen waved at its approach. She lowered herself to the small deck, where her magical bone-and-wood bow and quiver of arrows leaned against the railing. The doormat read *NO TRESPASSING* instead of *WELCOME*.

Should she put that inside for the dinner? By now, her guests knew that she and especially her father were on the skittish side when it came to people and preferred their privacy. Maybe Val and Matti wouldn't think anything of the unfriendly mat. Besides, Arwen planned to host the meal outside so everyone could enjoy the weather.

But why had they arrived so early? She hadn't expected her visitors until that evening. The turkey had hours left to roast.

After parking, Val hopped out. She lifted a finger, then pulled out a few narrow rectangular chocolate boxes as well as a ham wrapped in foil.

"Hi, Val." Arwen joined her in the driveway as the pregnant Matti got out more slowly, her due date fast approaching. "You didn't need to bring food."

"Well, Zav is coming, so you'll need a lot of meat. I assume you don't mind that I invited him, especially since he's promised to install powerful wards around your property to keep out strangers —especially *dark-elf* strangers."

Yes, Arwen had been glancing over her shoulder constantly since her run-in with the brother she'd never known she had. Even though she'd shot him in the back and watched him tumble into a waterfall, she doubted he was dead—or that he would stop troubling her.

"I appreciate that, and he's welcome of course."

"Sarrlevi is coming too," Val said. "He can't spend more than an hour away from Matti in her time of need."

Matti snorted but didn't refute the statement.

Arwen bit her lip, wondering how many people would show up for her dinner, one that she was only hosting because Yendral and Starblade had asked her to cook them a meal. Yendral, though he had nothing to do with the creation of the pool, had already flown past numerous times to check on the progress. Supposedly, he was hunting and might bring her something for the table.

In addition to Val and Matti, Arwen had invited Amber and Willard, mostly because they'd all been at the Coffee Dragon when Arwen had been thinking that having a dinner with only Yendral and Starblade present might be awkward. Oh, she would love a private meal with Starblade, one that featured soft music and romantic candlelight, but his half-dragon comrade added an element of uncertainty.

More than once, Yendral had mentioned admiring her squish, which Arwen had ambivalent feelings about. She wanted *Starblade* to admire her squish—or anything else on her that might appeal to him. Yendral was handsome and friendly enough, but she didn't want to have sex with him. However, as powerful as the half-dragons were, it had crossed her mind that Yendral could use magical coercion to convince her that she *did* want that. He didn't seem as bound by honor as Starblade. With more people present, many of whom were capable fighters and fearless in the face of dragons, the odds of Yendral doing something untoward seemed lower.

Still, her inherent fear of crowds, even crowds of friends, made Arwen grimace at the idea of numerous people on the property. The picnic table would only seat six, maybe eight if everyone got cozy. What would she do if more guests came? She couldn't ask Colonel Willard or Lord Zavryd to sit on a stump.

Matti walked around the Jeep to join them, her magical war hammer slung over her shoulder. As a good half-dwarf, she rarely left her weapon behind, even when she might need to be whisked off to the delivery room at any time. She also gripped a canvas grocery bag that rattled with empty jars.

"Thought I'd return these." Matti hefted the load. "I didn't realize quite how many of the jars of jam and pickled vegetables that Sarrlevi brought me came from *your* farm. Your food is really good. It's good that you're selling some of it at the Coffee Dragon now."

"I'm glad you like it," Arwen said.

"I have some news from Zoltan about your tattoo-removal recipe. Do you need help?" Val pointed to the roof where Arwen had left her bucket. "Or any assistance with dinner? I'm not the best cook, but I've gotten handy at making meat and poultry all different ways. And I can definitely pick berries."

Before Arwen could say that she had enough lingonberries, Val trotted up to the deck and pulled herself onto the roof, her blonde braid swinging. Between her half-elven agility and six feet in height, she made it look easy. Before harvesting anything, she looked toward the back of the property and smirked down at Arwen.

"Is picking berries what you were *really* doing up here?" Val asked.

"Yes, of course." Arwen pointed to the bucket, though she assumed Val had gotten a glimpse of the shirtless Starblade.

"There are only three berries in there."

"What? It was half full." Arwen pulled herself up, leaving Matti to head inside with the bag.

Father was working in the barn, so Arwen didn't worry about anyone running into him. He'd oozed disapproval at her admission to inviting people for a dinner party and wanted nothing to do with her visitors, so she doubted she would see him at all that evening. Starblade was the only person Father didn't mind; they'd bonded over tractor parts.

A crow cawed from the stove vent as Arwen made it up and peered into the bucket. There were more than *three* berries but perhaps not as many as she'd picked.

"Do crows eat lingonberries?" Val peered toward the bushes, vines, and trees that seemingly grew at random on the property but that had been planted to complement each other.

"Crows eat anything."

"I don't sense any goblins, at least. They love berries to go with their roadkill meals. I should warn you that I heard some might come by later. They were talking about it at the Coffee Dragon yesterday."

Arwen blinked. "Random goblins are going to show up at my dinner?"

"Nin tried to dissuade them, but they promised they would bring an appropriate gift and that you would love having them."

"Uh." Even though goblins were far from intimidating, Arwen's shoulders bunched at the thought of more people than she'd invited arriving. She decided to leave the *un*welcome mat out.

"I think I told you I showed that recipe to Zoltan," Val said, "and he's researching where the ingredients can be found. Some aren't that rare and can be easily foraged or purchased in markets on other worlds. Some are *very* rare. You might have to go on a quest to find them. Multiple quests."

"I expected that."

"Once you've got everything, Zoltan said he's capable of making the formula for your green-skinned tattoo artist to use. Have you seen him lately? Mark, isn't it? I remember he asked you out." Val arched her eyebrows.

"No. I'm not avoiding him, but... I'm not sure I want to have coffee with him." Arwen caught herself before she looked toward Starblade, but Val might have guessed her thoughts, because *she* looked.

"Not when you've got a half-naked half-dragon doing chores for you?"

"It's not a chore. It's a—"

"Huge commitment for a project that most people would only undertake if they're being paid handsomely?"

"I'm not paying him. I asked for a rejuvenation pool as a joke before I realized how much work it would be, and he... agreed."

"Maybe you *should* hold out for him and wave away the date requests from the half-troll."

Arwen shook her head. "He's not... He's told me..."

"I know, I know. He might be getting over someone else."

They'd discussed that possibility before, but Arwen had no idea if it was true. She hadn't asked Starblade.

"The fact that he's here suggests *some* kind of interest in you," Val said.

"He likes my food."

"Well, *everyone* likes that."

Matti walked back outside, giving Arwen a reason not to respond.

"It smells amazing in your kitchen," Matti called up. "If you want to expand your business and become the next Pepperidge Farm, we could put you in touch with some business-savvy people."

Val nodded. "Zoltan is an expert marketer."

"Your vampire alchemist roommate is an expert marketer?" Arwen asked.

"Yes. His YouTube following of infatuated female teenagers is so large that the company sends him plaques."

"I don't think teenagers would pay for my baked goods,"

Arwen said, though she'd made deals with Val's sixteen-year-old daughter.

"*Everyone* likes pie," Matti said, "and teenagers don't have to pay bills, so they have disposable income. But don't limit yourself. With some social-media marketing, you could reach people of all ages."

Val nodded. "You have a huge potential customer base. I'm positive. You could be shipping your desserts around the world to the masses and retire from picking berries. Or hire someone *else* to pick them while you oversee the farm."

"I only have two ovens." At the moment, those ovens were busy baking a couple of turkeys and cranberry-oat cobbler for her dinner guests.

"You might have to expand," Val said.

"I wouldn't want to work anywhere besides the farm. Especially this time of year when the view is magnificent." Arwen caught herself looking toward the back of the property again and blushed.

"Your crops are magnificent?" Matti asked.

"Of course." With her blush deepening, Arwen didn't look at either of them.

"Starblade is back there," Val said dryly.

"Oh, right," Matti said. "I sense him."

"This view *would* be hard to replicate at a commercial kitchen in town."

"Everyone knows rural properties offer more relaxing work environments," Arwen murmured, tossing berries into her bucket and pretending a lack of interest in the view. Why, she didn't know since she'd already confessed that she enjoyed it, but she worried Val would tease her.

"Relaxing or stimulating?" Val asked.

"Uhm."

"I thought so. Anyway, we didn't just come to discuss pies."

"That's why *I* came." Matti leaned against the deck railing, not interested in climbing onto the roof. Understandably so. She had a view of her own at home.

"I wanted to make sure you know Zoltan is willing to make the formula," Val said, "should you find all the ingredients, but you'll need to go over there to negotiate rates with him."

"Okay," Arwen said. "When is a good time?"

"He was sleeping when I left. I'll ask him tonight." Val's phone rang. She pulled it out, showed Willard's name on the display, and said, "*This* is why I came." She answered instead of explaining. "Hey, Willard. Yes, I'm about to ask. Yes, the dinner is this evening. Yes, I'm sure Gondo can come." Val raised her eyebrows.

Arwen hesitated but nodded. She didn't *want* more people on the property, but she didn't want to turn away new friends either. Oh, she might not consider Willard's assistant a *friend* exactly, but he had connected Arwen with the goblin clan near North Bend, and one of them had led her to her brother's lair. She owed Gondo.

Val hung up. "Willard wants to know if she can borrow your heritage detector. A full-blooded elf came by her office, asking to see the results of Starblade's blood test, specifically the part that suggested he's related to King Eireth."

"It's still at Imoshaun's workshop." Arwen was on the verge of saying Willard could see it any time but paused. "What elf wants to know? Do their people think it's good or bad that Starblade is related to Eireth?"

"I didn't see the guy, so I don't know. He introduced himself as a diplomatic envoy and kept picking up things in her office and poking everything like he'd never been to Earth before. Her Gondo-improved stapler is admittedly an odd knickknack. The elf thought so too and managed to staple his finger when he was prodding it with distaste. That resulted in Willard getting a blood sample from *him*. She wants to test it to see if he's related to any elf who's given us trouble. Like Matti's nemesis Slehvyra or Anyasha-sulin, a schemer who claimed to be my cousin and tried to get me killed when I fought the dark elves at Mt. Rainier. They belong to factions that want to overthrow Eireth because they think he's too accommodating to dragons—or they just want his power. It's possible they'd want to use Starblade—or his blood—to their own gain."

"When it comes to elves, he can probably take care of himself."

"I know he's powerful, but elves have plotted in the past and managed to take out full-blooded dragons."

"Well, Willard is welcome to use the device." Arwen opened her mouth to say more, but the roar of an engine came from the barn.

Her father rode out on Frodo. Their old tractor didn't have a lot of get-up-and-go anymore, but it accelerated down the driveway and onto the path that led past the chicken coop and corn crib and toward the back of the property. Just visible, pulses of blue light came from under the hood.

A soft cackle drifted back over the roar of the engine. Was that her father?

"Is your tractor enchanted?" Val asked.

"Just enhanced with a Gnomish part. Starblade brought it for my father."

"Oh, that's smart."

"Smart?" When the tractor wobbled as Father rounded a bend, Arwen worried that souping up Frodo to run at NASCAR speeds might not have been the best idea.

"Sure. Get in good with the father if you want to hook up with the daughter." Val tapped her temple. "*Smart.*"

"No, he's not interested in me. I thought he might be a little, but... he's not."

Val looked toward Starblade, and Arwen followed her gaze. Though he remained in his spread-armed, wide-legged stance in the future pool, his violet eyes were now turned toward them, as if he knew they'd been discussing him. With his pointed elven ears, he had to have hearing at least as keen as Arwen's, but she and Val weren't close enough that he could have overheard. She didn't think.

"Starblade just likes tractors?" Val asked skeptically.

"He likes *all* machines, as far as I can tell, but he's especially fond of Gnomish work. And siege engines."

Val blinked. "I guess you're lucky he's not building you one of those."

Arwen thought about bringing up how they'd discussed that Starblade, should he die, would like his airplane-refurbishment project to be delivered to Arwen's property. All she said was, "Yes."

Yendral approaches with fresh meat to be prepared for dinner, Starblade spoke into her mind.

Okay, I'll see if I can incorporate it.

You speak with Zavryd'nokquetal's mate.

Val, yes. They're invited to dinner. Is that okay?

His eyes narrowed. *That dragon is pompous and odious and thinks he's better than us.*

But we've learned he's a relative of yours, and he's agreed to help keep other dragons away from you. Maybe you should get to know him better.

Every time we interact, he wishes to duel or to punish me for being an abomination.

I don't think he'll do that tonight. And Val brought ham to share.

Starblade gazed silently at her without replying. Arwen remembered that his elven half meant he liked to dine on more than meat.

I'm also making a special roasted mushroom medley to go with dinner. I foraged a bunch of them fresh from the woods.

Starblade's eyes flared with a violet glow. That often indicated he was incensed about something, but Arwen knew how he felt about mushrooms, so she suspected another emotion was at play.

"Did you say something to piss him off?" Val must have guessed from Arwen's silence and Starblade's long gaze that they were communicating.

"No. He's excited. I told him I'm preparing him a special mushroom dish for dinner."

"And... he likes that?"

"Yes."

"He's a different kind of dragon."

"It's his elf blood." Arwen sensed Yendral approaching, flying over the trees in his dragon form.

"Is that one into fungi too?" Val pointed in the direction of Yendral's aura, though he wasn't in view yet.

"He said something that led me to believe he's not excited by Starblade's mushroom recipe." Arwen didn't know if the elven Mushrooms of Stamina even *had* a recipe. It was possible Starblade chucked them raw down Yendral's gullet to improve his health.

When the powerful silver-scaled dragon that was Yendral flew into view, Arwen wasn't surprised that he clasped something in his talons, but she had expected deer or elk. The white-furred game that he'd caught looked like—

"Is that a yeti?" Val asked.

From the deck, Matti looked skyward.

"I understand Yendral was hunting and bringing something to add to the dinner menu," Arwen said.

Once in view, Yendral reached them quickly, his strong wing-beats carrying him on a breeze. He dropped the dead yeti so that it landed with a thud on the gravel driveway three feet from the fender of the Jeep. Matti's mouth drooped open.

"It *is* a yeti." Val gripped her chin.

"Apparently." Since Arwen and her father lived off the land, she'd prepared all manner of game for the dinner table, but she had no experience with such creatures. Even though their kind had vexed the farm this past year, she hadn't been tempted to find out what they tasted like.

"What *course* is yeti?" Val asked.

"As a dark meat, I'd guess it goes after salad and mushrooms and turkey but before dessert." Arwen hesitated. "I may need to consult my Julia Child cookbook."

"Wouldn't you be more likely to find freshly hunted game discussed in *Buck, Buck, Moose*?"

"We have that cookbook. It only covers antlered meats."

"I guess you'll have to improvise then."

"Yes."

"It'll be an interesting dinner."

"Yes."

Yendral banked and flew circles—or were those victory laps? —around the property. He looked down at them, and his green eyes glowed as he met Arwen's gaze.

"Is he excited about mushrooms too?" Val asked.

"I'm... not sure." Arwen didn't know what to make of the long look and glowing eyes.

"An *interesting* dinner," Val repeated.

2

THE SUN WAS STREAKING THE CLEAR SKY WITH PINKS AND ORANGES, all the elements of the meal were almost ready, and Matti's elven mate, Sarrlevi, was levitating a log toward the picnic table to add more seating. If Arwen had been a relaxed and practiced dinner host, she would have been delighted that everything was going well. Instead, her frazzled energy had her tempted to hide in the kitchen instead of talking to anyone.

There were *so many* anyones. Even though all her guests were magical, so she could sense if someone approached her from behind, she kept jumping when someone came close.

In addition to Matti, Val, Sarrlevi, Zavryd, and Gondo, several goblins Arwen didn't know had arrived. Tinja, Matti's former roommate, was the only goblin besides Gondo that Arwen recognized. Amber had also arrived, parking in the comfrey near the beehives since the driveway was running out of room. Supposedly, Willard and her marsupial lion-shifter friend were on the way too. Where would *they* park?

Starblade had donned his shirt and stood with Yendral beside an outdoor fire that Arwen had hurried to make to accommodate a yeti haunch. Not sure what it would taste like, she had taken some liberties with the seasoning rub. Now and then, Yendral's nose twitched in approval, so maybe she'd gotten it right. He and Starblade were discussing the new spit that rotated the haunch.

"You've led armies and have power to rival dragons," Yendral said, "and yet you lower yourself to doing the work of gnome servants."

"It is not *lowering* oneself," Starblade replied, "to build something."

"Perhaps not to build something noble and elegant, but you constructed a cooking implement out of vines."

"Vines and *sticks*."

"Oh, yes. Such building materials often comprise the greatest of architectural endeavors."

"On Veleshna Var, it is so."

"Weren't you constructing the spit based on Gnomish design?" Yendral asked. "From something scribbled on the toilet paper roll that inventor gave you to get rid of you?"

"He offered his notes to me to honor me, and the spit was merely *inspired* by them. You gave Arwen a problem by dropping a yeti on her doorstep. *I* offered a solution to assist her in dealing with it. She did not know if yeti should be baked, roasted, or chopped up in a stew."

"The delivery of meat is *never* a problem, and Chef Arwen is quite experienced at preparing food, as attested by the spices now giving this meat its scintillating aroma. Your tinkering skills were not needed."

"I am certain she appreciates my ingenuity."

"In reading a roll of toilet paper. Oh, certainly."

Feeling strange listening to a conversation that involved her, Arwen hustled away, only to chance on Matti and Val discussing her tattoo.

Everywhere Arwen looked, there were people. It didn't help

that the encroaching twilight made the shadows deeper, giving her flashbacks to dinners in the dark-elf tunnels where she'd spent the first seven years of her life. Everywhere she'd gone, she'd had to worry about her mother's people reading her thoughts and finding them inappropriate. And then punishing her. She'd always had to worry about punishments.

"Arwen?"

She jumped and whirled, hand dropping to the foraging knife at her belt before she caught herself.

Matti stood in front of her, offering a can of carbonated water. "I came to ask if you want help with anything." She glanced at the knife on Arwen's belt. "I'd be alarmed that you almost pulled a weapon on me, but it has cute little bristles on the end, so I assume it's not that dangerous."

"Those are boar bristles, and this blade is mostly dangerous to mushrooms."

"I figured." Matti handed her the can. "Val found the silverware and is going to set the table and, uhm, log." She looked toward a second one that Sarrlevi was floating out of the woods from somewhere beyond the property line.

"That log is not sufficient for all the beings coming to dinner, elf," Zavryd stated, his arms folded across his chest. As usual, he appeared handsome and regal, the fluorescent yellow Crocs not quite ruining the stateliness of his elven robe. "Since your power is so feeble and inadequate for the task, I will find something more substantial."

"My power is *extremely* adequate, dragon," Sarrlevi said. "I am certain the half-dark elf does not wish giant redwood logs dropped at her doorstep."

"Bad enough someone already dropped a yeti," Matti murmured.

Arwen rubbed her face.

"You make excuses for your inability to find a large sturdy

bench?" Zavryd asked. "How is it that you ever dare duel a dragon?"

"Because my magical and physical skills are more versatile than those of a scaled behemoth who relies solely on raw power to win battles."

"You've witnessed the speed and strength of my talons and great maw and *dare* make that statement?"

"Are they going to duel?" Arwen whispered.

"Probably." Matti pointed to the open barn door, where two goblins were slipping out in the shadows, junk from the hayloft clutched in their arms. "You might be able to distract Zavryd by asking him to lay down his wards now. I'm not sure if Gondo even knows those goblins."

Arwen set down the can of water, gripped her knees, and sucked in a deep breath. This was too much. Too many people. What had she been thinking?

Gravel crunched as a new vehicle drove up. Willard's SUV, and, yes, there was a shifter in the passenger seat.

"Forester," Willard called in her Southern drawl as soon as she got out. "I need to talk to you about elf blood."

Arwen tried to nod to her, but the movement was jerky, and she struggled to release the grip on her knees. Her breaths were quick. Too quick. She tried to slow them down before she grew dizzy from too much air.

She sensed Starblade approaching from behind her and tensed, not certain whether another presence would be too much or if she wanted to run and hide behind him. Nobody was threatening her, she told herself. These were all friends, except maybe for the kleptomaniac goblins.

Are you ill? Starblade asked into her mind as he stopped beside her, gazing down with concern.

No, overwhelmed. Do elves get panic attacks?

I have seen many soldiers display various attributes indicating fear when approached by an enemy horde with superior numbers.

There aren't any enemies here. I just don't handle crowds well.

"Ms. Forester." A goblin bounced up to her. "Thank you for your hospitality. Your food smells delicious. We brought you a gift."

He thrust a stick toward her. Or... was that an arrow?

"One of our great shamans enchanted it. It's *magical*. When you fire it at enemies, it will glow in the dark."

"That ought to drive fear into the hearts of ogres and orcs," Matti said.

Arwen's curiosity overrode her impending panic attack, and she accepted it. The heft surprised her. Anything less than a magical bow wouldn't have had a shot at firing it.

"Is this made from metal?" she asked.

"Recycled materials, yes."

"Like traffic signs?" Matti asked. "It's red."

"Possibly." The goblin smiled brightly.

"That had better not have been one of the stop signs from in front of our house," Matti said.

More goblins flowed up to Arwen, rousing her panic again.

"Did she like it?"

"When can we eat?"

"Does she want me and Hamorock to build an automated food-delivery construct to serve the guests? Our design is quite clever. It allows you to make offerings to dangerous dragons without getting too close." The goblin speaker glanced at Starblade.

"Leave us," he told them, an eye toward Arwen's face.

Maybe it had gone pale.

"But the—"

"*Leave.*" Starblade's voice boomed not only with power but magical compulsion.

Movements jerky, the goblins hurried away.

Arwen shouldn't have wanted guests, even uninvited guests, to be cowed, but she was relieved to have fewer people around her.

Starblade rested his hand on her shoulder. "You will come for a walk with me. We will observe the progress I've made on your pool, and I will give you the lesson on creating a magical barrier that I once promised you."

She wanted to agree—and she *especially* wanted to learn to protect herself with magic—but Arwen felt obligated to stay. She was the host.

"Your guests will survive for a few minutes without your presence," Starblade said, as if reading her thoughts, though he'd said he couldn't do that outside of his sanctuary. "They are about to be enthralled by a dragon-elf duel."

Starblade shifted his hand to the small of her back to guide her away. He didn't use magical compulsion on her, but Arwen found herself going along with him without hesitation. She would *like* a quiet walk with him—and to escape the hubbub. What might turn into chaos. Hopefully, Val and Matti could keep their mates from destroying anything on the farm. Maybe Zavryd and Sarrlevi could duel in the road out front instead.

As Starblade and Arwen's path took them near Yendral and the cook fire, he stepped in front of them. Starblade's eyes narrowed.

"The food smells most excellent, Chef Arwen." Yendral nodded toward the yeti haunch dripping juices into the flames and toward the house where the turkeys had finished roasting and the cobbler was cooling on a rack.

"I hope you'll like everything," she said.

"I did not expect to share the meal with so many others. I wasn't even certain I wanted to share it with my commander." Yendral smirked at Starblade, ignoring the narrowed eyes.

"Were you going to gorge yourself alone in the forest?" Arwen barely kept from flinching when a cheer rose from several goblin throats. Zavryd had conjured his fiery magical blade to face Sarrlevi, who'd drawn his twin longswords.

"Not alone, no. I would have invited the chef to join me." Yendral rested a hand on his chest and bowed to her. "I suspect you will quite enjoy the fresh yeti. If you had dragon blood, I *know* that you would enjoy it. Were you aware that being fed tends to make dragons randy?" His eyes gleamed as he met her gaze, pausing before standing straight again.

"I enjoy many types of food, but they don't cause that, uhm, feeling in me." Arwen looked at Starblade, uncertain how to handle Yendral's flirtation, if that was what this was. Usually, she told men she wasn't interested and then fled to avoid further discomfort or pestering, but Yendral was her dinner guest and Starblade's friend. The rules might be different than with random strangers.

Jaw clenched, Starblade was glaring at Yendral and didn't notice her glance. They might have been communicating telepathically.

"That's a shame," Yendral said. "Perhaps it's only that you haven't experienced the pleasure of lounging naked in bed and having a mate feed you succulent morsels."

"Step aside, Yendral," Starblade said coolly. "She is not interested in being naked with you."

"We do not know that. And since you've said you have no interest in being naked with *her*, I do not know why it is any concern to you."

"She has proven herself an ally. I will not see her harassed any more than I would allow it with one of my troops."

Arwen glanced at Starblade's irritated face. Did his words and continued coolness suggest that had happened before? That there had been a time when Yendral hadn't taken no for an answer?

Arwen appreciated being called an ally, but she was less

certain about the comparison to Starblade's *troops*. It wasn't the first time he'd implied he considered her a subordinate.

"Never have I *harassed* a female," Yendral said. "I'm an enjoyable companion, and they *appreciate* my attention."

Knowing she needed to speak up, Arwen made herself lift a finger. "I'm not interested in your attention, but thank you for the yeti. It was very thoughtful."

Yendral gave her a puzzled look.

Are you okay? Val spoke telepathically to Arwen. She stood in the driveway with the other spectators watching what had turned into a sword fight, but she nodded pointedly at Yendral and Starblade, her gaze pausing on Starblade's hand. It was still on the small of Arwen's back. *They're not suggesting a threesome or something idiotic, are they?*

No. Yendral just wants... I guess to eat in the forest alone with me.

I'll bet.

I don't really understand, since I'm... Well, most guys with the power to sense it usually don't want anything to do with me because of my dark-elven blood.

You're pretty, you give them delicious food, and you've fought enemies at their sides. That's the way to a dragon's heart. Trust me.

But they're half-elven, and dark elves are... Everyone hates them.

You're not a very dark-elfy dark elf. And don't overrule the importance of food and beauty.

Arwen's mouth twisted. She'd never considered herself beautiful, but she *did* believe her food was good. After all, she'd won awards for her pies.

"You are not my commander anymore," Yendral told Starblade, his own tone cool now. They must have continued their conversation telepathically.

"I am aware," Starblade said. "You will step aside and leave her be because *she* does not want you, and it is honorable to respect a female's wishes."

Yendral stepped closer, not to Arwen but to Starblade. Alarm flashed through her as she envisioned a *second* duel starting. The urge to flee the chaos of too many people—too many emotions— swept into her again.

"It is not honorable," Yendral said, "to say you have no interest in a female but then monopolize her so others do not have time to charm her."

"With compulsion magic?" Starblade asked softly.

"I'm not a bastard."

"You've done it before."

"Not to a *female*."

"No, to her mate so that you were free to take her."

"Only because she wanted it."

"Arwen does not *want* it." Starblade lifted his hand to the back of her neck, gently rubbing her tense muscles. "Not from you."

Arwen didn't like being in the middle of their argument, even if it was about her, but she couldn't help but lean into Starblade's touch. She *did* want him and kept thinking that maybe it was possible he would want her eventually.

"You're an arrogant bastard, Azerdash," Yendral said.

"You've mated with enough females on this world. You don't need to *charm* an ally."

"*You* don't need to charm her either. You think it wasn't obvious what you were doing by standing half-naked working your magic?"

"It was hot."

"Please, the sun is so anemic in this place that I'm surprised anything grows."

"Stand aside, Yendral. Arwen needs a reprieve from over-whelming guests." Starblade shifted his hand to her back again and stepped forward.

Yendral rooted his feet to the ground.

Worried their confrontation would escalate, Arwen eased

closer to Starblade. She'd told Yendral she wasn't interested. What more did she need to say?

Jaw set, Yendral didn't look like he would move, but Starblade used his power to push him aside before their shoulders would have smashed together. Power swelled around Yendral, as if he would retaliate, but when Starblade looked icily backward, Yendral must have thought better of it.

He did bark, "She's not Gemlytha," after them.

Starblade stiffened, his face turning as rigid as the rest of his body.

"I'm aware," he said softly, looking forward again.

Arwen glanced at his face several times as they walked down the wide path to her cob home, the squash patches and the pool beyond it. Nothing in his expression invited conversation, nor was he looking at her now. He'd clammed up the last time Gemlytha, the half-dragon with dark-elven blood, had come up, but it had been clear she had died, and he missed her. And had regretted that they'd never hooked up?

"I'm not sure how to handle him," Arwen risked saying as they neared her home.

"He should respect your wishes so you shouldn't have to *handle* him."

"Will he?"

"I believe so. As long as you are clear with him. He isn't dumb, but he can be obtuse in some areas. Because few women have rejected him, he can't believe that *any* would want to." Starblade paused in front of her door, not yet taking the path that led to the back of the property. He turned to regard her. "If I claimed you, he would leave you alone. He knows he can't compel *me* to step aside so he can sate his urges."

"Claim?" Arwen mouthed, looking from him to the door, aware that they weren't ten steps from her bedroom.

What did he *mean* exactly? That he would take her to bed to get Yendral to leave her alone? Not because he *wanted* her but because he felt an obligation to protect her?

If he offered, what would she say? She'd rejected propositions before from men who'd only wanted to have sex, not to have a relationship, but this wasn't the same. Maybe it would even *lead* to a relationship, if he enjoyed himself. But would he? She had so little experience and wouldn't know how to make it good for him.

Still, she caught herself stepping closer and resting a hand on his chest as she waited for his answer.

"It would be... less than honorable, but I do not wish you to be bothered by foolishness when you must endure more dangerous threats from the dark elves and possibly others. The Silverclaw dragons might return, seeking a way around the Stormforges, and hunting down someone who could be a conduit to me."

"It wouldn't be honorable to be with me?"

"Not to say I've claimed you when I have not."

"Ah." Arwen lowered her gaze to his chest, realizing he *wasn't* offering to have sex with her. "Because you're not interested."

Even though he'd rubbed her neck twice, touched her hand, brought her father a present, and was making her a rejuvenation pool... he considered her only an ally. Maybe a friend.

She should have been honored to have him as an ally—it wasn't as if mongrels *usually* had powerful friends that would stand at their backs in battle and help them on quests—and she was, but she couldn't help but want...

"It is... complicated." Starblade looked toward the main house.

Arwen sensed Yendral changing form and turning into a dragon. As he sprang into the air, Starblade stepped close to Arwen, his chest brushing hers, and rested a hand on her hip. He bent his head to brush his lips to her neck as his hand shifted around to her butt, cupping it, and pressing her against him.

Hot zings of pleasure streaked through her body, and she leaned into him, wanting to grab his shoulders and plaster her body to his, but she glimpsed Yendral flying overhead. His green eyes flared as he looked down at them, at Starblade's warm lips on her neck, at a little nip as he moved his mouth, tasting her. That felt so amazing, but...

This was a ruse, Starblade wanting to make his comrade believe he would claim her.

Already aroused, Arwen almost didn't care. She wanted to wrap her legs around him and kiss him as she'd fantasized about doing almost since they'd met. To push her hands up under his shirt and feel the hard muscles she'd seen but never been able to touch. To trace them with her fingers, then scrape her nails along them. Maybe her enthusiasm would make him realize his complications weren't insurmountable. Maybe he would want to make the claim a reality.

But as Yendral flew past them and toward the forest, Arwen wrapped her dignity around herself like a cloak. "You don't need to sully your honor for my sake. I can take care of myself."

Maybe it was a dumb thing to say, since it wasn't as if she could beat a half-dragon in a fight, but neither Starblade's nor Yendral's words led her to believe she would have to *battle* Yendral to get him to leave her alone.

When she moved to step back, to make it clear Starblade didn't need to pretend to desire her, he didn't let go. A little growl emanated from him, as if he were the dragon and not the elf tonight. The *beast*, as he'd once called it.

Maybe he enjoyed holding her? Maybe he didn't want to let her go.

But he straightened and released her, then looked to the sky. Making sure Yendral hadn't lingered?

Flushed and confused, Arwen backed away from Starblade. More than ever, she needed a quiet moment to escape before returning to the dinner party. Turning her back on him, she hurried down the path, hardly caring where she went.

Starblade stepped away from her home and headed toward the edge of the property, toward the woods beyond. Had she irked him? Or was Yendral arguing telepathically with him, and he meant to go out and face him down again?

She didn't know, but she continued farther from her guests, needing privacy. Needing to escape.

3

A SCENT SIMILAR TO EUCALYPTUS WAFTED TO ARWEN, DRAWING HER down the path toward the pool Starblade had been working on. When last she'd looked, it had still been a hole in the ground. Had he managed to complete it while she'd finished dinner preparations?

A hint of soothing magic lingered in the air along with the appealing scent. Allowing it to calm her roused nerves, Arwen followed the path to the pool, which was indeed full of water now. Water with steam wafting from the surface. More, the ground on the side closest to her house had been covered in flagstones to create a patio. Near the edge, vines grew up from between the stones to clasp a weathered log that was carved flat to make a bench.

Just as when she'd been in Starblade's sanctuary, the magic and the eucalyptus scent, both promising relaxation and soothed muscles, made her want to peel off her clothes and slip into the water.

"Not tonight," Arwen muttered, not wanting Yendral or another dragon to fly overhead and catch a peep. Well, she might have wanted Starblade to do that, but he wouldn't want to. Apparently, his only interest was in keeping Yendral from pestering her. "Life was simpler before I met him. *All* of them."

As clangs came from the front of the property, peppered by elven and dragon insults, Arwen thought wistfully of when she'd hiked with Val's mother, Sigrid, and hadn't even known her daughter. But Val wasn't the problem; all these half-dragons were. And the newly arisen threat from the dark elves. Arwen hoped none of *them* were out there, keeping an eye on her. The memory of Harlik-van using a magical telescope to spy on her from afar still chilled her.

"Another reason not to slip naked into the pool." She did kneel at the edge and dip her finger in, letting the soothing steam wreathe her face.

Magic swelled a few feet above the water, a silver glow forming. A portal.

Startled, Arwen sprang back. She'd left her bow on the deck and only had her foraging knife. A poor weapon against anyone with the power to create a portal.

At least it didn't feel like dragon magic. Or dark-elven magic.

"Surface elf?" she guessed.

The only full-blooded elf she knew of in the area was Sarrlevi, and he was busy dueling Zavryd. Val had mentioned a diplomatic envoy visiting Willard, but he wouldn't know to come to the farm, would he?

The surface of the portal rippled, and an elf with long white hair leaped out, barely making it to the flagstones. As he landed, a glowing sword in his hand, he glanced in surprise behind him. He must not have expected his portal to form over water.

"It's a new addition," Arwen said while keeping her distance. She had no idea who he was or how he would react to her.

The elf whirled, his green eyes widening when he spotted her. Sword lifting, he barked something in his native tongue. Though he was older, with a lined forehead and creases at the corners of his eyes, his aura suggested he was a formidable wizard. The practiced fighting stance he lowered into demonstrated comfort with that sword too.

Arwen shook her head and held up empty hands. "I can read a few words, but I'm not that familiar with your language." Silently, she reached out to Val. *There's a strange elf that just came out of a portal back here. Is Willard with you?*

Flames in the driveway roared up thirty feet, visible above both houses, and distracted Arwen.

The elf said something else, then switched to telepathy. *Mongrel dark elf, what have you done with Azerdash Starblade?*

Nothing. We're... Arwen almost said *friends*, but she didn't know *what* they were, not at the moment. The memory of their embrace, his mouth on her neck, rose in her thoughts.

Arwen hadn't meant to telepathically share the image, especially not with a stranger, but the elf must have caught it. His eyes widened even further.

You seduced him? And then what? You slew him? Vile dark elf. The elf sprang for Arwen, swinging his sword as he erected a barrier around himself.

"No," she blurted, dodging the blow and leaping over the bench to get away. As if *that* would keep the powerful elf from reaching her.

Even as she cleared it, his power gripped her, keeping her from landing. With her feet hovering above the flagstones, Arwen couldn't run—she couldn't even duck when the elf raised his sword for another swing.

Starblade is a friend, Arwen blurted. *We were—*

A roar came from above her rooftop, and black-scaled and violet-eyed Zavryd flew into view. *Elf invader, you attack the friend of my mate in her own home?*

The elf must have been too distracted by Arwen—by her vile

dark-elfness—to notice the dragon's aura. Arwen also sensed Sarrlevi and Val running down the path toward the pool.

Releasing Arwen, the elf backed away. He lifted his sword, as if he might confront Zavryd, but he must have thought better of it. Even as Zavryd landed atop a tree whose branches extended over the patio and pool, the elf formed a portal and sprang through it.

Zavryd jumped down, shifting into human form as he landed. A second later, Val, Willard, and Sarrlevi burst into view, Val and Sarrlevi with their blades drawn and Willard gripping a gun.

"Are you all right, Forester?" Willard looked at the portal as it faded, all trace of the elf disappearing.

"Yes. He didn't hit me."

"Why did he *want* to?" Val asked.

"It sounded like he was looking for Starblade and thought I'd done something to him. I don't know why."

The half-truth made Arwen wince. Somehow, the elf had misread her memory of Starblade's embrace as *her* seducing *him*. As if. But it fit what people believed about dark elves—and those unfortunate enough to have some of their blood.

Though Arwen was rattled from the brief confrontation, it almost relaxed her, making her feel like things were normal again. Having someone like Yendral desire her was *not* normal and had her flustered.

"Ma'am." Arwen faced Willard, afraid the others would guess at the contents of her whirlwind thoughts. "What did the elf who visited you look like?"

"Older fellow," Willard said, "with long white hair, a gold-trimmed brown cloak, and a sword in a hip scabbard."

"Green eyes?" In the dark, Arwen had barely registered the cloak, but the rest fit.

"Yes."

"After dinner, we might want to visit Imoshaun's workshop so you can run his blood," Arwen said, "and see if the heritage detector knows who he is."

"A good idea."

"You still want dinner after being attacked?" Val asked.

"Well, I'm the host," Arwen said. "And it's ready."

"I am informing the half-dragon that you were assaulted by one of his kind," Zavryd stated. "I should not have engaged in an exercise duel when your property did not yet have wards, but I believed you were with Starblade and were safe. I did *not* believe he would leave your side, not when he has created for you a *yavasheva*."

"How about setting the wards now, Zav?" Val patted him on the back. "I'll make sure nobody takes your piece of ham."

"My large *chunk* of ham, and the leg of the roasting bird I have smelled, and the yeti haunch."

"I'll make you a plate." In the air, Val pantomimed what looked more like a giant tray.

"Yes, do this, my mate." Zavryd found space and transformed into a dragon again, then flew to the front of the property.

"You sure you're okay?" Val asked Arwen.

"Yes." Arwen nodded. "People jump to conclusions about me all the time."

"And try to kill you?"

"Sometimes. Usually, they aren't as powerful as that elf, so it's less worrisome." Arwen tried not to think about what would have happened if Zavryd hadn't flown over in time.

"Overly powered people from other worlds are pains in the ass," Val said.

"Tell me about it." Willard looked at Sarrlevi and in the direction Zavryd had gone before heading up the path. "We *will* check that elf's heritage, Forester, and find out what he wants on Earth."

Arwen already knew what he wanted. Or at least *who* he wanted.

4

OTHER THAN THE DUEL AND THE BRIEF VISIT FROM THE MYSTERIOUS elf, the dinner didn't prove to be as interesting as Val had expected. Yeti meat reminded Arwen of bear, the turkey was delicious, and everyone raved about the dessert options. Once people were sitting down and engrossed in the food, Arwen's nerves calmed somewhat. They were too engaged in their own pleasure to do more than nod and give her a compliment now and then.

Her father, who'd taken Frodo for a ride not only around the property but to the small store where he purchased beer, returned with a six-pack once the dinner was underway. Like a forest troll, he glowered over at the table—and logs—as he snatched a turkey leg, then disappeared into the barn.

Not wanting to worry him, Arwen didn't mention the elf. She would prepare a plate of leftovers for him to enjoy later.

Yendral returned but didn't make a pass at her, instead frowning when Willard described the elf.

"He said his name is Ambassador Rysharon."

"It's not familiar to me," Yendral said, "but Starblade may know. He always paid more attention to who is a who—that is the

Earth term, yes?—in the capital. And he has communicated of late with the king."

"Didn't he make *threats* to the king?" Val asked.

"After attempts at more friendly communication and negotiation were not accepted, he felt forced to deliver an ultimatum. You must understand we were backed up a corner."

"Where is Starblade now?" Willard didn't comment on Yendral's mangled idioms.

He looked at Arwen, as if she might know—or had been responsible for sending him on an errand?—but she shook her head.

"He will return," was all Yendral said.

"I have a video recording of the elf in my office," Willard said, "if you want to see if you recognize him."

"I can see his face in your mind and am certain I do not know him."

"You're reading my mind?"

"Naturally."

Willard gave Val a sour look. "Dragons are a threat to national security."

"And a peaceful meal," Val said.

"It is *elves* tonight who have interrupted the dining experience." Zavryd slanted a look at Sarrlevi to make the plural meaning clear.

"Do not accuse me of inappropriate behavior, dragon," Sarrlevi replied. "You drew your fiery blade and challenged me first."

"Hm."

"At least there are wards around the property now," Val said, "thanks to Zav."

"Indeed," Zavryd said. "Only the tracker, her father, and the friends she requested have access to the property will be able to walk over the boundary without alerts going off and the tres-passers experiencing a most unpleasant electrical charge."

"You might want to put up a sign," Matti told Arwen, "to instruct the mail person to leave packages at the box."

"Good idea," Arwen said.

"The uninvited goblins who appeared on the property," Zavryd said with a stern look toward the log the green-skinned visitors had claimed, "will not be able to return unless you adjust the wards to allow it."

"Thank you," Arwen said, though she wasn't that concerned about them. After all, they'd brought a dinner gift. How practical the heavy stop-sign arrow would be, she didn't know, but she'd tucked it into her quiver. The enchantment that kept arrows from falling out when she leaped and climbed had buzzed a little indig-nantly at such a hefty addition.

Near the end of the meal, Amber drew Arwen aside.

"You may need this more than I do." She opened her palm to reveal the spyglass-shaped camouflaging charm that she'd lent Arwen before.

"You're willing to rent it to me again?"

"You don't have to pay. Give it back when you get one of your own."

Surprised by the generosity, Arwen accepted it.

"Are you sure there's not a contract to sign? Or a bill that will come in the mail? You're usually—" Arwen edited the words that wanted to come out—*overly capitalistic*—to, "—a shrewd busi-nesswoman."

"I know, but I'm feeling generous and content after eating three pieces of your pie. Too bad Val said we need to have sword practice in the morning so I can burn it off. That isn't how I planned to spend my summer vacation. I don't suppose you'll need a driver soon? Or for any research to be done?" Amber raised hopeful eyebrows.

"Ah, I'm not sure, but I'll keep you in mind."

"Thanks. It's still ten percent for actual work, FYI."

"That's what I would expect."

After the dinner wrapped up, Willard promising to text over anything she learned about the elf, Arwen stepped into her father's kitchen and made a plate of leftovers for him. She also made a larger plate for Starblade in case he returned. After the silliness about *claiming* her, she wasn't sure she wanted him to, but she did want to warn him that an unfamiliar elf was looking for him.

When Yendral flew off, Arwen was relieved. She longed for the quiet of her little home and a book. But after the other guests left, the goblins taking the plates as well as the remains of the yeti meat, Arwen sensed Starblade. He landed in the driveway.

Arwen took his plate outside, aluminum foil covering the contents.

He stood in elven form, his hands clasped behind his back as he gazed up at the deck. "I came to apologize for my earlier... dishonorable action. At the time, it seemed like a logical choice, but you were not pleased by it."

"Don't worry about it. While you were gone, an elf came looking for you."

Starblade started to open his mouth, as if to state that he *would* worry about his behavior, but her last sentence made him pause.

"I'm not sure if he's a friend or a foe." Arwen walked down the steps and handed him the plate. "Probably a friend, based on how he reacted to me. Or at least someone who wants something from you."

"Given how few elven *friends* I have, the latter is more likely." Starblade looked at the plate but set it aside. "I will eat this later. I appreciate you preparing it for me."

"You're welcome."

He hadn't exactly said *thank you*, but for a haughty half-dragon, it was close.

"Those who *were* friends," he said, "or commanders who held me in good regard, passed in the years I was imprisoned in the stasis chamber. It was jarring to return to awareness in the Cosmic Realms only to realize that all those we'd once cared for, those we'd protected and served, were dead."

"I'm sure that was weird. And sad."

Arwen let her earlier irritation fade. Starblade's tiff with Yendral and plot to faux claim her were insignificant compared to what he'd been through. And to what she'd been through in her life too. Besides, he'd thought he was being noble, trying to protect her in a way.

"It was... sorrowful, yes. And I've since lost some of the half-dragons I was able to release from their own stasis prisons." Starblade gazed toward the beehives, their inhabitants slumbering in the dark. "If I'd known what would happen, I would have left them in the chambers to come out in another time, a better time."

He'd lost Gemlytha, Arwen thought but didn't say. "You couldn't have known."

"No? I believe I could have foreseen that the Realms wouldn't consider us heroes. But I was..." Hands still clasped behind his back, he shook his head and fell silent.

Lonely, she thought. He might not have said it, but she believed she was right.

He dropped his arms and met her gaze. "I believe I lured you away from your party with a promise to teach you to create a magical barrier."

He hadn't *lured* her but commanded her, but she'd needed a break so could hardly blame him. And she wanted to learn to protect herself with her magic, now more than ever, so she perked with interest.

"Before we begin instruction, will you show me your memory

of the elf?" Starblade lifted his fingers toward her temple but held them out, not presuming to touch her without permission.

No, that wasn't quite true. He'd touched her earlier... But this was mind reading, not neck nuzzling.

"Go ahead," Arwen said. "Willard got a blood sample from him and is having it checked."

Starblade raised his eyebrows. "A full-blooded elf from Veleshna Var voluntarily gave her a drop of blood?"

"He voluntarily gave her *stapler* a drop of blood."

"What is a stapler?"

"A clever device for attaching papers together, possibly of Gnomish origin."

Starblade smiled faintly. "Are you teasing me, Chef Arwen?"

She grimaced at Yendral's name for her. "Just Arwen, please. And, yes, staplers are made in factories by humans. Although I gather this one was goblin-improved."

"Arwen." Starblade nodded at her and touched his fingers to her temple to retrieve her memory of the elf. "You may call me Azerdash. I should have said that when we met. The galaxy blades are all missing, from what I've learned since waking in this century. When I was given my command, I received one—the great magical swords were crafted specifically for us half-dragons. Forged by multiple elven masters, they were meant to give us an edge so we might be as powerful as full-blooded dragons. I do not know that the elven smiths and enchanters accomplished *that*, but they were impressive magical weapons, and I was honored to carry one."

He imparted a memory of his own to her, of a beautiful sword with a night sky imbued into the metal. Another memory showed him wearing armor and a forest-green uniform, astride an elven riding bird and pointing the blade as he led his troops into battle.

"Only eight swords were made," he continued. "Those of us

who received them were all granted the surname Starblade. Without it, I am only Azerdash."

"Dash for short?" Arwen smiled, though when he flew in his dragon form, the great wingbeats that carried him far always seemed languid, not fast like a sprint or a *dash*. "That's a human name," she added at his head tilt.

"Hm." A flex of his nostrils suggested he wasn't a fan. "I once met an elf with the nickname Dasher. Would that help me fit in here?"

"With a reindeer herd, maybe."

That prompted another head tilt.

"Never mind. I'll call you Azerdash. It's a great name."

"It's... adequate." He sighed wistfully. Missing his sword?

"The galaxy blades are handsome weapons. I can see why you miss having one."

"Powerful weapons."

"Maybe you can find one again."

"I've heard there's one in the museum of the royals in the capital on Veleshna Var, but I doubt King Eireth will give it to me."

"No? Even when he learns that you're a relative?" Arwen had no idea if Val had passed that information along to her elven father—or, if Eireth had received it, if he'd believed it.

"I suspect he would regard me as... what is the human term? The charcoal sheep?"

"Something like that." Arwen smiled, the tension that had tightened her shoulders all night finally loosening. Wanting to help him, she did her best to accurately remember the elf. Thanks to his abrupt attack, the meeting had been a blur.

Starblade frowned. "He attempted to kill you. For no reason."

"He..." She stopped herself from saying he'd had a reason. It had been an idiotic reason that the elf had somehow misinterpreted because he'd rudely been reading her mind. "Yes."

Starblade lowered his hand. "It does not please me that beings who are seeking *me* out keep coming and threatening you."

"He went to Willard first."

Of course, he hadn't threatened *her*.

"Because he was looking for you," Arwen added. "Did you recognize him?"

"He's... familiar, but I can't place the face. Perhaps someone from the king's court?" Starblade didn't sound confident about the guess. "Unfortunately, his voice doesn't come through via a mental link."

"He didn't speak a lot anyway. I think just to cuss me out in Elven before jumping into my head."

"Unacceptable."

"I'm used to it."

He gazed at her, his mouth twisted in disgruntlement.

"You might remember that when we first met, you called me a vile dark-elf mongrel and tried to read my mind."

"That was also unacceptable."

"*I* thought so." Arwen smiled again and touched her chest. "But it's not atypical for me. I can't say I like it, but it's familiar at this point in my life." She didn't mention that she almost preferred hostility to Yendral's interest. She knew how to handle the hostility, but men wanting to eat with her in the forest flustered her.

"I will instruct you on magical barriers now. You have the power to learn to make a substantial one, perhaps one strong enough to keep away obtuse magical beings who bounce to conclusions."

The word *bounce* made her think of the one time someone had taken her to a toy store when she'd been a kid. It had been noisy, crowded, and moderately terrifying, but she'd briefly had a delightful time bouncing down an aisle on a space hopper with a cow head.

Whatever expression crossed her face must have convinced

Starblade he'd used the wrong word. "Leap to conclusions? Spring to assumptions?"

"Jump to conclusions. Maybe I can find you a book on American idioms."

And he could share it with Yendral.

"Yes, this would be acceptable. There are terms in the Study of Manliness that I have not understood. For instance, what is the man upstairs?"

"God." Arwen touched a cross necklace her father had given her as soon as they'd escaped from the dark elves, then pointed upward. "Our god here that we pray to, that is. Other humans believe in different ones, and I know magical beings have varied beliefs too."

"Yes, but why are stairs involved?"

"Because Heaven is considered by many to be in the sky."

Judging by his puzzled expression, he was imagining a very long flight of stairs, but he didn't ask for further clarification. "What is it to be tied to your mother's apron strings?"

"That's someone who's used to his mom doing everything for him and can't manage on his own."

"I may use that on Yendral. He called *me* a confirmed bachelor. This means I don't seek a mate, correct? This is not untrue, but he said it mockingly, and I suspected a dual meaning."

"It can imply a guy is into other guys, though I'm not sure where Yendral would have heard that."

"He loiters at bars and the werewolf-owned winery."

"I suppose that's one way to get an education."

"I prefer the books on your history, politics, and engineering."

"Especially the latter?"

"Indeed."

"I'm positive that if you visited Willard, you wouldn't inadvertently staple yourself."

He'd already admitted he hadn't encountered the office tool, but he nodded and said without doubt, "That is correct. I will lower my mental defenses, and you will enter my mind to observe me creating a barrier."

The abrupt transition made Arwen blink.

"Unlike Earth idioms, magic cannot easily be learned from a book," he added.

"Tell me about it," Arwen said.

"I am doing so."

"No, I mean... I'm ready."

Starblade—Azerdash smiled, so maybe he'd deliberately misinterpreted that one. "Come. I will sit, and you will rest your hand on my head to facilitate the observing. This is essentially mind reading, but I will deliberately share."

Arwen's vague memories of learning dark-elven magic as a girl had involved lectures, stern demands, and a short whip with tips like spider legs that was used for punishment. No dark elf had invited her to *observe* his or her thoughts.

"Is this... the elven way?" She followed him to the deck steps and explained the dark-elven way as she maneuvered to sit above him.

"The elven way also involves lectures and demands but not whips or physical punishment. Occasionally, to make a point, an instructor will grow a magical root up to entangle the ankles of an inattentive student, but that is not painful. If you wish, I can lecture you, but this is a shortcut, I believe is the term. Since it is somewhat intimate, it is only done between those who have a modicum of trust with each other."

"You trust me?" she blurted in surprise. She wanted him to but hadn't realized he might.

His smile returned. "You have not shot me in the leg for several weeks."

"I am trying not to let people manipulate me into doing that."

"Yes. Continue striving toward that goal."

"You like to give commands, don't you?"

"It is in my nature." He gestured toward the step above him. "Observe."

"Right."

Arwen rested her hand on the top of Azerdash's head, as he'd once done to her when he'd wished to read her thoughts. His shoulder-length black hair was softer than she expected, and she had to resist the urge to stroke it.

She also kept herself from touching his pointed ears, having heard that they were sensitive for elves, but it was hard not to find them intriguing. Oh, dark elves had pointed ears, so she'd seen plenty as a girl, but she couldn't remember ever touching any or getting close. With him, it was different. His were more... interesting.

You are paying close attention? Azerdash asked telepathically.

Arwen blushed. "Yes."

He looked back at her, eyebrows up.

"No," she admitted, "but I will. I am now."

Arwen closed her eyes and used her senses, trying to wrap them around his head instead of penetrating his skull. He'd said he would lower his mental defenses, but she didn't want to assume and drill right in. If that was even an apt verb. Never had anyone, not even her mother's people, attempted to teach her to read minds.

He drew upon power, both within himself and within the earth under the deck, then formed it all into a ball of energy at his core. From there, he expanded the ball until it extended beyond their bodies. The magic didn't affect the deck or railing but created a perfect sphere, an impenetrable wall that would keep everything from raindrops to fireballs to arrows from reaching him. At the same time, it would allow him to use his weapons against others.

That is the difficult part, Azerdash spoke silently. *Allowing fluctuations to accommodate one's surroundings as well as one's weapons is not automatic. Most beginners will knock over items when they create their first barriers. It is good to practice with walls or trees nearby so you learn how to allow the magic to flow around such things. Walls and trees you're not overly fond of, since you will make mistakes.*

Arwen opened her eyes, horrified at the thought of the side of the barn or her father's house being knocked down. And the trees? She wouldn't want to lose any of them. Nor would she want to take out the deck. Certainly not the greenhouse or any of the beehives.

As she looked around for something she wouldn't be upset about breaking, her gaze skimmed over the vine-and-stick fire spit.

They must have been linked closely enough that Azerdash could read her thoughts because he tartly said, *You will not practice on the magical spit that I crafted.*

Sorry. She hadn't truly been considering it, but she also didn't know if it would survive the stormier seasons. Due to the materials, it looked a touch fragile. But maybe the magic infused in it made it stronger than it appeared. *Maybe the mailbox. It's old. Or I could get some traffic cones.*

Hmmmph. Azerdash was eyeing her. Catching her thoughts about spit fragility? If so, he continued with the lesson without commenting on it. *Once you can create a barrier without knocking anything over, you will be ready to learn how to adjust the flow to fire arrows through it. Or stab with your... blade.* The glance he gave her foraging knife wasn't exactly scathing, but it did convey that she might want to find a superior weapon for hand-to-hand fighting.

Since she preferred staying back—*well* back—in battles and using her bow, she hadn't considered that. Besides, she often found the small blade and brush handy, not solely for cutting and cleaning foraged mushrooms.

Isn't it hard to fight for your life and keep a barrier up at the same time? Arwen asked.

Eventually, with practice, creating a barrier becomes subconscious, as does adjusting it to allow your weapons through. He dropped his magic, then formed it again, starting with the ball and pushing it outward.

Arwen watched him repeat the exercises slowly several times. It brought back memories of her mother's people. Even though they'd been a united clan living together in a complex of connected tunnels, there had often been spats, and the dark elves had created barriers whenever a confrontation threatened to escalate. Drawing upon the inner power granted by demons, they'd conjured defenses that had a red tint to Arwen's eyes, what had felt like an inherent evilness.

Maybe that had been her imagination, but she tried to make her barrier exactly as Azerdash did, wanting to do it like a surface elf, drawing upon inner power and the magic in the ground, nothing granted by demons who demanded sacrifices.

But when they moved away from the deck, and she tried to emulate what he'd done, nothing happened. She could form her power into a ball in her chest, but it refused to expand outward.

She envisioned trees and the earth offering her more power that she could draw upon, and she was able to pull more into her, the energy almost making her skin buzz as it intensified, but a weird urge to turn it into a weapon came over her. A memory popped into her mind of a dark elf hurling a red sphere of energy like a flaming cannonball.

Frustration infused her as she held the ball of power, not able to make it do what she wished. A whisper from the back of her mind promised a demon would prefer a weapon to defense and would reward her if she gave in and used her power like a dark elf.

Aware of Azerdash watching her, Arwen shook her head, refusing to give in to that urge. But she was also self-conscious and afraid she couldn't do it in the *elven* way. The ball of energy built until her head ached. She needed to release it but worried about nearby trees and her father's house and truck.

Feeling desperate and that she might lose control, she channeled the power into the ground, as she did when she helped trees. She used it to feed the roots of nearby plants and trees, twisting it into energy they could use for increased vigor. The branches all around seemed to sigh, pleased to receive the infusion.

"Sorry," Arwen said as the power bled out of her and lost its alarming edge.

"Perhaps the trees will rise to your defense if you are attacked," Azerdash said.

Her shoulders slumped with chagrin.

He lifted a hand. "Do not feel defeated. It takes practice, and it would have been surprising if you'd done it on your first attempt."

"I felt like I had the power but that it fought me."

His tone turned graver. "I saw."

Did he know that the demons of her heritage made everything more difficult? Maybe he did. He'd admitted that he had to fight his dragon half not to be overcome, to turn into a beast.

"I believe you are right not to give in to the temptation to use the power as a dark elf would," he said.

"Yeah. Not doing so makes everything harder, but—" Arwen shrugged. She'd long ago decided she wanted nothing of her mother's people or their ways. Even if it was hard, she would twist her magic into benign outlets.

"As Admiral Hruthia once said, 'Adversity shapes a man in a way that ease never could.'"

"I know. I'll try again. I—"

Azerdash looked toward the road, and Arwen paused.

She sensed magic beyond the property line. Elven magic.

Azerdash rose to his feet. "A portal forms."

"That elf might have returned."

"If so, let us find out what he wants."

5

BY THE TIME ARWEN AND AZERDASH WALKED UP THE LONG DRIVEWAY to the road, the portal had disappeared. The foliage obscured the view, but she sensed the same powerful elf who'd appeared earlier in the night. She slowed her pace, wanting him to see Azerdash before her.

But Azerdash looked back and created a barrier around them, waving for her to walk at his side. The silent gesture seemed more a command than a suggestion, but that was typical of him, and she didn't mind it this time. Walking at his side might convey that she was an equal, not a servant or lesser being. Or a horrible woman who'd seduced him, as the elf had chosen to believe.

They found their visitor in the center of the gravel road, the lack of streetlamps keeping it in darkness, save for the glow from his sword. It hung at his side and cast his face in a mix of light and shadow. He'd been eyeing the magical wards that now marked the property—Zavryd's work was invisible to the naked eye but detectable to those who could sense magic—but focused on Azerdash.

Lips parting with uncertainty, the elf looked from him to Arwen and back a couple of times before speaking in his tongue.

No, Azerdash replied telepathically, sharing his response with Arwen, *she is not powerful enough to compel me to do her bidding. Nor did she seduce me.*

The elf replied aloud, again speaking in Elven. He probably didn't know English and didn't want to use telepathy. That skirted the language issue, the base meanings of words coming through in one's mind, but he might not *want* Arwen to understand.

Eyes closing to slits, Azerdash replied, *You came onto her property and attacked her. I do not know who you are, but you will include her in this conversation since you made your presence a concern for her.*

The elf's mouth drooped. *You do not remember me, Commander Azerdash Starblade? I know it has been many years, but...*

Azerdash squinted at him. Earlier, he'd admitted the elf was familiar.

Azerdash created a globe of light to illuminate their visitor's face better than the glow of the sword. *You do seem familiar,* he admitted.

I served under you many centuries ago. The elf glanced warily at Arwen before smiling at Azerdash. *I'll admit I've grown older. I was a raw rookie then, barely old enough to swing a sword.*

A few thoughtful seconds passed before Azerdash asked, *Third Rank Rysharon?*

The elf's smile broadened, and he sheathed his sword and bowed. *Now Ambassador Rysharon, mostly retired.*

Mostly retired except for trips to Earth to attack the natives?

The elf's smile faltered, and he gave Arwen another wary look. *A mongrel dark elf is not— I did not expect to find such a one in your presence and was confused by the glimpses of you I saw in her mind. If she is... an ally, I apologize for incorrectly assessing the situation.*

You could have killed her.

The elf hesitated but didn't say what Arwen expected, that the death of a mongrel would be no loss to the Cosmic Realms. *Yes. I apologize.*

Azerdash looked to her. *Do you accept?*

Arwen shrugged, surprised he was asking since this probably had nothing to do with her except that the elf had found him at her house. *Sure. Especially if he's a friend of yours.*

Azerdash assessed the older elf. *We will determine if he is a friend. He was once a subordinate.*

With very poor sword skills. Rysharon managed to affix the smile again. *They improved somewhat, but, after the war, the king put me to work in a field using quills instead of blades.*

Arwen thought his swordsmanship had been adequate when he'd sprung after her like a twenty-year-old instead of... How old *was* this guy? The war between the elves and dwarves had been hundreds of years ago, if not a millennium in the past, hadn't it?

Wise, Azerdash said.

Yes. May I speak with you in private, Commander? It is not about the past or my career but about the future of our people.

Azerdash stood without replying—at least not giving a reply that included Arwen. His face was masked. Did the future of the elves concern him these days? When they'd done nothing to shelter him from the dragons who wanted to get rid of him and his half-breed kin?

I will hear what you have to say, Azerdash finally responded.

He didn't ask it, but Arwen walked back up the driveway to give them the privacy Rysharon wanted. None of this had anything to do with her, though she did worry that Azerdash, who'd barely gotten the Silverclaw dragon clan off his back—and possibly only temporarily—would allow himself to be drawn into some other trouble.

An owl hooted from the towering pines and firs to the east side of the property, and a bat flew past in search of insects. With her guests gone and the scent of snowberry blossoms in the air, a plant she cultivated for her bees, the night finally felt peaceful.

The lights were out in the barn, so Arwen assumed her father had gone to bed. She didn't blame him for disappearing during the busy dinner and wondered if he would have words for her later, reminding her of his preference for solitude on the farm.

A shadow stirred by the cook fire, her father leaning over the embers and turning the spit. Arwen had removed the meat to serve for dinner, so he could only be examining the craftsmanship. Or wondering who the heck made a spit out of sticks and vines.

"I put together a plate for you and left it in the oven to stay warm." Arwen stopped at his side.

He grunted, and she smiled, remembering when Azerdash had decided Father was a suitable role model for the type of person the Study of Manliness espoused. There had been a lot of grunting that day.

"Sorry about all the guests. It was more than I planned."

"I heard someone attacked you." He frowned at her. "Should I be following you around the property with my gun these days?"

"No. The dragon, Zavryd, put up some magical wards, so there shouldn't be any more attacks. On either of us. Though the goblin delivery guy will have to leave packages at the mailbox."

"Your life has gotten more dangerous of late. It might not be a good idea for you to work for that colonel."

Alarm quickened Arwen's heart. Would her father try to forbid her from taking further missions for the Army?

This last month had been chaotic, with her world turning far more eventful than she ever would have imagined, but she'd also gotten to know Matti and Amber and Val. If she stopped working for Willard, she might not see them much anymore. Even though she couldn't yet claim them as bosom friends, she liked having acquaintances who sensed magic and understood what it was to have strange powers—and who didn't care about her tainted blood.

Seeking a calm and reasonable tone, Arwen said, "The dark elves would have come after me whether I was doing odd tracking jobs for Colonel Willard or not."

"It was a dark elf who attacked you tonight?" Father sounded like he knew it hadn't been.

Arwen wondered who'd slipped into the barn to update him on the events he'd missed.

"No. A regular elf. It didn't have to do with Willard though. It was about, uhm." Arwen glanced at the spit, reluctant to voice Azerdash's name. She didn't want her father to forbid her to see him either.

Not that he would. He hadn't tried to *forbid* her to do anything since she'd turned eighteen. But he wasn't shy about making his disapproval known. And she didn't want him to disapprove of Azerdash.

"Did he make this?" Father pointed at the spit.

She didn't ask who. They both knew. "Yes."

"I caught it rotating by itself. If you touch it here, it stops." He demonstrated. "And then touch it again, and it starts. Like it's battery-powered. A battery-powered stick."

"It's magical. I'm not sure how long the, uh, self-rotating feature will last. He says he's not an enchanter."

That evoked another grunt.

Arwen thought the conversation was over, but Father added, "If you've an itch to... have a relationship with someone and have kids one day, it might be smart for you to consider humans."

Arwen blinked. "Humans?"

Father spread his arms. "We're not so bad."

"Of course not. I didn't mean that. I just— Well, I'm not looking for that."

"You're thirty now. I wouldn't mind grandkids eventually, but I understand that you've struggled with going out and meeting people. The Lord knows, I'm the same."

"Sigrid thought I should go to grocery stores and teach handsome but confused men how to choose ripe fruit."

He snorted. "I suppose that's an option. I worry about you being tangled up with these powerful magical people from other worlds. I taught you to be able to take care of yourself against *most* foes, but I don't have to be magical to tell how dangerous those dragons are. And the *half*-dragons."

"I thought you liked, or at least seemed to be okay with Azerdash—Starblade."

"Sounds like he's got people—and dragons—trying to kill him."

"That's not a reason to write someone off."

Father looked sidelong at her. "You sure?"

"Yes. But he's not interested in me anyway."

"No? I was planning to go to bed, but you two were sitting on the deck, fondling each other's heads, so I didn't interrupt."

Arwen's cheeks heated. "He was teaching me to create a magical barrier around myself."

"Through head fondling?"

"By sharing his thoughts and demonstrating—" Arwen's phone rang, startling her.

Her father frowned. "It's late for people to be calling."

"It's Val. It could be important." Arwen hurried away, relieved for the excuse to end the conversation. "Hey, Val. Everyone okay?"

"Yes, and sorry to call at midnight, but I talked to Zoltan. Since he's a vampire, he keeps strictly nocturnal hours. He said for you to come by before dawn if you want to engage his services. He informs me that he's a *very* busy vampire, and you're incredibly lucky that he can squeeze you in tonight. The rest of the week he's booked. If you come, he can tell you where the ingredients he needs for the formula can be found. All this is assuming you're willing to pay a reasonable amount for his time and effort."

"You said his services are expensive, didn't you?"

"Oh, yes. But if you turn to an amateur, you might end up with an ink-removal formula that takes your whole arm off with the tattoo."

"Uh."

"He's a little prone to hyperbole."

"Do *you* think I need an alchemist?"

"Well, it might not hurt. I can have Zav loom by your side as you negotiate rates with Zoltan. Zav still makes him uneasy."

"Does Zoltan take gold?"

"Oh, I'm sure."

"Amber doesn't. She wants me to convert the gold I've earned to digital currency—*real* money, as she called it—and Venmo her."

"Teenagers are interesting people."

"Yes. Okay, thanks for talking to Zoltan. I'll see if I can get over there tonight." Arwen stifled a yawn, thinking more longingly of her bed than Val's basement, but the sooner she got rid of the tattoo, the sooner she could stop worrying about dark elves controlling her through its magic. Maybe between that and Zavryd's wards, she would be safe for a while.

As she hung up, Arwen sensed Azerdash approaching. Her father had disappeared into the house. The light on in the kitchen suggested he was having the leftovers. Good. She didn't want to field more comments about head fondling.

Azerdash, a faintly dumbfounded expression on his face, didn't look like he had such activities in mind. There was no sign of the ambassador, but Arwen had a feeling her magic lesson was over for the night.

"Everything okay?" she asked.

"Rysharon believes he knows where a galaxy blade can be found and that it's here on Earth."

6

"DID HE HAVE ANY IDEA WHERE ON EARTH THE GALAXY BLADE IS supposed to be?" Arwen asked as the salty breeze whipped at her hair. Azerdash was flying her to Val's house so she could speak to Zoltan. "It's a big planet."

Coincidentally, Azerdash said telepathically, *he believes the dwarf who stole it brought it to this very area but that its specific location was lost when he was killed by highwaymen of the time.*

"Highwaymen?" The term made Arwen think of country singers from her father's youth. He had old records in the house that he played occasionally.

This was believed to be more than a century ago.

"Huh. And the sword might still be here?"

Rysharon thinks so. Researching the blades is something he started doing after he retired—mostly retired—and he's spent years gathering data and trying to locate them. He's been successful before. He found the one that is now secured in the elven capital, waiting in case it needs to be used to defend the world. They're extremely powerful and valuable weapons. From what I've learned, most disappeared after the war— after the half-dragons all fell or were imprisoned. When Rysharon came here seeking evidence for his hypothesis about the dwarf thief, he sensed Yendral from afar and, after asking around, learned that I was here as well.

"If the swords are so valuable, why is he telling you about this one? Other than that he remembers you from his youth?"

There had to be a catch. Again, Arwen worried that Azerdash would be embroiled in something dangerous.

Funny that her father was concerned about that for her, and she was concerned about it for Azerdash. She rested a hand on his scales and eyed Lake Washington as they flew over it, the city lights reflecting on the dark water.

Rysharon said he would have saved the other galaxy blade for me if he'd known I would return to Veleshna Var. He wants me to have one again because he desires something from me and believes I'll be more capable of achieving his wishes if I have the great sword in my hand.

"What is it?" Arwen imagined Azerdash being sent on some quest to slay a hydra hoarding treasure on a remote island. Something a retired ambassador couldn't take on himself.

Azerdash's black-scaled head turned enough for one of his violet eyes to regard her as they flew. *Help the elves drive the dragons off Veleshna Var and free our people from rule under the Dragon Council.*

It took a stunned moment before Arwen could respond. "Wouldn't that be an impossible task?"

His gaze shifted forward again as he stretched his wings, soaring toward the freeway and the Green Lake neighborhood beyond. *It has been tried numerous times over the years by factions of elves and also by other intelligent species who once ruled over their own worlds without outside interference. It has not been successful. Many elves were killed the last time a serious attempt was made. King Eireth rules today because the last king was put to death for being complicit in the insurrection.*

I trust you're not seriously contemplating trying to oust the dragons.

I had never considered doing so. Azerdash hesitated. *Rysharon pointed out, however, that the various intelligent species have never banded together to attack the dragons en masse with everything they had. Even weaker beings might overcome stronger opponents if they combine forces. Though their power is less substantial, there are far more trolls, ogres, dwarves, elves, goblins, gnomes, shifters, and others in the Cosmic Realms and on the wild worlds than there are dragons. Far, far more.*

You're contemplating it. Arwen stared at the back of his head in horror. *Just so he'll help you find that sword? How important a weapon can it be? What if I offer to make you something even better in exchange for* not *trying to piss off dragons all over again and get yourself killed?*

You could make something better than an elven galaxy blade infused with the power of the stars themselves?

My blueberry-crumble pies are really good.

He made a chuffing noise that might have been a laugh. *The yeti was delicious.*

I'm glad you found it so. Arwen had only tried a couple of bites, more out of obligation than because she'd wanted to eat a semi-intelligent creature. *But yetis don't have streusel. My streusel recipe is amazing. I'll make you four pies if you don't join the losing side in a war.*

Rysharon believes I might be a suitable person to assemble a joint-forces army and lead *our side.*

Even more horrified, Arwen barely kept from saying it would still be the losing side. A friend should support a friend in all endeavors, but...

It is possible he remembers me as greater than I am. He was extremely young and impressionable when he served, and he recalls being in awe when I and the other commanders led the troops into battle while wielding those swords.

"I can see that."

He believes that if I once again held a galaxy blade, people would more readily join the cause than when aristocrats and anarchists were plotting. He has, however, already given me the information he has on its location. He was not offering it in exchange for a promise to gather an army. Though I believe he thinks that if I find the galaxy blade as a result of his information, I will feel obligated to undertake his cause.

Undertake starting a war.

Yes. I did not agree that I would do so. It is... a daunting task, and I came here to retire.

Arwen thought he was too young, by elven standards, to retire but also that it would be suicidal to take on the dragons.

I obediently served those who created me, Azerdash added. *I am not an insurrectionist by nature.*

Good. Insurrectionists get killed. People who rebuild tractors and eat pie don't.

He gave her another one-eyed look as he descended toward the intersection by Val's house. *Even those without swords can die upon them.*

You're quoting Lord of the Rings now? Arwen well knew her father's favorite trilogy since she *and* the tractor owed their names to it. *I didn't know the works of General Tolkien were among your collection.*

I am not aware of that reference material.

Oh, a coincidence, then.

If this General Tolkien is a wise scholar of war that I should read, I would happily accept a gift of his selected works. Azerdash spread his wings and landed on the damp pavement, the streets empty at this time of night, fog muting the effect of the streetlamps. *And pie,* he added.

Blueberry-crumble pie?

You've convinced me that all other offerings would be inferior.

Yes, Arwen agreed.

Azerdash levitated her to the pavement before shifting forms.

"Will you come in and loom beside me while I negotiate with a vampire alchemist?" Arwen asked.

"Yes. Will you help me seek the galaxy blade?"

Arwen had taken a step toward the curb and almost tripped. "I... How could *I* help?"

If he hadn't mentioned that acquiring the sword could be linked to him suicidally starting a war with dragons, she would have answered *yes* without asking for details—after all, he'd politely agreed to her odd request. But what he'd told her already made her hope he wouldn't find that sword.

"This is your home world," Azerdash said. "You are more familiar with the names of places and how to research specific history, such as whether the location of a dwarf who visited a century ago is known. I find that the tomes I've acquired are suitable for the particular subject matter they cover, but I require, for example, bathymetric maps of the inlet to the west."

Arwen mouthed, "Bathymetric maps," only vaguely aware that those were for water. And inlet? Did he mean Puget Sound?

"Yes. The blade is believed to be underwater and guarded by a magical creature."

Maybe her vision of a hydra atop a treasure hoard hadn't been that far off.

"I'll help you. Write down anything you need looked up. If I can't find it, I know someone who loves research."

Actually, Arwen knew two people, Amber and Colonel Willard. At the least, Willard liked assigning her goblin assistant to do research. She, however, might feel as Arwen did that their resident half-dragon deciding to build an army and start a war wouldn't be a good thing to encourage, especially when he was hanging out on Earth. Amber, as long as she was paid, wouldn't care what Azerdash intended to do with the sword.

"Excellent." He stepped forward and clasped her hand with both of his as he gazed into her eyes. "I am relieved Rysharon failed to harm you."

A zing of pleasure ran up her arm at his touch. And the

earnest and appreciative look in his eyes made her entire body flush with gratitude. Or maybe something more erotic.

"I would not have expected it from our first meeting, but you have become an excellent ally."

"Yes," she whispered.

"A *loyal* ally."

"Yes," she repeated, remembering how much that meant to him. "I appreciate you too." Surely, he'd done far more to assist her than she had him.

"As you should." His half-smile almost made it a joke, but he was still full of himself.

Since he was rubbing his thumb across the back of her hand, awakening her every nerve, she forgave him for that.

Arwen might have enjoyed the moment—and the hand holding—for longer, but a wooden gate beside Val's house creaked open.

"You are invited in?" Azerdash released her hand.

Though disappointed, Arwen remembered she had a mission —and a vampire with limited office hours to see. "It seems so."

"I am prepared to loom."

"That's because you're also a good ally."

"Yes." He followed her to the walkway where the two dragon-shaped topiaries rose to either side, magic infusing their leaves, and their eyes glowing. Smoke wafted from their nostrils, and Azerdash paused. "These defensive shrubs are poised to attack."

"Yes, they do that to strangers who trespass."

"I may need to destroy them to gain entrance. Or perhaps alter them to serve me. My dragon half enjoys incinerating obstacles, as you've seen, but my elven half urges protection of nature, even nature corrupted to serve a haughty, uptight dragon. These are *sralietha* bushes, but they've been mutated to have thorns. What an odious display."

"Don't destroy or alter anything, please, or nobody in the

house will agree to work with me. One second." Arwen raised a finger. She didn't sense Zavryd inside, but Val was upstairs, and Arwen detected the magical aura of an undead human in the basement. Since she hadn't yet been introduced to Zoltan, she reached out telepathically to Val. *Azerdash is with me and would like to help ensure I get a good rate. May he come on the premises?*

Is he going to strong-arm my vampire roommate? Val replied, thankfully still awake.

I only requested looming. You'd mentioned that Zavryd would do that, but he's not here, right?

He's not. Zav showed me how to adjust the topiaries though. Give me a moment.

"Val is fixing them so you'll be able to go in," Arwen said, giving an update since Azerdash was eyeing the topiaries with speculation.

You can cross now, Val said a moment later. *I asked Zav to put Starblade on the guest list for the topiaries once we found out they're related, but Zav said blood alone isn't reason enough to allow one full access to one's nest. Starblade must prove himself worthy of such trust first.*

What does that involve?

Fighting nobly in battle at his side. Or, in lieu of that, kissing ass would probably work.

He just called Zavryd haughty and uptight, Arwen said. *I don't think the ass thing will happen.*

Well, battles are a weekly occurrence here, so we can wait for that. Zoltan says he's ready for you. I'm barefoot and in my nightie, but let me know if you need me to dress and come down.

Arwen waved that Azerdash could follow her to the gate in the fence. *We'll be fine, thanks. But you wouldn't have to dress on our account. It's your house, after all.*

It's a good idea to be fully clothed and possibly armored when one visits a vampire.

Arwen hesitated at the gate. She wasn't wearing the armored jumpsuit that Imoshaun had altered for her. *Is he likely to attack me?*

Just your veins.

Uh, is that a yes?

He's not a combatant, unless one counts his propensity for acquiring giant guard spiders and other security measures, but when he starts speaking longingly about how hale the veins of magical beings are while gazing raptly at your neck, you get a little uncomfortable.

Azerdash looked past her shoulder and into the backyard. "Is something amiss?"

"Val is giving me some information on her roommate."

He won't attack you if you point an arrow at his chest, Val assured her. *Do you have one that's rated for vampires?*

Rated, as if there were an agency that examined magical arrows and put stickers on them with details about their powers.

I have the new goblin one to try out. How do the undead feel about glowing arrows?

If Zoltan figures out it's made from stop signs, he might not be that intimidated, but I'll warn him that half-dragons can be cranky.

Azerdash does like incinerating obstacles.

That should be a sufficient deterrent to a vampire. You'll be fine.

Thanks.

"I think we're okay." Arwen nodded to Azerdash and continued through the gate. "Though Zoltan sounds as prickly as the thorny topiaries."

"Residing in the presence of a haughty dragon doubtless corrupts all around."

"Yes, I'm sure that's it."

A walkway led through a well-manicured yard to a patio that would have been considered large if it weren't taken up by a wood-sided hot tub attached to two enclosures, the sides made from reclaimed lumber, traffic signs, and corrugated metal. Arwen had heard from Sigrid that Zavryd had a sauna but not that it and whatever was attached to it were of goblin make.

"In addition to the fence, there are numerous wards and defenses around the perimeter of this yard," Azerdash said.

"More security to keep out assassins and thieves, I'm sure." Arwen, with her own property newly warded, had no trouble believing Val found heavy defenses necessary. "Zavryd has to keep his nest safe."

"Indeed. I sense the vampire down there." Azerdash pointed at cement stairs that led from the patio to a basement, a couple of small magical cannons mounted by them. The door at the bottom was made from metal with no window. "He may also be concerned about *his* nest."

"I think it's coffins when it comes to vampires." After descending, Arwen knocked.

The door opened, revealing a tiny dark room inside and another metal door. Arwen hesitated, imagining being trapped in the strange vestibule, but reminded herself that Azerdash could incinerate obstacles if needed.

She stepped inside with him, and the outer door swung shut, sealing them in darkness, no hint of light making it through gaps. She knocked on the inner door. It opened into a brick basement illuminated by panels of infrared lights and computer monitors set up by a workbench with alchemy tools and what looked like a witch's cauldron on top of it. Two cameras on tripods faced the area.

Elsewhere, the basement looked like a laboratory with counters lined with equipment Arwen couldn't name. There were cabinets above and below, and a huge glass display case near the door held skulls, jars of organs and fetuses in formaldehyde, and desiccated husks of things she also couldn't identify. And probably didn't want to.

Sensing the vampire around a corner made by the large brick foundation of an upstairs fireplace, Arwen called, "Hello?"

After Val's talk of veins, she had to resist the urge to take her bow off her back. Instead, she held out her hands as she stepped around the corner.

"Yes, you may enter, as implied by the open gate." A pale, immaculately groomed man—*vampire*—in a powder-blue suit leaned against a counter with a book open in his hands. He spoke with an Eastern European accent and, with black hair combed back from his widow's peak, looked exactly like Hollywood's vision of a vampire. "You are human-looking," he added.

"Uhm." Arwen looked over her shoulder at Azerdash. "Is that okay?"

"Rarely." The vampire—Zoltan, she reminded herself— sniffed. "I'd thought that if you were appealingly exotic, I might feature you in the instructional video that I will naturally do once you've gathered the ingredients and I am ready to, for a reasonable fee, create your formula."

"Videos," Arwen mouthed before remembering Val had said Zoltan had a YouTube channel. "What if I were *un*appealingly exotic?" she asked instead.

"It would depend on *how* unappealing. Great beauty can attract a higher viewership, but spectators are also drawn by freaks and mutants, as evinced by the early sideshow circus acts." Zoltan stroked his chin and considered his camera setup.

"Arwen is not unappealing," Azerdash said coolly. Silently, he added to her, *I do not like him.*

I don't think anyone likes vampires, she answered. *I'm just here for the formula.*

If he insults you, my dragon half may come to the forefront.

She probably should have been alarmed by the threat, but she liked that he wanted to defend her appeal. *If that means you'll incinerate him, I would appreciate it if you'd wait until I've gotten my tattoo removed.*

"No, no," Zoltan said, lowering his hand, "but she is, as I observed, *human*-looking. Not even points to her ears. I, of course, can sense in her aura her dark-elven blood, but auras don't convey through video. Only physical traits." His gaze shifted to Azerdash for the first time. "Your ears are pointed, and while you're not as undeniably handsome as the elf assassin across the street, you have a rugged attractiveness that teenage females like. Females of all ages, I imagine. Perhaps I'll allow you to stand in the video and hold my cauldron."

Azerdash glared at him, his body radiating tension. *When would you like the threatening looming to begin, Arwen?*

Not until we're negotiating prices.

Hm.

"The cauldron is merely for stage theatrics, of course." Zoltan set the book on the counter and picked up a notepad. "As a professional alchemist, I certainly do not use witch paraphernalia, but I have observed that overall views are higher when I employ such props. I draw the line at creating fake smoke and dangling bat wings over the worktable. A commentor requested that." Zoltan stepped toward them and held out the notepad. "I've translated the ingredients for the recipe into English for you, and I've placed a checkmark beside those I either have in my laboratory or am able to acquire through the internet without leaving my domicile." He waved toward a velvet curtain sectioning off a corner of the basement. His personal quarters? "I've also done some preliminary research and written down the locations of the harder-to-find ingredients. I trust you are able to travel by portal?"

"Ah," Arwen said.

"Yes," Azerdash said, then added telepathically, *You have agreed to help me with my sword quest. I will assist you with acquiring the ingredients.*

"Excellent. I believe the magical nightwater fungi may be acquired here on Earth, assuming you can find dark-elf tunnels where they are being cultivated, but you'll need to travel to the troll home world for *yagaroth* root and the fae realm for—" Zoltan glanced at his notes, "—the husk of fragolithian cave corn."

Though Arwen had already been warned that one of the ingredients could only be found in agricultural tunnels cultivated by dark elves, she grimaced deeply at the idea of sneaking into territory held by her mother's clan. "I suppose there's not a mail-order seed catalog that sells those fungi spores so I could order some and cultivate my own."

"If there is, I'm certain the catalog is delivered only to dark-elf mailboxes." Zoltan lifted a finger, as if an idea had come to mind, and his eyes glinted with humor. "Perhaps, if you hid in the bushes —er, behind stalagmites—near one of their mailboxes, you could pounce after a postal delivery and hope to get lucky rummaging through the contents. Of course, if you were caught, the repercussions might be unpleasant. How do dark elves deal with mail theft?"

"Theft of any kind is punished by cutting out one's heart and sacrificing it to the Soul Gatherer," Arwen said. "A demon."

"They're an unsavory people," Azerdash said.

"But I'll wager they have a low crime rate among their populace." Zoltan smirked.

Not amused, Arwen shook her head, "I might as well steal straight from their gardens if I'm going to risk the punishment for theft." She eyed her foraging knife, wondering if it could cut magical fungi.

"I know where to find *yagaroth* root," Azerdash said, "but the cave-corn husk may be more difficult to acquire since the fae are secretive about their farming practices and don't like outsiders in general. Is that the only recipe for a formula capable of removing magical tattoos?"

"It's the only recipe *I* have." Zoltan shrugged. "And, according to the book, it has a number of uses. It can be employed as a solvent capable of cleaning up all manner of messes, magical and mundane, so I believe I could bottle and sell it. I know that dragons complain vociferously if they get difficult-to-remove-substances, such as magical goblin pitch, on their scales." Zoltan pointed upward toward the turret bedroom that Val shared with Zavryd. "He and others of his clan might be buyers. Bring enough ingredients to make a large batch of this formula, and I will give you a discount."

Arwen started to nod, since this seemed reasonable, but she envisioned Amber negotiating for a better deal on her behalf. "If we bring enough ingredients for a large batch, I must insist that you provide the small amount that I need for free. I'll be happy to allow you to keep the rest since you'll be performing the work to combine everything."

"The great *deal* of work to combine everything, and let us not forget the value of the knowledge that guides my hands when I prepare my alchemical masterpieces. I have not even charged you yet for the time I spent researching the locations of these rare ingredients."

"Rare ingredients that you would never be able to acquire without our help." Arwen pointed at herself and Azerdash. "I am a professional forager. It's unlikely you could hire someone as skilled at finding things in the wilds. And will you not also gain income from preparing a YouTube video for your followers? It seems that you will be paid in numerous ways and need not charge me for a small amount of the formula."

"A small amount? I sense that tattoo. It's the size of a barn."

Arwen fought her instinct to hide the mark and pushed up her sleeve to display it. "We have a barn at the farm, and it is much larger in size than this. This is smaller than the door—than the *mouse* door the rodents dug under the wall last winter."

"Yes, yes, I was employing hyperbole, my foraging farmer. As to the video, scant few will be interested in watching me make a solvent. My followers desire to know how to cause warts to sprout on their teachers' cheeks, give debilitating stomach cramps to their ex-boyfriends, and make the hair of their schoolroom nemeses fall out."

That list sidelined Arwen, and she almost forgot their negotiation. "Those are awful things. You can't really do any of that, can you?"

"Of *course* I can. I am a versatile and talented alchemist. You would not be here otherwise."

"What if Azerdash holds your cauldron during your video?" Arwen smiled apologetically at him, but it was a much smaller price to pay than however many ounces of gold Zoltan intended to quote as his fee. "That'll increase your viewership. You said so yourself."

Azerdash didn't say he wouldn't do the task, but his eyelids drooped, and she didn't think he was delighted by the prospect.

Zoltan considered him. "He would have to hold it *shirtless* to ensure increased viewership. Especially female viewership."

"He... might be willing to do that during a brief appearance." Arwen raised her eyebrows at him.

Since she'd seen him wander naked into his rejuvenation pool, she didn't think he cared about nudity. Of course, getting naked for the sake of a vampire's internet followers might be another story.

A sigh that almost sounded like a growl came out of Azerdash.

"If he's unwilling," Zoltan said, "I would accept *you* holding my cauldron while wearing something to draw attention to your female assets. I have a small but growing number of male viewers also interested in the art of alchemy."

The art of cursing teachers with warts and enemies with hair loss, it sounded like.

"*I* will assist you with your video," Azerdash stated. "Your lascivious viewers will not ogle Arwen's female assets."

"Very well." Zoltan waved, indifferent about *whose* assets he employed. "I agree to your terms. I fear I made a mistake in admitting that I had uses for this formula, but I did not expect much negotiating acumen from someone with twigs sticking out of her hair."

Chagrined, Arwen reached for her bun, releasing it so she could comb her fingers through her locks. A single sprig of cedar fell out. That didn't count as *twigs*, in the plural, did it?

Azerdash brushed her hair behind her ear, a gesture that surprised her with its intimacy until he extracted a piece of a leaf. At least he smiled while doing so. Arwen would have felt exasperated, since she had no idea how long the forest had been riding along with her, but it was worth it to see him less irritated.

"General Mysolysar," Azerdash said, "advised his colleagues in war that there are times when you wish to sow fear in your enemies by making your forces appear greater than they are and other times to show only part of your forces, thus to be underestimated."

Was that about her? And her twigs?

"Indeed." Zoltan handed his translation of the ingredients and the locations to Arwen, then pointed at the cedar sprig on the floor. "Take that with you when you depart. The outdoors is full of dirt, bacteria, and other unclean microscopic organisms that do not belong in a laboratory." He curled a lip at them, as if he might also label Arwen and Azerdash as unclean organisms that didn't belong, but he only pointed them to the doorway. "I will be prepared when you return with the ingredients."

Outside, Azerdash surprised Arwen by wrapping an arm around her shoulders. She'd worried he would be irritated at having to hold a cauldron and take stage direction from a pompous vampire.

"My looming was not required," he said. "You negotiated well."

"Thank you." She leaned against him, glad for the compliment —and the arm.

"After you rest, we will begin the quest to acquire these ingredients. You will need to learn where to gain access to a dark-elf lair. Also, find an entrance to the fae realm."

"I have some resources I can tap." Arwen thought Val and Willard would know about active fairy rings—it was possible Val had one of those right in her front yard—but she vowed to send a detailed message to Amber, asking her to research the galaxy blade while she and Azerdash were busy with this. Whether he'd had to loom or not, he was helping with her quest, and she owed him help with his.

7

_____

I<small>T IS NOT NECESSARY TO PRIORITIZE THE FINDING OF THE GALAXY BLADE,</small> Azerdash said for the second time as he flew Arwen toward Amber's house in Edmonds the next morning. *We should locate the ingredients for your alchemical formula as soon as possible.*

This won't take long. I already told Amber about the sword quest so she could start doing research, but I thought you should share as much as you know. That'll give her more of a starting point.

This requires an in-person visit?

Are you sure you just don't want to see her because she was snarky about you riding in her car last time?

I am indifferent to the snark, but she insulted your choice in clothing.

A terribly egregious offense. Arwen wondered if she should mention how many people had denigrated her over the years and that comments on her *clothing* were the least hurtful type of insult she'd received. No, she didn't want to fish for sympathy from someone who'd been created by his people to be used in war, then locked away for centuries. That was worse than insults.

General Herathdor the Great suggested uniforms and homogeneity among troops to ensure merit was determined solely by actions and abilities.

Humans aren't into homogeneity.

Likely because of their lack of abilities with which to distinguish themselves.

I'm sure that's it.

Arwen's phone rang as they followed Highway 99 over Shoreline toward Edmonds, those in cars below oblivious to the half-dragon flying above. Well, *most* of those in cars. Someone with magical blood swerved onto the sidewalk and stuck his head out the window.

"Morning, Val," Arwen answered.

"Hey, I got your text. Sorry I was sleeping when you sent it."

"That's a thing normal people do at 3 a.m."

Thanks to her meeting with Zoltan, Arwen had only gotten a few hours of sleep herself. She might have snoozed longer, but a ticking at her window had woken her. A bird looking for seeds, she'd thought, but a black-scaled tail had been dangling down from the roof and bumping the glass. Apparently, half-dragons didn't sleep in, especially when perched on the rooftops of small homes that left some of their body hanging over the edge.

"As I've told Zoltan before," Val said. "To answer your question, yes, the fairy ring in my front yard can open a doorway to the fae realm. I've used it before. I can't particularly recommend the experience, but if you go, I can come along. I have experience there. And trust me when I say we'll want to take some boxes of chocolates for the queen."

"As an offering?"

"Offering, bribe, call it what you will. It might keep you from fighting a deadly assassin for the queen's entertainment."

"Is that the deadly assassin who lives across the street from you now?"

"It is. Strange world, isn't it? If we bring Starblade, that might work in lieu of dessert bribes. The queen is into elf ears."

"When you say *into*, do you mean... attracted by?"

"Yup."

Arwen eyed Azerdash's long neck. His wingbeats hadn't faltered during the discussion, but she was positive his keen ears caught everything. "Unless he wants to volunteer to seduce her, or be seduced by her, I'll plan to make a dessert."

"Make it with chocolate. She loves it."

"I can do that. I have a blueberry-chocolate-chip cookie recipe with orange zest that's delicious." Arwen imagined putting freshly baked cookies in a basket and skipping through the fae realm like Little Red Riding Hood.

"That might do it, but if not, elf ears."

"I'll keep your advice in mind, and I would be happy to have you as a guide, but do we *need* to see the queen?"

"It's a good idea not to sneak into her realm without asking her permission."

"Okay, thanks."

Arwen ended the call, put away her phone, and rested a hand on Azerdash's back as he descended. "What do you think? I was thinking of using my foraging skills to find the ingredient we need from the fae realm, ideally without encountering any of their kind." Admittedly, fragolithian cave corn sounded like a crop from a farm, not a plant found in the wilds.

The fae realm is a combination of pure magic and vast tunnel systems with numerous different climates, depending on where you enter into it. We may need directions on where to forage.

"I suppose that's true, but I'm not going to ask you to volunteer to... show the queen your ears."

You might volunteer Yendral's *ears,* came Azerdash's dry reply. *I believe a fae queen has seen them before.*

Ah. Is he willing to help?

If you give him some of those cookies, I deem it likely. He is currently seeking information about the sentiment toward dragons among the rulers of other intelligent species. He is a good troop.

Arwen, worried that Yendral's search indicated Azerdash was mulling Ambassador Rysharon's suggestion, didn't ask further questions. Was it a betrayal of friendship to hope that Yendral learned that nobody wanted to join in an insurrection?

When Azerdash landed on the roof, they found not Amber but her father in the backyard. He knelt beside a robot lawn mower with the housing off and a screwdriver in his hand.

Since he was fully human, he hadn't sensed their arrival, but if he looked up, he would spot Arwen and possibly Azerdash, depending on if he was making himself visible to the mundane this morning.

Despite a few visits to the house, Arwen hadn't spoken to Amber's father before and didn't know how he felt about people—and dragons—arriving via his roof. A cartoon twenty-sided die on his black T-shirt suggested he was familiar with hypothetical elves, dragons, and the like, but playing games involving them wasn't the same as having them alight on one's house.

Arwen sensed Amber in her bedroom. *We've arrived. Will your father be alarmed if he notices us on the rooftop?*

Duh. Normal people ring the doorbell.

I could ask Azerdash to do that telekinetically.

Just stay there, and don't do anything weird. I'm brushing my teeth, and then I'll be right out. Do you know how early it is for a Saturday?

The sun has been up for two hours.

Only because it's summer, and the sun is always up.

Arwen thought about arguing this dubious assertion—it wasn't as if they were in Alaska or Northern Canada—but since she wanted Amber to assist with research, she decided to wait without complaint. After all, they *had* arrived earlier than she'd intended. Dragons didn't have to worry about getting caught in traffic.

Azerdash, still in dragon form with Arwen on his back, was eyeing Amber's father. What was his name? Thad.

Before Arwen could ask if Azerdash found something off-putting about him, she realized his intent gaze was actually toward the robot mower.

Amber will be out in a minute to greet us, Arwen told him, hoping he wouldn't jump down and speak of Gnomish motors or drive-trains. *We can wait here so we don't startle her father.*

Azerdash levitated Arwen off his back and onto the roof. *While we wait for the mongrel youth, I will inquire about that device.*

It's a lawn mower. It won't be that interesting.

It is self-ambulatory?

I think so.

Intelligent?

No. It randomly rolls around the yard and cuts grass until the battery runs down.

Randomly? Are you certain? Programming true randomness into creations, whether magically or technologically, is not a simple matter. I believe Gnomish inventors rely on pre-set algorithms to emulate randomness. Perhaps we could discuss that later with your gnomish assistants.

Oh, I'm sure Imoshaun and Gruflen would love to chat about that with you.

Never mind that Imoshaun's scientist husband had hidden behind his wife the last time Arwen had visited their workshop with Azerdash at her side.

In the yard below, Thad plucked damp grass clippings out of the mower's innards, then prodded something with his screwdriver.

A curious contraption, Azerdash said. *Is trimming a single species of plant all it can do?*

It can probably mulch leaves too. Humans like to keep their yards tidy.

Your property is wild with dozens of species of fruit-bearing undergrowth and edible foliage in the open spaces.

We're not normal humans. And farms don't have a lot of use for decorative grass.

I will determine if the device has other purposes and is performing optimally. It appears to have a malfunction. Azerdash shifted into his elven form and leaped from the two-story roof to the patio.

Arwen groaned. Thad might not have noticed them on the roof, but he was sure to spot a stranger landing on his patio.

You might want to hurry, she told Amber telepathically.

You want me to come outside in socks and without deodorant like a hobo living out of her van?

Though Azerdash landed lightly, as if hopping off a two-story house was like stepping off a curb, Thad spotted him and let out a startled squawk. He tripped as he tried to scramble to his feet, and his butt hit down in the dew-damp grass before he managed to leap up.

At first, he stared in shock at Azerdash, who was wearing his Lord-of-the-Rings cloak, tunic, and leather boots rather than human clothing designed to help him fit in—not that jeans and a sports-team jacket would have changed Thad's reaction.

"Who the hell are you? What are you doing back here?" Thad stuck his screwdriver out as if it were a dagger while glancing toward the fence gates. Given its diminutive size, its value as a weapon was low. Arwen wasn't even sure about its value as a tool.

"I am Azerdash Starblade, a visitor to your planet. I seek to learn to fit in with the natives by engaging in suitably manly activities, and I also have an interest in mechanical constructs. What is the purpose of that device? I understand it is not imbued with an intelligence or any discernible magic."

Thad, screwdriver still raised, stared at him. His gaze took in Azerdash's pointed ears, but he didn't glance up and notice Arwen.

She didn't know if she should call out a greeting, jump down from the roof, or stay out of his sight. What would be least alarming and intrusive?

"It's a lawn mower," Amber said as she stepped onto the patio. "And didn't Arwen tell you about doorbells?"

After taking a few more steps, Amber peered up to the rooftop where Arwen crouched by the gutter, conflicted about the proper course of action.

"He's more interested in malfunctioning mechanical equipment," Arwen said.

"The doorbell doesn't always work if he wants to investigate that." Amber's nose wrinkle, as she glanced at Azerdash, suggested she would prefer he go do that.

Since Azerdash was striding toward the robot mower, an act that sent Thad scurrying back, Arwen doubted she could entice him away. Apparently not moved to defend his lawn equipment from strangers, Thad circled away from it and toward the patio.

"Amber, it would be nice if you warn me when you're expecting... company." Thad eyed Azerdash's pointed ears again as he crouched to investigate the mower, then shifted his gaze to Arwen.

"I wasn't expecting anyone this early, but this is Arwen, one of my employers. She's been by before. Remember those Gucci cherries?"

"I remember you wouldn't share them with me or Nin."

"They were too good for sharing. Anyway, I've been driving Arwen around, and she's got a research project for me now. We haven't negotiated rates yet, but don't worry. I know what I'm doing. I always get a contract signed."

Thad scratched his jaw as he looked at Arwen, his gaze lingering on her hair. Because she'd managed to get twigs and leaves caught in it again? Or maybe he thought the sticks she used to hold back her bun looked strange. When they'd first met, Amber had called Arwen's style *Davy Crockett*. But Thad, with his gaming T-shirt and Birkenstocks, didn't appear to be as cutting edge as his daughter when it came to fashion.

"Another employer who pays in cash and isn't going to give you a 1099 at the end of the year?" Thad guessed.

"Half the time, she pays in pies and pickled goods," Amber said.

"Hm."

"And Matti has a bookkeeper. She said she *would* give me a 1099." Amber looked at Arwen. "My dad is worried that I'm not keeping proper records about my income and that the IRS is going to arrest me for tax evasion."

"Not arrest, just fine and ensure you pay what you owe," Thad murmured. "For the record, you're supposed to report bartered goods and services. Even if you're a farmer receiving chickens in exchange for bushels of corn, that *is* a taxable event."

"I'm sure the government has better things to do than worry about how many pies I'm getting paid this year." Amber lifted a finger, but before she could continue, a small fire ignited at the lawn mower.

Judging from the calm way Azerdash crouched by the device and watched the flames, he was intentionally creating them for a reason—possibly to clean residue? But, understandably, Thad cursed.

"What's he doing?" He lifted his screwdriver.

Azerdash gazed coolly over at him, a warning glow to his violet eyes. Thad lowered the tool.

"I have removed the detritus clogging the chute of this clipping device," Azerdash said, the flames dying down but smoke trickling upward.

"His dragon half gives him urges to solve problems through incineration," Arwen explained.

Thad gave her an aggrieved look as Azerdash rested a hand on the mower, magic trickling from his fingers.

"Yup, the government has *much* better things to worry about than my pies." Amber gripped Arwen's arm. "Why don't we go into my office to discuss this new gig?"

Arwen almost mentioned Yendral's suggestion that he and Azerdash raise a goblin army to march on the White House and take over the country, but that might not put Thad at ease. And what was Azerdash doing to the mower now? Maybe he would improve it.

"Okay." Arwen nodded for Amber to lead the way to her office —presumably a corner of her bedroom—and waved for Starblade to follow them. He was the one who needed to decant what he knew about the swords.

Amber held up a hand. "It's a small office. Only room for one guest. Maybe he could go out to breakfast or something."

"For a dragon, even a half-dragon," Arwen said, "I think going out for breakfast means hunting something down and consuming it."

"Ew. You can't do that in Edmonds. This is a civilized city."

"There are sea lions and seals at the waterfront." Thad probably didn't wish the local sea life ill will so much as he wanted Azerdash gone.

The smoke had cleared, and Azerdash returned the housing to the lawn mower. He tapped a finger on top, and it started up, whirring happily around the yard, cutting grass.

Thad gaped.

"I used magic to sharpen and balance the woefully neglected blades," Azerdash said, walking to the patio.

"Oh, is that what it needed?" Thad touched his chin with the screwdriver.

"Dad can build computers from scratch, but don't ask him to fix things around the house," Amber said.

"I'm more of a programmer than an engineer or mechanic." Thad watched the mower as it vroomed around boulders in the landscaping with more accuracy and efficiency than Arwen had noticed from such contraptions before. Tiny grass clippings shot out of its chute.

"I also infused it with a modest sentience so that it will more effectively use its extremely limited power source," Azerdash said.

"A... sentience?" Thad asked.

"Yes. A very simple one. I am not an enchanter, and the magic will likely only last a few decades, but I believe the device will much more efficiently clip your grass now."

"I... Thank you."

"He did a service for you, Dad," Amber said. "Are you going to report it on your taxes?"

"I don't think I'm going to report anything about this morning to anyone." Shaking his head, Thad walked into the house.

Amber waved again for Arwen to follow her. She looked like she would reiterate the "eating out" suggestion to Azerdash, but Arwen held up a hand.

"The research I need done is for him—he's on a quest to find a magical sword that made its way to Earth—so he needs to be a part of our meeting."

"Oh. I'm *definitely* not getting a 1099 from him, am I?" Amber looked at Azerdash, who was eyeing a hose reel by the patio door, hopefully not considering how to infuse it with an *essence*.

"I don't think so," Arwen said. "And he'll pay in gold."

"Dad is right. Working for magical weirdoes makes it hard to be a stand-up tax-abiding citizen."

"Sorry. I'll throw in some pies if you can find a proper form for them."

Amber shook her head. "I may ask for more than ten percent this time. How much are magical swords worth? They've got to be valuable, right?"

Starblade's gaze shifted from the hose reel to Amber. "Centuries ago, the galaxy blades were enchanted by elven masters with ancient magic drawn from the stars to create blades rivaling those crafted by the great dwarven smiths. They have the power to prompt even dragons to quail before their might."

"*Super* valuable. And an antique. Are you going to pawn it, or sell it to a dealer, or what?" Amber pulled out her phone, bringing up the site she'd used before to create a contract.

"*Pawn* it?" Azerdash looked at Arwen, as if he might not have understood the word, but she thought he'd gotten the gist. "Should I succeed in this quest, I will wield it myself. Once, I carried a galaxy blade into battle. It is possible the one I seek is the very one I wielded, but if it is truly in this area, its aura must be muted or insulated somehow, else I would sense it from afar."

Contract up on her phone, Amber turned toward Arwen.

"Would five hundred dollars work?" Arwen didn't know how to value a sword Azerdash meant to find and keep for himself, but the research wouldn't involve driving around and using gas. If Amber could do it all from her home, it shouldn't cost as much as if she were to be in danger.

Amber lowered her phone and scowled. "My fee is ten percent."

"We don't know the value of the item we're seeking," Arwen pointed out.

"You've heard of appraisals, haven't you? Even without, I'm *sure* it's worth more than five thousand dollars. Trust me. He's describing some invaluable antique with magical powers. My twenty-year-old car with chipped paint and ripped seats is worth more than five Gs."

Arwen looked dubiously in the direction of the driveway, though they couldn't see the two-door red hatchback from the house. "Is it really?"

"Of course. I've upgraded it since I bought it."

"You mean the fuzzy seat covers?"

"*And* the new speakers. Haven't I played any bangers for you yet? I'm going to need a thousand dollars for the hours and hours of research this'll take, and two pies, four jars of pickled something good in season, and, oh, more of that jam for my croissants. Your jam is *amazing*."

Arwen looked to Azerdash, less for advice on whether the deal was fair and more because she was daunted by all the time she needed to spend in the kitchen when so much else was going on. But if she had to make cookies anyway to bribe a fae queen, maybe it didn't matter. She was an efficient cook.

"A thousand Earth dollars is an infinitesimal amount compared to what a galaxy blade is worth," Azerdash assured her.

"You're not helping that much with the negotiating," Arwen whispered to him.

"No? Shall I loom imposingly over her?"

"No. You can't do that to teenagers. It's illegal."

"What a strange world this is."

"We know."

"Weirdos," Amber whispered, tapping on her phone, then pulling up a signature box. "Feel free to read it first, but I didn't put in anything sneaky. And same deal as before. You only have to pay if I'm able to find the information that leads you to the sword."

"All right." Even though she trusted Amber, Arwen *did* skim through the contract before signing. She told herself that she'd saved herself whatever Zoltan's fee would have been for the tattoo-removal formula, so she could afford to pay to help Azerdash find the sword.

"I will reimburse you in gold coins," he told her as he watched.

"Don't worry about it," Arwen told him. "I owe you."

"You do not."

"I don't? Well, you can help me cook, if you want. I've got a lot of things to bake before we leave the planet."

"Are you sure you want the guy who lit my dad's lawn mower on fire to help you cook?" Amber tucked her phone away.

"Maybe you could *watch* me cook," Arwen told Azerdash.

"I will reunite with Yendral, learn what he has discovered from the other intelligent species in the Cosmic Realms, and inform him that he may be needed to seduce the fae queen."

Amber opened her mouth, then shook her head and closed it again. "Weirdos," she repeated to herself as she walked inside.

8

AZERDASH DIDN'T WATCH ARWEN BAKE. YENDRAL SHOWED UP shortly after she started, and the two half-dragons paced up and down the driveway, having a powwow. Now and then, Arwen took breaks to look out the window. Yendral gesticulated animatedly while Azerdash gripped his chin and listened.

Did Yendral *want* his comrade to leap into war? To raise an army and attempt a mission that could get him killed? It might get them *both* killed.

Arwen shook her head. After she'd gone through all the effort to gain Azerdash the protection of the Stormforge Clan—or at least Zavryd's Uncle Ston'tareknor—would Azerdash really pick a fight with every dragon in existence?

She hated the thought of him being killed. Hadn't he had enough of war and fighting in his life? Why couldn't he relax for a few decades? He'd even spoken of retirement. He didn't truly want this, did he?

Chagrined, Arwen tried to concentrate on cooking. Usually, the scents of vanilla and baking cookies wafting through the kitchen relaxed her, but not this afternoon.

She checked her phone often, expecting a text from Amber. Before leaving her house, Arwen had prompted Azerdash to relay everything he'd heard from the elven ambassador to Amber, so she would have as much as possible to go on for her research. But it would take a while before she dug anything up. It wasn't as if the location of an invaluable magical sword would be posted in an online forum.

As Arwen took two cookie pans out of the oven, she grew aware of Yendral's aura on the deck outside. He was alone.

A jolt of unease went through her as she swept out, searching for Azerdash's aura. Where had he gone?

She didn't sense him.

This glowing round button is what I push to request permission to enter, correct? Yendral asked telepathically from the deck.

Hearing it is what brings me to the door to see who's calling. Arwen set the pans on a rack to cool and removed her oven mitts.

Unless your senses are far poorer than I believe, you know *who's calling.*

Yeah. I'll be right out.

Arwen didn't want to invite him in, not alone. He was too interested in her. And she wasn't positive he would respect her wishes if she asked him to stay back. He seemed like the type who might not be able to believe a woman didn't want him.

"It smells fabulous in here," came Yendral's voice from the doorway before Arwen finished washing her hands.

She glanced into the living room toward where her bow leaned against the wall but didn't lunge for it, only watched him step inside, his height making him loom, his hair almost brushing the door frames.

"I'm hoping that blueberry-chocolate-chip cookies will convince the fae queen, or whichever of her people we run into first, to give me directions to find an ingredient for my formula."

"So I understand." Uninvited, Yendral ambled into the kitchen, his nostrils twitching in the air. "Azerdash has informed me that if the cookies are insufficient, I should flirt with the fae queen and invite myself into her bedchamber." He smirked, not appearing daunted or offended by the prospect. "I told him it was the *last* fae queen that I had sex with. As long-lived as their people are, the one in charge now is, I understand, not the same female we encountered early in our campaigns. They are, however, a libidinous people ruled by the desire for pleasure, so I expect she's similar." His twitching nostrils led him past Arwen to the cookies already cooling on the counter. "Will you allow me to sample your bribe?"

"Of course. Help yourself."

His eyes crinkled as he grabbed a cookie, inhaling deeply before taking a bite. "I do adore you, Chef Arwen."

"Uhm. Thanks."

"And I see I make you uncomfortable. Have no fear. I will respect Azerdash's so-called claim and not attempt to woo you, even if I am certain his embrace was for show and he's not joining you beneath the covers. Unless I miss my guess, he sleeps on your roof like a feral cat when he visits." Yendral smiled contently as he ate his cookie.

Arwen didn't know what to say.

"He'd be a lot happier and less moody if he *were* under your covers, but he's abysmal at letting himself be happy. He's too wrapped up in his head to enjoy a female without overthinking everything terribly."

"Yeah... So, where did he go?"

"Into the woods to brood."

"And he left you to, uhm..." Arwen extended a hand toward Yendral, not certain why he was here.

"Watch over you? Well, no. I believe his words were, *Don't pester her.* And then he reminded me that he's claimed you." Yendral smirked. "I think *you* would be happier as well if you two were having sex. You've a bit of the broodiness in you. The dark-elven blood, I'm sure. Gemlytha had a tendency toward melancholy too."

Arwen resisted the urge to ask him about Gemlytha. When she'd asked Azerdash, he had with reluctance spoken of her, saying she'd been a *subordinate*, but he'd clearly had feelings for her. Arwen had read between the lines that he regretted never acting on them.

"I am not here to pester you, of course," Yendral said, "but my curiosity about whether your research has uncovered any clues about the galaxy blade prompted me to contemplate the glowing round button by your door. Of course, eating your delicious food may affect me like alcohol and remove my inhibitions and wisdom." He gazed contentedly at her through his lashes as he ate another cookie.

Amazing that he could be so fit when he consumed so many desserts. Maybe half-dragons had fast metabolisms. Flying had to burn a lot of calories.

"If you invited me to spend the night on your property," Yendral said, eyeing her up and down, "*I* would not sleep on the roof."

"Since I prefer my privacy, I will refrain from inviting you."

"I will say with extreme certainty that you don't know what you're missing."

Arwen swallowed. Was he implying that he knew how little experience she had with men? Or just that he knew she lacked experience with *him*?

"Why is Azerdash contemplating trying to fulfill the ambassador's desires?" Arwen asked to change the subject.

"To right wrongs." Yendral hitched a shoulder. "We failed to win the war we were bred to fight. Thanks to betrayal, not a lack of our power or mettle, but Azerdash feels it was a failing not to suss out that betrayal ahead of time, not to anticipate it and be ready."

With his cookie hunger apparently sated, Yendral ambled toward her.

Arwen tensed, not certain what he would do. She stepped back but bumped into the pantry door.

"He's hard on himself." Yendral lowered his chin to gaze into her eyes. "We weren't gods, and we could only read the minds of the weak. Those who plotted against us from within were not that."

"I wouldn't think so," Arwen murmured, glancing toward the living room and her bow again, but she didn't want to attack Azerdash's ally. She didn't want Yendral to force her to.

He stopped close enough to touch her but didn't reach out, merely continuing to gaze at her. "This would be a chance for redemption for him. For both of us. It would be an even greater battle to win than the one our people pitted against the dwarves. Dwarves and elves were never even mortal enemies before that time. Outsiders instigated everything. Orcs, some say, but I suspect dragons. It has always been in the interest of the dragons to keep the lesser species, as they call everyone else, divided. They *know* that if all the worlds joined forces, they could make trouble. Maybe we couldn't kill the dragons completely, but we could hurt them and make them question whether it was worth it to proclaim themselves rulers over the entire Cosmic Realms."

Yendral lifted his fingers to Arwen's jaw, the brush of his nails startling her, sending a jolt of fear through her.

Trapped. She felt trapped. It was a different type of prison from what she'd experienced as a girl in the dark-elf tunnels, but fear surged through her nonetheless.

"If Azerdash does not get over his head issues and take you to his bed," Yendral said, "*I* will."

Arwen jerked her hand up to push his wrist away.

"I'm not interested." She tripped over her tongue in her hurry to get the words out.

"No?" His eyelids drooped.

Yendral had let her move his hand from her jaw, but he didn't back away, and her heart pounded.

"I can be a gentle lover," he said, "especially when I'm smitten and sated by delicious food. And when a female has stood beside us in battle. I find the thought of sex with you far more appealing than with some strange fae who considers it a sport and might require me to battle another like a gladiator before joining."

"I... you don't have to do that."

"No? I've heard those are the fae queen's preferences. If I make such a sacrifice for you, will you reward me?"

Arwen swallowed, wanting to run out of the kitchen and into the fresh night air. Why had Azerdash left Yendral here?

"With as many cookies as you want, yes," she said.

Yendral chuckled and stepped back. "A true reward."

"You don't have to sacrifice yourself to the fae queen. I'm not sure we need to talk to her at all. I don't know what Azerdash said, but you don't need to throw yourself on her bed for my quest. I would never ask that. I'll find a way to get the ingredient from the fae realm on my own. I'm going armed." Arwen gestured toward the cookies instead of her bow.

Yendral chuckled again and bowed to her. "You are indeed. My apologies for my forwardness. I would blame my dragon half, but I believe it is my elven tongue that so enjoys your food and finds it an aphrodisiac. You say you've had few mates in your life?" He cocked his head, as if he couldn't believe it.

"I specifically did *not* say that."

"But it is true. Why? You are attractive." Yendral glanced at her chest. "Have you not fed your wonderful food to the males that interest you? Certainly you are aware of how successful a tactic that would be."

Heat crept from her chest up her throat to scorch her cheeks.

Was he reading her mind? Or was her inexperience that obvious in how she reacted to him?

"I haven't— I mean, I don't." Arwen didn't want to admit that she'd never asked anyone she'd found appealing on a date. It wasn't as if she'd met that many people to practice on during her days of being homeschooled on the farm and spending most of her free time in the woods. Besides, so many who could sense magical blood had made it clear how unappealing her heritage was that she'd always been certain of rejection.

"Were you more experienced, I would suggest you put a cookie in Azerdash's mouth, clasp his hand, and lead him into the woods to seduce him."

"He's not interested in me."

Yendral snorted. "If *that* were true, he wouldn't have forgiven you for shooting him. Most people find that heinous, you know."

"It was heinous," Arwen whispered, reminded of why she so badly wanted to get rid of her tattoo.

"But not your fault. And you resisted a dragon's compulsion to avoid shooting him again." Yendral gave her a pleased look. "We *both* appreciate that. Because Darvanylar would have finished pulverizing me if Azerdash hadn't stopped him. He was a bully. I'm glad he's dead."

Arwen didn't admit it aloud, but she felt the same way. All the Silverclaw dragons she'd met so far made her understand completely why the various races of the Cosmic Realms might want to get out from under dragon rule. Even if Zavryd's clan wasn't *as* bad, weren't they all bullies? Using their greater strength and power to force weaker beings to submit to their laws?

"If you want him, try seducing him." Yendral took two more cookies from the cooling rack, inhaled their scent deeply, then slipped them into a pocket. "He won't object. He wants you. He's just hung up over Gemlytha sacrificing herself for him, and he regrets that he never took her off to show her that he cared. It wasn't *proper*." Yendral rolled his eyes. "I can't read his mind, but I'm *positive* he thinks it would be some kind of betrayal to her spirit if he claimed you—*truly* claimed you—but he's alive for now and needs to go on with his life. He *needs* to spend a night with a female's legs wrapped around him." Yendral gave her a frank look.

Arwen didn't know what to say. She'd lost half a batch of cookies to her unasked-for visitor, but if his information was accurate... would Azerdash eventually come to her? Or could she... do as Yendral suggested?

Unfortunately, he'd read her right, and she *didn't* have any experience with seduction. All she knew about sex was from books.

Besides, she didn't want to trick Azerdash into being with her. She wanted him to come to her of his own accord.

She looked bleakly toward a window. Was that asking for too much?

With his last two cookies tucked away for later, Yendral nodded at her and headed for the door. But he paused with a hand on the jamb and gazed speculatively back at her as if some new idea had come to him.

"I could bring him charging back to your farm to prove his interest in you," he commented.

Yendral didn't look at her chest again or give her a lascivious leer, but she caught the gist.

Again, her heart pounded as she imagined Yendral wrapping his arms around her and a jealous Azerdash rushing up to shove him away. She didn't want to play games, but a part of her was wistful at the idea.

With humor in his eyes, Yendral continued. "Let me know if you want me to lure out his beast—his *mating* beast. It wouldn't be the nicest thing to do to him, and it might get me beaten up and hurled against a tree again, but it would be worth it. You deserve to be rewarded for standing with us against a powerful dragon."

Arwen hadn't done anything—that dragon would never have found their lair if she hadn't inadvertently let him read her mind —and she shook her head at the idea of deserving anything for that.

"I'm not sure Azerdash is that great a reward, but I see that you believe he is." Yendral's lips twisted with wryness.

"He's a good ally, and I like his... quirky side." Arwen thought of Azerdash standing in ripped jeans and a high-school letter jacket to *fit in* with humans. And of how he'd found a gift from another world for her father to improve the tractor. And of him fixing the robot mower in Amber's backyard.

A further twist to Yendral's lips suggested he might have been able to read some of her thoughts. "*Most* women are drawn to his power."

"Oh." Arwen couldn't tell if that meant she should also find it his most appealing asset. She *did* notice it, especially when he was shirtless, with his aura crackling around him. "It's nice."

Yendral snorted again. "Nice."

He stepped forward and gripped her wrist, his return startling her. He leaned his head down, his cheek brushing hers, and she pressed a hand against his chest, not sure what he intended.

He whispered into her ear. "Since I am his friend, and you like him for better reasons than most, I won't try to steal you away, but if you aren't able to draw him out, and you find yourself lonely..." He nuzzled her ear, then kissed her cheek. "Come find me," he whispered, then inhaled her scent, released her, and walked out of the house.

Arwen slumped against the pantry door, a weird tremble coming over her. She was relieved when Yendral shifted into dragon form and flew away but confused by all the new information in her mind.

9

NIGHT HAD NEARLY PASSED BY THE TIME ARWEN BOXED UP ALL OF the cookies and pies she'd baked. She'd napped intermittently, woken often by oven timers going off. Maybe she should have gone to bed for better sleep, but she was nervous about her quest and doubted she would have rested well.

As dawn approached, Azerdash flew into range of her senses, and Arwen went outside to meet him. She needed to grab a bag she'd packed and put on her armored jumpsuit, but she was otherwise ready to go if he was done brooding in the woods, as Yendral had put it. Had he truly been doing that all day and night? Had he been contemplating starting a war?

He soared into view over the trees, a dark majestic form against the gray sky, his eyes flaring briefly violet when they met hers.

Arwen shifted uneasily on the deck. Could he know that Yendral had come inside and... and what? He'd touched her and nuzzled her ear, but he'd also backed off and grasped that she had feelings for Azerdash. She wouldn't complain or say anything about Yendral's actions, but she wondered if Azerdash would catch glimpses of the events in her thoughts.

As he landed, he shifted into his elven form, dropping into a soundless crouch on the gravel driveway. He nodded gravely at her and produced a pouch.

That grave face made her think of the times she'd seen him smile. She couldn't recall a time when he'd laughed in her presence. Had he ever done so? As a boy? Or had his tutors, knowing they were raising a leader for their people's armies, not permitted it?

Maybe Yendral was right that Azerdash needed someone to help him brood less.

"What's that?" Arwen smiled as he came up the stairs to join her, holding out the pouch.

"I gathered *yagaroth* root from the troll home world for your formula as well as some of the other ingredients the vampire would not easily be able to acquire from Earth." Azerdash placed the pouch in her hand, tubers and vials discernible through the cloth. "Only the difficult ingredients—the fae and dark-elven items—remain. I also asked around and learned that the fae queen, before she reached her current station, was the royal botanist for the *previous* queen. She may be precisely the person to point you to the fragolithian cave-corn husks you need."

Arwen swallowed a lump rising in her throat. Azerdash hadn't been out in the woods *brooding*. No, he'd been helping her. He was *always* helping her.

After accepting the pouch, she stepped close and leaned into him. "Thank you."

At first, he seemed surprised and didn't respond. She was on the verge of pulling back, but he wrapped his arms around her.

"Is everything all right?" he asked.

No, she thought.

"Yes," she said.

After a pause, Azerdash asked, "Did Yendral do something to disturb you?"

Arwen debated on an answer. He *had* disturbed her, but he'd also given her useful information. And even if she hadn't been comfortable alone with him in the kitchen, she didn't know if he'd crossed a line. She didn't think so. She also didn't want to risk starting something between them, not when they were, as far as she knew, the only two of their kind left, the only friends they each had from those distant days when they'd fought together. It was so strange that she, someone who'd rarely had the interest of *one* man, much less two, might have the power to, however inadvertently, come between them and cause a rift. She didn't want to do that.

"He liked my cookies too much," Arwen finally decided on.

A long silent moment passed, and she wondered how many of her musings he'd caught. She hadn't felt the telltale itch of someone reading her mind, but Azerdash always seemed to grasp some of her thoughts even through her tattoo's protection.

Finally, he rested a hand on the back of her head. "Perhaps I should not have encouraged you to bake for him."

His touch seemed an invitation, or at least a promise that it was okay to lean on him, so Arwen melted more fully against his chest. She appreciated his solid power and that she could use it for support.

"These were the cookies I made for the fae queen."

"He took them?"

"A sample."

A sample of six. Or had it been eight?

"Half a pan," she amended.

"His dragon blood makes him presumptuous," Azerdash said, as if his own blood didn't do the same.

"Being half-dragon sounds troublesome."

"Yes. It is perhaps even more troublesome than being half-dark elf." There was a smile in his voice, and he rested his cheek against the top of her head.

That was nice. She closed her eyes. "I think so. My blood doesn't make me presumptuous. It only drives me to want to worship demons."

"That... is a joke?"

"Yeah." Maybe it had been in poor taste. "Only when I draw upon the power from my heritage do I sometimes have urges to... I don't know. Not worship anything. But use the power in its original form instead of going through all the effort to twist it into benign surface-elf–like power."

"Hm. I am not certain what would happen if I attempted to alter my dragon power."

"Trees would burst into flames."

"Possibly so. I am able to use my elven power on trees when the need arises."

"I wish I had *human* power to draw upon for gardening and non-evil things, but humans are... disappointing when it comes to magic." Arwen resisted the temptation to add *when it comes to everything* onto the end. That would be an insult to her father, who was a good man and had many skills, as well as countless other people. She just continued to wish she had elven blood instead of *dark*-elven blood.

"It is possible your ability to make delicious sweets comes from your human half."

Arwen snorted softly. "I think it's the magic that I instill in the plants that makes the fruit and vegetables taste better, not any great cooking ability coming from my human blood."

"No? When I ate your strawberry dessert, the entire *short* cake tasted appealing, not only the fruit."

"I just follow recipes." Well, that wasn't entirely true. She added and adjusted, occasionally trying new ingredients. "Mostly."

Azerdash released her and lowered his arms. Arwen might have been disappointed, but he gazed at her and said, "You will allow me to taste the sweets you have prepared to bribe the fae queen."

"Yendral isn't the only one whose dragon blood makes him presumptuous."

"No." Azerdash nodded without any indication that he was offended. "I will determine whether it is only the fruit that makes the dessert appealing."

Arwen wouldn't have minded if Azerdash followed her into the kitchen, but, unfortunately, he *wasn't* as presumptuous as Yendral. He clasped his hands behind his back and waited on the deck. When she returned with a few cookies, he stood gazing toward the sky.

"They're blueberry chocolate chip. The berries are from the farm." Arwen pointed toward where the bushes grew interspersed with strawberry, thyme, and basil. "This climate is too cold for cacao beans though, so I can't make the chocolate chips from scratch. It's too bad because chocolates are a favorite at the markets." Half of her limited knowledge of pop culture was thanks to a colleague who sold candies created in molds that looked like the latest popular action heroes or cartoon characters.

As Arwen offered him the cookies, she recalled Yendral's suggestion that she might seduce Azerdash by giving him desserts and taking him into the forest for... she didn't even know what. Kissing, she supposed. And more amorous activities?

His hand brushed hers as he accepted them, and a zing of awareness zipped through her, with images of them entwined against a tree springing to mind. Maybe her subconscious mind *did* know what amorous activities with Azerdash would involve.

But she didn't want to seduce him with cookies or anything else. If Yendral was right and Azerdash *was* interested in being romantic with her, she wanted him to admit it to her and to himself. She didn't want to trick him into being with her.

"Do you wish me to fly you to an appropriate climate where you might grow the beans?" Azerdash asked, oblivious to her thoughts of entwinement. "If the plants do not need to be constantly monitored, you might tend them periodically, when I'm available for transport, and harvest them as needed."

"Are you offering to fly me to South America so I can grow cacao trees?"

"If you believe it would be useful in creating superior desserts."

"Does that mean you won't be busy going to war?"

Azerdash hesitated. "If I were to undertake such an endeavor, it *would* make me busy."

"Yeah." Arwen smiled sadly. It might also make him dead. "No chance you only want to collect your sword, ignore the entreaties of your old elf soldier, and retire, huh?"

"I have considered that." Azerdash nodded earnestly. "Sometimes, my mind is suitably engaged by studying this world's history and culture—and assisting you when I can be of use. Other times, I itch to do more. To do what I was created for— improving the world, if not the Realms as a whole, with my power." He bit into one of the cookies.

"I can understand that. I admit I don't *want* you to get involved in something that could get you killed, but if you're driven to do so... Well, I'll bake you cookies to help you win the loyalty of your troops. And if you need a tracker, I can join your scouting party, though maybe not every weekend, because Father gets grumpy when he has to do all the farmers-market visits by himself."

Azerdash chewed and gazed at her as she spoke, and she felt she had his undivided attention. A little thrill went through her that he might be so interested in her words. In her.

"Sometimes," Azerdash said softly, "Yendral is not a fool."

Her lips parted. She didn't know how to respond to that. She hadn't expected him to bring up his comrade.

"You *are* a superior female," Azerdash added.

"Oh." Maybe she should have thanked him or said something more articulate, but she'd spent her whole life feeling inferior for her tainted blood, so it was hard to believe someone might believe that. Especially someone with such great power and ability, someone who knew exactly what it was to be superior.

"And you are loyal." Azerdash stepped closer, clasping her hand.

Arwen nodded, willing to accept that descriptor, but the part of her mind that liked to sabotage her self-worth reminded her that she'd allowed herself to be manipulated and had turned on him. "I try," she managed.

"Yes."

Azerdash set the unfinished cookies on the railing and lifted his free hand to the side of her head. He brushed a wild lock of hair behind her ear, letting his fingers linger, and his thumb traced her jaw.

Pleasure radiated through her as she held his gaze. Would he kiss her? Should she do something? Purse her lips? Open her mouth? Would it be *that* kind of kiss? Would she need to respond in some way? Should she touch *his* head?

He smiled, as if he could follow her scattered and possibly overstressed thoughts, then bent his head and brought his mouth to hers.

When their lips touched, her body responded automatically, leaning into him again. She didn't need to think. She could relax and enjoy this—enjoy *him*.

At first, she simply let him kiss her, basking in the deliciousness of his touch as his lips caressed hers. But as her pleasure grew, an eager anticipation spread through her, and she kissed him back, exploring the feel and taste of his mouth. She lifted her arms to his shoulders, lightly gripping the hard muscles through his shirt, stroking their warmth before pushing a hand up into his hair.

It was cool and soft on the back of her hand in contrast to the heat of his body. She rubbed his scalp, hoping it felt good for him, hoping he liked her touch as much as he liked eating her food.

Azerdash groaned—or was that a *growl*?—as his arm wrapped around her waist, pulling her closer, locking her to him. Her anticipation heightened as she felt him, *all* of him, through their clothing. His kiss deepened, and a need stronger than any she'd known built within her, one she knew he could satisfy. One she *wanted* him to satisfy.

"Starblade," she whispered against his mouth. No, that came out as a groan as well.

Azerdash, he corrected telepathically, his lips stroking hers as he sent a tingle of magic zinging along her nerves.

Surprised by the intense pleasure it evoked, she gasped and arched into him. *Azerdash*, she agreed.

One hand lowered to cup her ass, rubbing her through her pants as his other hand massaged her scalp, his every move stimulating her body as he kept her close. Presuming she didn't want to leave. And she didn't. She wanted to touch him, every part of him, and she lowered a hand to his waist, slipping her fingers under his tunic to feel the hard ridges of his abdomen, the heat of his skin, the slight quiver of his taut muscles at her touch.

He was into it. He was into *her*. That made her feel wanted and desirable, even more than his words of loyalty and superiority had. Bodies didn't lie.

Her breaths quickened, images of them entwined against a tree returning to her mind. Or would he come to her home if she invited him? Not to her roof but to her *bed*. They could take off their clothes and—

A growl—and it was definitely a growl that time—emanated

from his throat, but it sounded more like irritation than pleasure, and he broke the kiss.

Arwen was on the verge of taking the opportunity to invite him home, but he'd looked away from her. When she turned her head, she caught the light on through her father's window and realized he would be out to cut vegetables for the market soon.

Azerdash wasn't looking at the light but at the sky, and she groaned as she sensed Yendral flying toward them.

A flash of irritation swept through her. Logically, she knew they had a date at Val's fairy ring. Further, Yendral's arrival might have kept Arwen and Azerdash from being in the middle of intimate groping when her father walked out of the house. But she wanted more time alone with Azerdash. He'd finally voiced his appreciation for her and *kissed* her. She longed for it to go on. She wanted him and couldn't keep from tightening her grip to keep him close, to continue what they'd started.

Azerdash turned back to her, his eyes flaring violet in the dawn light, and she froze, afraid she'd presumed too much, that she'd irritated him.

But he brought his lips back to hers for a demanding kiss even as Yendral flew closer. Her passion flared, her knees weakened, and she grew breathless again as she eagerly responded. In that moment, she didn't care that his friend might see them or even that her father might walk out. All she wanted was to be with Azerdash.

Only when the gravel crunched, Yendral landing in the driveway, did Azerdash give her a final caress with his lips—and his magic—and pull his head back. With her body more turned on than it had ever been in her life, Arwen dropped her face against his shoulder instead of looking toward their visitor. Heat and arousal flushed her, and she needed a moment to compose herself.

A chuckle came from the driveway, and she couldn't help but

glance over. Yendral, now in his elven form, looked from Azerdash to the cookies he'd left on the railing to Arwen.

A new flush heated her face, this one prompted by embarrassment. Yendral didn't think she'd followed his advice, did he? Trying to use her food to seduce Azerdash?

"My apologies for interrupting," Yendral said, bowing toward them, "but you told me to return at dawn, that we're meeting the half-elf at the fairy ring."

"I did." Azerdash had found his composure, and his voice sounded calm—far calmer than Arwen's would have been if she'd tried to speak so soon after those breathtaking kisses.

"Have you decided to claim Chef Arwen for yourself in *truth* this time?" Yendral's eyes twinkled.

With Azerdash's arm still around her, his hand cupping her and holding her close, Arwen felt claimed—deliciously claimed—and wouldn't have minded if he said yes.

"You will not disturb her with entreaties for her attention," was what he said.

Yendral's brow creased, as if that hadn't been the answer he'd expected, and he looked at Arwen. She couldn't read his thoughts but worried he would think she had complained about him. He didn't hold her gaze for long though, instead looking back to Azerdash.

"If she is not claimed," Yendral said, "she is free to decide for herself if she wishes *entreaties.*"

Before Azerdash could answer, a throat clearing came from behind them.

Father stood in the doorway with his rifle in hand—*clenched* in his hand—as he looked at Azerdash... and his hand on Arwen's butt.

Thanks to his mundane humanness and lack of a magical aura, she hadn't sensed him. Whether Azerdash had noticed him or not, he didn't give any indication of surprise.

Arwen was the one to blurt, "Sorry!" and spring away. What she was sorry about, she didn't know, but she hastily added, "I need to pack," and ran into the house.

She grabbed her bow, sprinted out the back door, and raced down the path to her own home before remembering she would have to go back to her father's kitchen for the cookie bribes. By the time she reached her front door, she felt ashamed that she'd left Azerdash—and Yendral—to deal with a cranky and protective father with a gun.

But they weren't humans, she reminded herself, and it wasn't as if he could shoot them. Not effectively.

Still, her actions had been cowardly. She should have stayed to explain... Hell, she didn't know how to explain them.

Shaking her head, she used the bathroom, put on her armored jumpsuit, and grabbed her pack. She needed to concentrate on her mission to eradicate the tattoo, nothing else.

"Easier said than done," she muttered.

10

As she rode toward Green Lake on Azerdash's back, Arwen decided she was relieved Val was coming along to guide them to the fae queen. After the strange events of the previous night, she liked the idea of a chaperone. With her magical tiger and sword and gun, Val would be perfect for swatting away the hands of overly forward suitors. More so than Arwen's mundane father. When she'd returned from gathering her gear, she'd found him still on the porch, glowering at Yendral and Azerdash, even though they'd changed into their dragon forms to wait. They'd appeared indifferent to his glowers and gun.

When Arwen had rushed to join them, deliberately choosing Azerdash to ride with, despite Yendral lowering a wing in invitation, Father had asked where she was going. She'd blurted a poor explanation, saying she had to gather ingredients for her tattoo removal, and had felt like a delinquent teenager as they'd flown away.

Even though she didn't think she'd done anything wrong, Arwen couldn't help but believe she'd screwed up. How, after an entire life of being largely ignored or outright shunned by men, had she ended up with two half-dragons interested in her?

You are loyal, Azerdash's words rang in her memory.

She'd only intended to be loyal to *him,* but maybe Yendral felt something for her because she'd been working together with Azerdash to free him from the dark elves? And he'd mentioned appreciating that she'd helped against the dragon Darvanylar.

Arwen hoped Yendral would end up wanting to have sex with the fae queen and vice versa, and that his randiness would be sated after that.

On the way to Val's house, neither Azerdash nor Yendral spoke to her, but she wondered if they were having a telepathic conversation, because they glanced at each other occasionally as they flew side by side. Their powerful wingbeats took them over the suburbs to Green Lake more swiftly than usual, and she sensed they were competing, if not outright racing.

It was with relief that Arwen detected Val waiting in the front yard. As promised, she was ready to go.

But as Azerdash landed in the street, a startling scream of pain or maybe fury came from Matti's house across the street. A tremendous *thump-crunch* followed it.

Arwen gawked in surprise, sensing Matti and Sarrlevi inside. They weren't *fighting,* were they?

Sarrlevi had been a deadly assassin before retiring and becoming Matti's mate, but Arwen had never seen him lose his temper. He was always perfectly polite—if haughty—when Arwen visited. And Matti... Well, *she* had a temper, but would she attack the handsome elf who doted on her, bringing her exotic cheeses from around the Cosmic Realms?

"What's happening?" Arwen slid off Azerdash's back as Val stepped onto the sidewalk, wearing a pack and her sword and gun.

She frowned toward Matti's house. "I'm trying to figure that out."

Another cry came from within, half screech and half roar.

"That's Matti," Val added. "I think."

"Are you sure?"

"It sounds like a dying yeti," Yendral said.

He and Azerdash had already switched to their elven forms. They wore cloaks, travel clothing, and their weapons, ready for whatever the fae realm threw at them. If Green Lake didn't throw something at them first.

Puzzled, they all gazed at Matti's house.

"I'll check." Maybe not receiving an acceptable telepathic response, Val started across the street.

But she only took a few steps before the front door opened, and Sarrlevi jogged out. His swords rode in their back scabbard instead of in his hands, but his concerned expression promised something was up. He ran up to Val.

"What's wrong?" she asked.

Another screech-roar came from the house.

"Mataalii has entered the time of birthing," Sarrlevi said.

"She's in labor?"

He blinked, puzzling briefly over the term before nodding. "Yes. She has rejected my offer to take her to the elven home world for assistance in this important endeavor and wishes her human doctor to oversee the matter." A disapproving sneer curled his lip before he nodded resolutely. "I am unaware of the doctor's current location, but she says you volunteered to drive her in your conveyance."

Another *thump* came from the house.

"That sounded like Matti breaking an orc's skull with her hammer," Val said. "Are you *sure* she's in labor? And not being attacked?"

"It is my understanding that Sorka attempted to advise her on the proper physical positioning and mental mindset for birthing a child with dwarven blood."

Sorka, Arwen recalled, was Matti's intelligent, and apparently opinionated, magical hammer.

"Matti's response was to hurl her at the drywall," Sarrlevi added. "Twice. I believe the advice was not appreciated."

"Ah. Yeah, I can drive her and call her doctor."

"Excellent. I will grab her bag and assist Mataalii to your conveyance." As Sarrlevi jogged back toward the door, he added something in Elven that might have translated to, "If she'll let me."

Val turned toward Arwen. "Sorry, can the quest to the fae realm wait a while?"

Arwen started to agree, but Azerdash spoke first as he stepped up to Arwen's side. "There is no need to delay. Yendral and I are capable of dealing with the antics of the fae, and we are ready to go."

Yendral stepped up to Arwen's other side, his arm almost brushing hers. "We'll find the fae ingredient and won't let them make a sex slave of Chef Arwen."

Arwen, who'd never considered that the fae might want that, could only stare in surprise.

"I'm sure you will," Val muttered, eyeing them and their proximity to Arwen. Switching to telepathy, she asked, *Are you okay? Do you want to wait until after Matti has her twins?*

Arwen hesitated, remembering how relieved she'd been at the idea of Chaperone Val, but she didn't believe Azerdash would do anything untoward—she *wished* he would—and as long as he was there, Yendral wouldn't either. It would be fine.

"I do hope everything goes well with the delivery," Arwen said, "but I'd prefer to get this out of the way while Azerdash and Yendral are available to help me. Later, they may be busy." If they found that sword and Azerdash joined the elf ambassador in starting a war, they would be. "Besides, my cookies are freshly baked. I wouldn't want to present the queen with stale offerings."

Val snorted. "That's the truth. Here." She shrugged off her pack.

As Sarrlevi levitated Matti through the front door, she with her hammer in hand and protesting that she could walk on her own two feet, Val handed a few sealed boxes of chocolates to Arwen.

"I know your cookies will be a treat for her, but just in case, she's known to enjoy truffles."

"Truffles?" Azerdash tilted his head.

"The chocolates, not the mushrooms," Arwen explained, accepting the boxes and tucking them into her pack.

"This way, Thorvald," Sarrlevi called, using his magic to unlock her Jeep and open the doors.

"I guess there's no need for me to get my keys, is there?" Val did retrieve them from the house before jogging to the Jeep where Sarrlevi was levitating Matti into the back seat.

"Good luck, Matti," Arwen called with a wave.

Even though she hadn't known Matti for that long, she felt guilty that she was leaving on a personal quest instead of staying for moral support. Birthing twins, twins with *dwarven* blood, sounded arduous.

"We will go now." Azerdash touched Arwen on the shoulder and headed for the ring of mushrooms growing on one side of Val's lawn.

"One sec." Arwen pulled out a container holding one of the batches of cookies she'd made and also dug into the first-aid kit she'd packed. It included a number of her herbal remedies, and she grabbed a muscle-relaxing tea and pain-relieving lozenges that she made using the magically enhanced offerings from her garden.

She rushed the items to Val, who stood by the driver's seat, about to get in. Sarrlevi had already joined Matti in the back of the Jeep, letting her use him as a pillow as she struggled to find a comfortable position.

"These are for Matti." Arwen held out the items to Val. "The ingredients for the medicines are written on the label, so her doctor can check if there are any contraindications. She may want to have them after delivering to help her relax and recover. And there are never any contraindications for cookies." Arwen held up the container. "She can have those any time."

The back window rolled down, and Matti reached out and grabbed the container. The cookies disappeared inside.

"I'm sure she'll appreciate everything." Val saluted Arwen, then hopped into the driver's seat.

"Good luck, Matti." Arwen waved again.

The snarl of pain that came from the back seat wasn't as loud as the previous roars, but it did prompt the windows to open on nearby houses as neighbors wondered about the early-morning cries.

Mataalii thanks you for the offerings, Sarrlevi told Arwen telepathically as the Jeep drove away, *and wishes you well on your quest.*

Is that how you translated that last scream? Arwen asked.

We are fused, the same as trees grown together in nature, so I am an expert at interpreting my mate's vocalizations.

You sound like an excellent mate and future father.

Yes.

After the Jeep disappeared from view, and the neighborhood fell silent again, Arwen joined Yendral and Azerdash on the lawn. At first, she was surprised the guardian dragon topiaries had allowed Yendral to set foot on the grass, but Val had known they were coming, so she must have arranged it.

"Are you concerned that you won't have sufficient cookies to appease the queen after giving so many away?" Yendral asked with amusement.

He stood with his arms folded over his chest as Azerdash walked around the outside of the mushrooms, invisible tendrils of magic whispering from him as he probed them thoughtfully. Did he know how to activate a fairy-ring doorway? Arwen had heard they could only be opened by fae or those with keys given by their kind.

"I made extras, thinking I'd have to bribe fae guards and half-dragons with bottomless stomachs."

"That does describe us," Yendral said. "Our elven commanders used to marvel at all the food we required after flying around."

Azerdash lifted a hand, the magic flowing from him intensifying. Pale green beams grew visible, one going to each mushroom and then pooling in the middle. The caps throbbed with matching light, and soon magic swelled in the center, not unlike that which formed portals.

"You've traveled this way before?" Arwen asked.

"I've rarely visited or interacted with the fae, but their enchantments are not that complex. Less so than Gnomish magic." Azerdash looked at her as a ghostly doorway formed in the middle of the ring. He looked a little proud of himself.

Arwen smiled encouragingly at him.

Yendral snorted. "If you hadn't figured it out, I could have gotten us in."

"You received a key during your previous liaisons?" Azerdash asked.

"Nope. Last time, I got naked and lay in the ring until an interested party on the other side opened the doorway." Yendral winked at them.

Do not believe all of his utterances. Azerdash rested a hand on Arwen's shoulder. *Possibly not any of them.*

Not even things he's told me about you?

Definitely *not things he's told you about me.* Azerdash nodded to Yendral. "Since you are a frequent visitor, perhaps you wish to lead."

"Certainly." Yendral lowered his arms. "I have no fear of going first." His eyes flared with green light as he met Arwen's gaze before striding through the doorway.

Not certain how long it would remain open, Arwen didn't want to dawdle, but she did ask, "Is he going to be a problem?"

Azerdash gazed at her, and she half-expected him to ask about what, but he seemed to know what she meant. "I wouldn't think so, but I am unsure. We've never..." He spread his palm toward her but didn't say the words that might have logically followed: *been interested in the same woman.* Maybe because, despite the kiss, he still hadn't admitted that he had that interest. "He ruts with many women," Azerdash said instead, "so I am uncertain why... No, that is untrue. I do understand why he desires you, but he does not usually go out of his way to irk me."

Arwen almost pointed out that Azerdash hadn't made his interest in her clear, either to her *or* his friend, and that might be part of the problem, but Yendral had been certain Azerdash liked her before *she* had.

"Perhaps it is the beast," he offered. "As I've admitted, it often threatens to rise up within us and drive aside our rational elven minds."

Yes, Arwen remembered the chilling story he'd told of being goaded into a duel with a comrade and inadvertently killing him during it.

"But I will not," Azerdash continued, his voice lowering to a growl, "let him have you."

A little shiver of foreboding and unease went through her.

"Come." Hand on the small of her back, Azerdash led her through the doorway to the fae realm.

11

WARMTH, HUMIDITY, AND THE HEADY SMELL OF GROWING PLANTS
and fungi washed over Arwen as they passed through the doorway, landing in a tunnel covered from ground to sides to roof in
vines. A green glow emanating from all around showed the plants
flexing and writhing, even undulating underfoot, and Arwen
almost reached for her bow before catching herself. Was she going
to shoot a *vine*?

She didn't sense any fae, or anyone at all, in the area, aside
from Azerdash at her side and Yendral, who crouched in a guard
stance a few feet away.

Magic infused the vines, and the earth underneath also
brimmed with it, as if both were alive. No, the vines were definitely
alive, but the ground... Arwen studied it with her senses. Its magic
wasn't like a growing plant but an inert element that had always
been there and always would be. It sang to her blood, promising
that she could use it if she called upon it.

Arwen had heard explanations about how weak magic was in
the ground of Earth and that it was greater on other worlds, but
this was her first time experiencing that.

"The magic in the fae realm is particularly strong," Azerdash said quietly, watching her. "It is one of the reasons they have managed to keep the dragons from imposing rule here. This is also a dimension rather than a world, so one cannot simply make a portal to it, at least not without learning a new kind of magical travel."

"So, this place is more like where the demons that the dark elves worship live?"

Azerdash nodded. "Yes. They are in a different dimension, but it may be easier to access it from here than from our worlds."

"That is one place I have no desire to *access*."

"Nor I." Azerdash considered a pedestal made out of earth that stood in the middle of the tunnel near where they'd arrived. Unlike everything else, it wasn't covered in vines. Though it didn't look like anything special, a hint of magic shrouded it. An empty tray made of gray spongy matter rested on the top, as if waiting for an offering.

For a moment, Arwen thought the fae might have somehow anticipated their arrival and set the tray out to receive her cookies and Val's chocolates. But there was no way they could have fore-told the future, was there?

Turning his back on the tray, Azerdash stepped toward Yendral before pausing and squinting back at Arwen. "Try to create a barrier around yourself. You may find it easier here."

"Oh." That was a good idea, and she would feel more comfortable if she had that ability to protect herself, especially here in a strange realm. Though she trusted the half-dragons could keep her safe, she preferred to be able to take care of herself.

Her previous failure at making a barrier came to mind, and she hesitated. She would prefer not to have any witnesses but especially not one who was quick to joke and tease. She looked at Yendral, wondering if Azerdash would send him ahead.

"She doesn't like having you give her orders." Yendral smirked at his comrade.

"That is not her complaint," Azerdash said with such certainty that she wondered if the magic here made it easier for him to read her thoughts. "She desires privacy to practice."

"There is an intersection ahead where we can wait." Yendral extended his hand down the tunnel.

Azerdash opened his mouth, probably to say that she only wanted privacy from *Yendral*, but Arwen patted his arm.

"I wouldn't mind trying without witnesses to see my, uhm, less-than-perfect attempts."

Failures was the word that came to mind, but Azerdash might want to correct negative thinking, as supportive teachers usually did.

"Very well." He nodded his understanding and joined Yendral. *We will not go far,* he added telepathically. *You are capable and have your bow, of course, but this realm has many threats. Call if anything alarms you.*

Thank you. I will.

The tunnel curved, and they disappeared around a bend.

When one of the vines undulated underfoot, Arwen jumped and almost called them back, but she frowned at herself and kept her mouth shut. She didn't need babysitters.

Besides, she would only practice a couple of times before catching up with them. She didn't want to delay the mission, especially when Azerdash's sword quest waited.

Recalling their last lesson, Arwen stretched out her arms, closed her eyes, and willed a barrier to form around her, as she'd watched Azerdash do several times. To her surprise, the ground shot power up into her at her first attempt to draw upon it. Magic surged into her, making her tingle all over, and she balled it up and thrust it outward, willing it to create an invisible barrier all around her. To her surprise, it worked.

As it formed, it pushed her away from the vines under her feet, causing her to float above them. Arwen would have to practice adapting her barrier to work around obstacles, but she grinned with pleasure at this success. It was *much* easier here than on Earth. The energy of the barrier crackled in the air around her, promising to keep arrows, bullets, and almost all other attacks from reaching her. Oh, how she hoped she could remember this feeling and replicate it when she was back home.

Five more times, she formed and released a barrier. It felt so good to manipulate the magic and get it to do what she wanted. Only the knowledge that Azerdash and Yendral were waiting made her stop.

Voices sounded in the distance, and she thought they were coming back to check on her. But those voices originated in the opposite direction, and they didn't belong to her allies.

They sounded female. Two fae women?

Arwen couldn't yet sense them, but the voices grew louder as they approached. She almost sprinted after Azerdash and Yendral before remembering she had Amber's camouflaging charm. She dipped into her pocket and rubbed it, then used her senses to check on the half-dragons.

She couldn't sense *them* either. Alarm jolted her. They'd said they wouldn't go far, and a sense of betrayal swept through her before she squelched it.

No, she decided, they must have also camouflaged themselves. Either they'd also heard the voices or they were lying low, not wanting any fae to detect them before they were ready to announce themselves to the queen.

Arwen thought about creeping away to join them, but might she learn something from the fae if they passed by? What were they talking about? Intruders they'd detected?

Biting her lip, Arwen stepped closer to the tunnel wall. When her back brushed the vines, they undulated, making her doubt the choice. The memory of Azerdash's security vines springing out to ensnare her popped into her mind.

In case they were sentient and thinking of such a thing, she used her power as she had before on countless trees and plants. Careful to be subtle, lest the approaching fae sense her magic, she willed extra vigor into the vines and helped them pull more nutrients from the soil behind them.

They pulsed. It might have meant they were pleased. It might have meant they were sounding an alarm in the nearest village.

With the pair of fae approaching, Arwen ceased her efforts and stood still, other than rubbing her charm again in case she'd inadvertently deactivated it.

The voices grew clearer as their owners rounded a bend and came close enough that Arwen could sense and see them through their camouflaging magic. She rolled her eyes at the realization that she wouldn't be able to understand them without a translation charm. Oh, well. She might be able to tell from their actions if they knew there were intruders or not. So far, they were walking, not running, and she sensed only tiny magical trinkets on them, nothing that felt like powerful weapons.

One of the women had brown wiry hair that stuck out in all directions, and the other had green hair that hung in ropes and was loosely pulled back from her face. The first had paler skin, the second darker, but both had freckles and green eyes. They trod barefoot across the vines, daggers in hip sheaths and bows and quivers across their backs.

Were they hunters like Arwen? She promptly felt a kinship toward them, but they might not feel the same way toward her. Especially since she was visiting uninvited.

Though she trusted Amber's camouflaging charm, Arwen held her breath until the fae looked at her without seeing her, their gazes skimming past as they settled on the pedestal and the empty tray. She still didn't breathe easily, aware of how quiet the tunnel was, nothing but the occasional rustle of the vines sounding, especially when the fae stopped talking.

When they reached the pedestal, they stood to either side of it, considering the tray before looking up and down the tunnel. As if they expected someone.

Arwen grimaced, suspecting they'd received a magical alert or sensed the doorway that had opened. Did numerous fairy rings lead to this spot? Or only the one that originated in Val's yard? If the latter, the fae would know right away where the visitors had come from.

One woman walked farther up the tunnel in Arwen's direction. Though she eyed the ground—searching for tracks?—instead of looking up, Arwen carefully scooted back, well aware the fae would see through her camouflage if they got close enough.

Have you completed your practice? Azerdash asked into her mind.

Yes. Arwen stopped moving when the fae female did and considered whether she should explain her situation. *I was able to make a barrier.*

Excellent. We are debating which of these tunnels leads to the queen's city. Azerdash must not have been close enough to sense the fae through their camouflage. *Your tracking skills may be of use.*

I'll be right there.

Arwen believed she could use her magic to determine which route saw more traffic, but that wouldn't tell her for certain in which direction the city lay. The fae would, of course, know, and she debated if she could learn that from them without understanding their language.

Bolstered by her success with the barrier, Arwen envisioned a magical cup around the head of the closest female, something to catch her thoughts. She'd done it before with Azerdash, but he'd been letting down his guard and intentionally sharing.

To her surprise, simply by willing her magic to help her read the female's mind, she *did* catch a few thoughts. Maybe not suspecting an enemy was close, the fae wasn't protecting herself with mental defenses. And, as before, the greater magic inherent in this realm assisted Arwen, increasing her ability to use magic.

The fae had indeed sensed the doorway opening. Usually, when that happened, it was Sarrlevi popping in to leave a couple of boxes of chocolates, the same kind of truffles that Val had given to Arwen. The female didn't know exactly why but understood that he had a deal with the queen and regularly left offerings.

Because the chocolates weren't on the tray, these two, who were scouts assigned to this territory, were suspicious. They would head back to the city to warn the queen that someone else may have used the fairy ring, someone unwelcome.

The closer woman said something to her companion, and they both turned away.

Briefly, Arwen glimpsed the route back to the city in their minds, but she was too worried her little group was about to be reported to do more than file the information away. Even though Arwen and the half-dragons had intended to walk openly into the city, not skulk about and spy, it would be better if the fae weren't alerted ahead of time and on edge, anticipating enemies.

As quietly as she could, Arwen removed her backpack and untied the flap. The two fae started walking away, and that forced her to rush. She grabbed two of the chocolate boxes, wishing she could lightly levitate them to the tray, but she'd never attempted to learn that ability, and this wasn't the time to try something new. She crept forward, intending to loft the boxes onto the pedestal, but the fae had already checked the tray and would find that suspicious. Instead, she tossed them so that they fell to the ground beside it, landing on the vines.

The lush plant matter insulated the sound, and the fae didn't hear the boxes land or look back. Arwen reached out to the vines, willing them to rustle or do something that would alert the scouts.

A tendril wrapped around one box. A faint crinkling of the plastic top sounded as the vine tightened. A second tendril lifted and flicked the end of the box with its tip. Puzzled, Arwen tried to figure out how the plants had interpreted her request as *beat up the box.*

The noise was soft, but the fae women heard, both turning curiously. The vines succeeded in opening one box and inserted a tip that attempted to manipulate itself to pluck out a chocolate. Did the plants want to *eat* the sweets?

Eyes widening, the fae women ran back. They bent, swatting at the vines and grabbing the boxes. One chocolate fell out, and a vine wrapped around it with the speed of a striking cobra.

The women shook their heads but didn't try to take it back. Boxes tucked close to their chests, they turned and trotted down the tunnel. One gesticulated and spoke, her voice irritated.

Trying to read their thoughts again, Arwen caught the gist. They were annoyed that Sarrlevi hadn't left the chocolates on the special protective tray that repelled the vines, vines that did indeed like sweets, however they consumed them. Absorption through their flesh?

Arwen had no idea. She hoped her actions didn't get Sarrlevi in trouble.

After the fae disappeared from her sight and senses, Arwen headed in the opposite direction to rejoin Azerdash and Yendral. They were already on their way back, probably wondering what had taken her so long.

"Sorry," Arwen said. "I was figuring out what the pedestal was for." Among other things. "You're supposed to leave offerings for the queen."

"How did you discover this?" Azerdash peered at the pedestal.

"The plants told me." Arwen eyed the spot where the chocolate had fallen but saw no sign of it. Absorption, indeed. "And I think we go that way to reach the city and the queen." She pointed in the direction the fae had gone.

"Did the plants also tell you that?" Yendral eyed the vines skeptically.

"Yup." She smiled.

Azerdash's eyebrows twitched, but he didn't look like he doubted her. "Lead the way, then."

Arwen did so, pausing at intersections to touch the vines rustling on the ground, seeing if they would confirm the direction for her. Given the numerous options, getting lost was a distinct possibility. She trusted Azerdash could form a portal to take them back to Earth if needed, but she didn't want to leave without finding her ingredient.

Maybe because of the vigor she'd instilled in the vines by the pedestal, or the chocolate she'd inadvertently given them, they helped, showing her images of a city in a great cavern as well as confirming which way the fae women had gone.

Arwen couldn't tell if there was only one vast organism of vines that ran down most of the tunnels or if there were many that communicated with each other, but they knew her each time she reached out. At the fifth or sixth intersection, however, the vine she touched withheld information. Instead, it inserted an image of a chocolate into her mind, a chocolate with a green tendril wrapped around it and throbbing.

It was hard to miss the message. Glad Val had given her the truffles, Arwen opened another box and dropped one onto the vine. A tendril shot out, wrapping around it.

The plant showed her that the fae women had headed down a tunnel to the left, but more tendrils rose from the ground, reaching for her wrist. No, for the box of chocolates.

Arwen yanked her arm back, not wanting to give up more when she didn't know how much farther remained, but another dozen tendrils shot out, this time from the tunnel walls. They stretched toward her arms and legs.

Magic surged from Azerdash, and the grasping vines burst into flame. A keening rang in Arwen's mind, and the rest flattened to the ground as ashes trickled down. The overall plant didn't appear that harmed, but he'd effectively cowed it.

"You say you've had success conjuring a barrier?" Azerdash asked.

"Yes, but it's not an automatic reflex yet."

"You will practice until it is." He rested a hand on her shoulder to take any sting out of the command. "It is unwise to allow sentient plants to take advantage of you."

"Sentient *anything.*" Yendral reached for the open box, plucked it from Arwen's grip, and sniffed the contents. He removed a chocolate and popped it into his mouth.

"Indeed." Azerdash gave him a baleful look, took the box, and returned it to Arwen. "Those are bribes for the fae queen."

"And her plants?" Yendral smiled happily as he chewed.

"Yes."

"You won't need to bribe her." Yendral rubbed his chest through his shirt. "I'm here to ensure she'll get something she wants."

"We'll see." Azerdash nodded for Arwen to continue to lead.

The vines didn't so much as stir as they trod upon them.

Arwen was relieved when the tunnel widened into a cavern and grew park-like with a high arched ceiling that beamed bright green light onto manicured paths winding between shrubs and trees. Ponds, statues, and fountains also dotted the area, with a wider path meandering through the middle.

Arwen knew from the fae woman's mind that this place was on the outskirts of the city. A good thing because she didn't think the vines would offer her any more information.

She was less relieved when two dozen male and female fae

archers with magical bows and arrows jogged into view on the wide path. Faces grim and suspicious, the fae spread out to face Arwen, Azerdash, and Yendral. They drew their bows and pointed them at the group.

Numerous arrowheads glowed, and Arwen's senses told her the projectiles possessed more power than any of her own arrows. If they'd been made using the greater magic of this realm, that made sense. Unfortunately. She didn't know if her armor or the barrier she could now make could deflect such weapons.

12

AZERDASH AND YENDRAL RAISED THEIR MAGICAL DEFENSES, attempting to extend them to include Arwen. But their barriers clashed, buzzing and spitting sparks since they couldn't *both* protect her.

With a grumble of irritation, Azerdash used his greater power to push Yendral's barrier to the side and ensure Arwen was covered. She might have tried to raise a barrier of her own, but there was little point with a much stronger one around her. Besides, she was busy worrying that she should have warned her allies that the fae might have known they'd arrived. Her trick with the chocolates must not have been sufficient to make the scouts believe Sarrlevi had come and gone, leaving only the offering.

Not deterred by the magical arrows pointing at them, Azerdash strode closer to the archers, waving for Arwen to stick with him. Yendral walked on her other side.

Beyond the archers, laughter came from alcoves Arwen hadn't noticed before. Partially hidden by foliage, they were spots where fae lounged in pairs or groups on benches the size of beds. More than a few occupants were engaged in romantic activities, some in *vigorous* romantic activities, unconcerned about the strangers encroaching on their city.

The archers, with their shoulders bunched with tension and their knuckles tight on their weapons, weren't nearly as carefree. A half-dragon—or *two* half-dragons—approaching wasn't something to brush off.

Intruders are not welcome into our realm without invitation, a green-haired woman standing ahead of the other archers said telepathically. *Especially not mongrel dark-elf intruders.* She sneered at Arwen.

Most of the archers did.

Arwen grimaced but didn't speak, intimidated by all the eyes upon them. Upon *her*.

I am Azerdash Starblade, he announced telepathically. *We have a proposal to offer your queen and seek an audience with her.*

The leader considered Azerdash and Yendral with far less disdain. Her gaze snagged on Yendral, and she licked her lips. Other fae, both male and female, eyed Azerdash.

The half-dragons' power emanated from them, their auras more substantial than those of anyone present. Though they weren't doing anything more than maintaining their barriers, the air tingled with their energy, especially to Arwen, who stood between them, but she had little doubt the fae were close enough to feel it too.

Yendral's comment that women were usually drawn to Azerdash's power came to mind. Even though Arwen liked him for other reasons, she acknowledged her own awareness of his aura, especially when he gazed into her eyes as he drew upon his magic. That always made her want to step closer to him, to bask in his power and reach out to touch him.

When Yendral saw the leader's interest in him, he propped a fist on his hip and used his magic rather than his hand to unfasten several buttons on his shirt, allowing it to fall open to show his fit pecs. He smiled, watching her through lowered eyelashes.

In other circumstances, Arwen would have rolled her eyes, but this *was* their plan. Or one of the possible plans. She was prepared to bring out her cookies, in case they would work as bribes, but she wanted to make sure she had enough left for the queen.

What do you offer? The leader's gaze shifted from Yendral to Azerdash, and she gave *him* a long look as well.

He didn't respond flirtatiously. If anything, he was more aloof and off-putting than usual. That didn't stop the perusal from the archers.

We have sweets the queen may enjoy, Azerdash said.

Not only sweets, I suspect. The leader glanced at Yendral again.

Azerdash hesitated, and Arwen sensed that he didn't want to trade sexual favors, even if Yendral was a willing volunteer, but he answered, *That is correct.*

Queen Dithara is attending meetings in her court and does not wish to be interrupted during such times, but I will see if she wishes to make an exception. We have heard of your quest, Azerdash Starblade. The leader bowed and stepped behind the line of archers, her gaze growing distant as she reached out telepathically to the queen or maybe one of her assistants.

Arwen looked at Azerdash. *She's heard you're helping me collect ingredients?* Arwen couldn't imagine how the fae would have found out in advance or why they would care. *Or... could she know about your search for the sword?*

I do not know. Azerdash watched the leader intently. Or was he trying to read her mind? *Her thoughts are guarded, and I do not wish to forcibly tear down her defenses when we seek a peaceful exchange with the queen.*

Arwen attempted to use her newly learned power to grasp thoughts but sensed what he'd said, that a wall protected the leader's mind. *All* of the archers had their mental defenses up, and she couldn't guess what they were thinking. The only fae who weren't guarding their thoughts were the ones in the park, busy with their entertainment and interested only in each other. When Arwen swept through with her senses, hoping to catch useful stray thoughts, she witnessed more imagery than she'd anticipated related to their sexual acts. Even those not participating had sex on their minds, and a group of three males and one female who were engaged with each other had particularly lurid thoughts.

Arwen stumbled back, tearing her gaze away and flushing with embarrassment.

Azerdash rested a hand on her shoulder again, his grip almost protective. She steadied herself, trying to mask her face, but it was hard to tamp down her embarrassment. She felt like she'd done something perverted by intruding; all she'd wanted was useful information.

Azerdash probably didn't know that she'd been reading minds, but he knew where she'd been looking. *Many other intelligent species are less private with sexual matters than elves, and I suppose humans in your culture are private as well? The fae are as libidinous as they are gluttonous—they openly pursue pleasure in many areas.*

It's fine. And I knew that, or had heard that. I just wasn't expecting — It's fine.

We will stay no longer than necessary. If the queen desires Yendral, I will encourage him to take her somewhere private.

The thought that they might *not* have gone somewhere private floored Arwen. Did the queen's court regularly watch their monarch engage in sexual activities for entertainment?

Arwen stepped closer to Azerdash, glad for his touch, glad that he wanted to protect her, not only from arrows but from experiences she wasn't ready to have. She didn't know if she would *ever* be ready to have some of them.

The archers parted so their leader could return to the front.

Arwen was impressed that they'd kept their bows at full draw during the entire meeting. None of their arms quivered.

The queen invites you to join her court and present your offer. The leader waved two fingers in what might have been a salute, then spoke to the archers in their tongue.

They lowered their bows. Several departed, heading down paths in the park, some walking toward structures among the trees that might have been guard towers. Guard towers that blended in because they were green and made from plant matter.

Arwen wondered if the fae and elves were related. They didn't look as similar in appearance as surface elves and dark elves, but their faces tended toward the same fine features, and their ears had points.

A dozen archers remained and walked down the wide path behind the fae leader, Arwen, and the half-dragons.

The auras of hundreds—no, *thousands*—of fae crept onto Arwen's radar as the trees thinned and dwellings dominated. When the inhabitants grew more numerous, she had to fight the urge to turn around and run back toward the solitude of the tunnels. Dealing with the persnickety vines would be more appealing than passing by so many people.

Though the half-dragons, with their notable auras, had to be the more interesting visitors, many fae frowned at Arwen, sensing her dark-elven blood, she had no doubt. That made the city worse. She barely noticed the architecture or anything about it, just the eyes of the disapproving fae.

Welling panic tightened her chest, bringing a flood of memories from her youth: dark and tight tunnels, grasping hands, and adults frowning at her for not doing things right. For not being dark-elven enough.

Arwen took a long slow breath, longing for it to steady her. She reminded herself that she wasn't a child anymore and could handle herself. Further, she had strong allies along to help her.

This was her quest, and she wouldn't fail it because a few people were watching. Getting rid of the tattoo would be worth any discomfort she had to endure along the way.

A wider and more ornate tunnel with vines creating majestic columns took them into a thankfully less populated part of the city. The ground shifted from the dirt path to mortared flagstones that led toward open silvery gates also made from plant material. Everything emanated magic, so Arwen trusted the gates were sturdy.

Bird chatter emanated from a more private park beyond them, this one without any couples—or groups—having sex. Insects also buzzed, and a three-foot-long, blue-scaled winged creature that looked like a minute dragon paddled about in a fountain.

Arwen attempted to loosen her tense shoulders, feeling slightly more relaxed in the natural setting. But she sensed more fae ahead, and some had very powerful auras. Was their magic strong enough that they could, if they combined forces, overcome Azerdash and Yendral?

The half-dragons were doing her a favor by helping with her quest. If this resulted in them being hurt—or worse—she wouldn't forgive herself.

Also worrisome, the archers stuck close to their group, their magical arrows nocked even though their bows were lowered. Strangers were not trusted in the least, their actions said.

Music drifted to them from a chamber ahead, a cheerful and invigorating tune played on instruments reminiscent of flutes and drums. Some machinery also emitted whirs and clanks.

Arwen caught Azerdash cocking an ear with curiosity. For the machinery, not the music, she suspected.

Looks like we're being invited to a party, Yendral said telepathically.

You will fit right in then, Azerdash replied.

Undoubtedly. I can fit in wherever I go. I don't even need to read books about how it is done. Yendral smirked at him.

Azerdash gave him a flat look before changing the subject. *I sense the aura of the one I believe is the queen.*

Good. Yendral's smirk remained. *I hope she's ready for me.*

I also sense a magical device. It may be the source of that clanking and whirring.

That sounds like something for you.

A wistful expression crossed Azerdash's face.

The park transitioned to a high-ceilinged chamber. Three blue-haired musicians stood on a stage to one side while other fae conversed in pairs and groups, some in travel clothing and others in green-and-silver robes with sandals. Some stood while others sat on large mushroom-like stools that grew from the ground in a circle reminiscent of a fairy ring. Could one of the fae doorways be formed in this chamber?

A horizontal cylinder on green wheels clanked as it moved slowly along a wall covered in fuzzy green growth similar to moss. A brush extending from the machine's side rotated as it swept along the stuff. Glowing magical bits on the contraption hummed and whirred. Arwen wanted to call it a tractor with a fertilizer attachment, but she had no idea what it was doing to the moss.

Azerdash looked curiously at it for a long moment before shifting his attention to the chamber's occupants. Knowing him, he would prefer to trot over and look under the housing of the machine.

Most of the beings inside were fae, and Arwen might have guessed them all courtesans or the realm's equivalent, but she also spotted a dwarf in a leather apron and an elf in greens and browns. Visitors? Diplomats?

Toward the back, a voluptuous woman with green-tinged white hair lounged on a giant gray mushroom chair—did one call that a throne? A small table next to it held two boxes of chocolates, one somewhat dented and crinkled from the vine. The female fae had a substantial aura, one that rivaled Azerdash's in power, and Arwen assumed she was Queen Dithara. Despite the mostly white hair, her skin was smooth, her cheeks pink, and her emerald eyes keen.

Two older female fae in robes and with staffs stood to either side of her seat. Advisors? A closed door behind the throne promised a meeting room or maybe the queen's chambers.

The leader of the archers stopped Arwen a couple of dozen yards away from the throne, then pointed to Azerdash and nodded. Indicating he could approach?

Yendral raised his eyebrows, but the leader shook her head, pointing again at Azerdash.

Before he could introduce himself, the queen plucked a choco-late from a box and spoke telepathically. *I have heard of you and your quest, Azerdash Starblade. What brings you to my court? My people observe the Cosmic Realms and know more than the races who dismiss us believe we know, but we are not aware of the locations of any of the galaxy blades.*

Azerdash had started to bow toward her, but he stiffened at the last sentence. His face was masked again, and he recovered and finished his bow, but Arwen could tell he hadn't expected word of his sword quest to have reached other realms.

I seek ingredients for an alchemical formula, Queen Dithara, he replied.

One that will aid you in amassing armies to challenge the dragons? There was no mockery in her telepathic tone, and she looked him up and down in assessment.

No.

But you are planning to do so?

Through whom have such rumors reached you? Azerdash asked.

Arwen shifted her weight, worried for him for a new reason. If the old elf ambassador—and who else could it have been?—had been blabbing all over the Realms that Azerdash would raise armies to march against the dragons, he would be in huge trouble soon. Everything Arwen had sought to do by learning of his lineage, and his link to the Stormforges, would be undone. Even though Zavryd's Uncle Ston'tareknor had seemed friendly and easygoing for a dragon, he wouldn't protect Azerdash if he was a threat to dragonkind.

The queen waved airily. *Such news gets around. You lack the power of dragons—though I sense that you have far more than an elf—and I wouldn't think you'd have a chance at such a quest, but it is possible other nations would unite and follow one with dragon blood. It presumably gives you insight into their kind that others lack. I trust you know of a dragon's vulnerabilities, for instance.* Her eyes narrowed thoughtfully.

Your source is not reliable. I am not seeking to raise an army. I have retired from making war.

Beside Arwen, Yendral sighed. Because he disagreed with Azerdash's retirement? Or because he was bored or feeling ignored? Thus far, the queen had barely glanced at him.

Arwen would be happy to be ignored. The queen had also barely glanced at her, but it had been a lip-curling, dismissive glance, and a number of the fae were eyeing her with distaste instead of watching the meeting.

You carry weapons and keep yourself fit. The queen smirked at Azerdash—it reminded Arwen of Yendral's earlier smirk. *Are you certain?*

Yes.

The dragons believe otherwise.

A chill went through Arwen. If that was true, Azerdash could already be in deep trouble. Very deep trouble.

13

AZERDASH DIDN'T RESPOND TO THE QUEEN'S COMMENT THAT THE dragons had heard of his quest, but Arwen knew he'd registered it and understood all the ramifications. More ramifications than Arwen was aware of, she had no doubt.

I am here, he told the queen, *because I seek to trade for the husk of fragolithian cave corn or its location and permission to gather it.*

The queen's lips parted in surprise. *That is all?*

Though Arwen was more concerned about Azerdash's fate than her tattoo-removal quest at the moment, she did note that the ingredient meant little to the queen. Maybe a couple dozen cookies would be a fair trade for it.

Azerdash lifted a shoulder. *Should you know where we might find dark-elf tunnels growing nightwater fungi, that is also something we seek.*

The queen nodded, as if she recognized the ingredient. If she had been a botanist, that made sense.

We have the corn in our gardens, and I might be convinced to tear off a husk for you. The queen rose from her throne and hopped off the dais, lithe despite her curvaceous build. *And the nightwater fungi... I am not aware of where the dark elves live currently, as their species is dwindling and their outposts are few these days, but I might have access to some dried powder. It is, however, extremely rare and therefore valuable. A sample of it would be costly.* Dithara smiled as she sashayed closer to him.

Azerdash raised his chin. *State what you desire for these items. If your price is unreasonable, I will gather them myself.*

Still smiling, Dithara walked closer, not stopping until she stood within his reach, then tilting her head back to gaze at his face. It looked like she was turning her cheeks toward the sun, not toward a man, especially when she spread her arms as if she were drinking in warmth.

No, Arwen realized. Dithara was drinking in the power of Azerdash's aura.

They stood close enough that their power rippled as their auras met. Hers reached out, half challenge and half caress as it interacted with his. Azerdash kept a barrier around himself, a wall that she couldn't penetrate, but that didn't stop her from stroking it with her aura.

The queen's eyes opened slightly as she regarded him. *What do you offer in trade?*

Without a doubt, Arwen knew what she wanted, and her fist clenched. She hadn't thought Azerdash might have to trade his body for her ingredients. They'd assumed Yendral, who enjoyed such things much more, would intrigue the queen. *He* was supposed to be the one she wanted.

Azerdash watched Dithara, his expression not changing. He didn't back away. Did he want to? Arwen couldn't tell, but she didn't think he wished to randomly hook up with a strange woman on a whim. No, not on a whim. For *barter*.

Arwen didn't want Azerdash to trade himself to Dithara. It would bother her. Maybe it shouldn't since he hadn't admitted feelings for her, and they'd only kissed once, but her clenched fist tightened further as she imagined Azerdash with the manipulative queen.

As I stated, he said, *we have brought delicious sweets that you would find enticing. My comrade, Yendral, is also an accomplished lover who enjoys experiencing sexual relations with women from other races.* Azerdash extended a hand toward Yendral, though not with any flourish that might have helped convince Dithara of his appeal.

Because Azerdash didn't want to do this. He didn't want to barter himself, and he didn't want to use his friend either.

Arwen closed her eyes. This was her quest, so she needed to be the one negotiating, whether every fae here hated her for her blood or not.

I am certain you are accomplished yourself and enjoy experiencing relations. Dithara lifted a hand, as if to rest it on Azerdash's chest, but his barrier kept her from reaching him. Unfazed, she splayed her fingers on it, her magic undulating like the vines, managing to convey her erotic interest.

His shoulders tense and his jaw clenched, Azerdash clearly didn't appreciate her entreaty, but he looked over at Arwen. When their gazes met, his face was less masked, his expression one of resolution. Abruptly, Arwen realized he might agree to the queen's wishes, whether he wanted to or not, to help her.

Anguish twisted her, and she shook her head. No. She couldn't allow that.

"It's my quest," Arwen blurted, walking forward.

The queen and several archers frowned, and a number of weapons shifted toward her.

It's my quest, Arwen repeated telepathically, realizing she'd spoken aloud, and held up her open palms. *I'm the one who needs the ingredients, and I've brought tantalizing treats to trade.*

Halt! several archers cried, as if she represented a threat to someone as powerful as Queen Dithara.

Arwen stopped and kept her hands open. *I should have negoti-*

ated with you from the start. May I offer you more chocolates? Or cookies that I've baked? She reached slowly for her backpack, aware of the arrows pointed at her.

A dark-elf baker? The queen scoffed.

I'm only *part* dark *elf. Humans love baking, just as they love making the chocolates you and your vines have enjoyed.*

Step back, mongrel. Dithara curled her lip. *I've already agreed to share the corn husk and perhaps more, and I've already chosen what I require in payment.* She managed to flutter her eyelashes at Azerdash as she continued to throw menacing glares at Arwen. *Entertain me for four hours, half-dragon, and I'll give you what you want. What your mongrel minion wants.* Dithara looked puzzled as she glanced between them. Wondering why Azerdash was helping such a lowly being with a quest, no doubt.

He's not on the bargaining table, Arwen said.

But I am, my queen. Yendral stepped up to Arwen's side, giving Azerdash a nod. *Trust me when I say you'd prefer my vastly more experienced company.*

Dithara flicked uninterested fingers at Yendral. *Entertain others of my court if you wish to sate yourself on a fae lover, half-dragon. I've chosen my prize.*

Azerdash's eyes flared with violet light, irritation tightening his jaw further. His aura crackled with barely restrained energy, and he looked like he was on the verge of incinerating the fae queen.

Dithara must have known she flirted with danger, because she'd erected a barrier of her own, but she hadn't stepped back from him. Her ongoing smiles promised she *liked* flirting with danger.

Azerdash didn't attack her. No, he held Arwen's gaze. Offering his dignity—his *body*—to another for her quest?

Again, she shook her head.

No, she told the fae queen. *You can't have him.*

Dithara laughed. *And why not?*

Arwen stepped up to Azerdash's side. *Because he's mine. I have claimed him.*

Afraid her presumptuous words would irritate Azerdash, Arwen didn't look at his face, but when she stepped closer, his barrier flexed to allow her in. Glaring at the queen, Arwen wrapped an arm around his waist.

He is mine, she added, emotion flushing her cheeks, *and I do not share with others.*

Are you telling me that a mongrel with weakling human *blood could claim one with the blood of a dragon?* Mirth danced in the queen's eyes.

Well, at least Arwen wasn't pissing her off...

I'm telling you that a mongrel with powerful dark-elven *blood could and* did *claim him.* Arwen glanced at Azerdash, hoping she wasn't pissing him off either.

No, a slight smile curved his lips. Was he amused? Or did he look the slightest bit proud?

That was probably her imagination. He might be happily daydreaming about examining the fae tractor.

Dithara eyed Arwen, considering her for longer than she had before. *You do have the power of their kind, however twisted and evil.*

Arwen clenched her jaw—she wasn't *evil,* damn it—but she had to play along. She lifted her chin as if in proud agreement.

Are you claimed, Azerdash Starblade? Dithara asked him.

We have claimed each other. She fights beside me in battle.

Oh? She will assist you in overthrowing the dragons and returning the rule of each world to its native inhabitants?

I have not *taken on that quest.*

The queen smiled. *I believe you will.*

Yendral was the one to look wistful. Arwen couldn't believe he wanted his comrade to hurl himself into that minefield.

Do you care about him enough to fight beside him in battle? Dithara asked Arwen. *Or have you simply seduced him because you*

*enjoy his power wrapped around you in bed, its skilled strokes even
more titillating than a lover's physical caresses?*

I— What was Arwen supposed to say to that? *I do care and
would stand with him.*

Right after uttering the words, Arwen wondered if she'd just
agreed to suicidally take on the dragons with Azerdash. What if
the queen had intentionally tricked her into saying so? There were
a lot of witnesses in the chamber.

Azerdash looked sadly at her.

Dithara stroked her chin. *I believe I must test you to see if you are
worthy to stand at a half-dragon's side.*

Who are you to judge that? Arwen asked.

*The ruler over this realm and one who has something you seek. Also,
it's important for the happiness of my people that I keep them enter-
tained.* Her gaze shifted to the quiver of arrows behind Arwen. *I
believe a challenge is in order. Should you win, I will accept your bribe
of desserts and give the information on* both *ingredients that you seek.*

Win?

Even with other concerns tumbling about in her mind, Arwen
couldn't help but wish she *could* acquire both ingredients here,
that she wouldn't have to venture into the tunnels of her mother's
people.

*It will not be an easy challenge to win. As I said, you must prove
yourself. And if you lose, or fail to entertain my people sufficiently, I
shall claim one or both of these half-dragons for myself.* Dithara smiled
at the men.

Azerdash folded his arms over his chest, his face flinty. Nobody
was going to claim him against his wishes.

Even Yendral, who might have objected less to being claimed
by a beautiful female, gave Arwen a worried look. *Do not accept her
challenge,* he said. *We'll find another way. If we must, Azerdash and I
have the power to hold off her guards and forcibly question her.*

Arwen looked at Azerdash and thought of the times he'd

spoken of honor. She doubted he would forcibly question anyone, not willingly. For a friend, he might, but she didn't want to put him in that position. Besides, the queen and many of the fae in her court had powerful auras, not to mention those magical bows and arrows. Arwen worried that Azerdash and Yendral couldn't come out on top against so many.

What is the challenge? Arwen asked the queen.

Dithara's smile turned smug, as if she knew she'd already won.

Simple. You are a hunter, as many of our kind are. The queen pointed to Arwen's bow. *I trust you've tracked down numerous kinds of game?*

I have.

Have you had to endure being hunted yourself?

Not... often.

Then this will be a new challenge for you. If you can avoid being captured by my hunters for two of your Earth hours, I'll give you what you seek.

How many *hunters?*

Ten should be sufficient, I would think.

And I just have to hide from them and keep them from finding me?

Keep them from finding you and dragging you back to this chamber, yes. Dithara waved toward the center of the ring of seats, and a hazy cloud formed, showing two fae with bows walking through a tunnel. Some of the hunters who would pursue Arwen?

When Arwen looked at Yendral, he frowned again and shook his head slightly. Saying she shouldn't do it?

Azerdash met her gaze solemnly, but he didn't nod or shake his head. Not presuming to give orders today? Arwen would have liked to know his opinion. How talented were fae hunters known to be? Ten was a lot of people to dodge in their own homeland, in tunnels that they would know well. Arwen did have the camouflaging charm, but what if those magical arrows could find hidden people?

I will confer with my allies, Arwen told the queen.

Of course. Leave me a sample of the food you brought while you do so. I wouldn't want to get bored. Her eyes narrowed. *I promise you wouldn't want me to get bored either.*

I'm sure.

Arwen removed some of the cookies and chocolates from her pack. A servant came forward and took them to the queen. Several of the fae in the chamber watched the desserts raptly.

As Dithara took another chocolate from the box on her armrest, she watched *Azerdash* raptly.

Arwen had a feeling the queen was setting things up so that no matter what happened, *she* would win.

14

AZERDASH DREW ARWEN PAST THE WATCHING COURTESANS AND TO the side of the chamber so they could have a private moment.

The wheeled construct was trundling into a tunnel, still brushing the moss growing on the walls, and would disappear from view soon. Nearby, the musicians continued to play, now a thoughtful tune that reminded Arwen vaguely of the *Jeopardy* theme song.

Instead of joining them, Yendral remained near the queen, his hand gestures and smiles suggesting he conversed telepathically with her. Maybe he would ensorcel her with his charm, and Arwen wouldn't have to worry about winning a game or suitably *entertaining* the fae.

"Do you think this is a bad idea?" Arwen asked Azerdash, switching to English in the hope the locals wouldn't understand.

"I do not trust her." He glanced at the magical tractor as it rounded a bend and disappeared from view but then focused on Arwen.

"Did you want to follow it and see if you can peek under the panels while we talk?" Arwen asked, only half joking. She wouldn't mind, but the fae might.

"That's not necessary." Azerdash faced her more fully, as if to say she had his undivided attention. But he somewhat sheepishly added, "I examined it thoroughly with my senses when we walked in. I believe it's placing a magical fertilizer on the vines. It may also be capable of seeding bare patches. The inside of the cylinder is largely hollow with two components piled inside. I am, of course, guessing at what they are, as I am not that familiar with fae magic."

"Is the machine of gnomish make?" Arwen, far more concerned about her own situation, hadn't examined the magic that closely.

Azerdash's eyes brightened. "It is an intriguing mix of gnomish *and* fae magic and engineering. But let us focus on your dilemma."

"*Our* dilemma." She extended a hand toward him as a reminder of the alternative option the queen offered.

"Yes. Normally, I would not allow a female to manipulate me into an encounter of any kind. It would be demeaning for one of my power and stature to let himself be used so." Azerdash rested a hand on his chest. "It would be demeaning to *me*."

Arwen remembered Yendral's advice that she should seduce Azerdash with cookies and was glad she hadn't tried.

"But if the alternative is a challenge which could result in your death, I can make myself available to her."

Arwen started to answer before his words fully sank in. "My *death*? She said it was a game, that they'd haul me back here if they captured me."

Azerdash shook his head. "You should not trust her. She did not like that you stepped in and interfered with—" He waved at himself.

"So she's going to arrange my *death*?"

"I believe that a possibility."

Arwen blew out a slow breath. "We could just leave. Maybe I can find the ingredients without her help. Or maybe I won't get my tattoo removed right now."

"Given that we spend time in each other's proximity—natural, since you've *claimed* me—" an eyebrow twitch was the only commentary he gave on that topic, "—I would prefer the tattoo not be a way for the dark elves to manipulate you."

"I know, but I don't want us to have to dance to her tune."

Azerdash cocked his head and looked toward the musicians. "No? It is not as lively as when we first arrived, but the music isn't unappealing."

"It's a saying. I mean that I don't want to give in and do what she wants. Entertain her people *or* her. Especially if your hunch is right."

"Ah. Many have been humbled by the fae and used for their entertainment. They are hedonistic but also a powerful people, thanks to the great magic of their homeland. It's possible that if we wish to leave without entertaining the queen, one way or another, we will have to battle her and her army."

"Oh."

Was that why Azerdash hadn't, like Yendral, shaken his head and tried to get Arwen to turn down the game? He thought they would have to fight, regardless?

"I would hate to just *give in* to her. And I apologize for the bit about claiming you. I didn't mean—" Arwen shrugged. "You know it was for show, right? Like you were trying to do with me to fool Yendral?"

"I know this, yes." Azerdash touched her shoulder, a trickle of comforting magic flowing from his fingers.

That made Arwen think of the queen's words about how enticing his power might be in bed. "Unless you want it to be real," tumbled out before she could think better of it.

Both of his eyebrows twitched that time.

"Never mind." Arwen lifted a hand. "It was a joke. Not a good one. Sorry."

"It was not a joke," he stated with certainty. "I understand."

Arwen spread her arms, not certain how to respond.

Azerdash sighed and looked toward the tunnel, then nodded for her to follow him into it.

The fae wouldn't likely give them all the privacy they wished, but Azerdash must have wanted to escape the watchful eyes of the queen and the courtesans. Arwen walked down the tunnel with him, trusting he wasn't looking for the tractor, until it opened to an underground lake. A couple of fae guards with bows stood on the far side and eyed them but didn't openly object to their presence.

Azerdash stopped at the edge of the lake, and Arwen joined him, their gazes toward the dark water.

I have told you of Gemlytha, he started, switching to telepathy to ensure privacy.

Yeah. Of how she was your subordinate. Arwen watched him, knowing from Yendral's words and Azerdash's face when he spoke of her that she'd meant more than that to him. Maybe a lot more.

Yes. When we were being trained as youths and beyond, our instructors raised us to follow the ways of the elven army—and, from my readings of your history books, I believe many human armies as well. Among other things, a commander was not supposed to allow himself to develop feelings for or have relations with his or her troops. It could make things complicated during the heat of battle. Officers in a relationship might protect each other to the detriment of the rest of the unit.

Arwen nodded, understanding in theory even if she'd never had a serious relationship with anyone.

I grew aware—somewhat slowly and obtusely, as Yendral has pointed out—that Gemlytha had feelings for me that went beyond those of a subordinate for a commander. And perhaps, after the many battles we engaged in together, fighting side by side, I felt something our instructors wouldn't have approved of, too. I never allowed myself to act on those feelings, even though... she would have desired that. She was less indoctrinated, perhaps, less obedient to the king and the generals who commanded us. Looking back, I am not certain why I was so faithful when, in the end, we were not treated that well. A character flaw, I suppose. Now, I regret...

Azerdash looked sidelong at her. Arwen nodded for him to continue, already knowing what he regretted.

During the battle in the mountain earlier this year, I knew we might all die. We faced many dragons, many superior opponents. But it didn't occur to me that Gemlytha might die and I might live. Azerdash swallowed and looked toward the water again, blinking a few times before continuing on. *I've regretted both that I put her in a position where she was killed and that we never... that I never...* He flexed his hand, turning his palm up with another glance at Arwen.

Had a relationship with her, she said with certainty.

She appreciated that he was being circumspect in regard to her feelings, since she would have preferred he hadn't loved—and maybe was *still* in love with—another woman. But she also didn't want him to ignore his past and couldn't expect him to forget someone he'd cared so strongly for.

Yes. I have regretted it many times since that night, especially since we weren't in anyone's army anymore then. It was after we woke from the stasis chambers and when nobody wanted anything to do with us. We could have... seen if we enjoyed having a physical relationship together.

When he looked again toward the lake, his eyes lost in memory, Arwen stuck her hands in her pockets. What should she say? Maybe she shouldn't say anything.

A whir-clank came from the other side of the lake, the tractor entering through another tunnel and passing through, or perhaps this was another one. Either way, the noise stirred Azerdash from his reverie.

Once more, he turned to consider Arwen. *When I encountered you, after I realized you were... not evil and not working with your kin...*

She bit down on the temptation to correct him and say the dark elves *weren't* her kin. Technically, they were. She just wished they weren't.

And after we battled Darvanylar, and maybe even before then, I noticed that you were attractive. His lips twisted wryly. *I believe Yendral noticed right away, but I did not wish to. I was still mourning the loss of Gemlytha—and my bad decisions.*

Having never felt attractive, Arwen didn't know how to respond. Instead, she wondered if she had any twigs sticking out of her hair. Or, here, it might be pieces of a vine.

Of course, unlike my comrade, it is your loyalty that attracts me more than your squish, at least on an intellectual level. And you are that. You also enjoy talking at length on things you are passionate about, such as mushroom growth. As you've seen, I also have passions that interest me, so I can understand that. Azerdash started to glance across the lake but caught himself and refocused on her.

I've noticed. You're doing a good job of not gazing over and fantasizing about the innards of that machine while having a serious discussion with me.

I am not *doing a good job. But only because I've never before seen a melding of gnomish and fae magic and engineering, and I'm thinking...* His fingers twitched, as if they were, independent of his mind, fantasizing about disassembling the magical tractor to study all the parts. *Well, such thoughts might be premature.*

I'm sure I would be distracted from you if we chanced upon a gnomish-fae garden filled with vegetables being grown with agricultural methods that I'm not familiar with.

Azerdash gazed thoughtfully at her. *I believe that is a truth. Were you to somehow win the favor of the queen, she might show you her gardens.*

Hell, now I'm definitely *going to accept her challenge.*

He laughed. It was a short, soft laugh but almost startled her because he'd so rarely done it in her presence.

Impulsively, Arwen clasped his hands, wanting to be close to him, wanting... more than he was ready to give.

He didn't step away, but he did look pensively at her grip. She almost retracted it, but he rested his thumbs on the backs of her hands, a partial return of the clasp.

Though I do appreciate loyalty and am capable of admiring female... squish—and you—I have been concerned that, if I were to engage in relations with you, it might not be for a good reason. You do not look *physically like Gemlytha, but there are similarities with your auras since you are and she was half-dark-elven. I'm not positive...*

I get it. It's okay. It wasn't, but Arwen understood. She longed to be wanted because of who she was, but maybe she wasn't enough, not for someone like him. Maybe if he hadn't had feelings for another half-dark elf, he wouldn't be drawn to her in the least.

A depressing thought, but she had to be realistic.

It would not be okay—*or honorable—for me to be with you while remembering another.*

No, Arwen agreed, though she wondered how much she would mind. Wasn't it possible their relationship could start out that way but that he would come to care about her, and only her, eventually?

It has not been that long since she passed. In time... I do not know if you will wait, but things might grow clearer for me when more time has passed. You have probably ascertained that I am not... uninterested in you. Azerdash shared a memory of her naked in the rejuvenation pool under his home as she rubbed a magical ointment over her hip—and other places.

Arwen blushed at the memory of her antics, at how she'd thought he might be there and had wanted to put on a show, to make him desire her. *I knew you were watching.*

I did not intend to.

But you were too captivated not to? Arwen smiled with self-deprecation, knowing he'd only come back for his sword, not because he was so drawn by her hotness that he couldn't possibly refrain from peeping.

I was captivated. His serious eyes were heated, his gaze capturing hers, and far more than her cheeks flushed at the admission. He lifted his fingers to her lips. *A part of me wishes to set aside worries about honor and feelings—and how* you *might feel if my thoughts drifted to another—and simply... have you.*

His touch sent a shiver through her as his admission of desire made her yearn for him.

But I do not want you *to regret our time together either,* he finished.

She almost blurted that she wouldn't, that she understood and was willing to take whatever he would offer, but he might not admire her for that. And, later, she might not respect the choice, either.

That makes sense, she said logically. Practically. Reluctantly.

Yes. Azerdash squeezed her hands, then released one of his so he could fish in his pocket. *If you do decide to take the queen up on her challenge, this may assist you.*

He withdrew a magical item of bone and steel that was crafted in a similar style to her bone-and-wood bow while reminding Arwen of the Leatherman multi-tool he'd found in Amber's glove compartment. A brush attached to one end was identical to the one on her foraging knife.

You once asked if I could imbue your tool with magic. Azerdash waved to the knife on her belt.

You said it was too weak a receptacle for your power.

Yes. This, on the other hand, has a number of enchantments. I worked with the half-dwarf Matti Puletasi to make it. I crafted the tool, inspired by the Earth version I saw, and she knew how to enchant it. I lent her my power so it would be strong and capable of holding many abilities. In truth, she is not weak, despite being a mongrel, and likely didn't need my power, but I thought a gift should have as much of the giver in it as possible.

Looking uncharacteristically shy, Azerdash offered it to her.

Thank you. Arwen accepted it and wrapped her arms around him, wishing she could kiss him—and that he would kiss her— but after their discussion, she refrained. She couldn't, however, keep from experiencing the emotion that welled within her. Besides her father, few people had ever given her anything— they'd certainly not *made* her anything. *Thank you,* she repeated and did allow herself to kiss the side of his neck.

He'd given her a valuable gift. He deserved a kiss. And she deserved... She didn't know what, but she lingered, enjoying his arms around her as she breathed in his pleasant masculine scent.

You are reminding me of my captivation, Azerdash spoke dryly into her mind. He brought his hand to the back of her head, threading his fingers through her hair and keeping her where she was.

Sorry. I'm grateful for your gift. Arwen would have drawn back if not for his hand suggesting he liked her closeness and wanted her to stay.

Even though I haven't told you yet what the enchantments do? He sounded amused.

Yeah. You made it for me. That means a lot. She kissed his neck again, letting her lips linger. Just for a moment.

A rumble escaped his chest, and he lowered his hand to her butt, drawing her closer to him. His mind might be conflicted about his feelings for her, but she realized his *body* knew what it wanted, and it wanted her. Maybe Yendral somehow grasped that and that was what had prompted his comment on seduction.

But Arwen didn't want to be with someone who wasn't sure he wanted to be with her. As hard as it was, she made herself draw back.

At first, his grip tightened, as if he wouldn't let her escape, but he sighed and let go, perhaps experiencing similar thoughts. He looked to the side, catching the aura of someone powerful approaching before Arwen did.

She glanced toward the tunnel in time to see the queen stroll out with Yendral and several of her archers. Yendral's hair was mussed and his shirt open, revealing his muscled chest and abdomen.

Only then did Arwen remember the fae archers on the other end of the lake. They'd been watching the show the whole time.

I see there actually has been some claiming here. Queen Dithara smirked at Arwen, then looked at Azerdash, not his face but his crotch.

Arwen stepped in front of him, not wanting the queen's brazen gaze roving all over him. Maybe Arwen *did* want to claim him.

Azerdash rested a hand on her shoulder.

I'm willing to accept your challenge on two conditions, Arwen told the queen, who continued to smirk. *First, if I win, you'll not only give me the corn husk but also acquire the nightwater fungi so I don't have to visit the dark elves. Enough of each for several batches of the formula I am having made.*

Dithara dropped her smirk and scoffed.

Arwen hurried to add her second condition before she spoke. *Second, you will give me a tour of your gardens so that I may see how your people cultivate their plants.*

A soft snort came from Azerdash, but when he squeezed her shoulder, it conveyed approval.

Surprisingly, the queen's scoff turned into a more thoughtful expression. *You have an interest in gardening?*

On Earth, I'm a farmer. And I bake and cook with much of what I grow.

The queen squinted at her. *You made the flat circles.*

The cookies? Yes.

I sensed your magic and thought they might be poisoned. But I determined that the berries were the only items with magic in them and that it was second-effect, as we say. Something was done to the plants from which they grew.

I tend the blueberry bushes with my magic, yes.

Dark elves do not have magic to work plants.

I make do with what I have.

Interesting.

Arwen was tempted to suggest they trade recipes and talk gardening while forgoing games, but Dithara said, *I believe I will enjoy watching your challenge more than others I've seen recently. Perhaps in a long time.*

Uh.

I agree to your conditions, but I have amended mine.

What? Arwen asked warily.

You'll run the challenge, to entertain my courtesans, and the other half-dragon will stay and entertain me during the two hours you must avoid my hunters. Dithara rested a hand on Yendral's bare chest, though she looked at Azerdash while she did so.

Yendral nodded at Arwen and Azerdash, as if this were all going according to plan, but calculation glittered in the queen's eyes.

Had Yendral's and Azerdash's lives been at stake, Arwen would have refused the game, but only she had to survive. She had her camouflaging charm, and she could now make an effective barrier. If one of the hunters caught her, he could carry her back to the chamber, but she would be ensconced in it. He wouldn't be able to kill her.

If he's okay with it, Arwen said, wondering if Yendral truly was, *I agree to your terms.*

Excellent. I am certain the half-dragon will be delighted to enjoy my body and my magic. Dithara's fingers curled to dig into Yendral's chest. *As he informed me, he had sex with my predecessor many centuries ago and wishes to compare.*

Simply experience another fae queen of great power. Yendral stepped closer to her and rested a hand on her stomach, brushing his chest against her shoulder. The archers tensed but didn't stop him.

Dithara's smirk returned, and she wrapped an arm around him.

Should you be surrounded or otherwise overcome, Yendral whispered into Arwen's mind, *do what you must to survive. I'll keep her distracted so she doesn't send more hunters into the tunnels than you've agreed to face.*

Are you sure you want to do this? she asked.

Usually. Yendral winked before extending a hand toward the tunnel, trying to guide the queen to walk away with him.

But Dithara lifted a finger and walked instead toward Arwen. *Remove what's in your pocket.*

Arwen tensed, afraid she meant Azerdash's gift, but she pointed to the pocket that held Amber's camouflaging charm.

You'll leave that with me while you are engaged in the challenge. It wouldn't be fair of you to be able to disappear magically.

It's not fair for me to have to face ten opponents.

And yet you agreed to the game.

Yes, before she'd known she would lose the charm...

It belongs to a friend. I can't risk losing it. Arwen flattened her hand over her pocket.

Give it to your claimed male to hold then. Dithara flicked her finger at Azerdash.

His face was masked again, but he held out his hand to accept it.

Surprised he wasn't objecting to this, Arwen couldn't help but feel panicked. She had the skills to blend into the forest, but these tunnels weren't natural, nor were they like the open wilderness of her home. She'd been counting on using the camouflaging charm.

You'll do fine with the skills and tools remaining with you. Azerdash widened his eyes slightly, as if giving her a secret message, but he didn't say anything else telepathically. Because the queen might be powerful enough to overhear even if they attempted to make their messages private?

Maybe he meant that the tool he'd given her had powers that would help her survive. Maybe *it* had a camouflaging element?

Hoping so, Arwen nodded to him. *All right.*

"What now?" she asked aloud.

You'd better run. Dithara smiled and pointed toward a tunnel on the far side of the lake. *I'll be generous and give you five minutes before I unleash my hunters.*

As if on cue, ten male and female fae walked onto the bank with magical bows and swords. They had strong auras and looked fit and capable. Evading even one might be a challenge.

With little choice, since she *had* agreed to this, Arwen headed for the far tunnel.

All who wish to watch the entertainment, come with me, Dithara spoke telepathically to her people, then glanced back, waving a hand in invitation to Azerdash.

He nodded, as if he intended to come, but he headed toward the tractor that had continued its slow crawl around the lake.

Are you going to study machinery while I'm hiding for my life? Arwen asked.

Like Yendral, I will seek to give you an advantage.

Not from the queen's bed, I trust.

Her bed *is not a melding of gnomish and fae magic and engineering.*

Arwen snorted as she jogged toward the dark tunnel, vines rustling underfoot. *If I have a gnome add cogs to my bed, will it clear up your complicated feelings about me and make you want to visit?*

That is a possibility.

Guess I'd better survive the next two hours so I can try that then.

I recommend it, yes.

15

Arwen passed another whirring tractor tending vines as she came to an intersection, randomly choosing the left-most tunnel. The queen hadn't deigned to give her a map or suggest which ways led to wilderness, where one might hide effectively, and which ways led back into their city. Not that Arwen couldn't hide in the fae equivalent of a Whole Foods produce section, but she would prefer more open spaces in case she needed to run.

After making sure nobody was yet chasing her, she pulled out Azerdash's tool. She should have spent less time hugging him in gratitude and more time asking how it worked. She had no idea how to activate it or even how to open what looked like multiple knives and other tools.

Hoping the queen was distracted by Yendral, Arwen risked reaching out telepathically to Azerdash. *How do I activate the camouflaging magic?*

He hadn't said anything to confirm that the tool offered such magic, but the look he'd given her made her ninety-nine percent certain it did.

Press your thumb to the oval indention on the side, he replied.

Don't dally. Dithara didn't wait the whole five minutes. Her hunters just took off after you.

Imagine my shock.

She is monitoring me. I will instruct you on the other enchantments layered onto the tool when you return.

So I have to live to learn what it can do?

Azerdash smiled into her mind. *Yes.*

Right.

Arwen checked the time on her phone, wanting to make sure she strode back into the queen's chamber at the exact two-hour mark. It buzzed in her hand and complained about the lack of a signal, but the display showed the hour in Seattle.

After activating the multitool's camouflaging power, Arwen glided down a tunnel, not as worried now about finding wilderness. As long as she was magically hidden, she had an advantage. She did want to locate a large area where there was enough space to ensure wandering fae wouldn't get too close and see through the camouflage.

In a wide, circular intersection where multiple tunnels joined, a merchant with gray hair and a green beard had a cart set up to sell knives. He was sharpening blades with a whetstone when Arwen entered, so she didn't worry much about him. There was enough room for her to stay far enough away for her magic to keep her hidden. Or so she thought. But when she stepped on a vine identical to hundreds of others she'd trod over, a startling *sluff-swisp* sounded.

She froze as the merchant whirled toward her.

He snatched a knife off the rack behind him and squinted in her direction without surprise, as if he'd been warned about the hunt taking place. Maybe every fae in the city had been.

He didn't look precisely at Arwen, so she trusted the camouflaging magic held, but when he hefted the blade to throw it, she ducked and moved away, lest luck favor him.

It thudded point-first into the vine that had alerted under her foot. A psychic keening came from the plant and rippled through the intersection and down the tunnels. Shouts in the distance suggested those hunting her had heard it and would rush to the area.

Moving as quickly as she could without breaking her camouflage, Arwen headed down one of the tunnels, leaving the merchant gripping another knife and peering around. The blade he'd thrown quivered where it had struck, the sharp point embedded in the vine.

Heart hammering, Arwen had to fight the urge to turn her jog into a sprint. Azerdash's hunch had been right. These people wanted her dead, not captured.

She took numerous turns, choosing passageways that her senses told her were empty, but she watched the vines warily now. Since they were magical, they could doubtless feel her walking on them. They covered the ground, so she had no choice.

A bare tunnel attracted her, no plants covering the ground, but before she stepped off the vines leading up to it, another *sluff-whisp* came from underfoot. This time, there wasn't anyone nearby to hear it, but that didn't make Arwen feel safe. The vines might have a way to communicate with each other—and the fae—from a distance.

The earthen tunnel, a path of flagstones leading down it, emanated reddish light from the walls. It led her to another lake, one filled with purple pads reminiscent of lilies, each with a red speckled fruit growing in the center.

Two fae in skiffs with paddles floated on either side of a bridge that arched over the lake to a short, wide tunnel on the far side. A bright yellow light beamed from a cavern beyond it.

The fae filled buckets between their legs with the fruit. This would have looked like a placid harvesting scene, except two or three spears with sharp tips rose from holders in the skiffs behind them. In case the lily pads got fresh? They did emanate a faint magic, not unlike the vines.

On the far side of the lake, one of the cylindrical wheeled machines ambled along a bank, brushing moss along the wall with one tool and spraying something onto the lily pads with another. Azerdash's fertilizer and seeds?

Another time, Arwen would have investigated, curious about the farming practices of another culture. Sadly, she was too busy being hunted for that.

Since the bridge was long and a place she could be trapped if fae started across from the other side, she turned, intending to go back and choose another intersection. But two hunters with bows walked up the tunnel toward her.

Youngish, with braided blue hair, they hadn't been in the queen's chamber, and they might not have anything to do with stalking Arwen, but she didn't know that for certain. And the tunnel wasn't wide enough for her to slip past them without being seen.

Reluctantly, she headed across the bridge.

Something stirred in the water, causing ripples that made the pads bob. She didn't sense any magical creatures, but that didn't mean there weren't the equivalent of crocodiles in the water. Maybe that was why the fruit gatherers had spears.

Quickening her pace, Arwen reached the halfway point on the bridge. From the elevated viewpoint, she could see more of the brightly lit area through the tunnel. It was another cavern with sun-like illumination beaming from the walls onto rows and circles of plants. Gardens?

If the area was as spacious as it looked, it might be the perfect place to hide.

As soon as she had the thought, two grim-faced fae strode out of the garden cavern and headed toward the bridge. They *were* from the queen's chamber, and the bows and arrows they carried emitted strong magic. Arwen's armored jumpsuit had deflected bullets before, but she didn't know if it was sturdy enough to withstand those weapons.

The hunters peered around, pointing and talking as they searched. For her.

Arwen glanced back, but the two young fae were heading across the bridge from behind. She cursed herself for walking into a situation where she would be trapped.

The hunters called to the youths, who waved their weapons and tapped their noses. What did that mean? They hadn't seen her, but they would help hunt?

Arwen had no idea, but both pairs of fae headed across the bridge with her in the middle. The fruit gatherers looked toward the newcomers, calling a query.

With little choice, Arwen secured her bow and quiver, then climbed over the railing. As the fae approached from both sides of the bridge, she lowered herself over the side, intending to drop down into the water.

But it rippled again, and something surfaced.

A large serpent with shark-like fins running down its spine moved through the water, heading straight toward her. Though Azerdash's tool ought to be hiding her aura from magical senses and her body from sight, it might not be camouflaging sound or scent. She didn't think she'd made any noise, but she couldn't help what she smelled like to a predator with a keen nose.

On the bridge, the fae drew closer, talking cheerfully, probably about how the youths would happily help the older hunters kill a mongrel intruder.

Slight ridges and a few indentions in the construction of the bridge allowed Arwen to find purchase below, hanging from her fingers with the toes of her moccasins wedged into a crease. If she'd only had to worry about sight, she was fully hidden from the fae above, but they would sense her when they walked over her. And that serpent *already* sensed her.

It circled under the bridge, and she imagined a dog following its nose, homing in on the location of a rodent. Arwen hung at least fifteen feet above the surface, but, with that long serpent body, it might be able to propel its jaws out of the water to grab her.

Since it was a mundane creature, as far as she could tell, her armor ought to offer some protection against its fangs, but her neck and face weren't armored. It could very well bite her head off. She *might* be able to create a barrier again to protect herself, but practicing magic alone in a tunnel was a lot different from drawing upon it when it mattered—and she was dangling from her fingers and toes.

This game of hide-and-seek was a lot more challenging than she'd envisioned. As she hung there, sweat dripping from her temple into her hairline, she decided she'd been crazy to do this for alchemy ingredients.

Both pairs of fae on the bridge stopped about ten feet from her location and twenty from each other. Arwen could no longer see them, but her senses told her where they were.

A query came from one. *Do you sense something?*

Arwen could only guess at their words, but it had to be something like that. They were close. She had to choose to face them or the serpent.

Neither option was appealing, but she doubted the queen would have her executed—any more than she was already trying to do—for killing an animal. Killing one or more of her citizens, even in self-defense, would be another matter.

Lowering her feet, her core muscles straining from the effort of holding herself from such an awkward perch, Arwen pressed her legs together, hoping she wouldn't make a big splash. She wanted to wait until the serpent was farther away but sensed the fae walking toward each other again.

Letting go with one hand, she pulled her bow off her back and managed to extract an arrow from her quiver, her selection precise. Quencher was enchanted with fire magic and worked well against water and ice creatures.

The serpent's head rose from the water, yellow eyes and a pair of long black fangs pointed at her. It had no doubt where she was.

In as acrobatic a feat as she could manage, Arwen let go of the bridge, her hands a blur. As she fell, she nocked Quencher, aiming for the serpent's eyes. The arrow released as her feet plunged into the water.

Gravity took her below the surface before she saw if the arrow struck, but an angry hiss sounded so loudly that she heard it through her splash. As cold water enveloped her, she reached for Azerdash's magical tool.

Certain the fae had heard her splash into the lake, and probably detected her aura too, Arwen swam away under the surface, kicking hard since her hands were busy. Struggling not to lose her bow or quiver, she opened one of the blades in the multitool. Since the serpent wasn't magic, she couldn't sense it behind her, but she *could* sense Quencher. It was moving rapidly after her. It must have struck true, embedding in the serpent's head. Not a killing blow, unfortunately.

Another angry hiss sounded, muffled by the water but audible. Under most circumstances, Arwen was a good swimmer, but her bow and quiver kept catching when she encountered seaweed-like tendrils rising from the lake bottom. The stalks of the lily pads anchored below. They gave somewhat but impeded her greatly, and it was too dark under the water for her to see and avoid them.

With the serpent drawing closer, Arwen turned and slashed at it. She glimpsed its yellow eyes as it tried to chomp her.

With the water and the tendrils fighting her, she cut for the serpent's head, needing to deter its fangs. The creature jerked away, and she would have missed, but she brushed the arrow sticking out of its skull. Bumping it made the serpent hiss again, its long body twitching in response to its pain.

Arwen grabbed for Quencher with her free hand, hoping to pull it out so she could use it again. Soon, she would need air, so she needed to figure out how to end this battle. Further, she sensed the four fae above, all on the bridge and looking down.

She caught the arrow, but, in the same instant, the back of the serpent flipped around and caught *her*. Much thicker and stronger than the stalks of the pads, it wrapped around her waist and squeezed, trying to crush her. Precious air escaped her lungs, bubbling away from her face.

The serpent's head jerked away, and she lost her grip on the arrow. Desperate, with visions of being dragged down to the bottom for her attacker to eat, Arwen stabbed its body with the multitool.

The magical blade sank in as if she were cutting room-temperature butter. More, branches of blue lightning streaked out from it, running up and down the serpent's long body. Fear blasted her at the thought that she would be electrocuted herself, but the magical attack only affected the creature. It shuddered violently and released her.

Relieved and craving air, Arwen swam away. She wanted to come up under the bridge, so it would hide her from the fae standing on it, but she'd lost all concept of her location in the water. Only her senses told her their vague direction—and that they'd split up. She imagined them leaning over the bridge with their bows drawn.

Before she breached the surface, something struck her from above, cutting through her armored jumpsuit and gouging her flesh. The last of her air escaped as fire lit the back of her shoulder. She almost dropped the multitool, but that would be a hundred times worse than losing an arrow. She clenched her grip on it as she kicked, trying to put distance between her and the fae.

But the tendrils continued to impede her, and she bumped her head on a lily pad before surfacing. It didn't give enough to allow her to force her way up.

She'd lost her air, and her lungs burned. She wanted to flail wildly until she found a way up, but common sense asserted itself, and she made herself grow still and find the button on Azerdash's tool. A faint tingle ran through her, hopefully indicating she was camouflaged again.

Even so, another arrow pierced the water from above. This one only grazed her outer thigh, but that didn't make it feel any better. Only barely did she keep from thrashing in pain, not wanting to break the camouflage she'd just activated, but they knew where she was. She had to move away.

With her lungs on fire, Arwen had to fight the reflex to gulp as she used the knife to cut tendrils and swim farther away. Once the pads weren't anchored, she could push them aside. Finally, she broke the surface. It took all her restraint to keep from gasping loudly and instead breathing in as carefully and quietly as she could.

A great splash came from less than ten feet away. *Now* what? Another serpent?

Dashing water out of her eyes, Arwen pointed her knife in that direction. Two more loud splashes came from farther away, and puzzled queries floated across the lake from the fae in the skiff.

Arwen's senses told her that the four fae archers that had been shooting at her were in the water now. At first, she thought they'd jumped in so they could swim after her, but seconds earlier, they'd been content to fill her with holes.

Sensing something magical above made her look up. The tractor was rolling along the bridge, its mass taking up the width, not leaving room for anyone to stand. Had it knocked all four fae into the water?

Though confused, Arwen didn't question her luck. With her shoulder and thigh burning, she paddled as quietly as she could toward the bank where the machine had been operating earlier.

Shouts came from the far side of the lake, and two more hunters with bows started across the bridge, but the tractor accelerated toward them, as if it had a mind of its own.

Or as if someone was controlling it? Azerdash?

The hunters backed off the bridge, pointing to each other and their comrades in the water. The machine stopped a few feet from the base and spat seeds into the lake on either side, as if it were simply doing its duty.

A shriek and numerous curses came from the water under the bridge. All four fae hunters swam toward the bank, glancing back as they did. Either the serpent Arwen had attacked had recovered, or another had shown up. One of the skiff fae rowed toward it, a spear balanced across his lap.

Trusting her attackers were suitably distracted, Arwen swam faster toward the bank.

As she approached, whirs floated from the short tunnel leading to the garden cavern. Her foot bumped the bottom of the lake, and she stood warily. She readied her bow again, glad it and her magical arrows weren't affected by water.

A tractor identical to the last rolled into view and up to the water's edge. A click came from it, and a door in the side of the cylinder unlatched and opened several inches. In invitation?

After making sure her camouflage was active, Arwen crept out of the water. The tractor *shouldn't* have been able to sense her any more than living beings could, but it did seem to be expecting her.

The swimming fae reached the bank, but they were pointing at the tractor on the bridge and the serpent that had been chasing them. With nobody looking in her direction, Arwen lifted the door. The dark interior smelled strongly of woodsy earth and held the mounds of seeds that Azerdash had hinted of, but there was room for her to crawl inside.

As soon as she did, the door clicked shut behind her, plunging her into darkness. She didn't mind since the scent was comforting and the fae might not think to look for her inside. The tractor clanked agreeably and whirred into motion.

She could tell it backed up, probably turning toward the tunnel, before rolling forward again. After that, she had no idea where it went or where it would take her.

Too bad there wasn't a window. Even though she was in pain, and it should have been the last thing on her mind, she would have loved to see the garden.

"Later," she murmured, slumping back onto a pile of seeds, the gashes she'd received throbbing.

If she stayed hidden the full two hours and returned to the queen's chamber, she would win the game. Dithara would have to show her the garden personally. Assuming she kept her word. Would she?

16

AZERDASH? ARWEN RISKED WHISPERING TELEPATHICALLY AFTER SHE'D
been riding in the belly of the machine for fifteen or twenty
minutes. Her recently doused phone hadn't come on when she
tried to check the time, but she didn't know if that was because of
water damage or it was simply irked at her. *Are you controlling these
magical tractors, or has the fae technology taken a liking to me?*

Sure. Even *human* technology didn't like her. After dropping
chocolates into their clutches, she'd thought the vines might be on
her side, but their feelings of appreciation had been short-lived.
Like everything else here, the plants served the fae.

*While Yendral distracted the queen and her advisors, I was able to
use my magic to tinker with them from a distance, yes.*

He's distracting her and *her advisors?* Arwen remembered the
older females who'd stood at the queen's side. They'd been attractive enough, she supposed, but she couldn't imagine a guy inviting
the whole forbidding group to bed.

*His libido ensures he is adequate for such challenging missions.
Other fae attempted to distract me, likely to ensure I didn't do what I've
done to assist you, but I am not easily seduced.*

That's good. Again, Arwen was glad she hadn't tried to woo him with cookies and soft caresses.

I discovered that the dresdalatha, *as the fae call them, communicate with each other through the vines and take orders from a central hub.*

Like a network connected to the internet?

I have encountered the term internet *on your world but am uncertain what all it entails. It is not covered in your history texts.*

No, it's kind of recent. We may need to get you an antenna for your underground home. Arwen imagined a big satellite dish affixed to the bench on his hilltop.

The Study of Manliness *has not mentioned such items as necessary to be a capable and suitably masculine human being.*

Oh, the internet is necessary. Even my dad has a satellite dish. He doesn't want to miss Jeopardy or football season. Arwen shared an image of the dish mounted on their corn crib.

I see. In this instance, I learned of gnomish central hubs via the notes the scientist presented to me.

You mean the toilet paper roll that Gruflen gave you to keep you from magically manhandling him?

The notes he presented me as a suitable offering for one with dragon power, yes.

I'll let Willard know, for the next time dragons invade Earth, that toilet-paper rolls are appropriate offerings.

Rolls covered in notes that are of interest to them, yes.

You're a unique half-dragon.

As I am certain you are aware, a mongrel heritage naturally connotes uniqueness. Azerdash shared an image of her with her hand resting on a tree, her eyes closed, and her spider tattoo glowing while she attempted to communicate with the forest in an elven way.

I guess that's true. Anyway, however you accomplished it, thanks for helping me out. I would prefer not to need *help, but the odds are stacked against me.*

Yes. When you return—

Arwen waited for him to finish the sentence. He didn't.

Azerdash? Everything okay?

She didn't receive an answer. Had Queen Dithara realized he was fiddling with her technology?

Though her wounds hurt, Arwen made herself rise into a crouch and reached out with her senses, trying to detect fae or anything that might hint of her location. Several more times, she tried to contact Azerdash, and he didn't answer.

Worry crept into her. If the queen had learned that Arwen had evaded her minions and lived, she would be irked. If she'd learned *Azerdash* had been responsible...

Did Dithara have the power to hurt him? Maybe not she alone, but she and all her people might, especially here on their home turf. Surely, Dithara had ways of defending herself from—and attacking—powerful visitors.

"I need to get out of here." In the dark, Arwen patted for the door that had let her in.

The tractor trundled on, its wheels in motion. There wasn't a latch or lever that she could find. Mounds of seeds and fertilizer were the only things inside with her.

Again, Arwen scanned the area outside, hoping to detect someone or something that might be useful, but she couldn't sense anything beyond the tractor's magic.

She leaned her unwounded shoulder against the door and pushed. It didn't budge. She drew Azerdash's multitool, selecting the blade that had shot lightning when it struck the serpent but hesitated, envisioning electricity ricocheting off the walls of the cylinder with her inside. She would feel like an idiot electrocuting herself with Azerdash's gift—*if* she survived.

"Wouldn't feel like an idiot for long," she whispered, imagining some fae gardener opening the cylinder days hence to reload seeds and finding the charred remains of her body.

Arwen opened the other tools and could sense their magic but had no idea what they did.

Next time you give me a gift, Azerdash, I'd appreciate it if it came with instructions.

Again, he didn't respond. Several minutes had passed now. Even if he was in a battle, wouldn't it have been decided in that time? Maybe the fae he'd mentioned attempting to seduce him had succeeded. No, something more concerning had to be going on.

Arwen put away the multitool and grabbed one of her arrows that had the power to punch through metal and magic. She lamented that she'd lost Quencher, though it wouldn't have helped much in this situation.

She leaned the arrow into the door seam, willing it to break the seal—or break the whole door. As seconds passed, she grew more and more impatient. And more certain Azerdash needed her.

The seal remained intact. The tractor even sent a charge through her arrow and up her arm. The buzz was painful enough to make her back away, her fingers numb.

"Where am I?" Arwen shook out her arm. "Fort Knox?"

Who would have thought a fae tractor had magical defenses?

After putting away the arrow, she flattened her hand against the door and willed her magic into it. In case the tractor had a sentience, she thanked it for the ride and asked it to release her. It continued trundling onward. What if it was heading farther and farther from the queen's chamber? From Azerdash?

"Damn it." Arwen groped through her repertoire of magic, trying to think of something that would work on a machine, but all the eleven magic she knew was for manipulating plants and the earth. And her dark-elven magic... Soul tracking wouldn't do any good. And the other powers her tutors had started teaching her long ago... She'd always shied away from them. They were too dark. Too beloved by the demons the dark elves worshipped.

Power built within her as she struggled to figure out how to shape it and use it. The magic inherent in the fae realm made it build more than usual. Soon, she ached with the energy within her, and it demanded a release.

Her forearm itched. The spider tattoo. Purple light from it seeped from under her sleeve.

Use your power, a voice in the back of her mind whispered. Hers? Or something that originated with the tattoo? *Dealing with this aberrant construct is a simple matter. The power to destroy is within you. It is far easier to access than the power to create.*

"Don't I know it," Arwen muttered. *Take me to the queen's chamber,* she spoke to the tractor, willing it to understand. Or for her message to get to that network hub Azerdash had spoken of and for *it* to have the capability to understand.

The image of a fire demon danced in her mind, amorphous and black but bordered by bright orange flames. *Embrace your heritage. Use your power, and learn the joy of destruction.*

Arwen bit her lip and shook her head, again reaching for the multitool. Better to risk using Azerdash's unknown magic than something dark-elven.

But a surge of power somewhere ahead made her pause. It was strong enough to detect through the tractor's muffling aura.

Because that had been *dragon* magic, not fae magic.

And was that a dragon's aura? Yes. A male. Whoever he was, she didn't recognize him, but a few seconds later, she picked up Azerdash's aura.

"Uh-oh." Arwen remembered the words of the Silverclaw dragons that Azerdash and Yendral had faced with Zavryd and his kin, the promise that if their clan ever found Azerdash away from Earth, they would kill him.

Had the fae queen, pissed that he wouldn't have sex with her, called one or more of them to come? Or had they heard the rumor that Azerdash sought the galaxy blade and might raise an army?

A screech of pain pierced the cylinder. Azerdash?

Somewhere ahead, Arwen sensed the dragon moving around him. No, *fighting* him.

More desperate than ever to escape the machine, Arwen raised the multitool, not glancing to see which portion of it she'd pulled out. She thrust it against the seam of the door, willing it to cut through. Or blow the whole thing up.

But it clinked and bounced off. Not a hint of lightning or other magic emanated from it.

Cursing again, Arwen almost threw it, but she couldn't do that to Azerdash's gift. More purple light seeped out from under her sleeve, and her forearm itched, the tattoo throbbing with the power still built up in her body.

Another pained screech sounded. That *was* Azerdash.

Envisioning a dragon and the entire fae court attacking him, Arwen slapped her hand to the door again. This time, when her dark-elven magic taunted her to use it, she did. She had no choice.

Combining her power with that which had flowed into her from the ground, she willed her magic to force open the door. It obeyed, striking with a great wrenching of chaotic energy.

The door blew outward. The light of the chamber outside showed black mist flowing out of the cylinder.

More, spoke the voice in the back of Arwen's mind. *Use more. Fully release your power.*

With her tattoo—no, her entire *body*—throbbing with magic, Arwen grabbed her bow and sprang outside. The tractor hadn't stopped moving, but she landed lightly, the green-scaled backside of a dragon not twenty feet in front of her.

To her surprise, she was back in the queen's chamber. The dragon had flattened a number of the mushroom seats, its taloned feet digging into mortar and tearing up flagstones as it faced a smaller black-scaled dragon. Azerdash.

Arwen sensed Yendral and the queen and her advisors in the chamber behind the throne, but the wall had collapsed, burying the door and blocking them from the battle. The courtesans had all left. Only one musician remained, crouching behind his drums.

Azerdash, with his back to the collapsed wall, spewed fire at the unfamiliar dragon. Two of the tractors had stopped near him, and they spat seeds and fertilizer at the great scaled intruder. All that did was cloud the air.

Stay inside, Azerdash warned. *He'll kill you by accident without even knowing it.*

"The hell he will." Still flush with the power she'd summoned, and with black mist roiling on the ground around her, Arwen lifted her bow.

She started to reach for an arrow but realized she still held the multitool. Though it hadn't helped in the cylinder, she pointed it at the dragon and willed her power into it, the same destructive energy she'd used on the door.

It flowed into the tool, as if it were a natural conduit, and ripped toward the dragon, leaving black mist in the air like smoke after a cannon fired.

The power blasted into the back of Azerdash's foe, and the barrier around the dragon wavered. Even with her magic enhanced by the fae realm's native energy, it wasn't enough to tear down the defenses of such a great foe. But it didn't matter because her attack startled the dragon. He whipped his head halfway around to look at her.

You! the dragon boomed into her mind. *Mongrel dark elf, your crimes are known to the Silverclaws. I will slay you!*

During the time he spoke, Azerdash took advantage of his distraction. He sprang, hurling power he must have been holding back and snapped his jaws.

Simultaneously, the two tractors drove at the dragon. They struck his barrier and exploded, somehow sabotaged to blow up using all the combined gnomish and fae power. The effect was enough to shatter the dragon's barrier, and Azerdash lunged in, biting with his jaws and raking with his talons.

Though Arwen didn't know if he needed her help in that moment, or if he ever had, she launched another blast of magic through the multitool. It hungrily accepted and even amplified her power.

The dragon's back was to her again as his wings thrashed and he clawed at Azerdash, so she didn't hit a vital target, but her power struck hard enough to make their foe stagger, his scaled body twitching in surprise.

Using her distraction, Azerdash whipped his long neck and found an angle that let him sink his jaws into the dragon's neck.

With a screech of pain, the Silverclaw leaped back, whirling and striking Azerdash with his tail. The dragon managed to pull his neck free but not without leaving a chunk of flesh and scales in Azerdash's mouth.

Again, the dragon screeched. He glanced at Arwen, then ran several paces. A portal formed between him and the hunkering musician.

Azerdash crouched, prepared to spring after him, but maybe he decided it was better not to kill another dragon. Another Silverclaw.

We won't forget you, mongrel! Did he mean Azerdash? Or Arwen?

She didn't know.

As the dragon leaped through the portal, escaping with his life, the collapsed wall behind the throne burst outward. Rubble tumbled all around Azerdash and the wreckage from the destroyed tractors.

Queen Dithara walked out with a staff, fury twisting her face.

Yendral—a very naked Yendral still in his elven form—walked out with her, carrying a sword. Her two female advisors, one holding a blanket to cover her nudity and the other holding a wall for support, peered out of the chamber.

Azerdash didn't glance at any of them, instead looking at Arwen with his violet eyes.

The black mist was fading, but she winced, certain he saw it and knew she'd used raw dark-elven power without twisting it in an elven way. His gaze shifted to her forearm, where the tattoo glowed purple, on full display. Her sleeve had been pushed back —or maybe blown back by the magic.

Dithara also looked toward Arwen and her tattoo. The dismissal on her face earlier had turned to something closer to wonder. Or even... respect?

The urge to tuck her arm behind her back swept over Arwen, but she'd used her power and couldn't hide it. Though she worried there would be repercussions, she lifted her chin and held out her arm, leaving the spider mark on display. Maybe if the queen believed Arwen had the power to be a threat, she wouldn't try again to deceive Arwen—to have her *killed*.

Only when Azerdash shifted into his elven form and walked toward Arwen did she lower her arm, chagrined that she'd been lured into using that power. Would he be disappointed? She'd helped him—or at least tried to assist in a small way—but he'd always been repulsed by dark elves and had seemed pleased with her when she'd used her power in the way of surface elves. What would he say now?

His eyebrows rose, and he pointed at his gift. "That is not the weapon I expected you to bring to a battle."

He didn't sound disappointed or upset. Instead, his eyes crinkled with amusement.

Arwen looked down. In the darkness of the cylinder, she

hadn't known which tool she'd unfolded, just that it hadn't done anything against the door.

"Is that... a bottle opener?" she asked.

"Yes. The half-dwarf enchanter said you were unlikely to need such a tool to aid you in your adventures, but the Study of Manliness stated that a multitool would be handicapped without that implement."

"I'm lucky I didn't pull it out to use on the serpent."

His brows rose higher. "Serpent?"

Remembering that it hadn't been magical, so he wouldn't have sensed it, she waved in the direction of the lake. "It was among the beings troubling me under that bridge."

"Ah."

What in all the rot-cursed realms was that dragon doing uninvited in my court? Dithara jammed her fists against her hips and glowered all around, though few fae remained to answer her questions.

Arwen certainly had no idea.

Azerdash, who might have thrown telepathic insults at the dragon while they'd been engaged, was the only one who had an answer. He squinted at Dithara. *Someone told the Silverclaw Clan that I am not only raising an army to pit against all of dragondom but that I was in your realm.*

Many are aware of that rumor, but I did not tell any dragons about your presence. Nor would it have given one of them the right to intrude here. He shouldn't even have been able to create a doorway through our defenses. Dithara scowled at the spot where the portal had been, though it had since disappeared. *We have a deal with their kind that they will not bother us, and we will not intrude upon their affairs. But that—* Dithara thrust her arm toward the rubble and her collapsed wall, *—is a bother. Especially when it came during my coupling time.* She glanced at Yendral.

It is tedious when enemies intrude upon coupling time, Azerdash said.

Very tedious. Disgusted, Dithara spat on the ground, then frowned at Arwen. *You are not dead.*

No. Arwen surreptitiously tucked the bottle opener into the multitool and withdrew a knife in case she needed a better weapon.

Azerdash walked to her side and stood shoulder to shoulder with her, facing the queen. *The two hours of* hide-and-seek *have passed. She has won what you wished to be a deadly game. Now, you must give her the ingredients, as you agreed.*

Dithara snorted. *With your assistance in suborning my machines, she won. Do not think that I saw nothing, even though I was enjoying your comrade's company until we were interrupted.*

I assisted her because she has claimed me, and it is my duty to protect her. Though he was in elven form, a growl emanated from Azerdash's chest as he rested a hand on Arwen's shoulder.

A tingle of satisfaction—or maybe that was pleasure—swept through her, both at his touch and at his words. Logically, she knew it was for show, an attempt to get the queen to leave her alone, but she liked his protection.

Dithara eyed him, less with hostility and more with the earlier look she'd given him, one of sexual interest. The way she folded her arms over her chest made Arwen worry that she was still plotting ways to get rid of her.

When a number of fae archers arrived via a tunnel, Arwen tensed, afraid she was about to have to fight again.

The fae trotted out around the rubble and pointed their bows in her direction.

17

OH, PUT THOSE DOWN, Queen Dithara snapped at the archers.

They looked hesitantly at her before lowering their bows.

We heard there was a threat to you. One male fae glanced at the rubble.

Yes, five minutes ago a dragon burst in here. Where were you then?

Er. The archers looked at Arwen—yes, they'd been busy hunting for *her*—but they didn't offer excuses for their tardiness.

The queen made a disgusted noise but looked at Arwen again and nodded. *Very well. I will retrieve the ingredients, as promised. If you can command the heart—or maybe the cock—of one with dragon blood, it's likely I underestimated your power and would be unwise to send my people after you again.*

Though Arwen was inclined to protest the idea that she *commanded* any body part of Azerdash's, she lifted her chin in what she hoped was perceived as agreement. She wouldn't verbally say *yes*, not wanting to irk him.

Azerdash only snorted softly, not appearing offended by any of this. He squeezed her shoulder before releasing her.

Dithara barked a few orders at her people in their language. A servant wearing an outfit that looked more like a towel wrapped around his waist than a piece of clothing scurried out of the half-destroyed chamber behind the throne room.

"How many people were in there?" Azerdash asked Yendral in dry amusement.

"Enough that you would have experienced... there is an Earth term." Yendral looked to Arwen. "Implementation apprehension?"

"You may mean performance anxiety, and I'm sure he wouldn't have."

Azerdash squinted at Yendral. "I am an expert and practiced implementer. Ask Arwen."

Yendral's eyebrows flew up as he looked at her again.

"I think he may be talking about his expertise with machinery. He helped me out of a sticky situation at a bridge." Arwen shrugged, which prompted a stab of pain from her wounded shoulder. In her concern for Azerdash and alarm at the dragon, she'd forgotten about her wounds.

"Yes." Azerdash opened his cloak and delved into an inner pocket.

"You are a strange male," Yendral told him. "I understand why you need instructions from that book."

Ignoring him, Arwen looked toward Azerdash's pocket, hoping he would withdraw his tin of elven regeneration pads.

The queen's shirtless servant brought the remains of the container of cookies to her. Dust covered it, but the contents had been sealed and weren't damaged.

Dithara nodded curtly at him and accepted the cookies, clutching them to her chest before pointing at a tunnel Arwen hadn't been down yet. *Come with me to the gardens.*

Instead of pulling out regeneration pads, Azerdash withdrew Amber's camouflaging charm and a familiar roll of toilet paper with gnomish scrawls in black ink all over the visible part. Or maybe all over *all* of it. After returning the borrowed charm, Azerdash unrolled numerous layers before pointing to diagrams and indecipherable—at least to Arwen—symbols.

Yendral lifted his eyes toward the ceiling, muttering that it was hard to tease someone who was so oblivious.

"The part on networks," Azerdash told Arwen with a bright smile, touching the diagram and looking pleased with himself for his successful implementation, or whatever he'd done, on the seed tractors.

Since two of the machines had saved her ass, Arwen couldn't mock him for that. "I'm glad you remembered it and were able to employ it here. I'm also glad the toilet-paper rolls in the public restroom that the gnomes were hiding in when they wrote those notes are so sturdy. Usually those kinds of places have one-ply." Only when she reached out to touch the roll did she sense the faintest hint of magic. Maybe Gruflen had enchanted the paper to be more durable.

"Ply?" Azerdash tilted his head.

Dithara had reached the tunnel and made a loud *harumph* as she looked back at them.

"Never mind." Arwen clasped Azerdash's hand and led him toward the tunnel. Once she had the ingredients and they returned home, she could bandage herself.

But she must have limped or grimaced because Azerdash frowned at her. "You are injured."

"Some fae guys were rudely shooting at me while I was trying to escape their serpent."

Hold, Azerdash told Dithara, as if he expected her to obey him.

He didn't wait to see if she would but stopped and held out a hand toward Arwen. He returned his notes to his pocket and patted around in another one. When he withdrew the tin case she'd seen before, she slumped in relief. Travel regeneration pads. He'd once used them to heal an orc.

Azerdash stepped around behind her and loosened her jumpsuit with a trickle of magic. Startled, she almost jumped away, since she wore only her bra and undies beneath it, but the damp fabric clung to her skin without revealing much. He peeled the top back only enough to access her wound. With a tingle of warm magic, he cleaned it and might have started the healing process before applying one of the green woven-plant pads. It formed to her skin, soothing and cooling the pain.

Arwen sighed as blissful relief swept through her. When Azerdash looked down, she hiked her leg up so he could reach her injured thigh. Sitting on one of the mushroom stools would have been easier, but a dragon's tail had smashed the closest of them.

Not fazed, Azerdash caught her under the knee, using his hand to support her leg, and she sighed again. Despite the pain of the injury, she enjoyed the gentle warmth of his touch. If they'd been alone, she might have snuggled closer, letting him have both legs, if he wanted. The better to treat her wounds, of course.

The arrow had sliced open enough of the leg of the jumpsuit that he didn't need to loosen the bottom half. He had no trouble cleaning the wound and applying the pad. Arwen hoped Imoshaun would be able to repair the jumpsuit, as she didn't think a needle and thread would work on the now-magical material.

"I will attend you more fully once we've completed your errand," Azerdash said gravely, an apology in his eyes. Because he hadn't noticed her wounds immediately?

"Thank you." Arwen rested a hand on his chest, wanting him to know there was nothing wrong with him being preoccupied by gnomish notes, machinery, and a dragon almost killing him—that latter especially.

He nodded, still grave, but she noticed he hadn't yet released her leg. He sent a warm trickle of magic along her nerves, the pleasurable sensation making her forget about wounds and witnesses. She gazed up at his face, at his lips, and wished she could kiss him. To thank him for his help and because... just because.

The way he held her gaze made her wonder if something similar might be on his mind.

But the fae servant who'd retrieved the cookies walked up to them, and Azerdash released her leg. Arwen resisted the urge to keep it up, maybe hooking it around his waist, and lowered it.

She turned, intending to hurry after the queen, but Dithara remained by the tunnel entrance. She was noshing on cookies and eyeing Yendral. He'd been in the process of levitating his clothing out of the abandoned bedchamber, but she was using her magic to block it from reaching him.

Yendral shifted their path, raising his clothes higher, but she conjured a burst of wind to bat them back. Their auras clashed as they tested each other, and sneers and defiant squints accompanied the magical outbursts. After Dithara created a barrier to keep his clothes from passing, Yendral shifted his power to her, and her trousers loosened and sagged off her hips. She caught them before they fell and glowered at him, though it looked like a mock glower.

"Is that how he flirts?" Arwen asked.

"One of many ways," Azerdash said. "His methods aren't subtle."

Once he and Arwen joined the queen in the tunnel, the flirting stopped. Yendral managed to retrieve his clothes and dress while the queen ambled off, another cookie in her mouth.

Should you tire of your half-dragons one day, she spoke into Arwen's mind without looking back, *send them to me. I shall find a use for them.*

Arwen almost answered that she had no power over them and they would have to send themselves, if they wished it, but remembered she'd supposedly claimed Azerdash. She didn't know what that entailed in the fae culture, but she may have implied she had authority over him. As if.

Assuming they survive attempting to start an insurrection against the dragons. Dithara glanced back as she walked. *Originally, I scoffed at the thought that half-dragons could do such a thing, but if Starblade obtains one of those swords again, other beings may follow him. The weapons have reached a legendary status over the centuries.*

Arwen didn't know what to say to that. It disturbed her that so many people—and dragons—had heard about a mission that Azerdash hadn't agreed to accept. That elf ambassador had to have told everyone he knew. Or maybe one person who was a huge blabbermouth. Would Azerdash be doomed, whether he wanted to battle the dragons or not?

And what of her? She'd agreed in front of witnesses that she would stand at his side.

How had her life gotten so complicated?

18

THE SUN WAS SETTING OVER THE OLYMPIC MOUNTAINS WHEN Azerdash's portal returned them to Earth. Apparently, it was easier for those with power to make portals and leave the fae realm than to get through their defenses and arrive without using a fairy ring. When they'd left, Queen Dithara, who'd been surprisingly generous about providing Arwen with the two ingredients she needed, had still been fuming about the disrespectful Silverclaw who'd shown up in her court uninvited.

Thanks to her disgruntlement, Dithara hadn't been willing to give Arwen a tour of the gardens or speak about fae cultivation methods. Given that she'd been arranging Arwen's death two hours earlier, maybe that had been too much to hope for. Arwen had, however, looked around at the beds of plants in the garden cavern and examined the magic permeating the crops with her senses. If her phone had been working, she might have taken a few dozen—or hundred—photos.

Azerdash had watched with knowing amusement as Arwen had sunk her hands into a corner of loamy soil, using her power to examine everything from the microbes to the fertilizer the fae used. By now, he understood her interests, just as she understood his. While the queen's servant had collected the corn husk, one of the magical tractors had ambled through the cavern and paused to loom at Azerdash's side, like a stray dog he'd tamed.

"Yendral isn't coming back?" Arwen asked when the portal disappeared and only Azerdash stood with her.

They'd come out in the intersection by Val's house, not twenty feet from the fairy ring they'd used to leave.

All was quiet, and Arwen didn't sense anyone magical around save for Zoltan in the basement. Matti and Sarrlevi weren't home, and Arwen assumed they were at the hospital or wherever one giving birth to half-elven, quarter-dwarven, and quarter-human babies went for delivery.

Azerdash's lips pressed together in disapproval. "He remained to finish his encounter with the queen."

"Did the arrival of the Silverclaw dragon interrupt their, uhm, relations?"

"It did. Leaving both unsatisfied, as he unnecessarily informed me."

"As your loyal comrade, he probably thinks he has to update you with the latest intelligence."

"The only kind of *intelligence* reporting I require is on enemy positioning and troop movements."

Arwen scratched her jaw. "Well, he's one of your troops, right? And there will presumably be movement."

His eyelids drooped. "Would *you* like the details of his sexual encounters?"

"No, but I'm not his commander. I don't need to know about any of his movements."

Azerdash's grunt suggested he had no interest in that area either.

"Let me give these to Zoltan." Arwen held up the pouch of ingredients but had only taken a step when her phone buzzed.

Surprised it was working again, she dug it out of her pocket. She expected little more than an announcement that it was back in service, now that they were in range of Earth's cell towers, or maybe an angry hiss and flash of the screen due to her rude treatment of it, but a long text from Val popped up.

I know you're busy avoiding fae orgies, and half-dragons who might be game to join in, but when you get back, let me know if you know where Amber is. Earlier, she mentioned doing some research for you, but she's not answering her phone. I called Thad, and he said she went to join us for Matti's delivery, but she never showed up at the magical-beings birthing center. I'm not worried yet, but if she doesn't come home tonight, I will be. It's not like her not to answer her phone. The thing is practically attached as a permanent fixture to her body.

Unease trickled through Arwen, and she stopped on the sidewalk. She flipped through alerts and found that Amber had called earlier but hadn't left a message. She dialed Val's number, hoping for an update—hoping that Amber had shown up.

"Problem?" Azerdash asked.

"I hope not." Arwen bit her lip as she waited for an answer, thinking of the calculation in Amber's eyes when they'd wrangled over a price for her services. What if Amber, motivated to earn her ten percent, had gone to check on something on her own? Something dangerous?

"Hey, Arwen," Val answered.

A wrenching scream in the background startled Arwen, and she fumbled the phone.

"Matti's still in labor," Val added.

"I thought you might be battling a harpy or a banshee."

"Nah. The birthing coach might feel like she is, but she's a half-troll shaman doula and can handle anything. She didn't bat an eye when Sarrlevi loomed with his swords at their first meeting, while detailing her inadequacies. You see, *he* wanted Matti to have her babies on his home world, but she refused to leave Earth. Specifically, she said she wasn't going to an elf hospital perched two hundred feet up in tree branches. Weird, huh?"

"Very much so."

"Anyway, the half-troll doula brandished some magical forceps and threatened to twist off Sarrlevi's nuts. Matti immediately liked her and chose her to deliver her babies."

"She sounds tough."

"Yes. Half-dwarves are into that. And things are going okay, despite the screams. I understand those with dwarven blood often let out all their aggressions during childbirth. Come to think of it, my human blood made me pretty aggressive too, though I've kind of blocked that all out. Speaking of kids, did you get my message? Do you have any updates on Amber? I'm tempted to go look for her, but I have no idea where she went."

"I don't know either. I was hoping she'd found you. Is it possible she went to a hospital instead of the magical-beings birthing center? I didn't even know there was such a place as that."

"Amber has zero interest in witnessing the birth of any baby or snuggling one afterward. Like me, she's not real strong on maternal instincts. I'm positive she told Thad she was coming here so he wouldn't worry about her. Which worries *me*. And, yes, there are a couple of magical-beings birthing centers in the greater Seattle area. Orcs, trolls, and lots of refugees from other worlds, especially those who came alone and don't have their people to lean on, use it. Given that the kids will only be one-quarter human, Matti wasn't sure what physical attributes they would be born with, so she figured it would be a good idea to avoid a normal hospital. This place is between a bowling alley and a tire shop in Lake City. Thanks to all the noises coming from the neighbors and some magical insulation, people don't even notice it's here."

"I did ask Amber to do research," Arwen said, "but I thought it would be on the computer. As far as I know, she's never gone anywhere before to look things up for me."

"What are you researching?"

"Where an ancient magical sword might be located here in the Seattle area. Is it possible she went to the library and silenced her phone so as not to be rude?"

Arwen's own phone issued a rude bleat. It was warming in her hand. Her tattoo itched, as if in indignation at its antics. She hoped the phone wouldn't turn off in the middle of the conversation.

"It's possible she went to a library, yes, but Amber isn't the most conscientious when it comes to not being rude."

Arwen refrained from saying, *I noticed.* Even if Amber was undesirably blunt, she'd helped Arwen a number of times now.

"Anyway," Val said, "she would still be able to answer her phone if she had the sound silenced. I'm *positive* she would still check for messages habitually. I may have to take a break from being supportive to go look for her."

Another scream sounded in the background, making Arwen wonder if Val might *want* a break from being supportive. But guilt made her hurry to say, "I can go look for her. I'm just dropping off my ingredients with Zoltan. Besides, it's my fault she's researching this topic."

"It is *not* your fault," Azerdash said quietly. "I requested your assistance in locating the blade."

"Yeah, but I brought her in because she's good at researching things online."

"With the *network*." He nodded, probably thinking of gnomish central hubs. "The mongrel human child is missing?"

"Yes. Will you fly me over Edmonds to see if we can find her?"

"She is mouthy and disrespectful to those with dragon blood, but if you wish it, I will do so."

"Thanks. And, Val?" Arwen asked. "I can track, remember. I'm the logical person to look for her."

Especially if Amber had gotten into trouble on her behalf.

"You can track someone in the city who would have left their house driving their car?" Val asked dubiously.

"Possibly. Amber lives in a suburb. There are trees I can consult."

"You're kind of a weird kid, Arwen."

"Amber tells me that often." Arwen thought about pointing out that she was thirty and didn't qualify as a *kid* anymore, even to her mother's people, but remembered that Val was in her mid-forties and could have been her babysitter if they'd known each other years earlier.

"I'll bet." Val's voice shifted as she asked, "Everything going okay, Sarrlevi? Matti's labor sounds difficult."

"She is birthing half-elven children with my blood," came his voice from the background.

"I guess that *would* account for the difficulty."

"Masterpieces are not created without duress," he said.

"Does Matti tell you that you're full of yourself?"

"Regularly."

"Good." Val shifted the phone closer to her mouth. "Arwen, I'll take you up on your offer. But if you don't find her in a couple of hours, let me know, and I'll drive up and join the search."

"We'll find her."

"Thanks for looking."

Arwen grimaced as she hung up. She didn't deserve thanks, not if she was the reason Amber was missing. She hoped this ended up being nothing more than Amber spending time with a boyfriend and not wanting to be disturbed, but she worried that wouldn't be the case.

As she walked through the fence gate, heading for Zoltan's basement door, her phone rang. She pounced on it, hoping it was Amber, but Colonel Willard's number came up.

"Yes, ma'am?"

"Have you seen Gondo, Forester?" Willard asked.

"Uh, no." Why would she have?

"I got back from a meeting down at Ft. Lewis to find an obscure note on my desk from him. It says he's doing research for you but will be back by three to finish the list of errands I left for him. It's almost nine, the errands haven't been touched, and nothing has been disassembled, invented, or otherwise disturbed since this morning."

"Amber was doing some research for me," Arwen admitted, "but I haven't seen Gondo since the last time I was in your office."

"What research?"

"Looking for the galaxy blade that the elf ambassador talked about."

"A super powerful invaluable weapon that could be used to amass armies willing to take on dragons?"

"It's powerful, yes," Arwen said. "I assume the amassing of armies relies on the motivations of the wielder."

Azerdash nodded.

"Either way," Willard said, "it sounds like something people would kill to get their hands on. A lot of people."

The unease grew heavier in the pit of Arwen's stomach. She hadn't considered that its value might prompt others to go after it. How many people had the elf ambassador told about it? As many as he'd told about his fantasies involving Azerdash overthrowing the dragons?

"We may need to talk to your elf acquaintance," Arwen whispered to him.

His eyes narrowed, and he nodded without confusion. Maybe he'd also been thinking that Rysharon must have been blathering if everyone from the Silverclaws to the fae queen knew about a quest he hadn't even agreed to take on.

"I'm going to look for Amber," Arwen told Willard. "I'll update you if I find Gondo. Maybe she called him in for advice."

"That's about as likely as tits on a bull."

"Maybe he volunteered himself for advice."

"That's more possible. Give me an update on that sword, whether you find Gondo or not. The last thing we want is some bloodthirsty murderer locating it and using it on the populace of Seattle."

"Ideally, Azerdash—Starblade will find it."

"I don't know if that's better," Willard growled before ending the call.

The screen flashed three times, then turned off before Arwen touched it. Given how technology felt about her dark-elven taint, she was lucky she got any use of the device at all.

Azerdash, whose ears were keen enough to catch both sides of phone conversations, arched his eyebrows.

"My employer is warming to you," Arwen told him.

"Like the *teeseerla* warms to a dragon snatching it up for dinner."

Though Arwen had no idea what a *teeseerla* was, she nodded in agreement.

For your edification, Zoltan spoke telepathically into Arwen's mind, *the clock starts when customers show up on my doorstep, even if they have not yet knocked. The presence of a half-dragon and a mongrel dark-elf is quite distracting and makes reading and other important tasks difficult to engage in.*

Clock? Arwen asked.

Yes, my dim dark-elf. A clock is an implement for tracking time and also tracking when a professional who works for an hourly rate will start and stop charging his fees.

You're supposed to be making this formula for me for free, right? Arwen descended the stairs, then knocked. Maybe that wasn't necessary when they were already conversing, but she didn't want to give Zoltan another reason to be cranky.

The formula, yes, but you may incur fees for time required outside of its preparation. I am, after all, a busy vampire.

Arwen looked at the empty yard, rain pattering softly on the patio. *Yes, I can see the lineup of customers waiting their turn.*

I do not solicit customers. The mere thought would make me shudder in my coffin. But I do important research, record videos for posterity—and my adoring audience—and write papers for alchemical publications.

"I had no idea there were alchemical publications," Arwen murmured.

Azerdash's eyebrows lifted again.

"Zoltan is talking to me," she explained.

"Instead of allowing you entrance into his laboratory?"

"For the moment." Arwen knocked again.

"Shall I incinerate his door?"

"No, he would charge extra for that."

Enter, enter. And do not bring in the rain. You may, however, bring in the blood of your comrade if you feel properly indebted to me for my work on your behalf. You are fortunate that I can take time from my schedule to perform such a menial service. Tattoo removal. Goodness. I will have to brace myself for mockery if my fellow vampires hear of this.

Arwen opened the door, not mentioning to Azerdash that Zoltan wanted his blood. That might make him even more inclined toward incineration.

They found Zoltan in a white lab coat and hunched over a Bunsen burner warming a beaker of pink fluid. Measuring tools, glass vials, and small ceramic jars of powders rested around it on the counter.

"Are you already working on the formula?" Arwen held up the ingredients.

"Of course not. How would I have known that you would arrive tonight with these items?" Zoltan looked back, lifting goggles and peering at her, glancing only briefly at Azerdash's wrists—at his *veins.* "Did you locate all of the ingredients? I admit, I'm intrigued by the descriptions of the nightwater fungi and have found other recipes that require it. Never would I have thought to obtain some."

"We did, and for the record, the fae queen has a stash, so you don't have to sneak into dark-elven tunnels to find it. Though you may have to sexually satisfy her if you want it or anything else from her."

Zoltan curled his lip. "I am over a hundred years old and far, *far* past any interest in such crude biological activities. It is bad enough that my upstairs roommate and her *dragon* engage so frequently and noisily in them." Zoltan strode forward and took the pouch from Arwen. A new thought must have crossed his mind because his lip curled further, and he held it at arm's length, barely gripping it between thumb and forefinger. "Did *you* engage in biological activities with the queen to receive this?"

Arwen thought about saying yes and that they'd rolled all over the pouch while doing so, but, after all she'd been through, she didn't want Zoltan to deem the ingredients tainted and cast them aside. "No. Someone else handled that."

Zoltan looked at Azerdash.

"Not him," Arwen said. "He was busy magically programming ambulatory seed-and-fertilizer distribution machines to save my butt."

Zoltan's mouth formed an, "Oh," but no words came out.

"I was not so much programming them as *re*programming them," Azerdash murmured. "The underlying gnomish magic already told the *dresdalatha* what to do and where to go."

"Either way, your aptitude at manipulating them was wonderful." And wonderfully timed. Arwen beamed a smile at Azerdash.

The words and gesture seemed to startle him because he blinked and... was that a hint of a blush?

He recovered quickly, cleared his throat, and said, "Yes."

Though he didn't offer a thank-you—maybe dragon blood

made men too supercilious for such social niceties—he did bow his head in what Arwen chose to interpret as gratitude.

"Hm," was all Zoltan said.

Still dangling the pouch at arm's length, he returned to his workstation.

"Once I complete this tonic to assist in what I understand is the arduous birth of a child—no, *two* children that are likely quite confused about their identities—I will start on your formula. It will take several hours, and then I must sleep while it settles. You may return tomorrow night, no sooner than an hour after sunset, to check on the results."

"Thank you," Arwen said.

"Hm," Zoltan repeated, turning his back to them.

Maybe those with vampire blood were also too supercilious for social niceties.

19

When Azerdash flew Arwen to Edmonds, they found Amber's father pacing in the driveway while checking his phone. Hoping for news about his daughter? Her car was notably missing from the driveway.

Arwen's guilt returned as Willard's words rang in her mind: *It sounds like something people would kill to get their hands on.*

"I never should have asked her to work for me," she murmured.

Technically, Amber kept volunteering to work for Arwen, but it didn't matter. Arwen could have said no. Amber was only sixteen, too young for work that could turn dangerous. Not that Arwen had ever envisioned that it might. This hadn't been a ride through a sketchy neighborhood at night to a tattoo parlor. All it should have involved was research done on a computer from the safety of one's room.

It is rarely wise to employ an inexperienced mongrel who is not properly respectful toward her superiors, Azerdash said.

"You remember that you're the one who offered to foot the bill, right? Land in the street, please. Not the roof. We don't want to alarm her dad."

I do recall that. My wisdom is occasionally questionable. Were it not, I would never have freed Yendral from that stasis chamber. Azerdash spread his wings, gliding toward the street in front of the house.

"Are you still annoyed that he shared information on his dalliance with the queen?" Arwen didn't believe for a minute that Azerdash regretted freeing his friend. More than once, he'd called Yendral a loyal troop.

Annoyed that he shared so many details of it. He was nattering telepathically to me while I was attempting to focus on healing your wounds.

"Ah. Do you sense Amber in the area anywhere? Since her blood is one-quarter elven, you'd be able to detect her, right?"

I do not sense her, but such a modest aura does not act as a great beacon. It is unlikely that I could sense her from more than a mile away.

A mile was an encouraging distance. If Arwen's attempt to track Amber didn't work, they could start a search from the sky. Though that would only work if she hadn't gone far. With a car, she could have driven across the state in the name of research.

Shall I allow that human to see me? Azerdash asked as he landed in the road a dozen yards from the driveway, tucking in his wings so he didn't brush any tree branches.

"Amber's father? Yes." Arwen slid off, intending to walk up to the driveway, but Azerdash continued.

What about that one?

Arwen paused, following his gaze. A mundane human holding something bulky in his arms was walking up the street. Whatever it was emitted magic. Scowling, the man turned at the driveway.

That wasn't a weapon, was it? Could someone believe Amber's father had information on the sword?

Arwen rubbed her camouflaging charm and pulled her bow off her back.

Hang on a second, she told Azerdash telepathically. *Let me see what's going on.*

"Mr. Stavropoulos," the newcomer said. "I understand that my grass was slightly taller than the requirements detailed by the HOA, but the lawn-maintenance crew is due tomorrow. It was *not* necessary for you to deposit your robotic mower in my yard. It went right under the fence gate and scared Muggins. She's a pure-bred Shih Tzu and has a delicate system that's easily upset. I don't appreciate such shenanigans."

Arwen crept around the corner of the driveway, though she realized the magic she sensed belonged not to a weapon but the mower that Azerdash had altered. *That* was what the neighbor held.

Behind Thad, the garage door was open, his BMW visible inside, and he jangled his keys as he dealt with the neighbor.

"I apologize for that." Thad, a distracted expression on his face, glanced at his phone again before accepting the mower. "It's been on the fritz."

"From what I've heard, it's been *overly* fritzed, vrooming up and down the street, mowing every blade of grass it can get its blades on. It terrified Mrs. Song's cat this morning, though there are rules against outdoor cats, and that thing is practically feral, so my only concern there was the caterwauling that woke me at five a.m."

"Yes, I'm sorry. I'll take it to the shop." Thad eyed the mower darkly. "Or the recycling center."

"See to it that you do. You don't want to become one of those neighbors that everyone talks about, do you? It's bad enough your daughter's jalopy is usually parked in the driveway."

"It's a Honda in good repair."

"It's older than she is."

"She's not that old."

"Clearly." The man sniffed and walked toward the street.

Though Arwen no longer worried about him, she stepped aside so he wouldn't come close enough to see through her camouflaging magic. He seemed like someone who might wet himself if he was startled. Or for many reasons.

Before he'd fully departed, Thad set down the mower, dialed a number, and raised his phone to his ear.

Arwen dissolved the camouflage and waited at the head of the driveway for him to notice her. She didn't necessarily want to talk to him, but since he was standing outside, she decided to get permission before attempting to track Amber. It might be in vain if she'd left in her car, but Arwen wanted to start at the house. Specifically with one of the trees near the driveway.

"No, Val," Thad said, "I thought *you* might have an update. I should have known she hadn't gone to lend moral support for your friend's delivery. She's a teenager. She thinks such things are gross. She may even think *babies* are gross. Val, she's much more like you than I ever expected."

Arwen didn't hear the reply and debated if she should walk up or continue to wait. But Thad chose that moment to turn around and glance toward the street.

"Shit," he blurted, dropping the phone.

Arwen bit her lip and lifted a wary hand. Maybe she should have returned her bow to her back.

Thad picked up the phone. "Someone just showed up. I'll ask her."

"Sorry." Arwen turned her raised hand into a wave before lowering it. "I didn't mean to startle you."

"You're the one employing Amber right now, aren't you?" Thad frowned. "Do you know where she is? She's not doing some work for you, is she? It's past her curfew for a weeknight. I don't care if it is summer." His gaze shifted past Arwen's shoulder.

Azerdash had shifted to his elven form and stood at the base of the driveway.

"*You*," Thad said in an accusing tone. "You're the one who supercharged my mower and made it think it needs to cut every lawn in the neighborhood."

Azerdash tilted his head. "That is not the desired function of that device?"

"*No*," Thad said. "It's only supposed to do my yard."

"That is highly inefficient and would require that every domicile in the area acquire a trimming device of its own. Since I enhanced the energy source to never need additional power input, it is capable of servicing all of the grassy areas nearby. Perhaps for miles around." Azerdash stroked his chin as he eyed the mower. "I could increase the speed at which the blades churn, and the device might be able to service this entire town."

"*No*," Thad repeated with even more exasperation.

Do you know what hang on *means?* Arwen asked Azerdash telepathically.

He regarded her with the same puzzled expression. *To grip a nearby object or perhaps person.* He looked her up and down. Deciding if she had something he should grip? *When I tended to your leg wound, I* hung on *to your thigh.* He smiled at the memory.

She caught herself blushing at the thought of him doing so again—especially with a witness. *Never mind.*

"I am—uhm, we are employing Amber to do some research for us right now, yes," Arwen told Thad. "We didn't ask or anticipate that she would leave your home to do it. If she did, I want to help find her. I'm sure she's fine—maybe she got caught up at the library—but just in case..." She waved at herself and Azerdash.

Thad's frown didn't lessen. "Are you going to program one of my yard implements to search for her?"

Azerdash looked toward the open garage. "If they are familiar with her aura, that might be a possibility. I am largely unfamiliar with the workings of human technological constructs, however, as my mistake with the foliage-trimming device attests. Allow me to consult the excellent notes I acquired from an esteemed gnomish scientist."

Thad's frown turned into a stunned stare as Azerdash pulled his roll of toilet paper from an inner pocket in his cloak.

"May I look around?" Arwen waved at the driveway and toward a stout maple as old as the house.

Its roots looked like they grew underneath the asphalt and perhaps under the street as well. It might have registered the departure of the car—trees tended to notice things that reverberated through the ground and shook their roots.

"I already checked her room." Thad frowned as Azerdash, hands clasped behind his back, strolled toward the garage. "You stay away from my car."

Azerdash leveled a cool stare over his shoulder, probably thinking about how disrespectful of dragons mundane humans were.

"I meant that I'd like to look around out here," Arwen said. "I'm a tracker."

"A tracker?" Skepticism twisted Thad's lips, but then he looked at her from moccasins to bow and quiver to the sticks pulling her hair back into a loose bun. The glittery gnome-modified jumpsuit might not fit people's notions of what a tracker should look like, but maybe the bow convinced him, because he asked, "Like Aragorn?"

"Ah, yes. I've not looked for Gollum here on Earth, but I've found any number of yetis, shifters, and lost hikers."

Thad blinked at the list. In truth, lost hikers accounted for most of the people Arwen had helped Washington State Search and Rescue locate. It had only been recently that she'd started working for Willard to find magical beings—usually magical *criminals*.

"Huh. You're a fan? Val has read the books but thinks they're slow and boring." Thad pressed a hand to his chest and made an aggrieved face. "I'm trying to turn Nin on to fantasy, but she prefers to read in her native language and says the offerings are slim. I hunted all over to find her a Thai translation of *The Lord of the Rings*. She wasn't as delighted as I thought she might be." He squinted at Arwen.

"I liked the books." She managed a smile, though the fact that her father had named her after a character from the trilogy hadn't always delighted her, especially since he'd used the same inspiration for naming the tractor and his gun. "My father read them to me when I was little. He alternated between *The Lord of the Rings*, *The Silmarillion*, the Bible, and *The Old Farmer's Almanac*. Considering how much he prefers non-fiction to fiction, I'm impressed I got as many stories as I did."

"You've read *The Silmarillion*? If I weren't already happily in love, I'd be asking you on a date right now." Thad grinned and waved away the comment as a joke, but it drew Azerdash back from the garage.

His shoulder brushed Arwen's as he squinted with new suspicion at Thad.

Thad waved again, ignoring—or oblivious to—him. "Look around if you want. Let me know if you find anything. I've called some of Amber's friends—the ones she's known long enough that I know their parents and have their numbers—but nobody has seen her. I'm telling myself she hasn't been gone that long, and it's probably fine, but..." He jangled his keys. "I'm going to drive around and check a couple of her favorite spots. Just in case."

"Thank you." Had Arwen known speaking about *The Lord of the Rings* could win Thad's favor, she would have brought up Tolkien's works as soon as Azerdash started tinkering with his lawn mower.

"You have referenced those books before," Azerdash said,

"and implied they are good resources similar to the human tomes on war, history, and engineering I've acquired and been reading."

"I implied that?"

"You did. I am a capable reader of your English, but if translations are available, I would be interested. Have they been penned in Elven?"

"Uh, maybe not *your* version of Elven." Arwen waved for him to step aside so Thad could back the car out of the garage.

Thad pulled into the street, looking like he would leave the garage door open, but after glancing at Azerdash, he firmly pressed the button on the remote before driving away.

"I'm sure you can borrow my father's copies of the books." As soon as they were alone, Arwen hopped over a manicured bush and headed for the maple she'd been eyeing.

"You will apply soul tracking to learn in which direction the mongrel child went?" Azerdash asked.

"Her name is Amber, and I'm going to try the tree first and elven tracking."

"I approve."

Arwen rested her hand on the trunk, about to start, but something in his tone made her look back at him. "Did you, uhm, *not* approve in the queen's court when I used my power without altering it?"

Maybe she shouldn't have asked. His good opinion meant a lot to her, and it would sting to learn that she'd lost it to any degree.

His hesitation felt like a cannonball dropping into her gut.

"I understand why you used it," Azerdash said, "and you came to my defense."

That wasn't quite an answer to her question, was it? She looked bleakly at him.

"Because of what you have admitted to me about the allure of that power, which sounds much like the allure of becoming a dragon—a *beast*—is for me, I prefer it when you do not require it. Or you can alter it."

"I do too," Arwen said softly, again remembering the story he'd told of how he'd accidentally killed a friend in a duel because they'd assumed their dragon forms and the battle lust had taken over their rational minds. He'd also spoken of another half-dragon comrade who'd loved being a dragon so much that he'd not been able to turn back and had been killed by full-blooded dragons.

"I do not *disapprove*," Azerdash stated firmly, watching her face.

"Okay, thanks." Arwen forced a brighter smile, though his hesitation—his concern for her—would haunt her. Maybe because it echoed her own concerns.

Hopefully, Zoltan would easily make the formula for removing the tattoo, and Arwen could further distance herself from her mother's people, and worry less about being driven to use their magic.

Arwen focused on the tree, letting her power trickle into it in an attempt to bond with it and see what it had recently experienced through its arboreal senses. Since the family presumably came and went often, it was possible the trees did not take notice, but she would start here before trying less desirable tracking methods.

An unexpected wariness came from the maple, and Arwen stared in surprise. Did it object to her because of her tainted blood? In general, nature had little love for dark elves, but it hadn't been her experience that trees prejudged magical beings by their heritage. Whether or not they carried axes and chainsaws concerned them far more.

The maple shared a recent memory of a robotic lawn mower whirring aggressively around the front yard and clipping one of its exposed roots, leaving a gouge.

Ah.

The tree is pissed at you, Arwen told Azerdash.

What? That would be unusual. He touched one of his pointed ears, as if his half-elven heritage should make every tree adore him. *Sometimes, they are less than pleased with dragons and their tendency toward spewing fire.*

Arwen shared the image of the mower and pointed at the root, though she couldn't see the gouge in the fading light. Having never experienced trees lying to her, she trusted it was there.

As she tried to tease out the maple's memories of the driveway and those who'd passed through that day, Azerdash came and rested a hand on its bark. Healing magic flowed from his fingers.

Mollified, the tree shared that a stranger had arrived a few hours earlier. A goblin. It did not, as Arwen had been thinking, always take notice of the family coming and going, but goblins were not common in the neighborhood. In general, they did not disturb trees, not the way axemen and bulldozer operators did, but they sometimes disrespectfully broke branches for firewood or to use in building their shelters.

Arwen received an image of Amber standing next to her car and facing a goblin holding a large piece of paper. Was that Gondo?

Since trees didn't have eyes, what they observed came across as blurry and vague, auras making more of an impression than physical features, and Arwen couldn't see any details on the paper. She was surprised the tree had noted it at all. Maybe it had some magic about it that had stood out?

After Gondo and Amber had perused the paper, they'd climbed into the car and left together.

Huh. Arwen hadn't realized they knew each other, but she supposed Amber visited the coffee shop and spent time in her mother's orbit enough to have encountered Gondo. Had she called him because he had goblin connections all over the state? Connections who were good at ferreting out information? And had he found that paper? Might it have been a map? Arwen didn't know what else of that size they would have been looking at. Maybe it was an *old* map, something that had never been scanned and uploaded to the internet.

Thank you, she told the tree, patting it before releasing it. That was more information than she'd thought she would get.

It radiated contentment toward her, probably because Azerdash was infusing energy into it. He'd already healed it; this appeared to be an invigoration spell similar to those she'd used on the plants and trees on the farm. And he wasn't only giving it to the maple. His power spread outward in a web that reached all the trees and shrubs in the yard.

Feeling guilty that your souped-up lawn mower nicked it, huh? Arwen hopped into the driveway again.

Yes. An unforeseen result of my improvements. I had not realized the sensor in the trimming device was so limited that it would crash into innocent trees and bushes. A rhododendron near the domicile was also damaged, and I am healing it.

You're a good elf.

One must take responsibility for one's actions and be careful with one's power. It is fortunate that I did not enhance the speed of the blades, as I suggested.

I think the whole neighborhood and *the trees would agree with that.*

Arwen rested her hand on the driveway where Amber's car was usually parked. In the past, her attempts to track vehicles had not gone well, and a car had no *soul* that would leave marks she could detect with her dark-elven power. Through the surrounding plants, she was able to tell that the Honda had turned toward Main Street after leaving, but it could have gone toward downtown Edmonds or toward the freeway from there. In virtually any direction.

"We may be stuck," she admitted.

Azerdash joined her in the driveway. "If the mongrel—Amber

—remains in this village, perhaps I could find her by searching for her aura."

"Let's try." The idea of flying around Edmonds and hoping to chance across her aura wasn't that appealing, but Arwen couldn't think of anything better at the moment.

After Azerdash transformed and she climbed onto his back, she tried not to be disappointed by her inability to track Amber. Even though streets and automobiles had always made using her skills difficult in the city, it was hard not to feel like a failure.

20

WHILE AZERDASH FLEW IN A SEARCH PATTERN OVER THE STREETS OF Edmonds, Arwen looked for Amber's red hatchback in parking lots and dug out her phone to update Willard on the Gondo situation.

"I'm in my pajamas, Forester," Willard answered.

"I'm... not sure what to do with that information, ma'am."

"It's to let you know that it's past my bedtime on a work night, so this better be an update on Puletasi's babies or our missing people."

"I believe Gondo came to Edmonds and is working with Amber. Or was working *for* her. I'm looking for them now."

"A witness saw them together?"

"Uhm, yes."

That *uhm* must have twanged Willard's senses. "A *reliable* witness?"

"A tree."

"A what?" Willard asked in a flat tone.

"A large maple in Amber's front yard. Trees tend to be very trustworthy and reliable. Lying isn't a part of their culture."

"Their culture. Forester, are you pulling my leg?"

"*Culture* might not be the exact right word, but they are in contact with the other trees in their area and can communicate on a rudimentary level. And they have similar attitudes and outlooks about certain things."

"You're an even stranger operative than Val."

"I have specialized skills, ma'am. I think that's why you hired me."

"I hired you to keep an eye on the dark elves and give me insight into their plots, not talk about tree culture."

Arwen didn't know what to say to that.

Willard sighed. "All right, let's assume Gondo and Amber are together. What next?"

"I think Gondo was showing her a map before they left the house. A physical map that might be magical."

"A map of what?"

"I don't know, but Azerdash mentioned needing bathymetric maps at one point because the galaxy blade was believed to be in the water—or had been at one time. So maybe a map of Puget Sound?" Arwen didn't know why such a thing would be magical though.

"Hang on. Let me make a call to the night sergeant at the office." Willard hung up.

Azerdash had been heading north along the coastline, but he turned back toward downtown Edmonds as what was probably the last ferry for the night trundled into dock.

Few magical beings live in this area. I have sensed intermittent humans with quarter- or half-elven blood, but they are ensconced in the domiciles rather than roaming the streets and seeking trouble.

Before Arwen could respond, Azerdash's wings froze mid-beat. He continued to glide, but his eyes locked onto something in the distance. The ferry?

Then Arwen saw what he'd sensed from afar, a portal forming

over the waterfront.

A dragon comes. I am camouflaging us. Azerdash descended to a rooftop with a view of the ferry terminal and downtown Edmonds.

Arwen hurried to activate her own camouflaging magic in case doubling up would help. As Azerdash landed, a green-scaled dragon flew out of the portal. The Silverclaw that they'd faced in the queen's court.

A growl reverberated through Azerdash's torso. *Hyrukorlin's wounds have been healed. Unfortunately.*

The dragon didn't fly far. As the portal faded, he alighted on the roof of a restaurant overlooking the waterfront. He faced inland, slowly scanning the buildings and trees of Edmonds, his yellow glowing eyes visible from Azerdash's residential perch.

I assume he's looking for you and didn't come for the seared ahi tacos at Arnies, Arwen said telepathically.

I believe that is accurate. After a pause, Azerdash added, *What are tacos?*

Corn tortilla shells stuffed with seasoned meat or fish.

Corn is... a cereal grain originally domesticated by the indigenous peoples of your southern Mexico.

That sounds right.

Is it appealing?

It's okay. Arwen decided Azerdash wasn't too worried about the dragon's arrival if he was thinking about food. *We grow some on the farm, usually heirloom varieties that people will pay a little more for. This fall, I could use the Bloody Butcher strain to make tacos with burgundy-colored shells.*

They taste like blood?

No, just corn. The color is unique though. I'm not sure who named them. It might have been a dragon farmer.

Dragons do not farm. They hunt.

I know. I was joking.

Possibly, a human farmer who wished to appease a dragon with a proper offering gave the cereal grain a name that would meet the approval of a mighty hunter.

I'm sure that's it.

Azerdash stiffened when the dragon—Hyrukorlin—looked in their direction and didn't continue his scan of the area. *He may be sensing me through the tattoo that marks me. My camouflaging magic can diffuse it but not completely eliminate the signal it emits.*

You wouldn't think he would want to tangle with you again after getting his ass kicked in the fae realm.

I do not recall kicking.

It's an expression.

You employed the bottle opener on his hindquarters.

I used my magic *on his hindquarters.*

Unleashed via the bottle opener. Dragon eyes didn't crinkle at the corners the way human eyes did, but when Azerdash turned his head, his violet gaze managed to convey his amusement.

I figured the Study of Manliness *would approve,* Arwen said.

Undoubtedly.

The dragon looked away without saying anything telepathically, at least not that Arwen heard. He settled his haunches more fully on the roof, as if he'd made a nest and intended to stay a while. Maybe he *did* want tacos.

Arwen's phone rang, and she flinched, yanking it out to silence it. The dragon had to be a mile away, but sound carried a long way over the water at night.

Though Hyrukorlin didn't look over again, Arwen whispered as she answered the call. "Yes?"

"It's Willard. My sergeant looked in the archives library where we keep translations, books from other worlds, historical Earth evidence that concerns magical beings, and various other texts we've acquired over the years. Gondo was the last one to sign something out. Bless his green hide for actually doing so. He used to just *take* things, but some of my yelling must have sunk in."

"Are you supposed to yell at your operatives?"

"Goblin ones, yes."

"What did he sign out?" Arwen asked.

"An old map of Edmonds, a stapler, a hole puncher, a calculator, a box of paperclips, scissors, a ruler, and seven envelopes."

"I'm not sure if that indicates plans to construct a new invention or if he's going to open a small office-supply store."

"I'm not either. The map is the only thing with a barcode on it that needed to be signed out. It *is* slightly magical, at least according to the notes on it, and it's over a hundred years old. It was drawn by a dwarven refugee working in the area as a logger."

"Dwarven?" Arwen looked at the back of Azerdash's head. A dwarf had supposedly stolen the galaxy blade.

"That's what the notes say," Willard said. "The map was brought in before my time here. It highlighted a couple of camps where magical beings lived at the turn of the last century."

"It's not a treasure map directing one to the sword, huh?"

"No. One rarely finds treasure maps in Army archives rooms."

"That's disappointing." Arwen nibbled on her lip. "Are magical beings *still* living in those camps?" She tried to guess why Gondo would have believed such a map would be helpful.

"Not unless they're leasing a room at the senior center or the athletic club."

"Is that sarcasm, ma'am, or are those buildings located over the former camps?"

"It *is* sarcasm, but according to my sergeant, those *are* the present-day establishments in those locations. He was stationed here when the map was brought in and remembered it. His former boss had him look up the locations of the camps, and he's got a digital copy of the map on his hard drive, so he double-checked his memory."

"We're in Edmonds now and can fly over those places in case

there's magic lingering. Oh, but ma'am? There's a Silverclaw dragon on the roof of Arnies."

Willard swore. "One of the ones who was after Starblade before?"

"No, this is a new one, but he's after Azerdash too. He attacked us in the fae queen's court."

"You didn't mention that earlier."

"I assumed you were more concerned about Gondo and Amber being missing."

"Had I known about a new dragon invading the Seattle area, I would have at least been *equally* concerned about it."

"Ah, sorry. I should have mentioned it, but we kicked his ass in her court, so I wasn't expecting him to show up here."

Azerdash looked back, that amusement in his eyes again.

Arwen pointed at him and almost told him not to say anything about bottle openers, but unless he roared, he couldn't comment anyway. Not so that Willard would understand.

"What's the Silverclaw doing in Edmonds?" Willard asked. "And why did Amber and Gondo want a map of the city? It's a lovely suburb, but I wouldn't call it a hub of paranormal activity."

"That's because you haven't seen the lawn mowers here."

"Pardon?"

"Never mind. Edmonds is on Puget Sound, and the elf ambassador said the sword was believed to be in the water, so maybe it's up here."

"I suppose that's as possible a place as any. There's a SCUBA park near the ferry dock."

"I doubt a powerful magical artifact is something that divers would swim past daily and not notice."

"Probably not, but it's got to be hidden, or someone would have found it by now. Especially if it's been there over a century."

"I'd like to talk to Gondo and Amber," Arwen said. "They might have more details than we do by now."

"It delights me no end when teenagers and goblins are the preeminent resources we need to consult." Willard sighed again. "You're searching for them now, right?"

Arwen decided not to admit that they were currently hunkering on someone's house. "Yes, we are."

"Good. Find them, and I bet you'll find some answers."

"Yes, ma'am. Oh, did you ever learn anything about the heritage of the elf ambassador? Rysharon?"

"Yes, he came up as a relative of a noble in Eireth's court. I can't confirm it yet, but I suspect he is who he said he is."

"Okay. Thanks."

"Keep me updated if you find anything new about Amber or Gondo."

"Even if you're in pajamas?"

"Yes, even if it's an obscene hour of the night. I might answer the phone with cursing, but I'll want to hear from you."

"Okay, thanks." Arwen remembered Val once saying that Willard was most pleasant in the morning when she'd had her first cup of coffee and had her fingers wrapped around her second. A lot of hours had probably passed since her last caffeine fix.

I suspect Hyrukorlin has also learned of the sword. Azerdash continued to watch the dragon, who remained settled on the roof like he planned to stay for a while. *And somehow determined its rough location. The galaxy blades are very powerful and can be sensed from afar, but they have the ability to camouflage themselves and their wielders. I never tried to camouflage mine when I wasn't using it, but I believe if the last person to wield it did so, that spell might still be active. It's also possible that a magically insulated box or other container may hold it.*

So is Hyrukorlin waiting for us to find it, then planning to kill us and take it?

He has not announced his intent to me or the area in general, but that is a possibility.

Can we risk getting closer to him? Arwen asked.

That would not be wise. The closer I get to him, the more likely he'll be able to sense me through this odious tattoo.

Arwen rocked back with a realization. *Will the formula Zoltan is making also be able to remove* your *tattoo?*

It is possible, Azerdash said without hesitation.

Had he already considered that? If so, that might be why he and Yendral had been willing to not only assist Arwen in her quest but volunteer Yendral to jump into the fae queen's bed. Oh, she believed they were genuinely willing to help her, as they both seemed to believe she'd helped them—and they liked her food—but it couldn't hurt that they also had a reason to want to see this formula be created. She didn't mind that at all and hoped it *would* work for them.

Good. Arwen patted his shoulder. *I need to get closer though. Will you wait here in case I get in trouble?*

You believe the missing beings are near Hyrukorlin?

I don't know, but I want to visit the senior center and athletic club to see if I sense anything or anyone magical. Or, even better, sense Amber and Gondo. After hearing about that map, I have a hunch they're near the waterfront.

Practically under the dragon's nose, probably. Arwen hoped *her* camouflaging magic would be powerful enough to keep Hyrukorlin from sensing her.

It is unlikely that refugees remain in camps that were used generations ago when the area was more primitive. Azerdash must have heard Willard's side of the conversation.

I know, but they could be starting points and offer clues.

Power wrapped around Arwen, levitating her off Azerdash's back. He shifted into his elven form to gravely face her.

I will permit you to go, he said, continuing to speak telepathically—maybe he was worried about sound too, *but I insist you take great care not to alert the Silverclaw dragon to your presence.*

I'm planning to, and, for the record, I go places whether half-dragons permit me to or not. I'm my own person, you know.

I do know this, and I respect your independence, but it is wise to make offerings and seek permission of powerful beings.

It might be, but my stubborn human half isn't interested in being that obsequious.

Azerdash tilted his head. *You said you would craft for me offerings of tacos.*

Not offerings. Gifts. Food made to share with a friend.

Hm. He squinted past her shoulder at the dragon.

Was he contemplating *not* letting her go? For her own good?

Maybe he worried that if Hyrukorlin spotted her, he would have to fly to her rescue and wouldn't come out on top in another battle against him. After all, he didn't have a couple of subverted fae tractors to hurl at Hyrukorlin this time.

I'll be fine, Arwen assured Azerdash. *I won't get close enough for him to spot me.*

How far are the locations you seek from his current perch?

Oh, super far.

Azerdash squinted at her.

I'm pretty sure the senior center is a ways anyway. Let me check on the athletic club. Before Arwen had met Amber, her only trips to Edmonds had been to sell at their farmers market. Everything had been tighter and more crowded than at her usual market in Carnation, and she hadn't received the locals discount, so she hadn't rented a spot there often. *It's kind of close to his current perch, as you called it. But nowhere near within the range of a camouflaging charm. I assume your multitool is as effective as the trinket Val gave Amber.*

My tool is extremely effective, but Hyrukorlin may have the means to see through such magic. He would have come prepared for us to be camouflaged.

I'll risk it.

Azerdash's squint deepened as he emanated displeasure.

If he sees me, I have your wonderful and effective gift to use against him. Arwen smiled and held out the multitool.

Azerdash reached for it and demonstrated opening one of the knives. *For the record,* he said, echoing her, *this is the appropriate implement with which to attack an enemy.*

Are you sure the knife is as good a conduit for my power as the bottle opener? Arwen asked, though she'd used the blade on the serpent and knew it was effective. The lightning would be handy against many enemies.

It is very good. Yes.

Perfect. She folded it, put it away, and started for the edge of the roof, intending to climb down and walk into the downtown area.

Azerdash caught her wrist before she could go, his warm fingers gentle but firm. *Do not touch the sword if you find it. It has defenses that may harm a user it doesn't consider appropriate. Touching it might also deactivate its camouflage. Once Hyrukorlin senses it, he will go straight for it. Many magical beings in the area may come for it when they sense it.*

I'm just looking for Amber and Gondo. If I find the sword, I'll call you over so you can touch it. I assume it considers you appropriate.

I shall hope it still does. Azerdash smiled sadly, as if he had doubts.

Arwen might have questioned that, but he surprised her by bending his head and kissing her on the cheek.

Warm pleasure swept through her, making her want to lean into him and stay there instead of traipsing off into the night. But she worried that Amber and Gondo were in danger and needed her.

Be careful, Azerdash repeated, then levitated her to the street.

I will be.

21

Arwen didn't sense a single iota of magic around the senior center, though a sign promised that registered members could enjoy boxed lunches between eleven and two, and she could envision older trolls, ogres, and orcs showing up for that. Chances were their kind wouldn't be served though. That was why they enjoyed the Coffee Dragon and the handful of other establishments that catered to the magical community.

With a soft summer drizzle falling, Arwen braced herself before heading farther south. Hyrukorlin remained on the restaurant, his height and great dragonness making him visible over the roofs of the intervening buildings. Despite the night deepening and rain, he didn't look like he would move anytime soon.

The athletic club wasn't *right* under his nose... but it wasn't that far from his perch. He couldn't know about the map, could he? He'd probably chosen that spot because it offered a view of downtown Edmonds, the waterfront, and the houses in the hills above. In short, everything in the area.

It was late enough that the athletic club was closed and pedestrians were few. After nervously reactivating her charm for the sixth or seventh time, Arwen padded through the parking lot.

Using her senses, she checked buildings that held tennis courts, exercise equipment, and a swimming pool. As with the senior center, she didn't pick up anything magical.

Disappointed, she bit her lip and turned a slow three-sixty. For a second, she thought she caught a hint of magic, not in the athletic club but to the south where a marshy wetlands lay dark and undeveloped.

Arwen pulled out her phone to look up the area, but it buzzed and turned off. She stuck her tongue out and restarted it. The map app refused to open until she threatened to chuck the phone in a pond.

Edmonds Marsh turned out to be the uninspired name for the tidal wetlands. The faintest trickle of a stream reached her ears, and, as she tried to sense that magic again, an owl hooted from a tree bordering the area. A critter scurried through, rustling the high grass.

"That seems like a more likely refuge for magical beings," Arwen murmured.

She padded to a trail along the edge of the wetlands. On a hunch, she rested a hand on a tree, trickling her power into it to ask if it had seen trouble lately.

While she waited for the flora to stir, she sensed magic again. No, magical *beings*. Only for a few seconds, and she didn't recognize any of them, but they had the auras of goblins. Could they live in the marsh? Arwen didn't see any huts or sign of habitation from anything besides birds and small animals, but magic could hide an encampment.

If she could find the goblins and question them, they might know something about Gondo. Maybe he'd even visited them, seeking information.

The tree shared something it had sensed earlier, a dragon

perching in its branches. It hadn't had the same aura as the Silver-claw on the restaurant, but might it have been from the same clan? Maybe the Silverclaws were taking turns keeping an eye on Edmonds, searching for the sword—or waiting for Azerdash to show up and find it so they could jump him.

Two tusked orcs came on the scene, standing at the base of the tree and communicating with the dragon. Receiving instructions? One carried an axe, a dangerous weapon that the tree always noticed.

After the meeting, the orcs walked into the marsh, and the dragon flew away. A different memory came from the tree, some-thing that had happened right under its branches later in the day, as the sun set over the Sound. A human girl had been walking with a goblin, an atypical pairing, so the tree had taken note of it. It had to have been Amber and Gondo.

Arwen hoped to see more, but the memory faded before showing where they'd gone. That was all right. If they'd been here and on foot, Arwen ought to be able to track them.

Shifting her hand to the ground, she called upon her magic again. Her tattoo warmed on her forearm, as if pleased she drew upon her dark-elven power. As always, Arwen would have preferred not to, but soul tracking was useful in the city where hard surfaces didn't allow for footprints.

As her vision shifted, allowing her to see the paranormal realm, numerous sets of glowing pale green footprints appeared along the path. Many were human-sized, but some were larger and some smaller. A *lot* were smaller. Goblin-sized. Did a whole clan live in the little marsh without the town's human inhabitants being any the wiser?

The larger prints had to belong to the orcs. That worried Arwen, and she hoped Amber and Gondo had been here at a different time, long after the orcs had gone.

Arwen knew Amber well enough to pick out her footprints

thanks to a hint of her aura—her *soul*—clinging to them. Cheerful, confident, and brazen. They headed along the trail adjacent to the marsh rather than through it.

Arwen followed them, keeping an eye on the dragon, whose gaze was shifting back and forth again, scanning Edmonds. A pair of small prints appeared alongside Amber's, and she recognized Gondo's cheerful and inventive soul. Oddly, a number of other small prints clumped around theirs, heading in the same direction. Had they recruited the local goblins for some reason?

Unease crept into Arwen when all the goblin prints disappeared, and Amber's and Gondo's tracks grew farther apart. They'd started running. The orc prints had left the mix, but something had scared them.

Even though Amber and Gondo had passed this way hours earlier, Arwen caught herself running, as if she might catch up with them and help fight whatever danger had stalked them.

Amber's prints turned away from the trail and the marsh and took to the street. Then they clumped together, turning left and right, as if she'd been dancing. No, not dancing. *Fighting.* The orc prints returned to the mix, their larger tracks aggressive and angry. Damn it. Had they jumped out of a car? Or a *van*?

Arwen remembered the orc mercenaries that her dark-elf brother had hired to attack tattoo artists. Maybe they were available for dragons to hire as well.

Amber's tracks didn't continue on from the skirmish point. Frowning, Arwen circled the area, trying to pick up the trail while worrying she might stumble upon Amber's dead body in the bushes. She didn't find either. If the orcs had driven a van, they could have grabbed Amber and Gondo and yanked them inside.

Or *had* Gondo been taken? When Arwen continued down the street, she spotted a number of small footprints again. It looked like the goblins had come back out of the marsh and headed south. Had they seen which direction the van went and followed?

With few other options, Arwen followed the goblin prints. None of the soul fragments left behind matched Gondo's, so she assumed he had indeed been kidnapped along with Amber.

The street ended at a park and off-leash dog beach, but the goblin prints continued, shifting from the pavement up to train tracks that continued south along the shoreline. Ah, and there were orc prints again.

Had Arwen not been worried about Amber and Gondo, she would have enjoyed the puzzle presented. Tracking was a challenge that she usually enjoyed. But not tonight. She hurried south along the train tracks, hoping she wasn't too late to help.

Once the dog beach ended, there wasn't much besides rocks and Puget Sound to her right and a bluff that rose up to the left. She glanced back numerous times to make sure a train didn't come barreling in her direction. To get out of the way, she might have to go for a swim.

With that thought in mind, Arwen shifted to a jog. She didn't know the area well enough to guess where Amber's captors had taken her. There were houses on the bluff, but they weren't accessible without climbing gear. Besides, the properties overlooking the water were expensive and luxurious—not the kinds of places where one stashed kidnap victims.

As she continued on, a few lights came into view out on a flat point full of huge cylindrical tanks. As a farmer, Arwen's first thought was that this was an odd spot for a bunch of silos. Then she snorted at herself. Not silos—oil tanks. An old refinery and storage area? She hadn't realized anything like that still existed in the area, but she had no trouble imagining someone stashing kidnap victims there. Not bodies, she hoped.

As she approached the point, Arwen searched with her senses, hoping to pick up Gondo's and Amber's auras.

A rumble came from the distance behind her, and the tracks vibrated faintly. A train coming.

Arwen turned her jog into a run, glancing back as she sensed something more alarming than a train. Hyrukorlin had left his perch and was flying in her direction.

In case her camouflaging magic had dropped because she'd been moving quickly, Arwen activated it again. Though the train headlights were visible, she made herself slow down.

The dragon came into view, his green body dark against the cloudy night sky. Two yellow eyes glowed as they tilted downward, looking toward the tracks.

Her camouflage *had* dropped, and he'd sensed her. Arwen was sure of it.

She might have pissed him off enough in the fae queen's chamber that he wanted revenge. Or he believed she knew where Azerdash or the sword was and wanted to question her. Or both.

Arwen almost reached out telepathically to Azerdash, but she worried the dragon would intercept her words, no matter how carefully she tried to pinpoint him.

Hyrukorlin slowed, wings barely beating as he continued along the tracks. He couldn't have seen her, or he would have dived for her. That was only somewhat comforting, because he was flying low enough that he might spot her through her camouflage when he grew close enough.

Distracted by the dragon and the train roaring closer, Arwen almost missed the prints veering off onto the asphalt of the oil-storage facility. Forcing herself to keep her pace slow, she left the tracks. None too soon. The train roared past, the wind of its passing tugging at her hair.

Hyrukorlin landed on the train. Good. Maybe he would let it take him to Seattle or wherever its final destination was.

But as Arwen followed the tracks between towering tanks and toward a wharf at the tip of the point, she sensed him springing off the train and flying back in her direction. His powerful aura drowned out any other magical beings she might have detected in the area. As he soared overhead, she barely resisted the urge to sprint away.

She thought of her brave words to Azerdash about how she would deal with Hyrukorlin if he found her. Yeah, right.

The footprints passed the last of the tanks and headed toward one of three docks leading to the wharf. Paralleling the shoreline, it held a building and fueling stations. The dread that Amber's captors might have killed her returned. They could have thrown her body into the water. What would she tell Val if her research request had resulted in Amber's death?

The prints scattered before heading out onto the dock, and Arwen paused. It looked like the goblins had abandoned their quest, something scaring them. They'd run off in numerous directions.

Hyrukorlin landed on top of one of the tanks and resumed scanning the area.

Can't imagine *what* scared them, Arwen thought to herself.

A couple of sets of orc prints continued, so she followed them out to the wharf. As they headed toward the old building, they grew denser, as if the owners had milled around and debated things. And then departed the same way they'd come?

A sign on the building illuminated by a light read Point Wells.

After making sure she wasn't in Hyrukorlin's line of sight, Arwen tried a door and was surprised to find it open. Despite the lights on around the point, the place had the vibe that it hadn't seen use for a long time.

Inside, there were no lights on. Arwen used a cement block to prop open the door so some illumination would seep in from the exterior. When she passed a bank of light switches, she didn't try them, not wanting to let her dragon spy know where she was.

The inside of the building was cavernous and largely empty, save for a few rusty metal barrels and storage crates that had been broken into, the contents removed.

More orc prints meandered across the floor inside, circuitous rather than direct. Arwen struggled to tell what their final destination had been but eyed the barrels. They were large enough that people—bodies—could have been stuffed inside.

She was about to search them when she caught the first hint of an aura. Gondo's aura.

Arwen spun and followed it toward the far side of the building. Soon, she detected Amber's aura too. She was relieved, because that meant they were alive, but their auras were muffled, less distinguishable than they should have been. More than the dragon's presence was drowning them out.

Arwen reached a pair of textured metal doors in the floor. Since she was on a wharf, she couldn't imagine that they opened to anything but the water below, but the auras were located under them.

Frowning, she knelt and groped for a handle.

A *thud-clank* came from the entrance, startling her. The door had shut, removing all light from the interior.

She froze and stared, doubting that cement block had moved on its own. Were the orcs still around? Or had the dragon noticed the open door and shut her in on purpose?

Her senses promised Hyrukorlin hadn't moved from his perch on one of the tanks, but he could use his magic to manipulate things from afar.

As she crouched in the silence with her hand resting on the cool metal trapdoor, it occurred to Arwen that he might have arranged the capture of Amber and Gondo as bait for a trap. A trap for her?

Azerdash? Arwen risked reaching out, focusing on his face in her mind, hoping the dragon wouldn't overhear. *Our Silverclaw buddy followed me to some oil tanks on a point south of town. I think he knows I'm here.* Reluctantly, she admitted, *My camouflage might have slipped while I was tracking Amber and Gondo.*

It did briefly, yes, came his soft reply from closer than she'd expected. *I was watching him and saw his head jerk up when he detected you. I did not expect that you would interest him, but...*

I figure that clan knows we're hanging out together now. Especially after I jumped into your battle in the queen's court.

Yes. That is unfortunate. I do not wish them to harm you to get to me.

Where are you now?

On the bluff overlooking the tanks. I am watching Hyrukorlin. Do not do anything else to draw his attention. Yendral has returned to Earth and is flying up here. If needed, we will attack Hyrukorlin together.

Knowing Azerdash was nearby should have made Arwen feel better, but she worried he would be hurt if he engaged with the full-blooded dragon again. Hurt or worse. She regretted that she'd let the camouflage slip.

Several yards away, a small light appeared on the ground between two barrels. Startled, Arwen reached for her bow before she recognized it. A smart phone.

Amber's?

She crept over and reached for it. The display went dark before she grasped it, but brushing it turned it on again. The screen was locked, but a recent alert popped up, a message from Val.

Arwen slid the phone into her pocket and returned to the doors. After more patting around, she found a latch, a semicircle set into the metal.

Though Azerdash had warned her to wait for Yendral, she envisioned Amber and Gondo caught in some trap that would fill with water as the tide came in. What if she didn't have time to wait?

Another train rumbled in the distance. As it drew closer, the noise intensifying, Arwen decided to risk opening the door.

Striving for silence, she popped the handle out and tugged. The heavy door didn't budge. She got to her feet to pull. Nothing.

She didn't sense any magic working against her, only the weight of the metal. She slid the tip of her bow staff under it for leverage and tried again. Finally, with the magically enhanced weapon helping her, she pried open the door.

The metal groaned, and she winced at the noise and hoped the passing train would keep the dragon from hearing it. Carefully, she pulled the door farther open and lowered it to the floor.

When she crouched to peer below, it was too dark to see anything. She activated her phone, tilting the display downward, then remembered the flashlight app. When she pointed the beam downward, it revealed not the rising water that she'd feared but a small windowless room, the only visible door the one she'd opened.

A few more barrels and two lumps occupied the floor, one long —tall—and one short. Amber and Gondo. But they were wrapped in some kind of magical mesh that covered them from head to toe. Could they breathe through that? If Arwen hadn't sensed their auras, still very faint, she would have feared them dead.

Arwen's phone buzzed. After the last call, she'd silenced it, but she jumped at the vibration, wincing at all the noise she was making.

She would have ignored the call, but Val's number popped up.

"Hello?" Arwen whispered, wishing she could use telepathy over the phone.

"Hey, Arwen. Willard said she heard from some goblins in Edmonds and that they tried to help Amber and Gondo hide from orc mercenaries. But it didn't work and the orcs snatched them. The goblins followed, but then a dragon showed up, and they scattered. They do know the orcs took Amber and Gondo to... ah, one second."

"Point Wells."

"Er, yes."

"I'm there now. I've found them, but they're down in... you might call this an oubliette." Arwen recalled a previous discussion they'd had about such prisons.

"Great."

"You were lamenting that there aren't many of them in America, weren't you?"

"Not lamenting. *Observing.* Are they okay?"

"They're enmeshed in some muffling material and aren't moving."

"Not moving? Shit, Arwen."

"It'll be fine. I'm sure." Arwen wasn't, but she didn't want Val to worry.

"I'll be up there as soon as I can."

"Let me check and figure out how to unwrap them, and I'll update you. I'll—" Arwen halted because Azerdash had abruptly registered to her senses. What was he doing?

Then Hyrukorlin's aura moved as he sprang from the tank and flew toward her, and she knew. Azerdash was going to risk his life to save her butt.

22

THE SECRET TO THE SWORD'S LOCATION IS MINE! AZERDASH CRIED AS he flew south from the bluff.

Hyrukorlin had been beelining for the building where Arwen crouched, clutching her weapons, and his direction shifted slightly, but he didn't take off after Azerdash. She was positive Azerdash wanted to lead the Silverclaw away, but the other dragon might not fall for that.

A roar from directly above the wharf made the building quake. A faint moan drifted up from below. Amber?

"I'm up here, guys," Arwen called down, doubting there was any point in stealth now. Hyrukorlin knew she was by his prisoners. "I'll come down in a second."

Assuming Hyrukorlin didn't tear the roof off the building to pluck her out. Bow in hand, Arwen aimed an arrow upward, worried about the possibility.

Another roar sounded, but the dragon turned and headed south, chasing after Azerdash's receding aura.

"It worked," Arwen whispered.

A great explosion came from the point. Metal wrenched, the

wharf trembled under Arwen's feet, and one wall of the building blew inward.

Shrapnel hit her, making her glad for her armor, but she wasn't safe. The missing wall revealed fire—a *lot* of fire. Hyrukorlin must have lit it before flying off.

It burned all over the point, flames so high that Arwen couldn't see the tracks or bluff beyond. Petroleum from a destroyed tank mingled with magic, creating more fuel for the fire than there should have been.

At least Hyrukorlin had left. Arwen hopped into the oubliette, trusting she could climb out. She patted Amber, trying to figure out how to unravel the mesh. A hint of magic promised it wouldn't be as easy as peeling away plastic wrap.

A groan wafted through the material. "Can't... breathe..." came Amber's muffled voice.

The other wrapped body squeaked.

Since they could make noise, they could breathe, but Arwen understood how it would be suffocating. She drew Azerdash's gift. Even as she worried about how his encounter with the Silverclaw would go, she silently thanked him for the versatile tool.

It sliced easily through the mesh, and Amber sprang out like a butterfly emerging from a cocoon. A very *angry* butterfly.

She sputtered and cursed before managing to articulate. "Where's my sword? I'm going to *kill* those orcs."

"I'm not sure where they went." Bent over Gondo, Arwen sliced open his mesh prison.

"They were the same mercenary bastards who shot up the tattoo shop in Lynnwood. They're working for that dragon now." Amber looked up and sniffed. "Is there a *fire*?" By now, the roar of the flames was audible, and smoke flowed into the building. She spun around, looking at the walls of their prison, then pointed upward. "Is that the only way out? Where the hell *are* we?"

"Freedom!" Gondo threw up his arms as soon as he could, then sprang away and put his back to them as he stood in the corner. "I've had to pee for *days*."

"It's only been hours since you were captured. Here." Arwen handed Amber's phone to her, then set aside her bow and multi-tool to cup her hands, offering a step up. "Climb out, and I'll lift Gondo up to you."

Amber glanced toward his corner. "Make sure his bladder is empty before there's any lifting."

Arwen hefted Amber upward, drawing upon her power to aid her.

Amber's six feet in height made it easy for her to reach the top, but as she swung her leg up and scrambled out, Arwen sensed an orc. And then a second orc. Then more. They were among the tanks, creeping around the fire and toward the building. The dragon must have ordered them to take care of the pesky mongrel freeing his prisoners.

"I'm so relieved," Gondo blurted, running over to Arwen. He glanced in the direction of the tanks—and the orcs. "No, wait. That's not the right word. There's no relief here."

"Tell me about it." Arwen grabbed the much lighter Gondo and hefted him up to Amber.

Once they'd cleared the oubliette, Arwen tossed up her bow, grimacing at the dancing orange light filling the building. With a running jump, she followed, catching the lip. Again using her power, she assisted her muscles in the pull. She scrambled out and grabbed her bow only to find that the fire had grown.

Fueled purely by magic now, it had roared up the docks and burned on the wharf. Flames and heat roiled through the missing wall in the building. The ceiling beams burned above, and a barrel at the other end exploded.

"Shit!" Amber barked, sounding like her mother.

Four orcs strode out of the flames, magical trinkets around their necks protecting them from the heat. Armed with crossbows and swords or axes, they broke into a run, heading straight toward Arwen.

"Go out the back door," she yelled to Amber and Gondo as she nocked an arrow. *Jump into the water,* she added telepathically, realizing the orcs would hear spoken words and might have men to cut them off.

Gondo spotted the door and sprinted toward it.

Fists balled, Amber looked like she wanted to stay and fight, but she didn't have her sword.

Go, Arwen repeated, trying to add magical compulsion, though she'd never learned how to do that.

Swearing again, Amber sprinted after Gondo.

One of the orcs broke from his buddies and ran after them. Arwen shifted her bow to fire at him first.

Clad in chain-mail armor and protected by a magical barrier, he sneered, not worried about her weapon.

Willing her power to infuse the magical arrow she'd chosen, she loosed it. It penetrated his defenses and sank deep into the side of his neck.

One of the other orcs pointed his crossbow at her. As she sprinted for a crate, Arwen tried to form the same type of barrier she had conjured on the fae world. It was far more difficult, the ground here not so eager to offer magic to draw upon, but a fledgling protection formed around her. Not one but two crossbow bolts that zipped at her were deflected away.

Relief flooded her as she ducked behind the crate for further cover. She nocked another arrow. She needed to keep these guys busy long enough for Amber and Gondo to escape.

"Watch out," Amber yelled from the doorway. "That one has my sword. You ugly bastard, that's mine! If Arwen doesn't kick your ass, *I* will."

A crossbow bolt shot toward her, but she ducked around the doorjamb in time to avoid it.

Two orcs shouted, raising swords, one Amber's stolen blade. The pair charged after her.

Calmer in battle than she was in crowds of people, Arwen leaned out from behind the crate and fired two arrows, one after the other.

The orcs must have seen their buddy fall, because they tried to dodge, but they weren't fast enough. One arrow thudded into a big male's shoulder, spinning him around. His sword— Amber's sword—flew from his grip and clattered across the floor.

The second arrow struck his buddy in the ear, driving into his brain. The orc was dead before he hit the floor.

Arwen grimaced, hating to shoot to kill, but she didn't have a choice. She had to protect Amber and Gondo.

A great burning beam snapped and fell, flames flying as it struck the floor. The entire wharf quaked under Arwen's feet.

"*Definitely* don't have a choice," she whispered.

The last of the orcs rushed to his injured ally, the one she'd hit in the shoulder. They crouched, arguing in their language as they pointed at her. Another pointed at Amber's fallen sword. Since it was magical, it was a prize.

"Back off, or I'll shoot again," Arwen called, showing enough of her body to line up her next shot.

One of the orcs had a crossbow, so it was dangerous to step out from behind cover, but they'd had enough. They sprinted back outside, charging through the flames, less worried about the fire than Arwen and her bow.

As soon as they disappeared, she ran toward the back door. The wall on that side of the building wasn't burning yet, but another beam snapped and dropped as she ran. When it slammed down, it brought a portion of the roof with it.

Arwen threw her arms up, only remembering at the last instant that she'd managed to conjure a barrier. She drew upon more of her innate power to reinforce it. Burning chunks of the roof landed on it, halting a foot above her head.

Relieved, she hurried for the door, pausing only to grab Amber's sword. She sensed more orcs on the wharf, blocking the way back to land.

Fortunately, they weren't coming toward Arwen. They were busy facing—was that Yendral?

His powerful aura registered to her senses abruptly, so he must have been camouflaged as he'd approached. A great roar sounded as he attacked the orcs, his silver dragon form visible through the flames.

Arwen sensed Amber and Gondo in the water below the wharf. They'd obeyed and jumped in.

"Good," she whispered.

She took a step toward Yendral and the orcs, intending to help with that battle, but another thunderous boom came from land— another tank exploding as fire wreathed it.

The wharf heaved, and Arwen half jumped and half fell over the edge. Gripping her bow tightly, she managed to land feet-first, plunging into the cold water.

So much for helping Yendral. The wharf was too far above to reach. Arwen might have climbed up one of the support posts, but with flames everywhere and tanks exploding like holiday fire-works, she wasn't eager to return to the point.

Another roar sounded, and Arwen sensed Yendral flying after the orcs, breathing fire of his own as he chased them. Since neither Azerdash nor Hyrukorlin had returned, she didn't think Yendral needed her help. But she did worry about Azerdash and what would happen if the Silverclaw caught up with him.

"This whole day has been complete bullshit." A few strokes away, Amber treaded water and wiped hair out of her face. "I need to start charging *way* more than ten percent."

"You said you only got two percent," came Gondo's reedy voice from farther away.

"I said I'd cut *you* in for two percent if you helped me."

"That's less than half what you're getting."

"I got groped by an orc. I deserve more than half."

"I would let an orc grope me for a greater percentage."

"No one wants to grope a goblin. Trust me."

"Is there any chance you learned the location of the sword?" Arwen hoped something useful had come out of all this.

"If we'd known that, the dragon would have killed us instead of using us as bait for a trap that you walked right into," Amber said.

"You're welcome for the assistance. I assumed you'd want to be let out of that prison."

"Hell, yeah, we did. But you shouldn't have come. That dragon has it out for your boyfriend, and he's happy to use you to get to him."

"I know." Arwen thought about correcting the boyfriend term, but weapons and clothing were dragging at her, and all she wanted was to climb onto dry land. Hopefully, dry land that wasn't a flaming inferno. She swam Amber's sword over to her, carefully handing it to her hilt-first.

"Thanks. Even if it was really dumb to walk into a trap, I appreciate you coming."

"The warmth of your praise makes me tingle all over."

"Ew. That sounds like some kind of weird nerve disease you should get checked out."

"I'll do that." Arwen paddled toward what she hoped was a safe beach. Though she was glad they'd survived, she couldn't help but be disappointed that it didn't sound like Amber's research had led to the location of the galaxy blade. All this had been for nothing.

23

"There's a big half-dragon coming," Gondo whispered.

"That's Yendral." Arwen sensed him landing nearby. "Hopefully with an update on Azerdash."

She, Amber, and Gondo had made it to a beach south of the refinery. Sirens in the distance promised someone had noticed that oil tanks were exploding on the point.

"We figured out," Amber said, "that more than you and Starblade are looking for that sword."

"When the orcs jumped out and kidnapped us, we figured that out," Gondo said.

"No, it was before that. Your green besties living *under* the marsh knew and tried to warn us."

"Shaman Hotok did say that," Gondo agreed. "They've lived many generations there and have seen much. And they've invented much! I did not know so many of their clan lived in the marsh under the water where humans cannot see their homes. And they have those clever breathing devices to protect them when the tide comes in. Goblins are very crafty." He sounded smug for someone who'd spent half the night having to pee in an oubliette.

"Do the goblins know where the sword is?" Arwen asked.

"Oh, no," Gondo said, "but a great clue is in the *museum*. Show her the poem, Princess Amber."

"Yeah, yeah."

Arwen would have asked about that honorific, but Amber brought a photo up on her phone and showed it.

"It's a poem in Dwarven," Amber said. "From my research—"

"*Our* research," Gondo interrupted.

"From *the* research," Amber continued, "we think it's instructions on how to make a key to open a chest or a door, whatever has been hiding the sword all this time. I'm going to send it to Matti."

Arwen squinted at the photo of runes carved into what looked like a mural or maybe a plaster relief on a wall located somewhere dimly lit. "She's a little busy."

"Well, I don't know anyone else who is part-dwarven and might be able to read this *and* enchant a key." Amber texted the photo to Val.

"Plumber Puletasi's mother is *all* dwarven and a very powerful enchanter," Gondo said.

"Uh-huh, and lives on another planet. I can't text her." Amber waved her phone at Arwen. "You should go to the museum in town. I didn't get all the photos I wanted to because the orcs showed up then, and we had to split. I think you might be able to figure out where the sword is from that mural though. Roughly."

"*Very* roughly. But it's good that we did not find all the answers because the dragon mind-scoured us." Gondo shuddered, and it probably had nothing to do with his wet clothes.

Amber did too. "Yeah, that sucked. I hope my mom kicks his ass when she gets here."

Yendral, now in his elven form, walked up to them. "You've

obtained information on the sword's location? And how to access it?"

"Just clues," Amber said. "That an old dead dwarf left."

"Clues for other dwarves," Gondo said. "But *we're* figuring them out."

"Sort of." Amber shrugged. "After I change clothes, I can take you to the museum and show you the mural. You'll need to see it for yourself. I'm pretty sure the location isn't there now."

"What?" Arwen asked.

"You'll see."

Arwen rubbed knots in the back of her neck. "I'm getting a headache."

"*You* are?" Amber asked. "We've been deprived of oxygen for *hours*."

"*Days*," Gondo said.

Yendral looked Arwen up and down. "Are you uninjured from the battle with the orcs? The dragon did not have time to pester you, did he? Azerdash only briefly apprised me of what was going on as he led Hyrukorlin off."

"I'm not hurt, thanks," Arwen said. "The dragon didn't get me, unless one counts lighting the entire point and wharf on fire as being *got*."

"I would," Amber said.

"Especially when you're locked up *in* the wharf when it happens." Gondo shuddered again.

Yendral's gaze turned toward the southern sky, and he didn't comment on their interjections. Maybe Azerdash was communicating with him. Hopefully, Hyrukorlin wasn't.

Headlights appeared, coming down a road that led to the beach.

Arwen reached for her weapons but stopped when she sensed Val driving the vehicle. "How'd she find us?"

"Magic." Amber waved her phone. "And I texted her. It's a good thing phones are waterproof."

"Yours may be." Arwen hadn't been able to turn hers on since falling in the water. Its second dousing in less than a day may have done it in. Or it was simply irked with her again.

"Yours is cursed. You should return it."

Arwen glanced at her forearm. "I don't think it's the phone that's cursed."

"Point. Your dark-elf weirdness is probably twisting its wires."

"I have no doubt."

As soon as she parked, Val ran down to the beach. Arwen stepped aside to give them room for a reunion. Even if Amber had only been missing for a few hours, and her parents had only begun to worry, Val wrapped her daughter in a huge hug.

Despite the oubliette and the oxygen deprivation, Amber wasn't as relieved and tried to squirm away. "Ew, Val. We're in public."

"I don't think Richmond Beach after midnight counts as public." Val squeezed Amber tighter before releasing her.

"Of *course* it does. There are *people* here." Amber looked at Gondo, Arwen, and Yendral, though the half-dragon wasn't paying attention to them. "Sort of people."

"I'm a people," Gondo said.

"You peed in our prison like an animal."

"It's not my fault it didn't come with a tree or shrub or other suitable place for unleashing one's bodily functions."

"A tree or..." Amber stared at him, then looked at Val. "I thought he worked in your boss's office."

"He does."

"Don't tell me an Army colonel has a bathroom full of bushes instead of toilets."

"No, I understand the bushes out back are somewhat damaged from Gondo's visits. He drinks a lot of soda."

"Gross."

Gondo gave them a toothy smile. "Human beverages are delicious."

"Azerdash is heading this way," Yendral said. "He is not alone."

"I suppose he's not being accompanied by a female dragon on a date," Val said.

Yendral looked toward Arwen before answering. "He does not *date*. The Silverclaws have learned of our quest and object to it."

"I gather there's a lot of objecting going on about that quest," Val said. "I think that's what Zav got called home about."

Again, Arwen worried that the Stormforges, who'd only recently accepted that Azerdash was a relative, would turn on him.

"Any chance he's coming back to Earth soon?" Arwen didn't know if Zavryd would help Azerdash after hearing whatever rumors had reached his clan's ears, but fighting what might end up being multiple Silverclaws without the help of other full-blooded dragons would be challenging, if not suicidal.

"Probably," Val said. "But I'm not sure how much assistance he'll be willing to give to this sword quest."

"The *sword quest* isn't the problem," Arwen said. "It's all the other beings lurking around interested in it."

A distant flash of silver in the night sky drew her eye. She sensed Azerdash out there but only for a second before he disappeared along with the light. Had that been a portal?

The Silverclaw dragon came within her range, but he also made a portal and flew through it.

"He led Hyrukorlin away to give us time to find the sword." Yendral pointed at Amber and Gondo. "You have discovered its location in a museum? And how to craft a key?"

"Like I said, we discovered *clues*, but, uhm." Amber looked at Arwen. "He's not the one cutting us in. We shouldn't give him the information, right?"

Yendral's eyebrows rose. "I can *take* the information."

Val held up a hand toward him. "Nobody's mind-scouring my kid."

"Too late." Amber grimaced.

Val frowned and gripped her shoulder. "What happened?"

"Nothing I couldn't handle. But we'd better all go to the museum. You'll want to see the mural."

"I wish to see all that you have learned," Yendral said. "Azerdash must be the one to claim that sword, not some Silverclaw dragon. Their kind would have it destroyed. A galaxy blade belongs in Azerdash's hands."

"Magical swords are handy," was all Val said.

"Especially when they are legendary, and people will eagerly follow he who wields such a blade." Yendral's eyes gleamed as he imagined the scenario.

Arwen tried not to grimace. She still half-hoped the sword wouldn't be here and that nobody would find it. Then people—and dragons—wouldn't try to kill Azerdash for something he hadn't done yet. Something he hopefully never *would* do. She didn't like the way Yendral wanted Azerdash to raise an army. As a friend of so many years—centuries—he might have the power to influence Azerdash, more than Arwen could.

"What is this, Amber?" Val held up her phone, the display showing the photo her daughter had sent.

"A Dwarven poem about how to enchant a key to open whatever is hiding the galaxy blade. The same guy who made a map that Gondo found was entrusted with hiding and protecting the sword."

"How'd you learn all that?"

Amber rolled her eyes. "By doing *research*, Val. I'm good at it. I dug around in the library archives—the *primitive* archives. I had to use a microfiche reader like a troglodyte from the Twentieth Century because they hadn't put all the old stuff about the original town online. And then we found the goblins, who've been here for more than a hundred years, though hardly anyone knows about them."

"*I* knew about them," Gondo said smugly.

"Duh. You're a goblin. And the mural in the museum, well, you guys can figure out if that'll lead to the sword. I'm not going for another swim." Though the summer air wasn't that cold, Amber shivered in her wet clothing. "I'll show it to you though. I work *hard* to earn my ten percent." She looked at Arwen. "Though I'm definitely going to start charging more."

"Azerdash is a generous tipper." Arwen remembered the stack of coins he'd left her for agreeing to bake desserts for him and Yendral.

"The museum is closed in the middle of the night, I presume." Val texted the photo to someone else. Matti?

"We will go regardless," Yendral stated. "There can be no delays."

"There'll be *some* delay," Val said. "Matti isn't going to enchant a key while she's in labor. I'm not sure if she can read Dwarven either. Willard may have to get this translated."

Yendral frowned his disapproval.

"We'll see if we can find the sword's location in the meantime," Arwen told him, not wanting to disappoint Azerdash's friend—his only ally besides her. "If we can't find it, well, the key will be moot."

"Very well." Yendral turned into his dragon form and levitated Arwen onto his back. *Direct me to this museum.*

"It's only fifteen minutes away." Amber pointed at Val's keys. "If you lend me your Jeep, I can drive us there."

"I promised your dad that you're done adventuring for tonight. He's going to be livid when he finds out you were kidnapped."

"Val, are you kidding me? We're integral. Arwen needs our help."

"Gondo can help her."

Magic swirled, and Yendral started to levitate Gondo and Amber toward his back.

But Val snatched Amber by the wrist and pulled her back to the beach. "She's going home."

Arwen couldn't blame Val for wanting to protect her daughter. Val didn't know the full story yet, but the oil tanks burning in the distance had to promise it had been an eventful night. Perhaps a testament to her harrowing adventure, Amber slumped and didn't protest further.

Val didn't object to Gondo leaving with them, and Yendral took flight with him and Arwen on his back.

As he flew north, Arwen couldn't help but look south toward where the portals had appeared in the night sky, but neither Azerdash nor the Silverclaw had returned.

24

"THE PICTURE IS IN THE BASEMENT," GONDO WHISPERED. "WE HAD to skulk around and *sneak* down earlier. Like burglars! This is much better." Gondo beamed a smile at Yendral, who had flicked a finger and unlocked the door to the museum, a brick building downtown that had once been a library.

"Unless the security system went off," Arwen murmured.

She walked beside Yendral with her bow in hand as Gondo led the way.

"I incinerated it before it could make a noise. It's useful to have a half-dragon around." Yendral gave her a smile that might have been flirtatious, but in the dim lighting, it was hard to tell.

Arwen thought but didn't say that Azerdash might have been able to disable or reprogram the alarm with his knowledge of gnomish engineering magic. She didn't want to irk her current half-dragon ally. Besides, Azerdash had been known to incinerate obstacles too.

She did say, "Alarms are usually remotely monitored. Bells could be ringing at the security company's home base."

"Should mundane human museum defenders arrive, they would be simpler than dragons and orcs to defeat."

"Defeating the police would get me thrown in jail and lose me my job with Willard." Arwen glanced at a logging exhibit that highlighted the origins of Edmonds.

"I would nobly rescue you from incarceration," Yendral said.

"Comforting."

"There is a jail cell in the museum." Gondo pointed off into the darkness. "We saw it earlier."

"In case someone steals furniture from the exhibit showcasing a Victorian parlor?" Arwen asked.

"The sign said the police department used to be located in this building when it was the city hall and also the library."

"I'll guess Edmonds wasn't very big back then," Arwen said.

"It was not. The ancestors of the goblin refugees in the area used to have much wilderness for their clan. They were among the first refugees to find their way to this wild world after fleeing the oppressive dragons." Gondo turned toward a dark corner. "This way to the secret stairs. The basement is not accessible to visitors. We were lucky to find it!"

Talk of dragon oppression reminded Arwen of the sword quest —and what Azerdash might be tempted to do if he completed it.

"May I ask a question?" she asked Yendral.

"You wish to know if I still pine for you despite being sated while fulfilling the demanding requirements of the fae queen?"

"I... cannot tell you how far from my mind that was."

"I thought you might be concerned," Yendral said. "My stamina and desires are quickly replenished, in case you're curious, but if not, what's your question?"

"Why do you want Azerdash to find this sword?"

"Because *he* wants to find it, and I'm a loyal comrade who supports him in his endeavors."

"Does he though?"

"I am certain he does." Yendral tilted his head. "Has he said something to you to indicate he does not?"

Arwen considered the conversations she'd had with Azerdash. "I guess not, but I *don't* think he wants to start a war to end dragon oppression."

"He doesn't, or you don't wish him to?" Yendral didn't sound perturbed with her, but his face had lost its humor.

Meanwhile, Gondo patted around on the floor, grumbling about secret trapdoors being too secret.

"I would prefer he not do something that could get him killed." That *would* get him killed, Arwen feared. "And I told him that, but I know I'm not..." She stopped herself from saying she wasn't anything to Azerdash. She hoped that wasn't true. "I haven't known him long and wouldn't sway him, but I got the feeling he didn't want to start a war either and is being pressured. And now there are these rumors that even the *dragons* have heard about. It seems like someone is trying to manipulate him. Or get rid of him. Or both."

"There are many who would like to see dragons out of their lives," Yendral said, "and there are some who'd like to see Azerdash achieve his potential instead of hiding out on this backward world."

Arwen spotted a train exhibit with a steam engine on display and was momentarily distracted by the thought that Azerdash would like to see that. "I should take him to the Northwest Railway Museum," she murmured as she coaxed her phone to life so she could take photos to show him later.

Yendral watched with a bemused smile. "You understand him, don't you?"

"He doesn't seem that hard to understand. He brought my father a gnomish *flikopdedorik*." Arwen said the word carefully, hoping she got the pronunciation right.

"Do you know what that is?"

"Not exactly." The phone flashed and heated in her hand, but she didn't go into her hate affair with technology. "I do know the tractor roars around the property like a race car now, and my father cackles with delight. He's had a rough life. I didn't know he *could* cackle."

"Would you stand with Azerdash in a battle against dragons? As you said to the fae queen? I know that was a ruse, but..." Yendral regarded her with steady, intent eyes.

Arwen almost blurted, *Of course*, but paused to consider her answer. She didn't approve of this notion of building an army and starting a war, but she had grown to care for Azerdash. Her instincts would likely drive her to stand by his side if trouble came, whether it was wise or not. Whether he'd *started* the fight or not.

Besides, in her short time interacting with dragons, and in her engagements with refugees from other worlds, she'd learned how much their kind interfered, imposing their rule to keep order in the Cosmic Realms. Order that *dragons* liked. Supposedly, it was for the safety and protection of all, but many said it was mostly for the benefit of their kind. If a warrior came along who could bind the various worlds together and drive the dragons out, would it be a bad thing? If they could succeed?

Her objection was more because Azerdash might *not* succeed and would die. She'd only just met him, but the thought of losing him saddened her greatly.

"Yes," she whispered. "I don't think I should, but I would."

Yendral didn't look surprised, but his smile grew a touch sad.

Before Arwen could contemplate his response, she noticed an exhibit on fishing and farming practices of the natives who'd lived in the area before loggers and settlers had come. Curious about the implements they'd used and what they'd grown back then, she read the signs by the dim nighttime lighting.

It turned out that the main *farming* they'd done had been of clams. The idea amused her, but she supposed it made sense for people living by the Sound. They'd even built gardens of a sort in the shallow waters, providing everything shellfish needed to thrive and grow.

Though she felt a little guilty about breaking and entering—or *incinerating* and entering—Arwen appreciated the chance to look around and read signs without crowds making her skin crawl. She'd entered few museums in her life, instead learning about history only from books. Maybe finally getting her tattoo removed would help her bury the suffocating memories of the past that always crept over her whenever she was around too many people.

"Ah ha!" Gondo lifted his arms with a flourish and opened a trapdoor, thumping it against the nearby wall. "Open caraway!"

Arwen stepped away from the exhibit and her musings. "Did you mean *sesame*?"

"Oh, maybe so. I knew the human saying involved seeds."

"Caraway actually isn't a seed," Arwen said, "though many people believe it is. It's a little dried pod that's the fruit of the caraway plant."

Gondo wrinkled his nose. "It tastes funny."

Arwen thought about mentioning the numerous delicious dishes caraway could be used in, but Gondo was peering into the dark space below the trapdoor, so all she said was, "Yes."

"When we came before, Princess Amber made light with her talking box." Gondo pointed at Arwen's phone.

"Princess? You called her that before. Why?" After a mere three restarts, the phone came on for Arwen, and she activated the flashlight function. The screen blinked, more in indignation at her touch than to be helpful.

"The Ruin Bringer is the daughter of the elven king, and Amber is the daughter of the Ruin Bringer, so I believe that makes her a princess."

"Amber didn't ask you to call her that, did she?"

"She said to never call her that, but I believe it is because she is shy and doesn't want her peers to grow jealous when they learn of her sublime heritage. Goblins are not shy." Gondo took the phone.

Afraid he would drop it, Arwen almost snatched it back, but it sighed, as if with contentment, in his grip. It stopped blinking, and the flashlight shone a steady beam below. Apparently, technology only objected to dark-elven auras, not goblin auras.

"Are you sure that's a basement and not a crawl space?" Arwen asked. "Or a dungeon?"

The so-called secret door looked more like an access panel with hinges, and the dark below reminded her of the prison she'd retrieved Amber and Gondo from. She supposed an old library/city hall wouldn't have a jail *and* an oubliette though.

"Yes." Gondo lowered his top half through and fiddled with something. "The *interesting* exhibits are down there, covered in dust."

A *clunk-clunk-clank* sounded as a foldaway wooden staircase dropped to the floor below. A cloud of dust wafted up, and Yendral sneezed. He gave Gondo a dark look but, fortunately, refrained from incinerating him.

Oblivious, Gondo trotted down the steps. "This way, powerful allies."

Though he appeared more irritated than delighted by the adventure, Yendral followed without hesitation. Eager to get a clue about the sword?

Arwen crept down after them. The basement had a low ceiling made from century-old wooden planks, and even at five-nine, she had to duck to keep from hitting her head on the beams. The taller Yendral couldn't stand straight even between them. Gondo whistled cheerfully, his three-and-a-half feet making the jaunt easy.

He trotted past boxes and bins, some modern and made from

plastic, some from rusty iron. Those boxes looked like they might have come across the country on covered wagons in the pioneer days. Gondo continued past disassembled exhibits, one on mining that proclaimed the area had once been the Gateway to the Gold Fields.

"Here's the picture." Gondo hopped on a box and pointed at a wall half-hidden by crates and exhibit pieces.

As Amber had said, it was a plaster mural, the paint faded from time. There were others in the basement, but Gondo focused on this one.

It showed the coast of what must have been Edmonds in the late 1800s. The view was from the north and displayed land and water. Old buildings made from wood included a sawmill and a foundry, and horses pulling wagons plodded through the streets. Where today's ferry terminal was, a quaint wooden dock stretched into the water. Out on a small rocky island to the southwest of the dock, a long chest rested as a bearded man stood with one foot atop it. He held a sword and glared skyward, as if battling an unseen enemy.

Surprisingly, the mural emanated the faintest tinge of magic. Dwarven magic?

Maybe the same person who'd created the map from Willard's archives had crafted this back when the building had been constructed. A couple of lines of runes that could have been Dwarven writing were etched in the plaster above the sword. The instructions that Amber and Gondo had found about making a key.

Yendral, who was looking at the same spot, sucked in a breath when his gaze fixed on the sword. Though the faded paint made it hard to tell, slashes around the blade might have indicated that it glowed.

Arwen leaned forward and used her sleeve to rub dust from the plaster. She couldn't tell if the tiny dots pitting the sword signaled rust and damage or were meant to convey stars, such as Azerdash had described.

"Is it buried on that island?" Yendral asked. "If you could call it that. It looks like little more than a heap of rocks jutting up from the water."

Arwen closed her eyes, imagining the current-day shoreline. She hadn't spent a lot of time at the local beaches in her life, but she *had* visited and couldn't remember any little islands. Especially not in the location this appeared to be.

"A heap of rocks that I don't think is there," Arwen replied. "At least not today."

Yendral squinted at her.

"It's not," Gondo said brightly. "After we found this, we looked. It was still light out then, so we could see. It's just flat water out there." He tapped the sword wielder in the mural. "I thought maybe a dragon was attacking him, and destroyed him and the island, and the chest sank to the bottom. Princess Amber said she'd never heard of dragons in Washington until Lord Zavry-d'nokquetal showed up to *tysliir* with her mother."

"Amber used the term *tysliir*?" Arwen had only heard the dragon word a couple of times.

"She said they smashed and then had a weird *situationship* until, all of the sudden, they were getting married." Gondo shrugged. "The dragon term is simpler."

Arwen looked to Yendral, thinking to ask him if dragons had visited Earth in previous centuries, but remembered he'd been in stasis for hundreds of years. Instead, she said, "I guess this is why Azerdash wanted bathymetric maps."

Yendral, his gaze fastened on the mural, nodded. "Ambassador Rysharon said his research suggested it was in the water, guarded by a magical creature."

Arwen had forgotten about the creature. As if it wasn't bad enough that Edmonds was being guarded by dragons. Even if

Azerdash had led Hyrukorlin off, the Silverclaw would be back. He knew the sword was in the area. His whole *clan* might be back.

Arwen stepped closer to the mural and drew her finger from the tiny island back toward land. The angle wasn't right for her to get a good idea of what exactly it might have lined up with, but it was farther south than the ferry terminal. The mural showed the bluff she'd run past earlier in the night, nothing but forest atop it back then, and no train tracks yet following the shoreline. The island looked like it was roughly west from the start of that bluff.

"I am hungry," Gondo announced. "Being imprisoned is harrowing and builds the appetite. It is unfortunate that the popcorn distribution machine that was working earlier is not producing warm buttery poofs now." Gondo rubbed his belly and looked wistfully toward the trapdoor.

Arwen's phone vibrated, Val's number popping up. "Hello?"

"Perhaps you could find it and turn it on." Yendral watched Gondo through lowered eyelids.

"Hey, Arwen," Val said. "Great news. Matti delivered her babies, a boy and a girl."

"Oh, good. Did you go back to the magical-beings birthing center?"

"Yes, with Amber. We got news that Matti was getting close, so I drove straight over. The babies are healthy, and they don't have pointed ears. At least not yet. Sarrlevi said it's possible that they'll develop some more obvious elven traits later on, since that's the predominate blood in their veins. I think he *wants* them to have pointed ears, Arwen. Can you imagine explaining that to your teachers all the way through school? And the teasing you'd have to endure? Assuming they go to school here. I suppose it's possible Sarrlevi will argue for sending them to some elven boarding school in Veleshna Var, but they'd be teased there for *not* having pointed ears, right?"

"It's not something I've considered. I'm glad the delivery was successful." And Arwen was, but her primary concern at the moment was finding the sword and getting out of the area so Azerdash didn't have to hang out in a place where the Silverclaws could sense him. "I'm sure Matti is exhausted, but is there any chance she'd like to enchant that key tonight?"

"Yeah, that's the other reason I'm here. I made sure she saw the Dwarven writing. I'll give you an update soon."

"Okay, thanks. Uhm, do you know anything about getting SCUBA gear and how hard it is to learn to use it?"

Unless someone came up with a better idea, their next step might have to be swimming around in Puget Sound and trying to find a chest on the seabed, buried under a collapsed rocky island.

"Oh, okay." Val must have been responding to someone else. "Arwen, Matti said yes to making the key, as she's actually feeling, ah, what did you call it, Sarrlevi?"

"*Fyleera lesh,*" came his voice from the background. "It is a term that conveys the infusion of power that mothers from races with magical blood experience during the delivery of their offspring. Since such births can be difficult, their bodies gain more ability to perform magic around that time. More power, essentially. It often combats the weariness they feel from the arduous birth. For several days, Mataalii may particularly excel at crafting."

"I'd just say she has a nice glow about her," Val said.

"Really," came the dry—or was that condescending?—reply.

"Anyway, she said she'd try the key after she rests a bit," Val continued to Arwen. "As far as SCUBA, you'd need an instructor. I guess I can roust Willard out of bed. She's certified in every form of athletic activity in existence, though her most recent foray is pickleball. I think she may be getting older, but don't tell her I said that. And, oh, Willard has access to a two-person submarine. I've actually used it before in Lake Union. Gondo has buddies with a jalopy capable of pulling it at short notice. Let me call her. You still in Edmonds?"

"Yes. We'll head to the waterfront. And I'll ask Gondo—" Arwen glanced around. "Where did Gondo go?"

"To seek popped corn, I believe." Yendral pointed upward.

Arwen nodded, sensing his aura on the main floor. "Okay. I'll see if he can arrange hauling for a submarine. That sounds better than trying to learn how to SCUBA dive tonight."

A yawn crept over Arwen, and she eyed the time. It was well past midnight. If Azerdash hadn't been in danger, she would have suggested everyone go to bed and that they could come back tomorrow to finish this adventure.

"I'll update you when I've got the key." Val hung up.

Arwen yawned again.

Yendral rested a hand on her shoulder. "I will take my dragon form and dive into the water around that area."

"Are dragons good swimmers?"

"They are adequate swimmers and can hold their breath longer than humans. Mostly, the form makes it easy to dive from a great height and use the momentum to plunge deep before buoyancy catches up. This inlet is not that deep, I believe."

"Yeah, Puget Sound is only..." Not certain, Arwen tapped a search into her phone. "Oh, it's actually up to nine hundred and thirty feet deep with an average of four hundred and fifty. Hm. Maybe it's not that deep near the shoreline." Arwen considered the island in the mural, estimating how far from land—from that *bluff*—it was, but realized the artistic rendering might not have been accurate. "We may actually need a submarine."

"I will dive to see what I can sense. You may rest. Once Azerdash returns, he can protect you." The hand on her shoulder shifted, turning the light touch into more of a massage. "Or *I* can protect you while *he* dives for the chest. He is the one who will carry the blade, after all."

"I don't need protection. Thanks." Arwen squinted at his hand and took a step away from him.

Yendral allowed it, his gaze toward the south. Could he sense Azerdash coming now? Or was the Silverclaw or someone else dangerous returning?

"Why don't we go upstairs and grab Gondo and go out to the dock to look at the water?" Arwen suggested.

"Of course," Yendral murmured.

But when Arwen started for the exit, wood snapped, startling her. She reached for her bow before the fold-down stairs collapsed, sending more clouds of dust into the air. The faintest hint of magic lingered around the area before fading. Dragon magic? Or *half*-dragon magic?

As if a gust of wind had rushed through the museum, the door slammed shut, trapping Arwen in the basement with Yendral.

25

"Unfortunate," Yendral murmured.

Arwen eyed him, the only light coming from her phone. Yendral watched her through drooped lids.

Had that been his magic she sensed breaking the stairs and shutting the trapdoor? It hadn't been Gondo. Arwen sensed him in the same spot on the main floor as he'd been in a few minutes earlier. In fact, he was in the *exact* same spot. They'd walked by it earlier, and she didn't remember seeing a popcorn maker there. It had been about where that old jail cell was located.

"Did you lock Gondo up?" Arwen asked.

Yendral smirked. "Certainly not. He is seeking food."

"Are you going to try to convince me that the popcorn maker is in the jail cell?"

"A cell is a fitting place for a goblin."

"A goblin who's been helping us?" Sweat dampened Arwen's palms, and she took another step back from Yendral before wiping them on her trousers.

What was he up to? He couldn't think that she wanted to have sex with him in a dank basement, could he? Or at all? Hadn't she made it clear that her interest was in Azerdash? Just a few minutes ago, he'd seemed to grasp that.

"Helping us for coin." Yendral glanced upward and toward the south again, though Arwen didn't sense anyone magical around besides the entrapped Gondo. Yendral took a couple of steps toward her and caught her wrist in his grip. "For more coin, he would help the Silverclaws."

"That's not true. He works for Colonel Willard." Arwen twisted her wrist and tried to pull it free.

Yendral's grip wasn't painful, but it did tighten, keeping her close.

Her hand dropped to her multitool, but she hesitated. Did she want to draw a knife on Azerdash's friend? The only half-dragon ally he had left?

No, but if Yendral tried to force her to do something against her wishes, she would.

"He was in the way." Yendral glanced toward the trapdoor, then took another step forward, wrapping an arm around Arwen and pulling her against him.

Instincts kicked in, and she stomped on the instep of his foot. He grunted but didn't let her go, instead lowering his mouth to the side of her neck and nuzzling her.

She reached for the multitool, but Yendral still had her wrist and kept her from grasping it.

"It's for his own good," he whispered, dropping a hand to her ass.

"Let go of me, you—"

The trapdoor opened, banging against the wall upstairs. Arwen abruptly sensed Azerdash. He dropped down, landing in a crouch to the side of the broken stairs, and stared at them, his eyes widening. With surprise? Betrayal? Anger?

Arwen shoved at Yendral, but his power and muscular arm

were wrapped around her. She couldn't find the leverage to force him away.

"What are you doing?" Azerdash demanded, stepping toward them.

"Showing her why the fae queen kept me in her bedchamber for hours, screaming with intense pleasure," Yendral said.

No, he's not, Arwen blurted telepathically to Azerdash, terrified he would believe the lie, terrified he would think she was betraying him. Even if they hadn't promised their romantic loyalties to each other, she didn't want him to believe... whatever he believed. Conflict twisted his handsome features. *Yendral locked Gondo in the jail cell so he could be alone with me. I don't want him. I want you.*

That last admission was more than she'd meant to blurt, but he already knew that.

Azerdash met her eyes, his blazing violet, then used his power to break Yendral's grip on her. Somehow, he managed to push her gently away from him while hurling Yendral across the basement. Azerdash strode toward her as he glowered at his comrade.

Yendral would have hit the far wall after tumbling into the boxes and junk blocking it, but he used his magic to stop his momentum and landed in a crouch. "You act like a child whenever she wishes to be with me, but then you do not claim her for yourself."

"It is not *childish* to protect a female from unwanted attention."

"But she *does* want my attention. She craves a half-dragon lover —why else would she continue to bring us food?—and you will not give her what she wishes. But *I* will." Yendral strode across the basement as if he would shove Azerdash aside to reach Arwen.

She raised a finger. "I don't crave any lovers." Maybe that wasn't true, but she was flustered and didn't know *what* to say.

It didn't matter. Azerdash had put his back to her to face

Yendral, who had his gaze locked on Azerdash. Neither was looking at her or her raised finger.

"You will give her *nothing* but support," Azerdash said.

"She wants far more than that from one of us. And if it will not be you—"

"It will not be you either," Azerdash snarled, crouching to spring.

"She *deserves* one of us." Yendral also crouched. "She has been loyal. She would even fight with you if you challenged the dragons. She's *already* fought with us against their kind."

"I am aware of that," Azerdash bit out.

"And yet you won't reward her. Then give her to me. Let *me* reward her."

Azerdash growled, more like a dragon than a man—or an elf—and sank lower, his muscles quivering. "Do not rile me, Yendral."

His power coiled within him, his aura growing stronger and more noticeable. Azerdash was focused on Yendral, but some of that power washed over Arwen, dangerous but appealing. Though she worried they would fight, she appreciated that he wanted to defend her, that he had the might to do so. She knew he would best Yendral in a battle and almost wanted to see it, to see him dominate another with his greater strength. Afterward, maybe Azerdash would make it clear to Yendral that he *was* interested in being with Arwen.

No, she couldn't want that scenario to play out. If Azerdash hurt—or killed—his friend, he wouldn't forgive himself.

"You *need* to be riled. Is a duel what you want? With the winner claiming the female?" Yendral flexed his fingers in invitation, a come-get-me gesture.

"I'm Arwen, not *the* female," she pointed out, but neither was looking at her.

Though ten feet separated them, they could close that in an instant if they leaped for each other.

Arwen raised a hand, tempted to grab Azerdash's shoulder to keep him from springing—or turning into a dragon. There wasn't nearly enough ceiling room for that. Regardless, she didn't want them to fight, not over her. How could she stop this?

"Her name is Arwen." Azerdash didn't spring, but he did blast power at his friend.

This time, when Yendral flew back, his own magic wasn't enough to insulate him and keep him from crashing. Dusty junk flew everywhere, and the wood of an old table snapped as he plowed into it.

Cursing, Yendral leaped to his feet as soon as he hit, not appearing injured in the least. He raised his arms, power of his own coiling around him.

Magic swelled, not in the basement but somewhere nearby. In the street in front of the museum. A portal?

Azerdash and Yendral paused, their defenses up but their attacks put aside as they considered what might be a new threat. Arwen sensed elven instead of dragon magic but didn't know if that meant an ally had arrived or another enemy.

"It is foolish for us to fight between ourselves when there are so many others who would kill us." Azerdash lowered his arms. Maybe he knew whose magic that was.

"It is *not* foolish when something of great value is at stake." Yendral looked toward Arwen, though Azerdash had positioned himself to block most of his view of her.

"She is Arwen, a *person*, not *something*. Do you speak of all your females such? Do they enjoy being so belittled?"

"They enjoy the pleasure I bring them in bed."

"Were you always this much of an ass?"

"Once, you would have corrected me for inappropriate behavior." Yendral said it in a challenging tone, as if he *wanted* that.

"Once, I was your commanding officer."

"You never *stopped* being that, you fool. You should be leading armies, not cowering on this backward pollution-wreathed world."

The aura of an elf registered on Arwen's senses, Ambassador Rysharon.

Instead of answering, Azerdash peered toward the street. Arwen shifted, thinking of all the people—and dragons—who'd found out about the sword and had heard rumors that Azerdash would raise an army once he found it. Who besides Rysharon could have let that information out?

"I have invited him to come down here." Azerdash straightened, flicking a hand as if to say he was done with Yendral's foolishness. "He has things to explain." He must have also wondered if his old soldier was the source of the rumors. "Hopefully, he will not be deterred by the lack of stairs leading down here."

Yendral snorted. "He is old but not weak. Surely, even if his bones are too brittle for jumping, he has the power to levitate himself down."

"We could go upstairs," Arwen pointed out, though the half-dragons were still bristling at each other from across the basement, not listening to her.

Soon, Rysharon arrived at the trapdoor.

Hello? he called down telepathically as well as aloud in Elven.

We are here, Azerdash replied.

Rysharon levitated downward, avoiding the broken stairs, and landing lightly. He wore the same clothing and carried the same weapons as the last time he had come to Earth.

Yes, I sensed you and... Rysharon glanced warily at Arwen. *Your female.*

Our ally, Arwen Forester, Azerdash corrected.

We are still determining which of us will claim her as his female, Yendral put in.

Rysharon looked stunned before his mouth twisted in distaste, but he waved a hand as if to dismiss the idea and said something aloud in Elven.

Yes, Azerdash replied silently, tapping his temple. *We will speak so she can understand. As a native here, she has knowledge we lack and is assisting us in our quest.*

As you wish, Commander, but I would prefer to speak with you privately. Also, did you know that a goblin is locked in a cell above?

I am aware.

He may be a spy, Rysharon said.

Yes, but for the human military leader, not the Silverclaws.

Rysharon's brow creased. *I do not fully understand, but I do not wish to delay. I have news you will find distressing and that I... I regret.* He grimaced.

If it is that Silverclaw dragons have learned the sword may be in this area and are hunting me, I am aware.

Rysharon rocked back. *I did not think they would strike so soon. They locked me away and used a* heethla *to temporarily weaken my aura and drain my power so that I lost consciousness. When I awoke, it was some time before I could conjure enough magic to form a portal and come here to warn you. If they have already harried you, I regret that.*

Where is Hyrukorlin now? Yendral asked Azerdash.

Azerdash waved to the south. *I took a portal to another world, letting him know where I was going, then made sure he appeared there before camouflaging myself, flying away, and returning here. Whether he believes I left Earth for long, I do not know. I expect he will return soon, possibly with others, to resume monitoring this place.*

Rysharon winced again. *I apologize, Commander Starblade. That is my fault. Though I told few that I was coming to see you, perhaps I told too many. I needed help with my research and spoke of the sword quest. Who might have told the dragons, I do not know, but a Silverclaw came to me and mind-scoured me to learn everything I knew.*

And what you hoped I would do? Azerdash raised his eyebrows.

Find the sword and use it to lead a combined army against drag-onkind? Yes.

Even though that was only your wish and nothing I'd agreed to.

Rysharon hesitated. *That is true, but I believed strongly that with the sword, you would feel compelled to fulfill your destiny.*

Yendral stirred, giving Azerdash an I-told-you-so look. *It is your destiny.*

It is not. I do not have a destiny. Azerdash snapped his fingers into a fist. *There is no such thing. There is only what those who created us wanted us to achieve, a victory for the elves against their enemies of the time.*

They wished you to lead our people to greatness, Rysharon said. *Perhaps they wanted you to begin with the dwarves, but I have read the works of the time, penned by the leaders and the very scientist-generals who created you. Once we'd defeated the dwarves, they wanted the half-dragons to help us defeat the dragons as well. To drive them away from our world so we could live in peace and rule as we saw fit, without kowtowing to their demands.*

Azerdash shook his head. *Whatever they wanted, the half-dragons are no more. I found those who were in stasis and freed them. All the others died in the time in which we were born. Only three of us survived the dragons attacking our base on Veleshna Var, and Sleveryn walked away, wanting nothing more to do with dragons or battles.*

It's possible there are more half-dragons, Rysharon said, *but we need only a leader, not an army. A powerful leader who wields a galaxy blade could unite—*

I know what you want, Rysharon. Azerdash chopped a hand to stop the elf's words. *And now the dragons do too, not only the Silver-claws but the Stormforges.* He looked to Arwen for the first time since he'd pushed Yendral away from her.

She nodded. "Val said Zavryd was called to the dragon home world on the matter."

Your thoughts are going to get us killed, Rysharon, Azerdash said, *before we can even find the sword.*

Yendral looked toward the mural. *Possibly not.*

Azerdash also looked, but he made another hand chop, this one for Yendral. Not wanting him to let Rysharon know they'd found a clue? If the elf couldn't keep dragons from reading his mind, that was understandable.

Arwen frowned, reminded that she also didn't have that power. She would do her best to make sure no dragons captured and mind-scoured *her.*

You've found a clue? Rysharon asked. *Was I right? Is it in this area?*

Azerdash walked to him, rested a hand on his shoulder, and turned him so that he didn't face the mural. He spoke quietly to him in Elven, his tone one of forgiveness rather than irritation. But he did firmly point toward the street.

Rysharon asked a question.

Azerdash shook his head.

After a glance at Yendral, Rysharon bowed to them, formed a portal in the basement, and departed.

"We'll have to go diving to look for it," Yendral told Azerdash when the elf was gone.

"The water is shallow?"

Their tones were calm, as if they hadn't been on the verge of tearing each other's throats out a few minutes earlier.

Arwen was glad. Even if a primitive part of her might have enjoyed seeing Azerdash defeat a rival, she didn't want them to hurt each other.

Yendral shrugged. "It may not be, but the remains of what was once that little island may remain not far beneath the surface. We will look."

Azerdash nodded. "Begin. I will follow shortly."

Arwen thought Yendral might object to Azerdash staying alone with her, but he nodded curtly and used his power to whisk himself over the broken stairs and through the trapdoor.

"I talked to Val before he got, uhm, weird. She said Matti can enchant a key to open that chest." Arwen pointed to it in the mural. "Val also might be able to get a submarine."

Azerdash's face was grave, but she tried a smile and envisioned a sub, telepathically sharing it with him, though she had no idea what the two-seater Val had mentioned would look like. Nothing like the U-boats in her father's history books, she was sure.

Azerdash smiled slightly. "I would enjoy seeing an underwater conveyance."

"And riding in one, right? It has to be better than the dragon-dolphin scenario Yendral was describing." Arwen's clothes were still damp from her last immersion in the Sound, and she couldn't imagine diving into the cold murky depths over and over. Even in the summer, the water flowing in from the Pacific Ocean wasn't warm.

"I might find that fascinating."

Arwen might find riding in a submarine claustrophobic and terrifying, but she could imagine Azerdash cheerfully pulling levers and opening panels to peer at the workings.

He stepped closer and gazed into her eyes. "Are you all right? I do not know what has gotten into Yendral, but his behavior is unacceptable."

"I'm okay. He didn't— Well, you came before he did anything." Arwen swallowed, thinking of what might have happened if Azerdash *hadn't* arrived.

Or... A thought occurred to her. Would *anything* have happened if Yendral hadn't known Azerdash had been coming? Arwen hadn't sensed him until the last moment, but he could have spoken telepathically to Yendral earlier. Or Yendral, with his greater power, might have detected him through his camouflaging magic. Maybe they could track each other through those dragon tattoos too.

Yendral hadn't been pawing her over or forcing his tongue into her mouth or anything like that. It had almost been as if the embrace had been for show. And afterward, had he been goading Azerdash? If so, *why*?

"He should not have done anything unwelcome under any circumstances, and I believe you that his grasp was not appreciated. Even if you had not said so to me, your face spoke of your distress." Azerdash's gaze radiated concern.

"Yes." Drawn by his warm eyes, Arwen stepped closer to him, but she resisted the urge to put a hand on his chest. He'd said he needed time to figure out his feelings for her, and she didn't want to push him. Why Yendral was pushing him, she didn't know.

Azerdash wrapped his arms gently around her and pulled her into the embrace that she hadn't presumed to initiate. He rested his face against her hair, his lips brushing the top of her ear.

Pleasure streaked along her nerves, and Arwen leaned into him. The memory of their kiss came to mind, and she wanted to tilt her head back to find his mouth with hers.

But that Silverclaw dragon could return at any time, and Yendral was out there searching for the sword by himself. What if he found it? Did he want to place it in Azerdash's hands, or was he scheming some plot of his own? Azerdash might have known Yendral for years, but *Arwen* hadn't, and she didn't know how trustworthy he was.

"I do not want to fight over you or play foolish games," Azerdash said softly, "but I was close to losing my... *gylersa*. You would say *humanity*."

"Elfity?"

"That is the rough translation, yes." He stroked a hand through her hair.

It had fallen from its bun, her sticks lost in the fight at the refinery, and he combed his fingers through its length. His touch was delicious, somehow relaxing and stimulating at once, and she longed to touch something of his.

"I don't want to be the reason you two fight," she made herself say, though his strokes were making it hard to form cohesive thoughts. The primitive part of her brain wanted to bask in this—and reciprocate. "I just want you to be happy." That sounded inane. She groped for something to say that was less of a dumb platitude. "I took photos of the train exhibit upstairs for you. I wasn't sure you'd make it back to the museum. It's not very much though. There's a museum not far from where I live with actual trains. I've never been, but I could take you if you're interested. When this is over. There are old locomotives you can climb around in."

"Arwen Forester," Azerdash murmured into her ear, "you've mentioned underwater conveyances *and* locomotives since I've returned. Are you trying to seduce me?"

"Someone suggested I would need to use cookies for that." She deliberately didn't mention Yendral's name. Azerdash had finally relaxed, and he was stroking her hair as his soft breaths whispered across her ear. Maybe to a normal woman who regularly engaged in relations with men, such a thing wouldn't have been that stimulating, but her entire body was awake to his touch—to him—and she didn't want him to stop.

His voice lowered to a rumble. "If you fed me your tasty desserts *while* guiding me through a fascinating engineering relic, I would be yours."

Arwen didn't know if it was a joke or not, but her body responded by flushing and shifting closer, molding her curves to his hard musculature.

Azerdash leaned his head back and brought his fingers to her chin, lifting it to gaze into her eyes. "You *do* deserve someone who will treat you well. You deserve—"

"You," she whispered, afraid he would say something self-deprecating or imply his mixed feelings made him less than ideal. "I don't know if I deserve anything special, but I want to be with you."

His gaze shifted from her eyes to her lips, and his fingers drifted to them, tracing them.

Hot tingles coursed through her, the longing to kiss him intensifying.

"I noticed a water gardening exhibit up there on my way past," he murmured, watching her reaction to his touch. "Did you also take pictures of it?"

"Not pictures, but I read about it. The natives used rock walls at the beach to build terraces and increase the amount of habitable shallows for the shellfish. They enjoyed little-neck clams, butter clams, mussels, and oysters, with barnacles being a delicacy."

His eyes crinkled. "You read the exhibit or *memorized* it?"

"I'm not sure. Would memorization be considered geeky?"

"Sexy." Azerdash finally lowered his mouth to hers. Exactly as she wanted.

Delighted, Arwen kissed him back, wrapping her arms around his shoulders and wriggling against him, relieved that he didn't find her passions off-putting. She still didn't know if he wanted to be seduced, if he'd made up his mind on his feelings for her, but as his hands ran through her hair and down her back while he kept her close, she could tell his body at least wanted to be with hers.

Never had I thought a female speaking of barnacles would excite me, he whispered into her mind.

The admission that she *excited* him filled her with a different kind of pleasure, and she felt beautiful and desirable. *Learning about the foods of other cultures can be stimulating,* she replied instead of admitting to her emotions. They were too private, too vulnerable to share.

Indeed. You *are stimulating.* His tongue stroked hers, arousing heat in her, making her hope dragons, elves, goblins, and especially his friend would leave them alone tonight. *I want you too.*

Even though...? Arwen didn't finish the question, not wanting to bring up the dark-elven comrade he'd had feelings for, not wanting to remind him of her. Maybe it was selfish, but she wanted him to think only of her right now.

I do not *know if I'm all that you deserve.* His thumb brushed her through her jumpsuit, making her wish she wore nothing, that he could touch her bare flesh. *But I want you, regardless. Seeing you with another... I cannot tolerate it.* A dragonish rumble emanated from his chest. A growl? *I will* claim you.

Excited by his words as well as his touches, Arwen whispered an amenable, *Okay,* and nipped at his lower lip.

That *really* made him growl. With a quick whisper of his magic, her jumpsuit loosened, peeling away from her shoulders. She pushed a hand under his shirt, scraping her nails over his warm flesh, his taut, hard body. She lacked the experience to know what to do to please him, but his muscles quivered under her touch, and he growled again.

The distant roar of a dragon reverberated through the building.

"No," Arwen groaned, tightening her grip on Azerdash, not wanting to let him go.

Maybe that had been Yendral, complaining about the cold water as he dove. Maybe they could ignore it.

Even as she had the thought, her senses identified the Silver-claw dragon. Hyrukorlin was flying up the coast at top speed.

This time, Azerdash's growl was frustrated. She understood the feeling perfectly and didn't want to let go when he broke the kiss.

His chest rose and fell with deep breaths, and he didn't yet release her. She knew he didn't want to. That was something at least.

"You need to go," she whispered as his head rolled back. Was the dragon speaking telepathically to him? Threatening him?

"We'll have to fight Hyrukorlin. He won't be lured away again."

Fear for Azerdash threw cold water on Arwen's arousal.

Finally, he stepped back, lowering his arms. "Yendral will help. If Hyrukorlin is the only dragon in the area, we might have a chance."

"I'll get your sword for you," Arwen blurted, though she had no idea how she would do that until Val returned with a submarine and a key. All she knew was that Azerdash would be more powerful with it in his hands—or his talons—than without, and he needed every advantage he could get.

"It's guarded, remember. Wait for me to finish, and we'll get it together." Azerdash cupped the side of her face. "Though it touches me that you want to help me, I'm not certain why you're giving me such devotion."

The roar of the dragon floated to them again. He had to go.

"I'm loyal," she hurried to whisper, because she knew that meant something to him, and it was less charged than saying she loved him, but as he kissed her a final time before leaving, she realized she *was* falling in love with him.

Azerdash ran out of the museum and changed into his dragon form.

Telepathically, she added, *Don't you dare get yourself killed.*

26

After tossing her bow through, Arwen leaped, caught the lip of the open trapdoor, and pulled herself up. Only as she ran for the front of the museum did she sense and remember Gondo.

"Chef Arwen," he called.

Feeling guilty, even if she'd had nothing to do with Yendral's shenanigans, she veered to the jail cell.

"Sorry, Gondo."

"The half-dragon rudely used his magic to *force* me inside here and lock the door. I did not even get to activate the popcorn machine first."

Yendral's magic had locked the door, but Arwen hoped the key on a large ring hanging from a peg would work.

"He *is* a rude half-dragon." She grabbed the ring and slid the key into the lock.

"*Yes.* At least this has given me time to communicate with my brethren in the marsh."

The lock turned, and Arwen swung the cell door open. "Come on. We need to head to the waterfront and—" And what? Take a swim and hope to get lucky? If the chest had gone undiscovered for all these decades, it had to be deep underwater. Even if magic hid it, it had to be far enough down that no ships had run aground on the remains of that island. "We have to get the sword while Yendral and Azerdash keep the Silverclaw dragon busy."

"Yes, I assumed that was still the goal." Gondo took the lead, running for the front door, as if he knew exactly how to accomplish their mission. "And now that Princess Amber has been taken away by her mother, if I successfully assist you, I am certain I will earn far more than two percent of the payment."

Gondo looked over his shoulder. Asking if Arwen agreed?

She hadn't been there for the deal-making between Amber and Gondo and didn't want to shortchange Amber but hazarded, "Azerdash is generous with his gold."

"Excellent. I am in need of funds. Did you know that Colonel Willard pays me only in sodas and candy bars from her vending machines?"

"Oh? I would have thought her a fair employer who would at least pay minimum wage. Although... how *many* sodas and candy bars do you consume a day?"

"She gives me all that I can eat. And drink."

Given his diminutive size, that shouldn't have been *that* many, but Arwen had heard stories from Nin and Val of the amazing metabolisms of the goblins who gamed at the Coffee Dragon. Arwen suspected Gondo might be receiving the equivalent of minimum wage. Maybe *more* than the equivalent.

"Usually, this is not a problem." Gondo pushed open the front door and waved to several short figures across the street. Goblins. Local *marsh* goblins? They lurked in the shadows between the streetlamps. "But I am thinking of following in the footsteps of Work Leader Tinja, the goblin who purchased a human dwelling on the street belonging to the Ruin Bringer and Plumber Puletasi."

Arwen almost pointed out that Matti and Val, despite having

bought houses in that neighborhood, did not *own* that street, but she was busy staring in puzzlement at the goblins.

"I wish to purchase a human dwelling for myself." Gondo trotted down the stairs toward their visitors. "This would make me more desirable to females. But I need to acquire many funds for the purchase of a home, even one located in a neighborhood that is less expensive due to terrifying dragons lowering the property values."

When he reached the goblins, Gondo switched to their tongue, a rapid-fire staccato with a lot of *pips, peeps, zirks, gluks,* and *geets.*

The leader handed something to him, then drew a wrench in the air with his finger, and departed. The group headed back toward the marsh while casting wary glances toward Puget Sound.

Arwen could sense Azerdash, Yendral, and the Silverclaw dragon flying out there, though she didn't think they had engaged in battle. She wished Zavryd would return to Earth and feel obligated to come help, though she worried his willingness to do so had changed by now.

"This will assist us in acquiring the sword." Gondo pressed two items that felt like mouth guards into Arwen's hand. "He gave me two of them, but I do not wish to battle dangerous foes for a magical weapon. My duty is research and the acquisition of helpful artifacts." He waved toward her hand. "Have you an ally who can assist you?"

"I... maybe, but what are these?" Arwen held up the devices, sensing their magic, but she couldn't believe they actually went into one's mouth.

"They are *girkleka.*"

"Uhm, naturally. And what does one do?"

"Allows you to breathe underwater. That is how the goblins can live not alongside the marsh but in homes under the surface, sneaky homes that the humans who birdwatch with binoculars never find. Even though the half-dragon so rudely incarcerated me, I continued to work on the mission, telepathically reaching out to my kin to ask if you could borrow these."

"You're a good goblin, Gondo."

"Yes, certainly. Which is why my efforts are worth at least *four* percent."

"Maybe even five." Arwen decided she would make up the difference if Azerdash wouldn't. Gondo would need a lot of gold if he wanted to buy a home in Seattle, dragon-depressed property values or not.

"Oh, fantastic. Perhaps the half-dragon will feel even more generous when he learns that I've arranged transportation for you."

Arwen almost mentioned that Val was working on a submarine, but who knew how long that would take? "A boat?"

"Indeed. One that the goblins keep camouflaged at the marina. They use it to go fishing to supplement their diet when they aren't able to acquire enough desirable human foods from the trash receptacles outside of restaurants."

"I... suspect that would be often."

"Indeed, true. Most human food is somewhat inferior. Fish is delicious, though, especially when simmered in garlic, bacon, and seagull blood."

Arwen had started to nod until that last ingredient came up. "How do they feel about barnacles?"

"Most tasty in a seafood bisque." Fortunately, Gondo didn't list the ingredients for that, which probably didn't involve the usual butter, cream, and white wine. "The boat goblin is not interested in paddling out when dragons are flying overhead, but you have permission to take the craft."

He waved for her to bend down to his height, then touched her temple and shared an image of the marina. The boat—no, that was a kayak—was tied to a support post under the walkway.

"Thank you, Gondo." Arwen kissed him on the cheek, then

jogged off toward the waterfront. "Tell the goblins to watch out," she called back. "There could be fireworks here tonight."

"Oh, they are aware. Fire is *always* in the works when dragons battle."

Arwen pulled out her phone as she ran, hoping for an update from Val. Hoping even more that Val was already on the way. But the text that came back said she was still waiting for Willard to have the submarine prepared for transport.

Fire appeared in the night sky. One of the dragons or half-dragons attacking?

The three combatants were far enough apart that Arwen didn't think so, but maybe they were strutting and flexing, each trying to intimidate the others. She was surprised the Silverclaw dragon, believing himself far superior to a couple of *half*-dragons, hadn't already attacked, but he'd probably heard that Darvanylar had died going after Yendral and Azerdash. Maybe that made him wary.

Even so, Arwen feared she didn't have time to wait for help from Val and Willard. She was on her own.

27

Despite the camouflage hiding it from mundane humans, Arwen found the two-person goblin kayak without trouble. It was painted green, with cogs, gears, and other bits of metal she couldn't name glued to the outside.

Paddling it around all the yachts tied up in the marina and out into the Sound wasn't as easy as she'd hoped. She'd been on fishing boats with her father but never a kayak, and maneuvering it took some getting used to. Especially when bursts of fire from the dragons flying overhead distracted her. Not to mention the sea lion that she startled awake. It barked and grunted like an incensed Rottweiler at her passing.

Arwen activated her camouflaging magic, hoping it would forget about her—and that the Silverclaw dragon wouldn't notice her either. She didn't want to give him any clues about the location of the sword.

You've acquired a watercraft? Azerdash spoke into her mind.

Of a sort. Arwen shared an image of the kayak. *I know you said to wait, but I can't. I want to get that sword before the Silverclaws or anyone else does, and I'm hoping you can use it if you have to battle the dragon.*

Your loyalty urges you to do this.

Loyalty or love? Or both? Arwen shook her head, replying only with, *Yeah.*

That conveyance is decorated with gears but is not itself mechanical?

That was what he was worried about most at that moment? *No, sorry.*

Hm. It is an inferior craft for what you are undertaking. If I can slip away without Hyrukorlin following, I will join you and assist.

How are you going to slip away when the three of you are in the middle of a pissing contest?

A what?

Seeing who can create the biggest stream of... fire.

Ah. We shall see.

Arwen paddled until the yachts in the marina appeared tiny behind her, and she could see most of Edmonds stretching along the coast and up the hill. By daylight, she might have picked out the top of Amber's house on the steep slope.

She angled to the south, trying to line herself up with the start of the bluff. The words *needle in a haystack* came to mind, but if the mural had been accurate, she at least had a starting point.

As the waves lapped at the kayak, Arwen sent her senses into the depths below. Before long, she realized how unlikely it would be to pick up anything. If the sword was buried in a locked chest, it was probably well insulated. If it was even down there after all this time. For all she knew, a SCUBA diver had found it fifty years earlier and had it mounted over his fireplace in Queen Anne.

Her phone buzzed, Val's number.

Hoping she was on the way with her submarine, Arwen stopped paddling to answer. In the air north of the ferry terminal, the dragons closed on each other for the first time, Hyrukorlin sprinting at Yendral. If Azerdash had been contemplating sneaking away, the sudden charge must have changed his mind because he flapped his powerful wings and arrowed in to help his comrade.

"Please tell me you have good news," Arwen said, her eyes locked on the encounter.

If the battle had begun in earnest, she might be running out of time to find the blade. It wouldn't necessarily change the outcome, but it might. Yendral had believed it had the power to tilt the scales.

"I called to let you know that I'm an unwilling prisoner in Val's Jeep and that I would have stayed to help if I could." That was Amber's voice.

"Okay. It's not a problem." Arwen hadn't wanted Amber to stay and be in danger.

"I'm still getting my ten percent, right? We did the research, and Gondo and I found the Dwarven mural and stuff about a key."

"Yes, of course," Arwen murmured, distracted by the battle.

All three dragons were breathing flames. She sensed barriers protecting each, but under the fiery assault, their defenses might be overwhelmed. Had she made the wrong choice in coming out here? From the ferry dock, she might have been close enough to help with her bow.

"It's not my fault," Amber continued, "that Val is being a *total* hypocrite by telling me to stay out of dragon affairs when *she* doesn't."

Arwen had a feeling Amber's rant was for her mother's sake. "She has a huge battle tiger and a majorly badass sword."

"Whose side are you on?" Amber asked.

"I want you to be safe. Researchers aren't supposed to be on the front line."

"Thank you," Val interrupted. She must have leaned over or grabbed the phone. "For that, I'll bring your sub personally."

"Soon?"

"Soonish. We're on our way to Lake Washington to pick it up, and then we need to navigate it through the Locks and up to Edmonds."

Arwen grimaced, afraid she didn't have that much time.

"There wasn't anyone available to drive it to the Edmonds marina, which might have been faster," Val added, maybe guessing her thoughts. "It's 2 a.m."

"It's fine. Come when you can."

"Matti is going to start on your key but said it will take a while. You might have to find the treasure box or chest or whatever the sword is in first."

"Okay."

"I could wait with Matti and drive the key up to her while you take the sub," Amber volunteered. "There's no traffic right now. It would be faster."

"Unless the Jeep gets snatched up by a dragon," Val muttered. "She's not going to need the key until after she finds the chest, and she needs the sub for that."

"You never know," Amber said.

Arwen peered over the side of the kayak into the dark water, wishing she *could* find the chest right away.

"You just want to get away from my supervisory eye," Val said.

"*Duh.*"

"We'll be up there as soon as we can, Arwen," Val finished and hung up.

A screech of pain came from the dragon battle. Azerdash or Yendral?

Arwen hadn't witnessed the blow and couldn't tell, but she glanced up in time to see Azerdash wheeling away from the big full-blooded dragon. Hyrukorlin cast a gout of fire after him.

Yendral arrowed in from the opposite side, talons raking toward their nemesis. Though Hyrukorlin's barrier remained up, and the attack never reached him, it did cause him to veer toward Yendral, his flames halting.

Azerdash flexed his back and tail like a dog shaking off water, then rolled in a somersault and headed back toward the battle.

Arwen dug out one of the goblin mouthpieces, not sure how it worked and wondering if there was any point in diving below. Probably not unless she knew she was in the vicinity. With no idea how precise that mural had been, she might be miles from the former island.

Again, she stretched below with her senses, searching for something. Anything.

For a heartbeat, she thought she caught a hint of magic. Dwarven magic?

Her breath caught. Could the same dwarf who'd made the mural and the map have been responsible for crafting the chest? Maybe he'd been the person featured in the display, what Arwen had thought was a bearded man—human—instead a dwarf. It wasn't as if there had been anyone else nearby for context.

She lost track of the magic as soon as she detected it and turned the kayak around, hoping to pick it up again. It had come from below but not hundreds of feet below, as she'd feared. Maybe the Sound wasn't that deep in this area, or, more likely, some of that island remained below the surface.

"Where are you?" Arwen whispered, her brain aching from the effort of searching with her senses.

Too bad her tracking magic, neither elven nor dark-elven, wouldn't be useful in finding traces of someone who'd traveled this way a hundred years earlier.

A surge of magic formed in the sky over the water to the south. *Dragon* magic. Arwen glanced warily in that direction as the silver disc of a portal appeared.

"Please be Zavryd coming to help," she whispered.

But a green and a blue dragon flew out. One she didn't recognize, and one she did. The Silverclaw dragon who'd tried to kill her and Val in North Bend when they'd been searching for Harlik-van. Arwen had to assume both were Silverclaws, here to join in against Azerdash and Yendral to slay them.

They flew lazily out of the portal, as if they had all the time in the world, but they headed north toward the battle.

Trouble incoming, Arwen warned Azerdash telepathically, though he had to know.

She peered over the edge of the kayak, once more contemplating the dark water. Though she hadn't sensed the magic again, she was tempted to use the goblin device and dive down. If she got closer to the source, the magic would be easier to detect.

Yes, Azerdash replied. *We're outnumbered and will have to flee. Are you camouflaged?*

I am, she replied, though she didn't know why he was worried about her when the Silverclaws wanted to kill *him*. Then she realized why. If he and Yendral fled, the other dragons might remain, and if they detected her, they would come after her and mind-scour her. Or worse.

Is your water conveyance camouflaged?

Uhm, no, but I'm about to get out of it.

Arwen, we need to abort this quest. There are too many dragons. Even if you found the sword, they would take it from you.

Not if I can get it to you first. Having it would help you, right?

To defeat three dragons? Unlikely.

Just hold out for a bit, Arwen urged him. *Val is on the way up here.*

Unless she brings Zavryd'nokquetal and his uncle and sister, the odds will not be tilted by her presence.

I'll tell her to invite them. You go ahead and run for now. Escape, camouflage, and come back if you can. We'll get the sword.

Arwen, do not risk your life on this. It's not worth it.

Yendral said it's your destiny.

He also said, when I demanded to know why he couldn't keep his hands off you, that you have a hot ass.

He's not wrong, is he? Arwen didn't smile at the joke. She was busy grabbing her weapons and slipping over the side. The frigid water made her gasp, and the kayak rocked alarmingly at her weight shift. "This may be a bad idea."

Swimming with her bow would be awkward, especially diving underwater. If not for the dragons, she would have left her weapons behind. Still, maybe the goblin-made arrow that glowed would be useful in the dark water. She didn't have goggles and wouldn't be able to see a thing down there without magical aid.

As she sank in, the icy water wrapped fully around her, making her shake with cold. It was her second time in the Sound that night, but she'd been running and fighting before her first plunge, and she hadn't noticed the chill as much. Now, with her body already cool, the Sound sucked the heat out of her instantly.

The shoreline looked farther away than it had in the kayak. Her father had taught her to swim, and she'd played in many lakes in the summers, but she doubted she had the endurance to stroke all the way to shore. She would have to hope the kayak didn't float too far away—and that she could lever herself back into it.

Realizing Azerdash hadn't answered, Arwen looked toward his battle.

He and Yendral hadn't fled; they continued to team up against Hyrukorlin. Surprisingly, the other two Silverclaws hadn't joined in. The green dragon perched on the ferry terminal building. The blue flew back and forth over Puget Sound, less than a mile from Arwen.

He was searching for the sword. Or waiting for someone else to find it. Could the new dragons know she was out there? Despite her camouflage?

As if in answer, the blue banked and flew toward her. His eyes glowed green-yellow against the dark night, and they locked onto the kayak. She might be camouflaged, but *it* wasn't.

If the dragon got close enough, he would see her.

With little choice, Arwen tucked the goblin device into her mouth. It molded to her top teeth, like the dental guard she'd originally thought of, but a concave bubble of magic also formed over her mouth and nose. She breathed through it, to make sure she could, then dipped her face in the water. The bubble kept it from reaching her lips and nose. Her instincts told her *not* to breathe, but she inhaled experimentally. The device must have filtered oxygen out of the water because she received almost normal air, though it was heavy—humid—and briny with the taste of seaweed.

Aware of the dragon flying closer—he was undoubtedly checking out the kayak—Arwen submerged, the cold water covering her head. After assuring herself with a few more breaths that she would have enough air, she tipped herself upside-down and swam farther from the surface, the weight of her clothes, moccasins, and weapons helping her sink.

It was utterly black below, and little light filtered down from the night sky above. Arwen might have been swimming straight into a rock—or a kraken's mouth—and wouldn't have known it.

She drew the heavy goblin arrow, mentally dubbing it Glow, but she was hesitant to fire it into the depths. Just because the magic she'd briefly sensed hadn't seemed that far down didn't mean the Sound wasn't eight hundred feet deep under her. She would lose the arrow forever if she fired it into those depths. And she didn't sense the magic now.

Aware of the dragon's aura drawing closer, she couldn't dawdle. Hoping she'd descended ten or fifteen feet, she started stroking sideways. Pressure built in her ears, and she didn't know how deep she would be able to go without the protection of a submarine. Probably not far. But if she could sense that magic again…

Yellow light flared above her. Arwen flinched, almost dropping the arrow. That was dragon fire.

Afraid it would penetrate deep into the water and fry her, she balled up and tried to form a magical barrier around herself. But it was much harder here than in the fae realm, and fear and distraction made her fail.

Fortunately, no flames penetrated the water to engulf her. They weren't even aimed in her direction.

With a sinking sense of certainty, Arwen realized the dragon had toasted her borrowed kayak.

28

THE DRAGON'S AURA REMAINED ABOVE THE SURFACE OF THE WATER, near where he had destroyed her kayak. Arwen swam farther away, hoping her camouflage stuck, but his presence was another reason not to wantonly fire an arrow. While her weapons were on her, the camouflaging magic hid them, but once she released something, its magic would make it detectable.

Mongrel dark elf, the dragon boomed into her mind, *we know you are there and that you presumed to unleash your weak magic at one of our clan. The punishment for attacking our kind is death. Once we have the weapon and the mongrel half-dragons are destroyed, we will also rid the Realms of your treacherous presence.*

Ignoring the threat and willing the Silverclaw to fly away, Arwen angled herself deeper, but now that his fire had faded, there was no light. Only the fact that she had to fight the buoyancy of the saltwater helped her identify up and down.

Growing weary, she was about to risk heading to the surface to try to find her bearings when she sensed the dwarven magic again. It was so faint that it would have been easy to miss. Did the dragon sense it? It seemed like he would have checked it out if he had, but he might be far enough above that, even with his keener abilities, he hadn't caught it.

Without hesitating, Arwen angled lower and stroked toward it. The pressure built in her ears. Would she be able to swim deep enough to locate the source of the magic? What if it was a hundred feet down? Or more?

Her knuckles bashed against something, pain almost making her gasp and lose the breathing device. She clamped her jaw down and drew her battered hand to her chest. Carefully, she reached out with the other and felt rock covered with algae or seaweed and barnacles.

Ignoring the pain in her hand and the blood seeping away, possibly attracting sharks, Arwen patted her way along the rock. Hopefully, this was the remains of the island from the mural. If she could find the chest...

What? She couldn't open it without a key. And it would be too heavy for her to haul up. Even if it were magically lightweight, she would have nowhere to haul it *to,* since the kayak had gone up in flames.

She would have to call to Azerdash and hope he could dive down and haul it up. Maybe he could immediately form a portal and take it to another world. They could figure out the key later.

Arwen nodded to herself as she followed the rocky protrusion. If he could get away from his battle, that would be the plan.

She shifted her grip upward when she brushed against something spiky, and her hand swept through empty water. She'd found the top of the rocky protrusion. It was surprisingly flat. *Unnaturally* flat. As if someone had taken a giant axe or saw and cut off the top.

Maybe that was exactly what had happened. The dwarf, or some rival of his who'd wanted to hide the island holding the chest, could have destroyed the top. If not with a blade, then with magic.

Her hopes lifted as she circled the protrusion, finding the top flat all around. She began to believe it *was* the remains of the island. If so, was the chest below? Her senses told her that the dwarven magic originated from a deeper position. They also told her that the dragon who'd destroyed her kayak had flown to the north. He hadn't completely abandoned the area, but he might have been drawn closer to the battle, being called to help by Hyrukorlin.

That thought didn't reassure Arwen, since that would mean more enemies for Azerdash and Yendral to fight, but she could take advantage of the dragon's distraction.

Deciding she could risk firing her arrow if there was a land mass down there, she pulled out Glow again. She found a couple of bumps with her feet and anchored herself sideways, her hair floating around her head. It hardly mattered if it was in her eyes since she couldn't see anything anyway.

As she nocked the arrow, relieved her bow's magic made the string as taut and strong as on land, she remembered something else that had momentarily slipped her mind. A creature. Rysharon had warned Azerdash of a guardian for the sword.

If Arwen got close to the chest, whatever it was might awaken. Of course, whatever it was might have left or died after a century too.

Find the chest first, she told herself, and then worry about it. And then shout for Azerdash to come help.

She sensed him miles away, now closer to Mukilteo than downtown Edmonds, but trusted he could reach her quickly if needed. He might have dragons on his tail, but... he would come. She was certain of it.

At that moment, as she drew back her bow, she realized he cared for her. He might not have figured that out for himself yet, but she knew it to be true.

She released the arrow in the direction of the dwarven magic.

Glow flared yellow as it streaked into the depths, the light illuminating its red recycled-stop-sign shaft. The arrow slowed down more quickly than it would have in air, and Arwen worried all she'd done was fire it into the depths of Puget Sound, where it would land too far down to retrieve. Then it flared brighter as it pierced barnacle-covered rock and stuck.

The distance and the water made everything blurry, and Arwen wished she'd thought to ask those goblins for goggles.

Drawing magic into her, she willed it to sharpen her eyesight, to allow her to pierce the gloom. Since she'd never learned to do such a thing, she didn't expect much, but her vision *did* sharpen slightly. The arrow stuck out of one of four parallel cracks in the rock. Those cracks didn't look natural.

Excited, Arwen swam lower.

Weariness and the pressure increasing in her ears made her want to turn back, to go to the surface to rest, but she willed her magic to help again, to form a barrier that would protect her fragile body from the increasingly hostile water. Her forearm itched and warmed. It wasn't the tattoo's magic that she wanted, but in her precarious situation, she had to take whatever help she could get.

Fish flitted by, not disturbed by the pressure or her presence. An eel slithered between her and the arrow. As of yet, she hadn't seen any sharks and hoped there weren't any in Puget Sound, but she doubted she would be that lucky.

As she neared her arrow, she spotted something square, an angle that one wouldn't find in nature. It was *under* the parallel lines, sticking out from—that almost looked like a foot carved from stone.

A memory of the concrete Fremont Troll under the Aurora Bridge came to mind, a car clutched under its grip.

Pausing, Arwen followed the foot upward with her eyes. Was that a barnacle-covered leg? Or her imagination? That might be a torso above the leg... She was almost even with it. If there was a head and face mounted against the natural rock of the former island, she couldn't tell, because sediment, vegetation, and barnacles covered everything. Even so, she had a feeling she'd found a slumbering golem. No magic emanated from it—the dwarven magic she sensed came from under the foot—but that might change if it woke from its nap.

Arwen descended closer to the arrow and patted the corner she'd spotted. Instead of a car, this stone guardian held a chest. So much silt and grime covered it that she couldn't tell if it was made from iron or another material, but whatever it was had stood up to time and retained its shape. If there was a keyhole, she couldn't see it. She couldn't see *most* of the chest, not with that huge stone foot over it. Her arrow had landed between two of its toes. Only fortune had kept Glow from hitting the golem in the stony flesh.

As much as she wished she could use her magic to blast away the lid, defeat the golem, and free the sword she hoped lay within the chest, she wasn't delusional. A golem would smash her. She'd found the chest; she needed help for the rest.

Azerdash? If there's an opportunity for you to slip away, now would be a good time. As far north as his battle had taken him, Arwen didn't know if he would hear her telepathic words.

She thought about swimming up and leaving her arrow to be a beacon to guide her back—its magic was stronger than what emanated from the chest. But it would be a beacon not only for her but the dragons and anyone else who could sense it.

Grimacing, she stroked close enough to grab her arrow and pull it from between the toes. As it came away, a grinding noise emanated from the island. No, from the *golem*.

Cursing silently, Arwen swam backward as fast as she could with her arrow clutched in her hand.

The great stone creature stirred and pushed itself from its rocky perch. Though sediment clouded the water, she had no trouble seeing the face now. A pair of glowing gray eyes opened twenty feet above her.

The golem woke abruptly, and between one blink and the next, a tremendously strong aura popped into existence.

Arwen kept swimming, not wanting to fight anything with the power of a dragon—maybe *more power* than a dragon. She angled for the surface, but before she'd gone ten feet, a whoosh of magic came from the golem. Its power wrapped implacably around her, halting her instantly.

Trapped, Arwen could only stare in horror as the golem reached a huge stone hand for her.

29

THE GREAT BLADE IS IN MY PROTECTION, A TELEPATHIC VOICE LIKE grating rock boomed in Arwen's mind. The golem. *Only the rightful owner shall have it. All thieves shall be crushed.*

Even as the golem's power pinned her in place, holding her suspended in the water, a hand bigger than her stretched toward her.

I know the rightful owner! Azerdash Starblade. He's in the sky above. A half-dragon warrior. I'm friends with him. She'd no sooner shared the words than she realized she couldn't sense Azerdash anymore. Yendral was still in the sky to the north, battling one— no, *two* of the Silverclaws, but what of Azerdash? Had he been forced to make a portal and flee?

Horrible timing.

The hand didn't move quickly, but it was inexorable, and the barnacle-covered fingers flexed, ready to crush her.

Arwen couldn't swim away, but she *could* move her arms. Desperate, she nocked Glow and pointed it between the golem's eyes. She released it, the water muffling the twang of the bowstring. The arrow streaked past the grasping hand and toward the golem's face. Even with the water resistance, it hit where she'd aimed. Right between its glowing gray eyes.

But the magic of the arrow wasn't enough to overcome that of the powerful golem. It hit and bounced off.

The fingers of the hand spread to grasp Arwen. Desperate, she kicked and flailed, but she couldn't tear away from the invisible power that held her in place.

Groping for calm and concentration, she drew upon her magic and attempted to funnel in more from the water around her and the earth far below.

As she'd done in the fae realm, Arwen created a ball of energy within her. Her forearm throbbed, the tattoo lending her power of its own.

Even as the golem's great magic threatened to crush her, Arwen pushed her ball of energy outward to form a barrier, willing it to drive her foe's power back. The two magics clashed, the golem's threatening to subsume hers. She focused, drawing upon every scrap of power within and without. Groaning around the mouthpiece, she finally had enough to drive back the golem's power as a full-fledged defensive barrier wrapped around her.

That didn't keep the stone hand from trying to grab her. Summoning every bit of concentration she had, Arwen swam backward as she kept her barrier around her.

Azerdash's aura returned to her awareness, startling her. Still in his dragon form, he arrowed between her and her enemy and bit into its thick stone arm.

As large as Azerdash was, the golem dwarfed him, making him appear small. His jaws could only wrap around part of that great stone arm. But his magical fangs sank in as he used his power to strike the grasping hand. The fingers that had been reaching for Arwen halted.

Azerdash's power flared as he summoned more magic. A battering ram of energy slammed into the golem's chest.

That's Azerdash, Arwen said telepathically to the creature, though it might not be inclined to like him at the moment. *The rightful wielder of a galaxy blade. You can give him the chest.*

With the golem focused elsewhere, Arwen stopped swimming away and considered how she could help Azerdash. Its focus had turned toward him as he battered it with his power and bit deeper into the stony flesh of its arm.

The dwarf who found the abandoned blade, the golem said emotionlessly, *and claimed it for his own summoned me to protect it until a great warrior of their kind came, one worthy enough to wield it. It will not be given to an enemy of the dwarves.*

That's what it thinks. Azerdash released the arm, tearing off a chunk before he did, and swam toward the golem's head.

But a great wall of power emerged from the stone creature and slammed into him. Even though a barrier protected Azerdash, it knocked him sideways. He thudded into the remains of the island, wings mashing against the rock.

Elves and dwarves aren't enemies anymore, Arwen yelled telepathically. *That war ended a long time ago.*

The golem did not reply, only turning to go after Azerdash. She doubted her words would change its mind.

Swim to the surface, Azerdash told Arwen, not glancing at her as he pushed away from the island.

None too soon. The golem slammed a fist into the spot where he'd been. Barnacles and shards of rock tumbled away, and sediment clouded the water, further dimming the view. If not for the golem's glowing eyes, there wouldn't have been any light now that Arwen's arrow had tumbled away.

I can't hold my breath much longer, Azerdash added. *I'll have to go up to the surface too. But I want it focused on me instead of you.*

Arwen sensed one of the Silverclaw dragons in the air above their battle and grimaced. *You'd better not go up there. Come over here. I've got an underwater breathing device.*

Even as she told him about it, she realized it wasn't shaped correctly for a dragon's maw. Would it work if he held it between his fangs? She didn't know.

As Azerdash tried to swim around the golem and toward her, it blasted him again.

Even though her last arrow hadn't done anything to it, Arwen nocked another, choosing one with the power of fire. If this golem had been created to live in the sea, maybe it would be vulnerable to flame.

Azerdash struck it with magic of his own, aiming for its head this time instead of the stout chest. His power ripped into it, tearing away a layer of its magical protection, but it didn't do anything to damage the golem itself. Its head turned toward him, and twin beams of gray shot out of its eyes.

Azerdash's barrier deflected them, but he grunted, bubbles escaping his maw. The sheer power of those beams had to be hard for even him to defend against.

Arwen wanted to target the golem's eye, but with the head turned toward Azerdash, she had to fire at its ear instead. Surprisingly, the arrow passed through its defenses and burrowed deep. Azerdash must have weakened its barrier.

The beams shooting from its eyes halted. Azerdash took advantage and swam back in.

Your air? Arwen dug out the second goblin device, not certain how long dragons could hold their breath.

She also sensed the Silverclaw above, closer now, right above the surface. Had he detected the chest? Or was he waiting to take advantage of Azerdash?

Fortunately, Arwen sensed Yendral flying in. *Un*fortunately, she sensed the other Silverclaw chasing him.

Guilt surged through Arwen as she realized she might have made things worse. She'd forced them to abandon any advantage they might have had in the battle to come help her. And now they had a golem to worry about as well as the dragons. A golem who didn't care that it was guarding a sword that hadn't rightfully belonged to the dwarf who'd buried it down here.

With fury mingling with her guilt, Arwen fired another arrow.

It chipped the golem's cheek but glanced off, disappearing into the murk. Frustrated that she was losing arrows, she drew the multitool and swam in.

Azerdash reached the golem's torso and raked it with his talons as he sank his fangs into its thick stony throat. It didn't breathe or have arteries, so Arwen didn't know if that was a vulnerable target, but the golem didn't like the attack. It raised both arms and battered at Azerdash. The blows didn't keep him from gouging it deeply with his talons.

Arwen avoided the golem's moving arms to swim in from behind. By now, her limbs ached with weariness, and she felt like she wasn't getting enough oxygen from the goblin device. With a last spurt of energy, she dove in. Knife portion of the tool extended, she stabbed the back of the golem's head as Azerdash assailed it from the front.

The magic of his gift was enough to let the blade sink in. As it had against the serpent in the fae realm, it sent streaks of lightning all around the body of their enemy.

Whether it was enough to hurt the golem, Arwen didn't know, but Azerdash also tore away a chunk of its throat. He turned his head, spitting it out, and lunged in for another bite.

The golem battered him in the sides, blows that had to hurt, if not crush scale and bone, but Azerdash hung on to their foe, again sinking his fangs in.

Arwen drew the blade out and stabbed it once more. She doubted the golem had a brain or any organs at all that she could pierce, but she doggedly attacked its stone head. Streaks of lightning brightened the water all around as they battled.

With so much light, she almost missed seeing a burst of orange from above. Dragon fire. A lot of it.

The two Silverclaw dragons remained above the surface, waiting for the golem to finish off Azerdash. At first, Arwen thought Yendral might be attacking them, or at least distracting them, but she sensed his aura shooting past. More like a dolphin than a dragon, he dove deep, bypassing the battle completely. Arwen was confused until his talons clasped the chest.

With a cracking of stone, he pulled it away from its rocky tomb.

A portal formed underwater. Yendral's.

Go, he commanded Arwen. Or was the order for Azerdash? Azerdash who was still holding his breath and fighting?

Arwen sank the knife in again, this time at the base of the golem's neck, desperately seeking a vital target.

Go, Yendral repeated, compelling her with his power as lightning streaked out from the multitool again, a branch burrowing into the golem's ear beside her arrow.

A whoosh of magic wrapped around her, and she barely retained the tool, pulling it out as Yendral's power drew her away, then pushed her toward the portal.

Yendral, the chest clutched in his talons, swam through it ahead of her.

Azerdash, Arwen cried telepathically as momentum carried her toward the portal even after Yendral disappeared.

Terrified Azerdash would stay behind and sacrifice himself so they could escape, she tried to stop. But the momentum carried her through, and the dark cold water of Puget Sound disappeared as she plummeted through the portal to another world.

30

Arwen landed hard on her shoulder in a grassy field, brilliant sunlight in a pink sky startling after the murky black water. Before she'd done more than rise to her knees, barely able to see over the grass toward a purple mountain range in the distance, a dragon tail wrapped around her.

Yendral.

He sat on the chest like an egg in a nest, but his tail captured her. Protectively? Possessively?

He peered intently toward the portal, the silver disc floating above the grass nearby. Waiting for Azerdash? Or afraid the Silver-claw dragons would follow him through?

"If he doesn't come out," Arwen said around the goblin breathing device still in her mouth, "we have to go back for him. We can't let—"

A black-scaled form somersaulted through the portal and tumbled into the grass. Azerdash.

He gasped in air, somehow hacking water from his lungs at the same time.

The portal disappeared.

Arwen wanted to collapse on the ground in relief, but Yendral's tail kept her upright. Maybe it was just as well. If either of the Silverclaws had the ability to track portals, they might know where Azerdash had gone and follow him.

"You can let me go now," she told Yendral, wanting the freedom to draw arrows if she needed to, though she'd lost several back in the Sound.

He didn't. He wasn't even looking at her. His gaze fixed on Azerdash, who'd recovered and risen to all fours.

Azerdash shook his wings and body, water droplets flying into the tall grass. Turning, he faced Yendral. Blood streamed from gashes in his sides, and some of his black scales were damaged, scorched by flames and cracked by golem fists.

Also wounded, Yendral didn't look any better. But for some reason, the two half-dragons stared at each other like adversaries instead of allies, allies who'd barely escaped Earth with their lives.

The sword is within this chest, Yendral stated, speaking telepathically. *Once we have a key to open it, perhaps I will claim it as mine.*

Is that so? Azerdash replied coolly.

I am the one who snatched it out from under the Silverclaws' and the golem's noses.

While we *battled them.* Azerdash inclined his head toward Arwen, including her. *Release her. She is not your prisoner.*

No, but I am thinking of claiming her, the same as the sword. She is a worthy ally and a mighty female warrior.

She is that, Azerdash said, stepping forward, *but you will* not *claim her. The choice of mates will be hers, and she does not desire you.*

She will come to appreciate me in time. Especially after I wield a galaxy blade.

Azerdash growled and crouched low to spring. Yendral released Arwen and stepped off the chest but only so he could face Azerdash fully and also crouch, prepared to attack.

"Guys," Arwen said. "There's no need to fight. Let's go back to

Earth and figure out what to do with those Silverclaws, okay? *They're* your enemies, not each other. Right?"

They didn't look at her. As one, they roared and sprang for each other's throats.

As dirt and grass flew, Arwen scrambled back.

She pulled an arrow and started to nock it, but the half-dragons came together, fighting like cats in a back alley, clawing and biting as they wrestled and writhed. She might have gotten off a shot, but she worried she would hit the wrong one. She wasn't even positive she *wanted* to shoot Yendral. He was being an ass, but couldn't they work it out? They needed each other, not to kill each other off.

"Guys," she called again, wishing she had a huge bucket of water to throw on them, as if that might stop the battle.

Roars and screeches floated across the grassy plain. At least there didn't appear to be any enemies around to take advantage of the distracted combatants.

Arwen lowered her bow. Though it was her nature to want to help, something told her this had been building and that they needed to fight it out. She hoped they didn't kill each other. The story Azerdash had told of inadvertently killing a friend in the heat of battle continued to haunt her.

Their wild wrestling and biting carried them away from the chest. Thinking she might find a way to open it and draw the sword, she checked it. Maybe *that* would stop the fight. She could leap upon the chest and claim that *she* would wield it.

"Yeah, right," she muttered.

She'd never wielded a sword in her life. She would need to join Amber for lessons from Val first.

The lock on the grime-covered chest wasn't even visible. She could only guess where it might be and doubted poking the chest with an arrowhead would release the clasp. Matti, with the key she was enchanting, might be the one who could open it.

Maybe her half-dwarven blood would entice the sword, and *she* would end up wielding it. But, no, that had been the golem, not the sword, that had been loyal to dwarves.

A screech of pain came from the half-dragons. Arwen couldn't tell which one had issued it but jerked in horror as blood flew from the battle and spattered her.

She stared over the grass to where one combatant had come out on top. The black-scaled Azerdash crouched atop Yendral, who lay flat on his back, blood running from a dozen wounds. Azerdash's talons pinned Yendral as his magic further plastered him to the ground. His great fanged maw hovered above Yendral's long exposed neck.

Terrified she was about to watch Azerdash kill his friend, Arwen almost cried for them to stop.

But Azerdash spoke first. *You will* not *claim Arwen like some mindless minion who doesn't have rights of her own, and you will also not take that sword. I am the stronger warrior in this form, and I've defeated you in the way of dragonkind.*

Yendral showed his fangs and emitted what Arwen thought was a growl, but, no... That was almost a laugh. Or what passed for a dragon version of it.

I'm glad you finally remembered that, Yendral replied. *The talons sinking into my gut were worth it for you to do so.*

What are you talking about, fool?

You have a destiny, but you needed a tail whack to the back of the head to accept it. Did it work?

You've been doing this on purpose? Azerdash looked not only toward the chest but toward Arwen.

Of course. You've been sulking and slumping around like we've been defeated forever, not like the great warrior and leader you were meant to be.

Azerdash made a disgusted sound and stepped off Yendral. *I could have killed you.*

It would have been worth it if you'd found your yeylesta.

Arwen had no idea what the word meant, but her mind filled in *cojones*.

Azerdash shifted into his elven form and walked over, looking at her and barely glancing at the chest. "Are you all right?"

"Better than you, I think." She eyed his ripped tunic and trousers, blood leaking from deep wounds and staining the clothing, as if he'd been wearing them in dragon form.

"Good."

Yendral also shifted forms, but it took him a moment before he could grit his teeth and push himself to his feet. When he walked over, it was with a limp, an arm wrapped around his ribs.

He nodded at Azerdash, then grinned at Arwen and thumped her on the shoulder. She had no idea what to say to that—or him —though she remembered her earlier thought that his embrace in the museum basement might have been for show. Maybe this was the reaction he'd hoped to bestir in Azerdash all along.

Azerdash sighed, gave Yendral a dark look, then crouched to examine the chest. He probed it with his magic.

"The enchantment is old and has faded," he said, "but I think you are right that we will need a key."

"With luck, there's one waiting for us back on Earth." Arwen remembered that Val was headed up to Edmonds with the submarine. If she arrived now, all she would do was run into two irate Silverclaw dragons. "We might want to go back sooner rather than later."

"Yes," Yendral said. "I, for one, need a long soak in our rejuvenation pool."

"If we return to that town," Azerdash said, "the Silverclaws may be waiting."

"Let's go to Val's house. From there, maybe someone can call her and keep her from going to Edmonds." Arwen dug out her phone and wasn't surprised when it didn't come on. Though she'd gotten it wet several times before, she'd never taken it swimming fifty or a hundred feet down, or however far under the surface she'd been. At least she hadn't left it in the kayak where it would have burst into flames with the rest of the craft.

"The half-elf female does not have a rejuvenation pool." Yendral curled a lip.

"She has a goblin-made hot tub," Arwen said.

"That is *not* the same."

"Let's get the chest open before we worry about healing ourselves." Azerdash eyed him without humor. "Assuming you have *yeylesta* enough to survive those small wounds for a couple of hours."

That word *definitely* meant *cojones*.

"Small wounds? Azerdash, you left fang marks all over me. *Deep* ones. Is that my spleen over in the grass?"

"You are a fool."

"Yup." Yendral thumped Azerdash on the shoulder, the same as he had Arwen.

Azerdash formed a portal, then levitated the chest into the air and led the way through with it.

Yendral looked at Arwen before following.

"Are you done trying to claim me?" she asked.

"Yes. You're meant for Azerdash. And he you. Nobody else could *possibly* find his babbling about gnomish engineering interesting. And you burbling about clam gardens? Only he would tolerate that." Yendral gave her a lopsided thumbs-up before leaping through the portal.

Maybe Arwen should have been insulted, but she was mostly relieved.

31

ARWEN CAME OUT OF THE PORTAL IN THE STREET BETWEEN VAL'S and Matti's houses, almost running into a black Jeep that was parking. *Val's* black Jeep.

Blinking in surprise, Arwen looked at the driver. It wasn't Val but Amber. Surprisingly, she also sensed Matti and Sarrlevi in the Jeep with two tiny new auras that had previously been on the *inside* of Matti.

After parking, Amber rolled down the window and leaned her head out. "Uhm, Val is piloting a sub up to Edmonds to meet you." Amber looked Arwen up and down. "You look like some bedraggled rat a cat fished out of a sewer and chewed on for a while before spitting out."

"Make it a golem, and that's about right." Arwen glanced toward the sidewalk, where Yendral and Azerdash stood, glaring at the dragon topiaries that were glaring at *them.*

The shrubberies' eyes glowed orange, and smoke wafted from the nostrils. Had Zavryd revoked permission for Azerdash and Yendral to come onto the property again?

The half-dragons didn't appear too worried, not after they'd battled real dragons—and each other. The chest floated in the air next to Azerdash, with Yendral making no more suggestions that he would keep the sword for himself.

"Can you let your mother know we had a change in plans and don't need the sub?" Arwen asked Amber.

"She and Willard will both be pissed about that." Amber stepped out of the Jeep. "They had to jump through a lot of hoops to find it. It's 3 a.m., you know."

"I'll apologize to them. Also let her know that there might be Silverclaw dragons up there. It would be best to avoid the area completely."

"The area of... Edmonds?" Amber made a face. "My *house* is there."

"Sorry. Hopefully, when they realize Azerdash and Yendral—and that sword—aren't up there anymore, they'll leave." With luck, the dragons had *already* left. "I don't suppose you have the key we need?" Arwen suspected Val had taken it with her.

"Actually, I think we do, right?" Amber looked into the Jeep.

Arwen watched as Sarrlevi formed a protective barrier around his family and stepped out, taking the babies while glowering suspiciously at the half-dragons. He didn't look like he'd expected to come home to *activity* around his house.

"Will you allow me to levitate you into our home, Mataalii?" Sarrlevi leaned forward as his mate scooted off her seat, his eyes intent with concern, as if he could barely restrain himself from presuming to do so.

"No, I will not." Matti pushed herself out of the Jeep and to her feet, then leaned back and grabbed her big war hammer. She'd taken that to the delivery room? "I appreciate your concern, but I've got feet of my own. I can even see them again now." She looked down. "Almost."

"Capable feet, yes." Sarrlevi smiled at her. Then one of the babies cooed, and he shifted his focus to the bundles in his arms, offering them a comforting caress of magic.

Matti walked over to Arwen while Amber moved off to call her mother.

"Are you okay? The delivery went well?" Arwen felt guilty that she hadn't been able to visit during it but was glad Matti and the babies were healthy. Though Matti appeared weary, with bags under her eyes, she also looked happy and content.

"It was a little rough, and I might have thumped a few people around—"

"Indeed," came a dry interjection from Sarrlevi.

"—but we all survived." Matti smiled fondly at her new family before handing Arwen the magical key she'd enchanted. She looked curiously at the chest, Azerdash's foot on it now as he waited.

Arwen held up the gift. "This is an odd-looking key."

"I had to work with what was on hand."

"Is it made from... a scalpel?"

"Among other things. I felt like a goblin recycling bits to twist into a key. It should work though." Matti waved toward the chest, then headed toward her house. Despite her earlier words, she let Sarrlevi levitate her up the stairs and inside. The door shut behind them with a firm thump.

Amber waved her phone. "Mom left the submarine at the marina up there. The other dragons must have taken off, probably because Val isn't alone. She said Zavryd and his sister, Zondia, just came from their home world and are with her."

"That's good," Arwen said.

Key in hand, she joined Azerdash and Yendral on the sidewalk. The chest had settled to the ground, layers of mineral deposits, caked grime, algae, and barnacles making it hard to determine how large it actually was, but its length promised it could hold a sword. The magic the dwarf had infused it with kept them from sensing what lay inside. For a moment, Arwen worried that the sword might not be in there, that someone had found it long ago and stolen it. But the golem wouldn't have guarded the chest so assiduously if that had happened.

"I hope," she murmured.

Azerdash raised his eyebrows.

"I'm not sure where to put the key." Arwen waved it at the chest. She couldn't even tell which side was the front.

"Ah." Azerdash flicked a finger, and fire sprang from the chest.

Startled, Arwen jumped back into the street, but the flames were concentrated. They incinerated the grime and growth, leaving the rusty iron chest visible. The keyhole was *also* visible.

Arwen eyed it dubiously. It was much larger than the key, and she worried the instructions had said nothing about dimensions and spoken only of the enchanting magic needed. Would that be enough?

When Arwen knelt before the lock, Azerdash crouched beside her, his shoulder brushing hers. He looked intently at the chest.

All along, Yendral and others had seemed to care more about the sword than he, but now he scarcely breathed. Maybe he also worried that after all that effort, the weapon might not be inside.

"What does *yeylesta* mean?" Arwen asked lightly, bumping his shoulder.

"Fangs."

"Oh? Are you sure? Going by the context, I thought it might mean something else."

Azerdash looked curiously at her.

"We have an expression about finding one's *cojones*. Uhm, balls, basically."

His head tilted.

"Like testicles." Her cheeks heated. Why had she brought this up? She'd only meant to distract him from his concern. Shaking her head, she slid the small key into the large hole.

"Dragons do not have external genitalia." Azerdash appeared more puzzled than enlightened by her explanation. "They have a cloaca."

"Yeah, I know. I mean, I didn't know *exactly,* but you know." Flustered, Arwen waved a dismissal and attempted to turn the key. It didn't turn, but a *click* sounded, accompanied by a small surge of magic.

"Elves have genitalia similar to humans," Azerdash said.

"Good to know."

"Everything is compatible for mating purposes."

"Yes, I'm glad."

Yendral snorted. "Is it going to be this awkward when you two finally have sex?"

"No," Arwen blurted, her cheeks scorching now. "We wouldn't — I mean, if Azerdash wants to, I doubt there'd be *talking.*"

Was that right? Most of the romance novels she'd read involved a lot of grunting and growling and groping of various body parts.

"Uh-huh," Yendral said. "There'll probably be coital chitchat about trains and gardening."

Azerdash squinted at him. "You will stand farther away when we are engaged in private discussions, or I will not hesitate to use my *yeylesta* on you again."

"Not that. I'm still bleeding from last time." Yendral lifted his hands and stepped back but only a pace. His gaze turned toward the chest, his interest as keen as Azerdash's.

Arwen withdrew the key and stepped back, waving for Azerdash to try the lid. He wiped his palms on his trousers first. Nervous? She couldn't blame him.

As soon as the lid cracked, Arwen sensed extremely powerful magic inside. Relief flowed through her. The sword was there.

When Azerdash pushed the lid all the way back and gazed into the chest, his jaw dropped. In surprise? What had he expected?

The sword had black metal with pinpoint stars all along the blade that glowed like those in the night sky. The hilt was pure black, save for a comet streaking from the cross guard to the pommel. Despite its century or more in an underwater coffin, it gleamed as if it had been recently cleaned and oiled.

"It's beautiful," Arwen said.

"That's your sword," Yendral told Azerdash, also appearing stunned.

"Wasn't the plan always for it to become his sword?" Arwen asked.

"No, that's the very sword he carried that was given to him by our commanders. One of only eight that were made by the greatest masters of the time, one he personally carried into battle."

A long moment passed before Azerdash reached in to grasp the hilt. At his touch, the blade flared with blue light, and the stars gleamed brighter. Its aura hummed with pleasure at being reunited with him. A surge of power came from the blade, and magical fireworks shot from the tip and exploded in the sky high over the houses, looking like shooting stars as they streaked away from a flash of white.

"Wow." Arwen's bow did not feel that strongly about her.

"To us, it seems like it's only been a while since Azerdash wielded it," Yendral said. "How strange to think that centuries have passed. How many other wielders did it have in that time? How did it end up here?"

Arwen almost mentioned the dwarf, but that was only part of the story. How had he gotten it? Why had it been brought to Earth? And who had he left clues for about its location?

"Now that you have it, what are you going to do with it?" Arwen asked Azerdash.

He let out a long sigh. "Before this, I would have said I didn't believe in destiny, but maybe... maybe I was meant to find it." He looked at her. "Or *you* were meant to find it and give it to me," he added, acknowledging that she'd been the one to locate it.

Arwen shrugged, not sure she liked the talk of destiny, especially since Yendral had folded his arms over his chest and appeared pleased by Azerdash's reasoning. This was what he'd wanted, wasn't it? And what the elf ambassador wanted?

"I only helped because you went foraging for ingredients for me," she said.

Azerdash snorted softly, lowered the weapon, and wrapped an arm around her. Arwen leaned in to him, glad he'd found his sword, even if she worried about where it would lead him.

He smiled contentedly down at her and bent his head toward hers. For a kiss?

She parted her lips, pleased that finding it had put him in the mood for that, but Amber's phone rang before their lips touched.

Azerdash pulled back and frowned toward the north. "Zavryd'nokquetal and his sister come."

"Yeah, they're here," Amber said to whoever was calling. Val? "Okay, I'll tell them."

Though Arwen couldn't yet sense the dragons, her earlier concerns came to mind, that Zavryd would have heard from his queen the same rumor that was circulating everywhere else about Azerdash and his intentions.

"Here you go." Amber walked the phone over to Arwen. "It's for you."

"Val?" Arwen assumed.

"Yeah," her voice came from the phone. "We're on the way back, and Zav wants to know what the hell exploded at the house."

"Uhm." Arwen eyed the happily glowing sword. "It was *over* the house."

"Well, if any half-dragons were responsible, you might want to tell them to beat it. Apparently, the queen heard some news about their plans. I don't know if they're true or not, but she wants them incarcerated."

"Even though Azerdash is her relative now?" Arwen asked.

"I believe that's why there was talk of *incarceration* and not simply execution. But if Zav finds Starblade, he's going to be compelled to collect him, especially if Zondia is with him. She's... well, flying next to us, so I'll just stop there."

Zavryd must not have been too eager to *collect* Azerdash if Val was riding on his back while warning Arwen, but if Zavryd found Azerdash on the sidewalk in front of his house, asking him to pretend not to notice would be too much.

"We'll be home soon," Val added.

"Okay, thanks."

"I'm not going to get to soak in our rejuvenation pool, am I?" Despite all his bloody gashes, Yendral didn't look too upset about that.

"Not tonight." Azerdash smiled sadly at Arwen, then delved into a pouch and pressed heavy coins into her hands. "To pay your assistants."

Arwen glanced at Amber, though she was texting and didn't notice. "They'll appreciate that."

"I'd tell *you* to keep some, but I suspect you are too proud to accept coin for helping a... friend."

Friend, right. He knew he meant more to her than that. She hoped she meant more than that to him.

"Yes," was all she said.

"I will thank you for your help though." Azerdash looked at her lips but, instead of kissing her, glanced to the north, toward the approaching dragons. "Unfortunately, we must go now."

Arwen nodded, though emotion welled in her throat, and she didn't trust her voice. She had a feeling *going* wouldn't mean returning to the sanctuary up north, and she worried she wouldn't see him again for a while. Hopefully, a while wouldn't be forever.

"We have... work to do anyway." Azerdash gave Yendral a significant look, and Yendral nodded firmly back.

"Amassing armies?" Arwen asked.

"The less you know the better." Azerdash touched her cheek. "I'll return when I can."

A moment before Zondia and Zavryd registered on Arwen's magical radar, Azerdash and Yendral stepped away and camouflaged themselves, disappearing from sight as well as her senses.

She gazed glumly down at the empty iron chest, tears threatening to form.

Your loyalty has meant everything to me, Azerdash told her telepathically as he moved away. *I owe you.*

You don't. Arwen wiped her eyes. *Just... don't forget me.*

I will not. I'll return as soon as I can.

When you do, I'll make you tacos. She would make him anything he wished but smiled at the memory of the discussion.

Excellent.

EPILOGUE

"Zav might not be happy about that ugly chest on his sidewalk," Amber said.

She and Arwen stood alone in front of Val's dark Victorian house, but Zavryd and Zondia were visible in the night sky, wings outstretched as they glided down for a landing.

"I'm sure he can have his shrubs incinerate it." Arwen wiped her eyes, afraid she might have to be tough and stand up to questioning. Especially from Zondia. Arwen didn't know her well but had gotten the gist from Val that she was much more of a hard-ass than her older brother.

"I don't know if they're that powerful." Amber waved at the topiaries. "I think they also only zap people. Uhm, where did the guy with the gold go?"

"He didn't tell me. But here. Split this with Gondo, please." Arwen dropped the coins into Amber's palm without looking at them.

"Wow, those are heavy." Amber held one up to the light from the streetlamp at the corner. "I'd complain that this mint isn't on Earth, but I think you can melt down gold. I much prefer digital money, but maybe Gondo knows how to get this exchanged. I'm going to watch him though. You can't trust a goblin not to take more than his fair cut."

"He was really helpful, just FYI."

"So I should give him more than two percent?" Amber's nose wrinkled.

"Azerdash would have wanted him to have five." Arwen doubted Azerdash even knew Gondo's name, but she didn't think he would object.

Amber sighed theatrically but also didn't object.

As the dragons came in for a landing, a portal formed in the air above the intersection. The lilac-scaled Zondia flew through it instead of staying to chitchat—or question Arwen. That was one small relief.

Then Zavryd alighted on the roof of his home, his scaled face grim as he skewered Arwen with his gaze. He turned a baleful eye on the empty chest before levitating Val to the front lawn.

"Am I in trouble?" Arwen asked quietly, envisioning a dragon mind-scouring session.

"Probably not if you cook him some yeti," Val said.

"I did put some in the freezer since it wouldn't all fit on the spit."

"Perfect." Val paused before stepping onto the sidewalk and frowned back at the house. "Zoltan went somewhere?"

Arwen realized she hadn't sensed the vampire's aura at any point. He hadn't been on the top of her mind so she hadn't thought anything of it.

"I haven't seen him, but we—uhm, *I* haven't been here long." The word fumble made her glance toward Zavryd, though she suspected he already knew Azerdash and Yendral had been here. It wasn't as if Matti, Sarrlevi, Amber, and the topiaries hadn't seen them.

"He doesn't go out much," Val said. "He's a homebody. And he's been busy working on your formula since he got the ingredients. I don't sense Dmitri either, so maybe they went out together, but..." Val held up a finger and headed toward the gate in the fence.

Busy with the sword hunt, Arwen had almost forgotten about the tattoo-removal formula. Hoping nothing was wrong, she followed Val into the backyard and down the steps toward the basement.

Val stopped halfway down. The door stood ajar.

"He never leaves this open or even unlocked," Val said in a grim tone.

"How would someone have gotten past the wards and defenses around the property?"

"Powerful people can get past them—or destroy them if they're in the way." Val walked inside.

The inner door was also open, revealing the usual red lights illuminating the laboratory in a way that worked for Zoltan's sensitive eyes.

Glass crunched under Val's boots, and she stopped again. Arwen stepped up to her side and looked around in growing horror. Vials and glass and ceramic jars were broken all over the floor. The cauldron on Zoltan's workstation was upturned, the contents forming a puddle that hadn't had time to dry. Faint smoke wafted from it.

Val checked his living quarters and found the coffin over-turned. Arwen's gaze locked on a small spider-shaped crystal resting on a counter, a hint of dark-elven magic clinging to it. Her stomach sank into her moccasins.

Val must have sensed it too, because she whirled and pointed her semi-automatic pistol at it. "Is that a damn dark-elven artifact?"

Arwen closed her eyes as dread settled over her. "Yes."

"Shit."

"I don't know what it does, but I wouldn't touch it."

"No kidding," Val said. "What does it mean? That dark elves kidnapped him?"

Kidnapped him? Or had put a permanent end to him with a wooden stake to the heart?

"I don't know." Arwen slumped against the doorframe. "But it's my fault."

All along, her mother's people—*her mother*—hadn't wanted her to remove that tattoo, and Arwen had tried anyway.

Val eyed her. Though she didn't lower her gun, she forced a smile. "Don't worry about it. We'll find him."

"Sure," Arwen said, though she would do nothing but worry.

"He's a tough vampire. And this isn't the first time he's been kidnapped."

Arwen made herself nod as she wrapped a defensive barrier around herself, picked up some tongs off the floor, and used them to pluck up the spider crystal. Whoever had been here had left a clue. She would use it to track the person down, and she would get Zoltan back.

                          THE END